Reunited . . .

"A woman of your beauty should never be left unattended," a deep voice said over her shoulder.

Katherine's heart seemed to stop for a moment.

Nicholas.

She even remembered the thickness of his voice. His breath was warm and delicious on her bare skin. She was afraid to turn and face him, afraid he might not like her appearance. Afraid his eyes would find her every flaw.

"Is leaving a woman unattended on a crowded ship anything like leaving a girl of fourteen alone on River Street?" she managed to ask.

She waited. Breathing became a task. The conversations and laughter of the other guests seemed to fade. The sun began spilling magnificent colors—purples, pinks, and reds.

"Katherine?" he responded finally. "I knew you were promising, but . . . you're stunning!"

She wanted to laugh aloud with joy . . .

*Stories of Love on the Great Lakes from
The Berkley Publishing Group*

TWILIGHT MIST
by Ann Justice

TEMPEST WATERS
by Nancy Gideon

SECRET SHORES
by Kelly Ferjutz

SUMMER STORM
by Teresa Warfield

SUMMER STORM

TERESA WARFIELD

B
BERKLEY BOOKS, NEW YORK

If you purchased this book without a cover, you should be aware that this book is stolen property. It was reported as "unsold and destroyed" to the publisher, and neither the author nor the publisher has received any payment for this "stripped book."

SUMMER STORM

A Berkley Book/published by arrangement with
the author

PRINTING HISTORY
Berkley edition/August 1993

All rights reserved.
Copyright © 1993 by Teresa Warfield.
This book may not be reproduced in whole or in part,
by mimeograph or any other means, without permission.
For information address: The Berkley Publishing Group,
200 Madison Avenue, New York, New York 10016.

ISBN: 0-425-13820-8

A BERKLEY BOOK ® TM 757,375
Berkley Books are published by The Berkley Publishing Group,
200 Madison Avenue, New York, New York 10016.
The name "BERKLEY" and the "B" logo
are trademarks belonging to Berkley Publishing Corporation.

PRINTED IN THE UNITED STATES OF AMERICA

10 9 8 7 6 5 4 3 2 1

To Jack, my husband, friend, lover, chocolate provider, and computer repairman. Thanks for putting up with my obsession and giving me the space to do what I must do.

And to my husband's coworkers, my fans long before I could boast of a manuscript sale.

Acknowledgments

When I first heard of Berkley's Great Lakes historical romance project, I wondered if I was a skilled enough writer to pay tribute to one of the Great Lakes and write a captivating romance, all in one book. Even after mailing the first draft of the manuscript, I wondered. Certain people helped dispel my fears: Judith Stern, Donna Rogers, Barbie White, Shannon Flores, Michelle Brocious, Peggy Widder, Bobbie Smith, Colleen Culver, and Joyce Flaherty. The list could go on... Gloria Dale Skinner always encouraged me and was as excited as I was when the manuscript sold. Ginny Anikienko, Debbie Krauss, and Peggy Musil all deserve some of the credit for the polishing and shaping of the book; they devoted time to reading and commenting despite busy schedules.

Mr. Alexander B. Cook, Curator of the Maritime Museum of the Great Lakes Historical Society, provided valuable information on 19th-century Great Lakes vessels. And, dear staff of the Cleveland Public Library, how can I thank you enough? Yes, I know my taxes help pay your wages, but you were always there, patiently reloading the microfilm when I messed it up. You dug out such material as *The Great Lakes Wooden Shipbuilding Era* by Captain H. C. Inches and entrusted it to me for a time. The West Park Branch librarians must be acknowledged, too, for showing me how to obtain books from other areas of the country through inter-library loan.

Acknowledgments

Finally acknowledgment must be given to that great body of water—Lake Erie. So many times, dear lady, I have sat on your shores, watched your beautiful waves, admired your calm, your temper, your depths. You have astounded me with your fury and thrilled me with your elegance. You provided much of the inspiration for this book.

Teresa Warfield
February 1992

SUMMER STORM

Part One

Next day, when we stopped at Cleveland, the storm was just clearing up ... we had one of the finest views of the lake that could have been wished. The varying depths of these lakes gives to their surface a great variety of coloring, and beneath this wild sky and changeful lights, the waters present kaleidoscopic varieties of hues, rich, but mournful. I admire these bluffs of red, crumbling earth. Here land and water ... meet to mingle, are always rushing together, and changing places; a new creation takes place beneath the eye.

Repose marked his slow gesture ... but it was a repose that would give way to a blaze of energy when the occasion called. His voice, like everything about him, was rich and soft, rather than sweet or delicate. He loved to have her near him, to feel the glow and fragrance of her nature.

It is a curse to a woman to love first ...

—*Summer on the Lakes, in 1843*
MARGARET FULLER

Prologue

1853 CLEVELAND, OHIO

NICHOLAS CUMMINGS SAT back in an elegant velvet-cushioned armchair. He had taken a chance coming here. Werner Kraus, the balding German banker seated behind the huge mahogany desk near a small window, was a close friend to Lemuel Cummings, Nicholas's father. What was to stop Werner from running straight to his friend and revealing what Lemuel would undoubtedly think of as betrayal?

Of course, Nicholas wouldn't call this meeting a betrayal. He was showing financial independence. But his father would never understand. Lemuel Cummings couldn't think beyond schooling his only son to someday take over Cummings Ironworks.

Kraus's elbows rested on the arms of an upholstered chair, his fingers intermittently locking and unlocking as he seemed to weigh Nicholas's request. Several years ago Nicholas had funded the building of his steamship, *Ontario*. Today he meant to use the *Ontario*'s impeccable records to convince Kraus to invest in the next two Erie Line ships.

"As I said . . . *Ontario* has done well these past two years. Her account books are there," Nicholas said, inclining his head toward the small stack of documents he'd laid on the edge of Kraus's desk no more than ten minutes ago. "You'll see that she's more than recovered the cost of building her. She's made a sizable profit."

Kraus made no move to survey the documents and reports. Sighing heavily, he reached for a water glass and drained it. Nicholas tried to read the man's movements. Would Kraus turn him away without fair consideration because of who he was? Surely not. The evidence that his investment would come back to him many times over was within arm's reach.

"You won't regret investing," Nicholas said.

Kraus's gaze shot to his. "Have I agreed to invest?" he asked, his voice containing the hint of a German accent.

"You have doubts?"

"Only of a personal nature."

Muscles tightened in Nicholas's jaw. "I see . . . My father."

"Why not go to him, Nicholas? He would be honored," Kraus said.

"Honored?" Nicholas countered. "Honored, or satisfied that he has control over some part of me again? I think not, Mr. Kraus. Let's keep Lemuel Cummings out of this. I'm here to do business with you. If we can't do business without the shadow of my father between us, I'll go elsewhere."

They sat in silence for a time, then Kraus spoke, a touch of regret and weariness in his tone: "Business . . . yes. And yet . . . Ah, Nicholas! I met your father shortly after I arrived in Cleveland years ago. He worked as hard as I for success. Oh, yes. I was not blessed with a son, but if I had been, I would have worked these past years with him in mind, as Lemuel has for you. Why do you hurt him by refusing what he offers? Why come to me? *Unverstandlich*. I cannot understand."

Nicholas didn't bother to respond. Quarreling with Kraus was not what he had come here to do. Obviously Kraus could not see beyond his devotion to Lemuel Cummings. Nicholas moved from the chair, lifted the *Ontario*'s records from the desk, and started for the heavily polished door.

"Wait," Kraus said.

Pausing, Nicholas tipped his head back and prepared to listen.

Summer Storm

"I will invest in your Erie Line, Nicholas. I do not need to look at papers to know how well you have done. When you built the *Ontario*, I knew you would do well. I watched you grow up, remember? You were always strong-headed, always filled with a hunger to succeed."

Exhaling a breath of relief, Nicholas faced Kraus and found the man's blue eyes regarding him with admiration. Yet there was also a touch of sadness Nicholas felt certain was for the relationship between father and son that had turned sour years ago. But that relationship would never again be what it had once been. Never . . .

"Good," Nicholas said in a clipped tone. "The ships will be built at the Erie Line shipyard. I've already laid the plans if you want to see them or perhaps have someone you trust look at them."

"No need to have someone else look at them," Kraus said. "But I want to talk more, get some idea of what is involved in the building. Unfortunately I have an appointment soon at the Weddell House. Could you return in the morning?"

Nicholas nodded. He searched Kraus's face for some sign of reluctance and found none. "Thank you," he said, then turned again to leave.

The door flew open, cracking him clean across the forehead. The force of the blow stunned him and drove him backward. He reeled, catching the edge of a table to avoid a fall.

"Don't you know better than to stand behind a closed door?" he heard a voice demand.

Steadying himself, Nicholas caught sight of a young girl peering at him with narrowed blue eyes. She stepped inside and shut the door. The lump on his head throbbed and swelled . . . and she stared, the infuriating hint of a grin playing on her mouth.

A wisp of a thing, she wore smudges here and there—on a torn blouse that might have been white a year or two ago, and on a pair of baggy black trousers rolled up at the ankles at least ten times and fixed to her waist with a lengthy piece of rope dangling halfway down her legs. Her hair was a mess of filthy curls that might appear blond after a good scrubbing. To call her disheveled would have been too polite. What the hell she was doing barging into Werner Kraus's elegant banking office, Nicholas didn't know. But he certainly intended to find out.

"What are you starin' at?" she asked.

Nicholas gave a snort of disbelief. "I should be asking you that. You just hit me with that door. But then, you know that, don't you?"

She tossed her little chin in the air. "If an apology's what you're wantin', I don't apologize to no one."

"Is that so?"

"That's so."

Nicholas glanced at Kraus for some sign that his host recognized the girl, and as he had thought, there was none. Kraus looked as shocked by the intrusion as Nicholas felt. But the man wasn't rising behind his desk to demand that the ragamuffin get out, and that bewildered Nicholas.

The girl made a move toward the desk. Nicholas stepped in her path, glaring, refusing to allow her to take another step. He meant to wring a few apologies from her first, then accompany her to the outside of the building, where she belonged.

"You know who I am?" She tipped her head back and fixed a cool gaze on him.

"I've no idea, and I don't especially care to know."

"Well, you better start carin' or you might just find yourself in a kettle of hot water." She pursed her lips as if to say, "So there," then drifted toward a shelf of books and hunched for a better look at the selection. Whistling low in appreciation, she ran a hand over gold letters on bindings. Finally she stood and lifted an expensive oriental vase from the top shelf. A dirty finger touched exotic, painted flowers.

Kraus gasped. "No—"

"Put that down!" Nicholas demanded.

She shot a grin of defiance over her shoulder, making no attempt to do as she'd been told.

Nicholas took determined steps in her direction, maneuvering himself between her and the shelf. He snatched the vase from her hand. "What is a rumpled piece of baggage like you doing barging into this office, handling Mr. Kraus's belongings

Summer Storm 7

like they're your own? Apologies. Now. For myself and for Mr. Kraus! Then you can get out."

"Rumpled piece of baggage?" She laughed bitterly. "You all dressed in your fine cloth . . . Well, no matter. I told you, I don't apologize. And if you lay a hand on me, I'll dunk you in the river."

Nicholas's brows shot up at the threat. "Will you? Just like that? A little thing like you?"

"I'm not so little. Now leave me be. I came to ask my—"

"Leave *you* be? *You* disturbed *us*, not to mention the way you grinned after hitting me with that door. Apologies . . . now."

Something flashed in her eyes. She was stubborn, obviously a little fearful, but determined not to back away. Such a small thing, and yet the tilt of her chin and the sparkle in her eyes revealed a spirit Nicholas found admirable despite his anger. She would fight to the end. Wrenching an apology from her would be difficult . . . but not impossible. Few things were impossible.

Like the rhythm of a ticking clock, her head rocked in refusal. She grinned smugly at him, then at Kraus, who had clasped his hands behind his head and appeared to be watching the scene with great interest.

"Better tell this idiot that stands behind doors who I am," the girl told Kraus.

Kraus shrugged and lifted his brows as if he hadn't the slightest notion who she was.

Nicholas plopped the *Ontario*'s records in a nearby chair and replaced the vase on the shelf. "Idiot" was the final insult. His hand lashed out and grabbed the girl's wrist. "Listen . . . I have a throbbing head because of you, and I never like being called names or having a tongue wagged at me. I've had quite enough of your childish game. We'll see who's going to dunk who in the river."

"Let go, blast it!" she cried. Wriggling like a freshly caught perch, she used her other hand to try to pry free of Nicholas's grip. When that didn't work, she kicked at his legs and tried to bite his arm.

Nicholas glanced apologetically at Kraus, ready to give up the fight in a second if he spotted the least amount of displeasure on the banker's face. But he spotted humor instead. Kraus rose from his chair and crossed the room to open the door obligingly.

A mix of black walnut, gilded trim, and shimmering brass sconces gave the bank lobby a look of elegance. Several employees rose behind desks, shock frozen on their faces. One woman giggled behind a hand covering her mouth.

Once outside, for the sake of an easier journey to the river, Nicholas grabbed the girl and swung her over his shoulder—quite an undignified position for a female of any age. A *genteel* female. But this one was anything but genteel. She was extraordinarily brash and insolent. She kicked and screamed and pounded his back with her fists.

Nicholas headed west on St. Clair Street, humming as he walked, drawing stares from passersby. The girl called him every foul name he had ever heard and some he had never heard. He reached the railroad, crossed it, and stepped onto dusty River Street, artisan and merchant shops filling the many warehouses on either side. Just ahead, side-wheelers, brigs, and schooners cluttered the Cuyahoga River. The girl quieted on Nicholas's shoulder, as if she suddenly realized how serious he was about dumping her in the river.

"Don't do it," she said, so low he barely heard her. "Don't know how to swim."

He grinned. "You just want me to put you down so you can call me more foul names, then run off."

She kicked again. "Throw me in an' I'll drown. I will. Don't. Do-on't!"

Nicholas heard a sniff. As if . . . no . . . no. She was merely trying to trick him. A group of men gathered near a dilapidated two-story gray warehouse pointed and laughed. The girl stopped kicking and sniffed again. "Put me down. Please?"

Please? There was something about the plea. Sincerity . . . desperation. It gripped a soft spot inside Nicholas. As angry as he had been with her, as much as knew he shouldn't give in, he slowly lowered her.

She stood unmoving before him. Her shoulders slumped slightly, and she bowed her head. He reached to lift strands of tangled hair so he might see her face. She jerked away.

"You really *can't* swim, can you?" he asked in disbelief, feeling a twinge of guilt. Absurd! Why should he feel guilty? She had needed to be taught a lesson.

"No. Satisfied?" A tear slipped from her cheek, landing on one of her dusty, tattered boots.

"No." Nicholas cursed low, shifting from foot to foot, wondering what he was supposed to do with her now. He couldn't believe she was crying. For all her defiance back in that banking office, she now seemed like nothing more than a defeated girl. Well, he couldn't leave her here in the Flats, the warehouse district. It was not a safe place for anyone to wander alone, much less a young girl, no matter how tangled her hair or dirty her face or coarse her language. "Where do you live?" he asked. "I have a gig parked in front of the bank. I'll take you home, and we'll forget this happened."

She shuffled away, her voice trailing. "Don't live nowhere, not really. Not now. Ma died when I was four. Pa died a few weeks ago. That German in the bank says he's my uncle, says he's responsible for me now. I just want to be left alone."

Nicholas stood frozen in shock. She was related to Kraus? And the man hadn't objected to his rough handling of his niece? Since Kraus had taken her in, he must care something about her. And yet he hadn't seemed to care at all. Of course, if she had been acting as she had this afternoon ever since Kraus had taken her in, no wonder he was so willing to let someone else take charge for a time.

She walked. Nicholas followed. "You really want to be left alone—that's why you just told me all that?" he asked.

No response.

He sighed heavily. "I'm taking you back to the bank."

"Leave me alone. I ain't never goin' back there. I'm sorry. There, you got your apology. Now go away."

Half a block ahead, River Street connected with Superior. More warehouses, rough-looking lake men... He was *not* going to leave her here. "You can walk back to the bank with me, or I'll toss you over my shoulder again. It's up to you."

"You're not carrying me like that again!" she blurted.

"Then you'll walk back?"

Suddenly she stopped near the edge of the street, where vines, scraggly bushes, and trees clustered. A thick log lay parallel to the river. She stomped over, sat, and folded her arms. "And just what's that German going to do with me? I got dropped on him by mistake. He don't want me."

"What happened to your parents?" Nicholas asked, walking over to the log. He sat near her, watching her closely.

"Ma died of some lung sickness. Pa got some stomach sickness."

"There's only your uncle? No aunts? No cousins or grandparents?"

"That German and my father, that's all there was. If everybody'd leave me alone, I'd do just fine by myself. Could go back to the farm and plant the fields. There's cows and chickens and hogs. Got a good farm. That German says he's sellin' it. What's that leave me with?"

"How old are you?" Nicholas asked gently.

"Fourteen."

"Your name?"

"Katie."

"You really think you could manage a farm by yourself, Katie?"

Her chin shot up. "I could. And don't you try and tell me I can't! Been arguin' with that German about it for weeks now."

Nicholas chuckled, then studied her again. Wild blond curls, crystal blue eyes . . . If she was telling the truth, she was rough, willful, and temperamental because life had made her so. She was bruised and battered, yet determined to march forward with that strong chin stuck in the air, daring anyone to oppose her. She had no way of knowing, but she was a lot like him. Again he felt a flare of admiration for her. "You know, with a little soap and water, you might be pretty. Have you ever tried to be a girl, Katie? I mean—have you ever washed and brushed your hair and worn a dress?"

Summer Storm

"Never any need to. Pa needed a boy to help him on the farm. I could do the work of two boys," she promptly responded.

Nicholas sighed. She was obviously proud of doing the work of two boys. "You can't go back to the farm, Katie. You'd be alone. Besides, what about school? Do you know how to read?" he asked, thinking of the way she had gone directly to the bookshelf in Werner's office.

She was silent for a time. Presently she said in a low voice, "A little. I like it. I went to school some, when I could."

"Can you write?"

"Never learned much. Pa—"

"Needed you on the farm," Nicholas finished in disgust. Had the farm been more damned important to the man than his daughter? "What about going to school? Would you like to?"

She kicked at the grass. "Think that German would let me? He thinks I ain't worth nothin'."

Nicholas winced at her English and at her way of referring to Kraus as "that German." "I'll speak with him. But if I do, and he enrolls you in a girls' school, you must promise to work hard. Does it bother you that he doesn't like the way you are?"

Katie nodded. Reluctantly, Nicholas thought.

"Then make him like you, Katie. Make him proud to call you his niece. Make me proud to have met you."

Tears swelled in her eyes again. Nicholas stood and started back toward St. Clair, knowing Katie's pride would take another blow if she discovered he knew she was about to cry again. He suspected he had won her affection in an odd sort of way during the last few minutes. She had certainly won his.

"Gonna wait or do I walk back by myself?" he heard her demand.

Amused, he stopped and glanced back at her. Her head was tilted again, but this time she peered at him with those pretty blue eyes around a tangle of curls.

Then she shuffled toward him.

1

1858 SANDUSKY, OHIO

AT THIS POINT along her glorious shore overhung with trees and other foliage, Lake Erie looked tranquilly beautiful. Pink hints of forthcoming daylight touched the water as Katherine sat forward in the little boat, propped her elbows on her knees, and stared across at Alexandra Owens.

Alexandra's dark hair fluttered around her pretty ivory face. Her eyes glittered as she stared back and smiled. "Remember how we hated each other?"

Katherine gave a little laugh, although sadness swelled inside her. Their last day together. No . . . their last morning, their last hours. "I remember," she said softly. "We almost tore each other bald one night over supper. I didn't like the way you looked at me."

"And I did not like the way you *looked*."

"Unruly."

"Horrid."

"Frightening," Katherine concluded, loving their familiar play of words. They giggled together, remembering.

Alexandra reached to untie the rope that moored the boat to a tree. Katherine had saved her allowance until she had enough to purchase the little boat. Through an acquaintance she had arranged to have the boat brought here, to the "secret place" along Lake Erie's shore.

Summer Storm

Enemies at first, she and Katherine had caused much trouble during Katherine's first year at the Sacred Heart School for Young Ladies. The instructors, a group of ancient nuns, had permanently separated them, assigning Katherine a room at one end of the school hall, Alexandra one at the other end. Katherine always sat at one far corner of the huge dining table. Alexandra sat at the opposite corner.

The nuns *thought* they had permanently separated the girls.

"All right, I was horrid," Katherine admitted. "But you were intolerable, thinking you were queen of the school."

Alexandra giggled. "I was the prettiest girl until you arrived. Suddenly I had competition. The day you smashed that egg on Rose Thompson's face, I knew we were on the same side."

They shared another moment giggling. Katherine took an oar, Alexandra grabbed the other, and they rowed the boat out from the shore a ways. Not too far, for they knew the dangers of Lake Erie. She was huge, a sister to the other four Great Lakes. Her opposite shore was never visible. Katherine had heard that even a storm-tossed ocean couldn't match the fury of a sudden Lake Erie gale. She and Alexandra had sometimes escaped the confines of the school to sit near her during storms. Nothing could compare to her beauty.

"Rose hated us both," Katherine said. "Besides, you and I had to become friends. We nearly bumped into each other that day we both sneaked from the school. If we hadn't started talking and become friends, we would have been discovered and sent back."

"Back where there is nothing," Alexandra said, a touch of sadness in her voice.

Katherine shut her eyes, emotion rushing through her again. She had dreamed of the day when she would return to Cleveland and see Nicholas Cummings again. He had never visited, preferring to send occasional notes and books through the years and "not distract her from her studies," he had written in one missive.

Yes, she wanted to see Nicholas. But leaving Alexandra . . . Katherine could hardly breathe. "I-I'm sorry, Alexandra. I will not go. I'll stay in Sandusky and—"

"No." Alexandra stopped rowing and reached for Katherine's hand, looking deeply into her friend's eyes, her only friend in the world. She would not take this opportunity from Katherine. Katherine had worked hard, sometimes sitting near a window and studying by moonlight. She could read as well or better than Alexandra, who had had years of schooling. Katherine had worked hard so she could someday make Nicholas Cummings proud of her. This afternoon Katherine would leave for Cleveland, and Alexandra would do nothing and say nothing to make Katherine alter her plans.

"You go," Alexandra whispered. "Nicholas cannot help but fall madly in love with you. Look at you. You are lovely. He will see that and he will see the lady you've become and he will want to marry you."

Alexandra sat back, battling tears. She had been through much worse then losing a close friend in her lifetime. She had lost her Mama when she was five—a young age, but she remembered the accident well. Mama had fallen on the stairs and died hours later, leaving Alexandra desolate. Two years later, Papa had enrolled Alexandra in the school. After they had started talking, she and Katherine had realized how similar their troubled lives were, and they had grown close. Now Katherine would be gone, and emptiness would be her companion again. But she loved Katherine. She wanted her happiness. That was all that mattered.

Silence fell between them. The sky lightened in shades of purple and red. Lake Erie stirred, coming slowly awake as the little boat moved along. Alexandra rowed more.

Katherine followed suit. She watched Alexandra, knowing she would feel an empty spot inside after she left, a spot Alexandra had occupied. She would miss these secret outings, miss Alexandra's smile and laughter, miss their many conversations.

The boat rocked and creaked. A distant gull's cry pierced the morning. "What will you do after you leave the school someday? Where will you go?" Katherine asked.

"I'll teach. Perhaps in Toledo. I've even thought of going to Cincinnati," Alexandra answered.

"Cleveland is growing all the time. Nicholas says so in his letters. Surely there are many schools," Katherine suggested.

Alexandra smiled. "Then perhaps it will be Cleveland. I will teach, and you will marry your Nicholas, whom you have fantasized about for five years now."

Katherine stared beyond Alexandra, at the vast expanse of water and at the gulls soaring above Lake Erie. "I love him," she said. "I have loved him since the day he talked my uncle into giving me a chance. Uncle Werner was finished with me. I don't know exactly what he had planned, but it wasn't a proper school, to be certain. Perhaps an orphanage far east. I really was horrid."

"We must go back now," Alexandra said.

Katherine caught Alexandra's gaze and held it. She dropped her oar. Alexandra dropped hers. They flew together and embraced, emotion finally overcoming them. Alexandra sobbed unashamedly. Katherine inhaled sharp breaths, her entire body shuddering.

"I will write . . . always," she managed in a thin, weak voice.

"And I will join you someday," Alexandra promised. "Our friendship will never end."

They parted and grabbed their oars again. They turned the boat, guiding it back to its haven beneath overhanging trees.

Once they had climbed the embankment, Katherine didn't dare look back.

2

THROUGH THE CARRIAGE window the sight of Cleveland's River Street, cluttered with shipyards, factories, and wholesale grocers, flooded Katherine with memories of a summer day when Nicholas Cummings had pulled her from the throes of self-pity. She smiled, admiring the cluster of ships in the Cuyahoga River near River and Lighthouse streets. She remembered how she and Nicholas had sat together on a log and talked. The conversation had not lasted long, yet it had shown her that someone—Nicholas—cared. It had shown her that she had not been left alone in a huge, overwhelming world.

Nicholas.

He was special. So very special. Katherine tingled with anticipation when she thought of seeing him again. She flickered an ivory fan before her face. The temperature inside the carriage was oppressive, perhaps more so because of her nervousness. Uncle Werner sat opposite her, busily looking out the carriage window.

Would Nicholas be pleased by the change in her?

The question had been in her head for days, plaguing her, keeping her awake at night. She smoothed the sheer overskirt of her yellow gown, hoping she looked lovely enough this evening to at least catch Nicholas's eye. She and Alexandra had made the gown, employing the expert stitches they'd been taught at the school. Despite the invention of the sewing machine, there was still a certain pride to be found in delicate, handmade stitches. The gown's bodice, modestly cut and off the shoulder, was trimmed with frothy black lace. The long skirt beneath the overskirt was decorated with matching lace flounces and silk roses. Brushed away from her face and pinned, her hair fell in a cascade to graze her bare shoulders—the only manner in which the unruly curly mass could be managed on a humid summer day.

A slight breeze caressed her face. Wispy curls tickled her neck. The fan flickered faster. "He knows we are coming?" she asked suddenly, gathering her shawl of black lace more securely over her forearms.

Smiling, Uncle Werner nodded. "Nicholas has been waiting for your homecoming."

Katherine's eyes widened slightly. She quickly composed herself, determined to be realistic. She knew Nicholas didn't love her the way a man loved a woman. He had merely taken an interest in the filthy, unmannered girl he plucked from Uncle Werner's banking office, writing her letters now and then and sending books occasionally through the years. But she adored him. She loved him. She had loved him since that fateful day five years ago, and she hoped in time Nicholas would return the sentiment.

The carriage slowed. Katherine glanced out the window. The sun was a huge ball in a clear sky, bathing everything in an orange glow and promising a glorious sunset. Ships roamed up and down the Cuyahoga, making their way in and out of the river mouth and Lake Erie, decorating the water with an array of pilot and paddle-houses and tall masts with sails unfurled or secured. Black and brick-red stacks puffed black smoke. All this against the background of warehouses with signs boasting a variety of services to be found within. There were sail makers, carpenters, insurance and shipping agents... Katherine could have read the many signs and words painted on the sides and fronts of buildings for an hour. But one title in particular, amid the many ships and buildings, caught and held her attention.

Morning Star.

The lettering followed the arc of a paddle-house on the side of a ship docked near Front Street. The *Morning Star* nestled lazily between a schooner and a barge. Each of her three deck railings were decorated with red, white, and blue banners for this evening's Independence Day celebration.

Katherine's heart fluttered wildly. Within minutes she would see Nicholas again.

She recalled how she had sat near him in Uncle Werner's banking office and listened to him argue for her future. Of course, Uncle Werner had not thought she was worth bothering with. He'd said she was "obscenely improper," "horribly dirty," as well as "intolerably willful." There were a number of other descriptions, all of which had made Katherine brood in her seat, glancing hopelessly about for some way to slip from the office. She remembered thinking that expecting a man who didn't like her to consider helping her was ridiculous, senseless.

But no . . . Nicholas had continued, talking about this school and that school. There was one in Sandusky his mother had recommended for his cousin several years ago. Perhaps a convent might even do. That suggestion brought Katherine straight out of the chair. She would have something to say about being shipped to a convent! Nicholas had told her to sit and be quiet. She had. She adored him even then.

Finally, after what seemed hours, Uncle Werner had agreed to the Sandusky school, wanting her away from Cleveland, out of his sight. "I've endured enough embarrassment," he had said, and had gone into accounts of things she'd done during the last two weeks. Climbing out an upstairs window and slipping down a tree. Tripping Peggy, the housekeeper. (The tripping would have been bad enough, but she'd tripped the woman while Peggy was carrying a tea service!) She refused to wear anything but the clothes she'd come to Cleveland in, refused to bathe, and . . . well, he had gone on for some time.

Katherine had squirmed, fearing the accounts would destroy whatever faith Nicholas had placed in her. Instead he had stood and said, "Sandusky it is then." Within a month, she had been on a train bound that way.

Summer Storm 19

Smiling at the memory, Katherine noticed that guests had already gathered on the ship. Gay music and gowns of red, lavender, orange, green, and a host of other colors made the festivities seem that much more exciting. And there was the coaxing sound of a violin's strings being stroked. Lifting a brow, Katherine looked questioningly at Uncle Werner. "Musicians?"

"Of course. Nicholas is a thorough man."

Werner watched the driver assist Katherine from the carriage. He followed, offering Katherine his arm, certain he would be envied as soon as they boarded the ship. "Stunned" was the only word that could describe his reaction when she had arrived yesterday. He had felt somewhat meek, remembering how he had treated her the day Nicholas had convinced him to send her away to school. Not once had he gathered enough courage to go visit her, fearing she had the same unkempt appearance.

He chuckled to himself. A rather ridiculous man he had been, frightened of a girl to the point where he had not even believed the reports Sister Dorothy had sent him from the school now and then. When he had gone to the station yesterday, he had truly expected the same scraggly girl in dirty boys' clothes Katherine had been five years ago. The sight of the clean, well-dressed, lovely young woman stepping from the train had pleased him immensely. And while he and his niece still had a great deal to learn about each other, they had gotten off to a pleasing start over supper last evening. They had shared conversation, and later they had discussed a few of his many books.

He patted her hand, inquiring, "You learned dancing at the school?"

She nodded. "That and many other things. I speak French. And . . . I requested to be taught German. *Und Ich erfahren gut.*"

Werner was touched that she had learned the language of the old country. Part Irish she might be, but her mother had been German, and he was pleased that she knew her mother's native tongue. "Now to celebrate the new country," he said, guiding her to the ramp leading to the ship.

Once on board the elegant *Morning Star,* Katherine visually searched the mingling guests. She was certain she would know Nicholas; she had studied him long enough, watching him that day in Uncle Werner's office. His face was forever imprinted on her mind. His eyes were a rich emerald, slightly turned down at the corners and fringed with short, black lashes. The lines of his jaw were straight and long, joining at a proud chin. His nose was perfect, chiseled and angled in the right places. Thick black hair curled slightly at his nape.

"Nicholas will be amazed at the change in you," Uncle Werner said. "Perhaps he is inside or below. I will get refreshment. You will do well alone for a moment?"

Katherine nodded, still searching the crowd. Men glanced her way, and she averted her gaze as she'd been taught to do. Still, from beneath her lashes, she searched. All around her people mingled, talked, and laughed, sometimes passing, sometimes pausing. Hands held glasses, and fans fluttered to ward off the July heat. The ship stirred, swaying slightly.

"A woman of your beauty should never be left unattended," a deep voice said over her shoulder. "You came with the Harrises? Edmond said he would be bringing a guest."

Katherine's heart seemed to stop for a moment.

Nicholas.

She even remembered the thickness of his voice. His breath was warm and delicious on her bare skin. She was afraid to turn and face him, afraid he might not like her appearance, afraid his eyes would find her every flaw.

"Is leaving a woman unattended on a crowded ship anything like leaving a girl of fourteen alone on River Street?" she managed to ask.

She waited. Breathing became a task. The conversations and laughter of the other guests seemed to fade. The sun began spilling magnificent colors—purples, pinks, and reds.

"Katherine?" he responded finally. "I knew you were promising but . . . you're stunning!"

She wanted to laugh aloud with joy. Stunning? Yes, he had said that. She had accomplished her first goal—grabbing his interest.

He moved around her, and she caught a glimpse of his wavy black hair before dropping her gaze to the ivory fan she gripped in one hand. An instant later she mustered enough courage to dare a glance at him from beneath her lashes. After all, she had dreamed of this day, dreamed of seeing Nicholas again. She would not stand here the entire evening with her eyes downcast, making him think she was a foolish girl.

He spoke her name in a low voice that was strangely thick and slightly raspy.

Katherine watched him as he assessed her while adjusting the black stock fastened around a collar that barely grazed the strong jaw she remembered well. He wore black except for the white shirt beneath his vest. His coat hung open, and his trousers tapered at the ankles and were secured by straps passing under black shoes. He was dressed exactly as most of the male guests were, yet she could easily have picked him from the crowd.

Still, there was something different about him this time, something that had not existed five years ago, when they had first met.

It was in his eyes, those mesmerizing emeralds. They were darkened, narrowed, concentrated on her in a way that made her tremble.

Katherine recalled her and Alexandra's many whispered conversations about "the act between a man and a woman." Alexandra had once said she'd heard a man's eyes changed when he desired a woman. Was that it then? Did Nicholas truly desire her?

Yes, she thought so. And that knowledge made her heart pound all the faster.

He shifted his position, exhaled a long breath, and looked off at a group of guests just boarding the *Morning Star*. "They taught you a lot at that school, didn't they?" A throaty chuckle escaped him. He shook his head. "Save that demure look for the man you want to marry, Katherine. It's far too enticing to be used on me."

Katherine didn't know whether to smile or frown. Obviously she would have to make her feelings for him known very soon. She must let him know she wanted him to love her as she loved him. She wanted to "entice" him.

"Nicholas . . ." She glanced around the crowded deck, heard the voices, the laughter, the many conversations.

Uncle Werner appeared with two glasses of punch, handing one to Katherine. "Ah, Nicholas. I see you have reacquainted yourself with my lovely niece."

"Yes . . . lovely. I didn't know her," Nicholas mumbled.

"No? Do not feel alone. I did not know her at first either. Your parents are here?"

"*Mother* will be here," Nicholas replied. He was conveying a meaning to Uncle Werner, Katherine guessed, but she didn't dwell on deciphering it. She'd received a number of lectures about patience from Sister Dorothy through the years, none of which had done much good. In fact, she seemed to have less patience now than ever. She wanted to get Nicholas alone and make her feelings for him known as soon as possible.

He exchanged more conversation with Uncle Werner. Apparently Nicholas's mother had won a great deal at the track two days ago. His face, as it turned this way and that way, was a combination of well-defined planes and angles catching shadow and light in the evening glow. He brushed aside the skirt of his coat, buried a hand in a pocket, and leaned casually against the deck railing, laughing deeply at something Werner said about the woman having the most luck of anyone he had known, for she knew nothing about horses.

Nicholas was what Alexandra would call an exciting man, handsome and confident, Katherine thought with a surge of pride.

"Yes, unfortunately, Mother beat us all out of that purse," he said. "Even Kevin, who was sure he had the winner. Amazing, isn't she?"

"Irritating, that is what she is," Uncle Werner said, pretending indignation.

"With the parade and festivities in Public Square, how was the ride here?" Nicholas asked, shifting the topic.

Werner grunted. "*Schrecklich*. Harrowing. Godard's foolish contraption, you know. People crowded everywhere to see that blasted balloon go up." He waved a hand in a pantomimic way. "Sailing away. And to where? I will not be surprised if we hear it has spilled into a mess of trees or—God help that fool—into the lake. He will drown before anyone can reach him."

"Ah . . . a critic," Katherine couldn't resist teasing over her glass of sweet punch. "I'm fascinated with Mr. Godard's balloon. I would like to have questioned him." *Exchange some of that curiosity for a little patience*, Sister Dorothy had often advised. But curiosity, as well as a lack of patience, seemed forever embedded in Katherine.

"The sky is for birds," Uncle Werner scoffed. "Godard will realize that soon enough."

"You echo Peggy's words from this morning. What if Mr. Godard manages to land his balloon safely? He'll be heralded as a genius then, no doubt. I saw it from the house, you know, a beautiful mix of dark blues and reds. I waved and shouted from the balcony. All seemed well."

Uncle Werner grumbled something more. Katherine suspected he really wanted to see Mr. Godard succeed, for she knew just enough about Uncle Werner from their time spent together in the library last evening to know he possessed his own store of curiosity. Why else would he have so many books, many philosophical in nature?

"Contraption, eh?" she teased further. "Can you deny any more than I, Uncle, that you wonder how he keeps the thing in the air for even a moment?"

Uncle Werner tapped the edge of his glass. "Bah! Foolishness."

"And yet your brow is wrinkled. Not so much with annoyance, I think, as with curiosity. Even if Godard 'spills into a mess of trees' or into the lake, he has at least made some of us ask questions. And questions, when turned this way and that, often lead to answers. And answers lead to progress."

"She has you, Werner," Nicholas said, chuckling. His gaze met hers again, this time sparkling with surprise and admiration.

The beginnings of a grin twitched one corner of Uncle Werner's mouth. "Very well. I do wonder."

"We'll investigate the subject together soon," Katherine said. She sipped more sweet punch, smiling over the rim of her glass.

Nicholas excused himself, then wandered off to greet a few more guests. Moments later, he wandered back while Uncle Werner turned to converse with someone to his left. Nicholas glanced at Katherine, and again he narrowed his emerald eyes.

Her gaze faltered, then flicked, to the deck railing, to her skirt, finally settling on the glass she held. Despite her earlier success at conversation, she was still nervous. "Is it so difficult to believe?" she asked softly.

"What?"

"That I'm really Katherine."

"I'm staring. I apologize. I don't usually get caught at it."

She laughed. "A sneak. But don't apologize. I truly enjoy your gaze."

He said nothing.

She was still trying to muster enough courage to glance up and assess his response to her bold statement when Uncle Werner turned back to them.

"The profits from the canal boats are plentiful so far this year, Nicholas. You are making me a rich man."

Nicholas shifted. Both hands sought pockets. "You should take over managing them for a while. I need a vacation. I've been thinking of going to Canada."

"Oh, no. No, no. I would never think of managing those canal boats. Or the ships."

Katherine's gaze darted between the men. "Canal boats? I thought you owned side-wheelers, Nicholas."

"Both. Canal boats and side-wheelers. Three years ago, I proposed a partnership to your uncle. We ship grain and other goods up and down the canal."

Werner grunted. "Yes . . . As you know, Katherine, Nicholas has a persuasive way about him, particularly in the area of business ventures. How can I say no? But I do not care for this latest proposal. Running off to Canada and leaving me to manage—bah! We would be ruined in a month's time."

"Nicholas!" someone called through the throng.

A tall red-haired man in the popular black evening attire drew near and paused before Katherine, wearing a smile that froze in place as their gazes met. His blue-green eyes were murky, but there was a warmth to them, a depth.

"Dear lady," he said, bending to place a light kiss on the back of her hand. "Never have I been so enchanted in my life. Your name, please, so I may store it in my brain."

"That is, if he has one," Nicholas muttered, drawing up behind the man. "Stand up, Kevin, and stop making a fool of yourself."

Katherine returned Kevin's smile, wondering at the sharp way Nicholas addressed his guest. Nicholas obviously found Kevin a bother at the moment; she found him dramatic yet charming. "Enchanted? You do have a way of getting a lady's attention, Mr. . . ."

"Riley," he provided, straightening.

"I'm Katherine McDaniel, Mr. Kraus's niece."

"Reserve a dance for me this evening, Miss McDaniel?"

She laughed. He certainly wasted no time. "Of course. I'll enjoy—"

"Would you mind telling the captain to move out, Kevin?" Nicholas interrupted.

"Aye." Kevin released Katherine's hand and started past Nicholas. "Face it, man, she's one lass you won't be having all evening. There'll be others besides myself vying for her attention," he said loud enough that Katherine heard. Then he wove his way through the crowd until she lost sight of him.

"He has a brash way about him," Nicholas commented dryly, staring after Kevin.

More dashing than brash, Katherine thought. He had swept through with irresistible charm. Nicholas had been rather rude to him, but at this point, moments after her precious reunion with Nicholas, she wasn't about to say so and risk making him angry with her.

Uncle Werner waved to someone. "Tom Jenkins! I have been trying to meet with the man for a month. I fear I must be rude, Katherine, and leave you with Nicholas. If you do not mind?"

"Of course not."

Uncle Werner wandered off. Nicholas offered Katherine his arm, his gaze resting briefly on her mouth, then lifting to her eyes.

Katherine felt a pleasant heat creep up the back of her neck. She placed her hand in the curve of his arm, feeling firm muscles beneath the smoothness of his coat. "Where are we going?"

"I need to talk to the cook, make sure everything is going as scheduled. I'll show you the ship after that."

Katherine felt as if she were on a cloud, sailing through a clear sky. Nothing else in the world mattered at the moment but being with Nicholas. Even if he didn't love her right now, he would soon. She would make sure of that. She would use every feminine charm she and Alexandra had ever talked about to win Nicholas Cummings.

He was the only man in the world for her.

She was entirely too attractive, entirely too innocent for her own good. Never had Nicholas been so startled by anyone's appearance in his life.

While he spoke with the cook regarding the supper that was scheduled to be served in another half hour, Nicholas watched from the corner of his eye as Katherine wandered the dining saloon, touching the dark mahogany walls then a crystal goblet on one of the many tables covered with white linen. She touched a fork at the next, a dark blue napkin at yet another. She walked with an unmatched air of grace, the reddish-gold highlights in her hair shimmering in the dancing light provided by dozens of oil lamps. She possessed pure ivory skin, lips the color of ripe strawberries. The once insolent, willful girl had grown into a devastatingly beautiful and poised young woman.

Summer Storm

Her gown, though modestly cut, was trimmed with black lace, flounces, and roses and revealed tantalizing glimpses of her full breasts. Nicholas's eyes returned to her hair—that incredible mass of alluring unruliness. It softly framed her face and spilled from the back of her head to dance on her tempting, bare shoulders whenever she moved her head. Black lace draped over her forearms in striking contrast to her skin as she paused to look at a huge painting of white-tipped waves rolling onto a section of the Lake Erie shoreline.

She had a small nose and large blue eyes, lined with light curly lashes that nearly touched her eyebrows as she looked up. Her profile was delicate and lovely, a mix of soft curves and shadows.

Good God. She was bewitching.

He finished his conversation with the cook. The man slipped away, and Nicholas approached Katherine from behind, wanting to tell her how he had hired a European artist to do this painting. Art was one of her interests, he had discovered long ago. Art and books.

She apparently didn't hear his footsteps. She turned around just as he reached her. Her hands flew up in surprise and planted themselves, palms out, against his chest.

Their eyes met and held. Hers were the color of the lake on a clear day. Sparkling blue. Fathomless. Incredible. Nicholas inhaled deeply. Her perfume . . . something flowery . . . something sweet.

He couldn't seem to back away; in truth he didn't want to, not just yet. He was lost in her eyes, could lose himself even more. Her lips parted in breathlessness as he planted a hand on the wall above her shoulder, just beneath the painting. He leaned closer, felt her warm breath on his face, and wondered if he could ever withdraw.

"Nicholas. I have waited so long to see you," she whispered. She was so bold as to touch his jaw, then the hair at his nape.

Nicholas caught his breath. This couldn't be the same girl he had wanted to drown in the river five years ago! Couldn't be.

But she was. That "rumpled piece of baggage" had been transformed into the vision before him.

He had never expected this attraction to her, and he wasn't sure how to deal with it, how to counter it. He knew it wasn't right. He shouldn't be feeling this for her, for any woman but Sarah Preston . . . his fiancée.

3

NICHOLAS FORCED HIMSELF to withdraw. "I'll . . . I'll take you back upstairs. The ship is moving now. You'll want to see the sunset over the lake."

Seeing the stunned look in her eyes, yet confident he was doing the right thing, he turned away.

"Nicholas?" she queried softly.

He reluctantly turned back. She stared at him. He offered his arm as if nothing were wrong, hardening himself against showing any sort of response. Her gaze faltered. Finally she placed a hand on his arm.

In silence they returned to the *Morning Star*'s middle deck. Nicholas spotted Kevin maneuvering his way through the crowd and wanted to hide Katherine somewhere. The Irishman was closing in like a wolf on the hunt. But immediately Nicholas felt guilty. If Katherine chose to see Kevin, that was her business, and he had no right to interfere.

So he relinquished Katherine as the ship moved out into Lake Erie. The setting sun tossed orange and silver flecks on the water, and conversations and laughter from Nicholas's many guests filled the air. He mingled in the crowd, lifting feminine hands to his lips, giving ladies the smile he knew would leave them blushing but thrilled when he turned his back and walked away. He took empty glasses to be refilled and nodded responses to the many thank yous. Later he spotted

Katherine and Kevin standing near the stern, laughing together. Obviously spellbound, Kevin couldn't take his eyes off of her.

A prickle of annoyance flickered through Nicholas. Whether or not she wanted to see or involve herself with Kevin was Katherine's business, he again told himself.

Ten minutes later, Kevin made the same mistake Werner had made a mere hour ago: He left Katherine alone while he fetched more refreshment. In a flash she was surrounded by eager-eyed suitors vying for dances later in the evening. Some of Nicholas's closest friends made absolute fools of themselves, just as Kevin had, sweeping down over her hand, flashing dashing smiles and glances and rattling off what they doubtless thought were clever words. They looked like a bunch of preening male peacocks, spreading their feathers before the female, Nicholas thought. He couldn't deny that he was irritated.

"I'm thinking I should've taken her with me," Kevin said in disgust as he joined Nicholas near a door that led downstairs. Laughter drifted from Katherine's group of admirers. "Wouldn't stand a chance if I went over now. Punch?" he asked, offering a full glass.

"No."

Nodding, Kevin drained the glass himself, then sighed. "Prestons coming tonight?"

Nicholas shifted his eyes from the peacocks to Kevin. "No. And if you came for the sole purpose of lecturing me about my decision to marry Sarah, don't. Your words in my study yesterday were quite enough."

Always a bit cocky, and more than a little sarcastic when he wanted to make a point, Kevin leaned against the deck railing. "Lecture you? My friend, why would I lecture you? Why would anyone lecture you about anything? You build perfect ships. You have a perfect house with a perfect housekeeper and a perfect butler. Oh, and let's not forget Harold, the perfect driver. Now for a perfect little wife, one with social skills and an education to challenge almost any man's."

"I don't think I have the stomach for you tonight." Nicholas turned, preparing to walk away. "Try to behave the rest of the evening. The engagement will be announced at the supper in a few days," he tossed over his shoulder.

He hadn't taken three steps before Kevin had eased his way in front of him again, forcing Nicholas to halt. Both glasses were gone now. "Of course, it's the perfect match since you and Sarah were raised together. Quite a perfect world all the way around."

"It's more than a feeling of obligation," Nicholas snapped.

Kevin raised a brow. "Is it now?"

"It is. I love Sarah."

"Love . . . oh, yes . . . love! And what a perplexing thing love is, having many different sides."

"Kevin, you're making a fool of yourself. People are beginning to stare." Nicholas started to the left.

Kevin gripped his arm. "There's passionate love, the kind that seizes you so you can't put a woman from your mind. You want her day and night. You want to feel her hair and skin, listen to her voice and her laughter. Then there's platonic love, the kind that exists between you and Sarah. A simple touch of affection now and then, a few words of—"

"That's enough." Nicholas shook his arm free and tugged at his stock. "I would sincerely hate to have you tossed off this ship."

"Ah, I see I've made you a little nervous. Quite a telling habit you have there, always fumbling with neckcloths or cuffs when something ruffles you."

"What exactly do you hope to accomplish with these rantings of yours?"

"To bring a friend to his senses," Kevin grated. "What did you hope to accomplish by sending me the note telling about the upcoming announcement of your engagment? Did you think I wouldn't be concerned? We've had conversations about Sarah before."

"I wanted you to be one of the first to know about the engagement. If I had known you would react like this, however, I—"

"What did you expect?"

"That you would act like my friend and wish me well."

"I *am* acting like your friend. If you marry Sarah Preston, you'll be making a mistake. The biggest of your life."

Nicholas gave him a scathing look. "Don't try to dictate my life based on opinions you've formed about marriage."

Kevin clamped his jaw shut, narrowing his flashing eyes. A moment passed. They glared at each other. "That's not what this is about," he finally responded.

"No?"

"No."

"I think it is."

Kevin gave him another long look, then stepped back. "Make your perfect world then, if that's what you think. But don't expect me to support what you're doing. Don't be expecting me at the wedding."

Nicholas inhaled deeply. Kevin was like a brother. He wanted him at the wedding, wanted him by his side. They didn't always argue like this. In fact, before yesterday Nicholas couldn't remember the last time they had spoken to each other so sharply. "You don't mean that," he sputtered, searching Kevin's face for some sign that he didn't.

"I do." Kevin nodded, backing away. "Yes, I do." His gaze slid from Nicholas's as he turned.

Then he slipped into a cluster of people and out of sight.

Kevin miraculously found an uncrowded place amidship. There were one or two people here and there, but at least it was a quiet place where he might gather his thoughts and put a smile back on his face. He did, after all, intend to stay the remainder of the evening. He *had* come for the sole purpose of talking to Nicholas, but several young beauties, including Katherine McDaniel, had caught his eye, and he wanted to explore them a bit.

Nicholas was going to marry Sarah Preston for all the wrong reasons.

Damned fool, Kevin thought.

He'd traveled a bit more than Nicholas, had led a different life. The son of a bootmaker with a rickety shop in a west-side slum, he'd felt hunger pains many times as a child and knew the agony of a half-frozen body. Too many times there'd been holes in the walls and in the ceiling of his family's two-room shack. Winter on the shores of Lake Erie could be brutal, and no one knew that better than Kevin. Some six years ago, he'd struggled to start a dry goods store. Now he owned a small but prospering hotel. He'd never begrudged Nicholas anything, despite the fact that Nicholas had at least had the influence of his family name to help him become a success in the shipping business—part of Nicholas's perfect world. And Kevin was certainly experienced enough with the sort of passionate love he'd described to offer Nicholas a bit of well-intended advice.

The tinkling of a bell announced supper. Kevin straightened his coat and merged with the crowd, taking the stairs that led to the dining saloon. Musicians played a soft tune while servants in black and white assisted guests. To Kevin's dismay, he found he was seated across the length of the saloon from the lovely Katherine McDaniel. Suitors fluttered around her. A Negro waiter tried to convince them to take their seats. As anxious as Kevin was to continue a romantic evening with Katherine, he realized any effort to get near her would be fruitless.

But there were others. Indeed, there were always others. A bounty. Kevin lifted his wineglass and turned his attention to the delights of the coy, ebony-haired creature to his right.

Ah, yes . . . The evening, it seemed, was just getting under way.

Much later, the notes of yet another waltz filled the main saloon. Katherine had danced for hours. Her feet ached, her back ached, her head ached. Nevertheless, she smiled at Henry Roberts as he swept her around and prattled on about the magnificence of the railroad. His father was heavily involved in expanding the railroad west. Henry felt certain the railroad would soon replace travel and shipping on the canal. "Trains are faster than ships or barges," he said. "They make more sense if you think about it."

While Katherine was sure he was right, she didn't want to think about the railroad versus the canal right now. She wanted to think about Nicholas and his odd behavior in the dining saloon earlier.

She had given him full opportunity to kiss her; in fact, she'd never been so bold with a man. She had offered him her lips, yet Nicholas had pulled away. Could she perhaps have mistaken the look of desire she had seen in his eyes upon first encountering him this evening? No . . . As she recalled the heat of that look, she was certain she had made no mistake. For some reason, Nicholas was reluctant. She intended to learn why.

The problem was, she hadn't seen him for hours. She had thought he would request a dance with her. Scores of other men had. Not Nicholas.

The hour was growing late. After several more dances, Katherine excused herself from the men still waiting to dance with her and headed toward the ladies' saloon. From there she managed to escape onto the dim, deserted upper deck, she hoped without being noticed.

Waves splashed gently against the side of the ship. A night breeze had kicked up. July it might be, but out on the magnificent Lake Erie, Katherine had learned long ago, night was often cool. She shivered, watching a lantern rock gently from its hook on the railing. She was glad to be away from the noise of the crowd. Here there was only the occasional creak of the ship and the splashing of water as Lake Erie stirred from her evening doze. The moon was a silver sliver, casting its magical reflection on the shimmering water. A number of lights in the distance indicated other vessels. The sounds of music, conversation, and laughter seemed faint now. Crossing her arms and rubbing them for warmth, Katherine closed her eyes and tilted her head back, listening to the peaceful sounds of the night.

Something slid over her shoulders. A man's coat? Yes, she smelled champagne and a faint masculine cologne. Her eyes flew open, and she jerked to attention, wondering who lurked behind her. Perhaps she shouldn't have come up here alone.

She should have known she would be followed.

Hands gripped her upper arms, firmly but gently. "Relax, Katie. Were you preparing to fight me again?"

Hearing the richness of Nicholas's voice, she did relax. "You frightened me," she said, laughing nervously at herself.

"Sorry."

She smiled. "No one has called me Katie in years. They called me Katherine at the school."

He chuckled.

Shivers raced through Katherine. The cool lake breeze didn't cause them. Nicholas did. Nicholas . . . with his overwhelming presence, with his sheer masculinity.

"You'll always have a little of that spirited girl in you," he murmured, as if recalling the day of their first encounter. He settled the coat more securely on her shoulders. "Cold still?"

"A bit," she admitted. His breath smelled of tobacco. He had obviously just finished smoking.

Nicholas shifted to her left, turned his back to the rail and leaned against it, settling his gaze on her. Her eyes were wide and glistening; her rapid breath was audible. He tilted his head. "Afraid? Apprehensive? Of me?"

"Oh—"

"I wanted only to warm you, Katie," he assured softly.

"I-I'm sorry. You'll think I'm silly, but I've never been so alone with a man," she said.

This was a mistake, being out here with her. There was the bewitching glow of the moon, the soft splashing of the water, the magic of the night. There was her scent and the gentle breeze that fluttered wisps of hair about her face. Voices of apprehension whispered in Nicholas's head. He ignored them, preferring to reach up and brush strands of hair from her cheek. Just as he had thought—her hair felt like silk.

"Surely you've had a number of suitors, lovely as you are," he said.

"None I wanted. None I would even walk with through a garden."

They stood in silence for a time. He turned and faced the rail. Together they watched the moon's glitter dance on the water. The ship was turning. In the distance the bright light in the lighthouse tower beaconed across the lake.

"Why didn't you dance with me?" she asked softly. "You never even asked. You just seemed to disappear."

"I was there. Some. I much prefer to watch everyone enjoy themselves."

"But not even one dance?"

Nicholas debated how best to answer her question. Why hadn't he danced with her? Because he did not yet have his desire for her under control, though he couldn't tell her that. So instead of answering the question, he chose a different course, thinking he understood her reasoning for being so bold. "You owe me nothing, Katie. Nothing at all." He moved away slightly, putting a few more inches between them. He had encouraged her a bit, he thought, first with open looks of admiration he hadn't had the power to restrain, and now by standing here with her, telling her how lovely she was.

Katherine maneuvered a hand, sliding it over his on the deck railing. His gaze shot to their hands, and he stared, but made no effort to withdraw. What was he thinking? she wondered. That she wanted to give herself to him as payment for a debt? Certainly that wasn't her motive at all. No. Loving him was her motive. Loving him. She moved closer and traced his fingers with her forefinger.

Nicholas shut his eyes. She tortured him with her touch, tempted him in a way she knew little about. Her finger traced his knuckles, the bones of his hand, his fingers.

"We should join the others," he said, burying his hand in a pocket. That seemed the only safe place.

"You're wrong, you know, about me feeling like I owe you," she whispered. "That has nothing to do with what I'm feeling."

Nicholas stepped back, staring at her. This had gone far enough. It wasn't right. "Nothing can come of this, Katherine. Nothing."

Her yellow gown glowed under the moon and oil lights. Her eyes shimmered and sparkled—beautiful blue pools of

Summer Storm 37

innocence. "I would love to have you kiss me. I've never been kissed, you know. Never."

Good God. Nicholas breathed deeply. This was madness. How easy kissing her full red lips would be! He felt drawn to her, this woman who had suddenly swept into his life on this magical, starlit evening. Her satiny voice slithered around him. *I've never been kissed, you know. Never.*

He took a step, wetting his lips with his tongue. He was just lifting a hand to touch her, caress her face, when the sound of approaching voices jolted him back to his senses.

She did not belong in his life. Not like this. Why was he even thinking of kissing her when his engagement to Sarah was three days away from being announced?

"Let's go inside," he said in a sharp tone he didn't intend.

She stared at him, obviously not understanding, obviously hurt again that he had put her off. Well, he didn't care to explain. What had almost happened should never have almost happened. He meant to take her back inside and forget it.

He delivered her to Werner, who offered her his arm. Katherine took it, and they wandered away. Nicholas involved himself in another conversation regarding Godard and the balloon—the man and his contraption, as Werner had called it, seemed to be the talk of the evening. It was not a new thing overall, but it was certainly new and exciting to Clevelanders. While Nicholas listened and even shared in the conversation from time to time, he glimpsed Katherine occasionally. She and Werner and others were dancing a quadrille. Now and then she tossed baffled looks Nicholas's way.

He felt like a man who had barely escaped danger. Indeed he had, hadn't he? She was the only woman he had ever felt such a powerful urge to kiss. Not that he hadn't kissed others. He had. He had just never been so drawn to a woman.

A heavy feeling that he really had not escaped settled over him. It was like a dark cloud, wrinkling his brow, snuffing his enthusiasm for the celebration during the ensuing hours. He wandered the various saloons. Cards here, smoking and politics there, billiards, private conversations around small tables . . .

He finally wandered back to the main saloon. Katherine laughed at something someone said, and for a suspended moment her light laughter seemed to be the only sound in the noisy room.

A ridiculous notion, Nicholas thought, turning away. A waiter paused before him, offering a tray of goblets filled with champagne. Nicholas lifted one of the glasses and drained it, something he did not often do. Normally he slowly savored his choice of drink, whether it was champagne or wine or lemonade or punch. Something odd had come over him, something very odd indeed. He approached the door leading outside, casting one last look over his shoulder in time to meet Katherine's shimmery blue gaze as it settled on him.

Then he pushed the door open and stepped outside, feeling as if he no longer had a firm grasp on his "perfect little world."

Near the very spot on deck where he and Katherine had stood earlier, Nicholas stared across the dark water. Growing up, his family had consisted of not only his mother, father, and Werner Kraus, but also Sarah's parents, Alistair and Myra Preston. He couldn't remember many days when they hadn't been about; his father, Werner, and Alistair still often gathered in one or the other family library for pipes and conversation while his mother and Myra visited or shopped or some such thing.

He'd been nine years old at the time of Sarah's birth. She'd been weak and frail, but cute, too, and he'd been unable to resist the infant who turned into a toddler, then into a little girl with bouncing auburn curls.

If, as a little girl, she hadn't followed him around, he might have followed her around. She was still sickly, still had a tendency to fall and hurt herself; he felt a need to protect her. He didn't miss the whispers between her mother and his—the hope that one day he and Sarah would marry. He adored both women and didn't want to disappoint them. So by the time he was nineteen and Sarah was ten, he *knew* the two of them would wed someday. It was only a matter of time, of waiting

Summer Storm

for Sarah to reach an appropriate age and for him to build his life enough so he could give her a comfortable, if not wealthy, existence.

She was twenty years old now and would be the wife of one of Cleveland's more well-to-do and respected citizens. The time for the marriage had arrived. It was a perfect match, and certainly both mothers would be happy. He and Sarah would be happy.

Passionate and platonic... Nicholas shook his head. Kevin liked not knowing what life might bring next, but Nicholas preferred order in his. He preferred a plan, laid out much like the plans he carefully constructed for his ships, and even for the house he had designed. He didn't like disorder; it confused him, upset the balance.

4

NICHOLAS PULLED THE old, gray, hooded cloak securely around his body. The thing was wool and insufferably hot, but he would rather be hot than have someone recognize him.

At three in the morning, this section of Cleveland, just south of the junction of the Cuyahoga River and the Ohio Canal, was eerily quiet.

Like spirits in the night, two figures moved from the carriage to the side-wheeler *Ontario,* where they would hide away in the cargo hold. The hold was dank, no doubt, for the *Ontario* had sprung a small leak on her last voyage and had just been repaired.

Perhaps disease lurked in the darkness, too, Nicholas thought, but which was the worse evil—disease or bondage? Many were willing to take dangerous chances for the sake of freedom, himself included.

The majority of Clevelanders were anti-slavery. Fugitive Negroes were frequently hidden in basements of city homes, in barns, sheds, and farmhouses. But despite the majority, there were still those in the city who would eagerly reveal the whereabouts of escaped Negroes in return for the five dollars a head offered by slave hunters. Whenever someone spotted a fugitive, the bell in the Old Stone Church in Public Square chimed an alert. Anyone caught harboring an escaped Negro was threatened with prosecution under the Fugitive Slave Act.

Summer Storm

In silence Nicholas led the Negro man and woman across the *Ontario*'s deck and to the hold hatches, their footsteps like whispers in the night. The only light was the dim flame flickering in a small lantern hanging amidship. A husky lake man had already opened a hatch cover and lowered a ladder. Nicholas nodded to the seaman, then stepped aside so the man and woman could lower themselves into the hold. The woman suddenly flung herself on Nicholas, hugging him tight. When he glanced down at her, he saw the gratitude in her wide, white-rimmed eyes.

He knew why she felt so grateful, and the reason had to do with much more than just the fact that she was escaping bondage. Nearly a year before, her husband and young son had successfully traveled the points of the Underground Railroad. Nicholas had put them aboard the same ship he was putting her aboard now. Soon she would join them in Canada.

The woman withdrew, gave him one last look of gratitude, then hurried down the ladder into blackness. The man followed. Food and drink were stored in one area of the hold. Grain had been loaded more for appearance than for profit. In the morning passengers, excited about their journey, would board and everything would appear normal. The *Ontario* would then depart for another voyage.

The hatch was shut. Nicholas inclined his head to the lake man, feeling thankful yet again that he had easily found fellow abolitionists to work the *Ontario*, men who could be trusted explicitly.

Once he disembarked the ship, he walked three blocks east to Vineyard Street, where the carriage awaited. His driver, obviously anticipating his arrival, already had the door flung open.

Nicholas smiled as he climbed in and discarded the cloak. "You're timing me again, Harold," he said low, settling on one of the seats. In the dim light provided by the carriage lanterns, he saw Harold grin.

"Indeed, sir," Harold said, tugging at the edge of his tall, broad-brimmed hat. "I fear we are getting quite good at this illegal business. I know exactly how many minutes it takes you to complete your task."

"And how many is that?"

"Seventeen, sir."

Nicholas chuckled. "You're very good, Harold. I hope you never think of leaving my service."

"No, sir," came the response. Then the door clicked shut.

Within minutes the carriage moved north. Nicholas stared out the window as the vehicle crossed the quiet Ohio Canal. Boats and barges often littered the canal. At Champlain, Harold turned the carriage east, then south on Canal Road, which was no more than a dirt road with an abundance of foliage on either side. An inconvenient but necessary way home, thought Nicholas, feeling the night breeze waft through the open window. Canal Road was infrequently traveled at night. There were few farms and houses, therefore the chance of arousing suspicion was less.

Nicholas stared out at the farms and houses they did pass. He knew he placed his personal and public life in jeopardy by transporting the escaping Negroes across Lake Erie to freedom in Canada. But his personal sentiments against slavery could be traced back many years.

At fourteen he had fallen under the influence of an abolitionist Cleveland schoolmaster who planted seeds of antislavery sentiment in him. The following summer, Nicholas accompanied his father to a South Carolina plantation to visit one of Lemuel Cummings' friends. There Nicholas befriended Samuel, an old Negro field hand, and discovered that Samuel had secretly learned to read and write. He and Samuel spent a number of evenings together in secret, sitting by a stream reading and fishing. One day Samuel disappeared. Nicholas witnessed the organized slave hunt and the cruel and inhuman beating that followed. Samuel didn't die from the beating, but days later he died from infected wounds.

At a plantation supper on the evening of Samuel's death, Nicholas revealed his disgust and anger. He became so distraught that he called his father's friend a murderer. The man laughed and said Nicholas was a boy whose opinions mattered little. Nicholas was infuriated. An argument ensued, voices

Summer Storm

rose to shouts, and Nicholas was dragged from the room by his father. Lemuel Cummings made his stance clear that day: He forbid his son to speak another word against Justin Shannon, his friend.

Once Nicholas and his father returned home, discussions regarding slavery became heated ones, for Nicholas refused to allow his thoughts and feelings on the subject to be changed by Lemuel. He hated Justin Shannon, and lost respect for Lemuel for allowing Samuel to be murdered. Every time Nicholas closed his eyes he saw Samuel tied to that tree, saw the bleeding cuts on Samuel's back, and heard Samuel's cries of agony. Nicholas was set in his belief: Slavery was wrong. Samuel had been a person beneath his black skin. He had had feelings and a good mind, as did other Negroes. Lemuel never responded to Nicholas's statements, but his behavior told Nicholas enough: As a slave, Samuel had been nothing more than property. As a captured *runaway* slave, he had been killed to give a warning to other slaves. And as Samuel's owner, Lemuel's friend had been within his rights to punish Samuel.

The carriage turned onto Euclid. The homes here were of classical and colonial design, elegant, almost haunting in the moonlight. Presently the carriage stopped in the drive of the two-story stone home Nicholas had planned himself three years ago. The "perfect home," Kevin had said. His remarks on the *Morning Star* still troubled Nicholas. Not attend the wedding? Kevin couldn't be serious. Harold flung the door open, and Nicholas stepped out.

Rubbing his rough jaw, he entered the house. A deep blue carpet runner spanned the length of the passage before him. He planned to go to his study, savor a glass of wine, then go up to bed and sleep away what remained of the night.

As soon as he opened the study door, he smelled tobacco, sweet and pungent. His gaze was drawn to the pipe lying on its side on a table nestled between two maroon velvet wing chairs, their backs to him. He stiffened. Near the pipe sat a dirty glass. The servants never left dirty glasses about. Besides, he hadn't been home all day to dirty one. And he certainly didn't smoke a pipe.

But Lemuel Cummings did.

The last thing Nicholas wanted to do with the remainder of the night was quarrel with his father. And how well he knew they would quarrel; they always did when their paths crossed. The years immediately following Samuel's death had only deepened their ill feelings toward each other: Nicholas wanted to build ships; Lemuel wanted him to devote his time to Cummings Ironworks. Nicholas had this opinion; Lemuel had that opinion. He wanted a son he could mold to his idea of perfection. What he had was one with a strong mind and a thirst for independence.

Moving to a small sideboard nestled between two sections of shelves, Nicholas poured a glass of port. He wondered briefly why Lemuel had come here. They had an unspoken rule never to visit each other. Nicholas's desire for complete financial and personal independence nearly eight years ago had finished off what little relationship he had had left with his father. When he visited his parents' home, he went only to see his mother. He never, ever, ventured into the library there. It held too many stormy memories, for Lemuel had made a habit of summoning Nicholas to the library for scoldings and punishment.

Preparing himself for the inevitable encounter with Lemuel, Nicholas sipped port and gazed about the room. To save fuel, he had instructed the servants to leave only the mantel lamps burning whenever he was expected home late, and so they had. The soft orange-and-blue flames flickered shadows on the beige walls, on the moderate selection of books not quite filling the shelves, and cast the small secretary nestled in one corner of the room in deep shadow. His gaze finally settled on the portrait above the mantel.

The scene depicted Cleveland's Public Square, the four sections enclosed by white fences. Three years old, the picture was already outdated. People roamed the greens within each square, and horse-drawn carriages graced the streets. That was fine. What wasn't quite right were the few business buildings. There were more now, overshadowing homes and infuriating residents. What had become known as the "fence war" between

Summer Storm 45

businessmen and residents had been fought since the early fifties. Businessmen, of course, wanted more buildings. Residents wanted Public Square utilized as a "grand central park." Cleveland was growing at a rapid rate; the residents couldn't possibly win, but they would hold on as long as possible, Nicholas felt certain.

While he was a businessman in his own right, he wasn't sure which side he would take if ever asked. In order to progress, the city needed viable business districts. He didn't advocate pushing people out of homes, but what better place for a business district than the heart of the city?

"I wasn't aware your business kept you occupied until the morning hours," came a low, gruff voice from one of the chairs.

Nicholas's jaw tightened as his gaze skittered from the portrait back to the goblet in his hand. He had been trying to distract himself, not really prepare himself for this little tête-à-tête, he realized. He never anticipated a conversation with or a visit from his father.

And tonight, of all nights.

Lemuel's presence here so soon after the fugitives had been put on board the ship was really somewhat ironic. Sadly ironic, considering the event that had driven father and son apart.

But he could not force his views on his father any more than Lemuel could force his on him. That was the basic truth they had long ago seemed to accept.

"Would you like a drink? Wine? Brandy?" Nicholas offered, trying to figure out why Lemuel was here.

"I had three glasses of wine while waiting for you."

Nicholas didn't miss the sarcasm in the remark. It lashed him the way it always would, no doubt. He was not entirely indifferent to his father. He sipped port again, one hand resting casually on the sideboard, and asked sincerely, "I trust the wait was comfortable?"

"Hospitality, Nicholas? I expect less from a son who has hated me for years."

Another lash. "I don't hate you."

There was a moment of quiet. Then Lemuel spoke again: "My wait was more than comfortable, thank you. Your servants are impeccable."

Nicholas knew his father was waiting for him to indicate that he was pleased by his approval, but the words would never come. He had long ago stopped seeking or acknowledging paternal approval, knowing that if he did seek or acknowledge it, Lemuel might feel as if he had some sort of power over him again. Nicholas was no longer a child to be praised or scolded.

"Damn you, Nicholas! Will you not bend even a little?" The exclamation was soft, the question loud.

Cradling the goblet in his hand, Nicholas moved to the chairs. The glow from the mantel lamp cast shadows on Lemuel's deeply etched face and heightened the silver of his hair. His gray eyes were those of a weary man, the lids heavy. As always, he was properly dressed and groomed, his gray neckcloth arranged to perfection, his legs properly crossed.

"I'm surprised. But I must say I'm also curious. Why the visit?" Nicholas asked, sitting down heavily in a chair. He leisurely sipped his wine, ignoring his father's outburst.

Lemuel Cummings studied his son—a young man who had accomplished more in his twenty-nine years than most would in a lifetime. He and Nicholas had been at each other's throats since the ugly business about that slave. And some years ago Nicholas had intentionally set out to free himself of any responsibility to Cummings Ironworks. Perhaps Nicholas didn't hate him, but he certainly had no desire to be called his son any longer. Nicholas's every action proved that.

Lemuel had watched Nicholas's business ability grow these past years. The young man was brilliant, snatching opportunity as it presented itself, carefully weighing the possible risks and calculated gains. He had somehow avoided heavy financial losses during the depression of last year, at a time when others were being ruined. And before that, along with a number of businessmen Lemuel knew well, both he and Nicholas had bought into the Cleveland Iron Mining Company, based at the newly discovered Marquette mines near Lake Superior.

Summer Storm 47

Three years ago, when the opening of the Sault St. Marie Canal had connected the upper and lower Great Lakes, the company had sent the brigantine *Columbia* down to Cleveland with its first cargo of ore. Others had followed. Now the company flourished.

The Cleveland Iron Mining Company was not in the business of building ships, however. But Nicholas was. So the news that he had followed his investment with wanting to build a ship to carry ore from Lake Superior had not surprised Lemuel. Nor had the reluctance of local businessmen to invest in the ship. The ore business was rapidly taking off, but never far from anyone's mind lately was the recent financial scare. But, Lemuel saw past the risks to the fact that more ships were needed. And Nicholas did build fine, sturdy ships.

That, and the fact that Lemuel had no doubts about his son's business ability, had brought him here tonight. Clearly Nicholas was bitter about the past and wanted nothing to do with him. But as businessmen surely they could work around the past.

Bracing an elbow on one arm of the chair, Lemuel leaned toward Nicholas slightly. "Why the visit, you ask? You have been inquiring around Cleveland for investors in a ship, a venture no one but Werner Kraus seems willing to fund. I will invest. Werner, myself, and you . . . ," Lemuel said, knowing that Nicholas, depending on how badly he wanted to build the ship, had little choice but to accept the offer.

Nicholas gave him a hard stare. "No."

Lemuel sat back in the chair. He had not expected such a hasty response. Oh, he had known Nicholas would be rather reluctant, but to say no so quickly? Back when the mining company had formed, neither of them had known at first that the other was investing. When they learned of each other's interest, neither had backed out. Like that, this would be just another business venture. "Nicholas, think about—"

"I've thought about it as long as I care to, which is less than a moment."

"You would desert a very promising plan because I am making the offer?"

"I didn't say I would desert it."

"There is no other way, Nicholas, you must know that by now. You have been asking people for months. You have presented plans. Only Werner and myself have come forward."

"I don't care to have your hands in my company," Nicholas said, not bothering to ask how his father had learned of the ship. He knew. Lemuel Cummings had been the starving son of Easterners who had come to disease-ridden, budding Cleveland because it held promise. Lemuel had first become a merchant, then through numerous investments had risen in prosperity. For the last fifteen years, he had owned and operated Cummings Ironworks. He had risen from his poor childhood to become one of Cleveland's wealthiest and most prominent businessmen, and through his circle of friends had come his knowledge of the project.

"I have no desire to have my hands in your company, as you say," Lemuel responded in disbelief. "My interest is in the ship. You want to build it, I want to invest in it."

"No," Nicholas said again, feeling his father's sharp gaze. He met it evenly, refusing to be swayed. He reached to the back of his neck for his stock buckle, undid it, then tossed his stock and buckle on the table between the chairs.

Lemuel sighed, a raspy sound that seemed to vibrate through the room. The lamp flames flickered softly. "I see. You cannot let your personal affairs interfere in your business affairs or you will fail, Nicholas."

"I've succeeded so far without your advice. I've also succeeded without your money."

"I would not be giving you anything." Lemuel reached for his pipe and bent to tap it gently on the edge of a nearby spittoon. "I will expect a return from my investment. Business, you see . . . And contrary to what you obviously believe, I have no interest in snatching your company from you. If I did, I would have done so five years ago, when it was an infant and still weak. Consider that, Nicholas. I've resented the fact that you've wanted nothing to do with the ironworks, but to ruin you . . . my own son . . ." He straightened. "Well, if I had wanted to, if I had been the monster you think I am,

I could have, I suppose. A few words in the right ears, money in the right places . . . quite an easy task if I had wanted to, you see."

Nicholas studied him, knowing his father spoke the truth. At the time he had stepped out and built the *Ontario,* he had wondered if Lemuel would attempt to sabotage his ventures. Nothing had happened. Nor had anything happened when he built the other two side-wheelers with the help of Werner's investment. So while Lemuel privately objected to Nicholas pursuing his own business, he had never stood in the way.

"Why are you so eager?" Nicholas asked cautiously. Much more than the promise of money would be needed to convince him to accept his father as an investor.

"Distrust. It is always between us. We are two stubborn men." Lemuel produced a pouch and stuffed the pipe bowl with tobacco, then put away the pouch. He struck a match. Clouds of smoke twirled around Lemuel's head as he puffed on the pipe stem and narrowed his eyes at Nicholas. "Why am I so eager? Because I have glimpsed your business mind these past years and I like what I have seen."

"You were angry when I built those ships, angry that I no longer expressed an interest in Cummings Ironworks."

"Is it wrong of a man to want his son to follow in his footsteps? We are speaking of business, not personal matters, Nicholas. My company needs more ore. Besides, the whole damned country is excited about the Superior mines. The services of any ship venturing up that way will be in demand."

Nicholas was thoughtful. He had already considered those things. For once he and Lemuel agreed on something. Lemuel was right about something else, too. Distrust could very well keep him from building the ship. "I don't know . . ."

The personal and business sides of this proposed arrangement troubled him. They would intermingle, no matter how hard he tried to keep them separate. He would see Lemuel frequently, keeping him abreast of the ship's construction. Could they work together? Lemuel had treated him as an equal tonight; in fact, for some years now they had sat near each other at meetings of the investors of the Cleveland Iron

Mining Company. Still . . . Nicholas didn't want the ship to be half-built and the two of them decide they couldn't work together because of personal differences.

"Tell me how you're expecting the ship to be built," he said cautiously.

"The obvious. A well-constructed hull that will withstand even the worst lake gales. Hatches that latch more securely than most. As you know, in a lake storm a certain amount of water will seep into the holds. I won't try to tell you how to build a ship. You sketched the plans for those side-wheelers and you did a damned good job, Nicholas. I would like to be informed of progress now and then, perhaps see it myself."

"I have final say?"

"You are the shipbuilder."

"I have your word?"

"You have my word. So it is agreed?"

Nicholas drained his wineglass and turned his attention to the portrait of Public Square again. Its gilded frame glowed softly. "I would like time to think more."

"Of course," Lemuel responded, rising. "I felt the matter was important enough to be addressed tonight." He moved from the chair.

Nicholas rose, intending to see him out.

Lemuel raised a hand to stop him. "No need to show me out. You look comfortable. And tired. I know the way to the door."

Settling back in his chair, Nicholas watched his father leave. He couldn't help but be excited by the thought that he might now have the investors he needed. Lemuel had listened to him, listened with the glow of respect in his eyes. Still . . . such differences he and Lemuel had had over the years. He couldn't get too excited and fly into this just because he had shared a few moments of peace with his father.

He remembered Lemuel's words about not wanting Erie Line. With his powerful influence in Cleveland, Lemuel could easily have squashed the company in its infancy, just as he had said. He hadn't. And he actually seemed confident of Nicholas's ability to construct a worthy ship.

Summer Storm

Nicholas moved to the small secretary, lit a lamp there, and lifted a folder—plans for the ship, one he wanted to see launched on the Cuyahoga River.

He removed the sketches. They consisted of lines and circles, curves and exact dimensions, from the length of oak planks to such details as the binnacle, where a lamp and compass would be stored, and the fife rail, to which rigging would be belayed. Nicholas wanted to see this ship built. He wanted to watch it disappear on the Lake Erie horizon, bound for Lake Superior, and later he wanted to watch the first shipment of ore be unloaded from its bowels. Lemuel needed the ore. Others did, too.

Nicholas replaced the ship's plans on the secretary, fairly certain what his decision would be.

5

FROM THE TOP of the mahogany staircase, Katherine heard booming, merry voices coming from somewhere below. She slowly descended, giving Peggy, the housekeeper, a look of puzzlement. "Who is that?"

Peggy smiled. "Why, it's your uncle, miss," she said with a heavy Irish brogue. "Your uncle and his friend. Believe they've had a bit much."

"A bit much?"

Peggy nodded, her round face framed by light orange curls. "Yes. A bit much to drink, that is. They do it occasionally, have a grand time together, drinkin' and singin' the old songs. Harmless sort of fun, ye know. Mr. Baum comes all the way from Toledo. Was unexpected this time. Woke up this mornin', an' there he was on the doorstep."

The deep male voices boomed through the house again, rising in pitch, then lowering as they slurred the words to the old festive German tune. They blended one moment, were way off-key the next. Katherine frowned. "What about the supper tonight?" she asked, of no one in particular.

"Supper, Miss?" Peggy inquired, busying herself with a feather duster and some tables.

"Yes. Uncle Werner told me last evening that we were invited to a supper at Nicholas Cummings' home this evening."

"Well . . . I'm afraid he won't be in any shape to go, miss.

I've seen 'em this way before. Give 'em an hour and they'll be passin' out."

Katherine sighed, then turned to go back upstairs. Uncle Werner was certainly entitled to his day of fun with Mr. Baum. But he had promised to take her to a few shops, then accompany her to the supper later.

What harm would come from venturing out alone? Katherine wondered. None. She quickly decided to ask Peggy where the nicer shops were and stay in that area of the city. She could get the stockings she needed for this evening and the camisole she had in mind, then come home, no harm done.

She dressed quickly in a plaid basque—a bodice with tails ending just below her waist. Her crinoline skirt was rose-colored with white lace flounces, and her bonnet was of matching rose velvet, decorated with more white lace and secured beneath her chin by a wide bow. Clasping the handle of a ribbon-decorated parasol as it dangled by her side, she went downstairs.

Uncle Werner and Mr. Baum were still booming away at the top of their lungs. They hit one particularly high note, their voices went shrill, and Katherine smiled. Intending to ask Peggy about the shops, she found the housekeeper in the parlor, dusting more furnishings.

"Could you locate my uncle's driver and have the carriage brought around?" she asked.

Peggy lifted an eyebrow. "Ye sure, miss? Wouldn't be proper, ye know, goin' out alone."

"Yes, I'm sure."

"Very well then," Peggy said, sweeping haughtily by Katherine and out of the room.

Katherine had gotten on Peggy's bad side yesterday by intervening when Peggy would have rudely sent away a woman caller from Uncle Werner's church. Uncle Werner had apparently missed the last service, and the woman's visit was a friendly "we missed you" call. Katherine had known Uncle Werner had just finished looking over some books he had brought from the bank and was relaxing in the gardens out back. She had sent Peggy to fetch him. Peggy had gone, but the look she had tossed over her shoulder at Katherine had not been a friendly one.

"A woman after the position of mistress of this house, that's what she is," Peggy muttered after the woman left.

"Is it your task to pick and choose Uncle Werner's callers?" Katherine countered, unable to subdue her temper.

Peggy had lifted a fine eyebrow at her then, too. Katherine had not even thought of looking away. Peggy had moved on without another comment.

So Peggy's snootiness toward her today didn't surprise Katherine in the least. Nor did it change Katherine's feelings about what responsibilities Peggy's position did and didn't include. Katherine was certainly not trying to fill the role of mistress of the house; she simply didn't agree with Peggy meddling in Uncle Werner's private affairs. Or in mine, she thought.

"It's comin', miss," Peggy said, appearing in the parlor again moments later. She resumed dusting.

"Peggy, there's no need for my uncle to know I've gone out alone," Katherine said, watching her.

Peggy stopped dusting to stare hard at Katherine. "Very well, miss," she responded finally, turning back to her task.

"Good." Breathing easier, Katherine left the parlor for the front entrance.

The carriage waited in the drive. Katherine recognized the driver standing beside the open door as the same man who had driven them to and from River Street a few evenings before.

"Mr. Jackson, I'd like to go shopping." She hoped he would know where to take her since she hadn't asked Peggy where to shop.

The stout Negro driver inclined his head and grinned. "Well, you ain't dressed fo' the farm market, so I figure I know where you need to go."

"Do you?" Katherine asked hopefully as she stepped up into the carriage.

"Got a brother who drives fo' the Prestons just down the street. Takes the ladies ever'where."

Summer Storm 55

"Wonderful. We should have a splendid afternoon together, then."

Soon the carriage was moving along Lake Street. Between houses and businesses, Katherine glimpsed Lake Erie, lazing beneath a bright mid-morning sun. The magnificent lake spread her blue-green water northward to the horizon, and east and west to join hands with her sisters Ontario and Huron. Ships speckled her water, decorating it with sails and smokestacks. They were ladies gracing the inland sea.

Katherine lifted her ivory fan and moved it gently before her face. This evening she would see Nicholas. She couldn't wait. Already, she felt a little quiver of anticipation at the thought.

The carriage turned south, and Katherine could no longer see Lake Erie. Now her attention focused on businesses—a hat shop, a jeweler, a real estate company, an optician, a druggist, and a bookbinder. Hawkers peddled their wares.

Suddenly the carriage pitched forward and crashed to a stop. Katherine grabbed the leather strap above her head to keep from falling onto the floor. She heard Mr. Jackson trying to soothe the horses, then the tipped carriage stilled. Katherine breathed deeply and slowly in an effort to calm her heartbeat. Moments passed. Then the door eased open, and Mr. Jackson peered in with wide eyes.

"You hurt, Miss McDaniel?"

"No. No, just a little shaken." Katherine shifted, and the carriage shifted with her, creaking and groaning. She was scared to death to move again. Something was horribly wrong. "Mr. Jackson . . ."

"Now just . . . just sit there," he sputtered. "Gonna see if I can get somebody to steady this thing so's I can get you out. Horses are unhitched now, but you got to be real still."

"I won't breathe, Mr. Jackson. Just hurry," Katherine said, displaying calm she didn't feel. But she wouldn't panic. She wasn't a swooning female, no matter how tight her corset.

Mr. Jackson shook his head. He had just stepped away from the carriage door when Katherine heard the thud of horse's hooves, then Nicholas's deep voice: "Broke an axle, did you, Jackson?"

"Yessir. I got—"

"There's nothing we can do about that at the moment, but let's get Mr. Kraus out before the thing crashes over."

"Yessir. But it ain't—"

"On second thought, maybe I can use this predicament to bargain about that vacation I mentioned the other evening," Nicholas said loudly.

"Mr. Cummin's, Mr. Kraus ain't in—"

"How about it, Werner?"

Nicholas surveyed the tipped carriage. Jackson had unhitched the two horses. They were standing peacefully to the right of the carriage, dipping their heads and swishing their tails. Jackson was wide-eyed and jittery, shifting from one foot to the other, making Nicholas suspicious.

"What is it, Jackson? Is Werner hurt? Why the devil are you just standing there?" Nicholas marched forward and stuck his head inside the carriage.

The sight of Katherine clinging to the leather strap nearest him, a look of fear in her blue eyes, chilled him.

"Nicholas. Oh, Nicholas, would you please stop jesting and help Mr. Jackson get me out?" she pleaded, sounding half-scared and half-annoyed.

Nicholas withdrew. He looked around, saw several men walking in front of a boardinghouse, and shouted, "We need help here! There's a lady inside."

The men responded immediately, crossing the street to help.

"Jackson, take them to the other side," Nicholas said. "Make sure this thing doesn't move while I'm getting her out."

Once the men were positioned where he wanted them, he poked his head and one arm inside the carriage. "Let go of the strap now, Katherine, and take my hand."

If anyone but Nicholas had been at the door coaxing her to let go of the strap, Katherine wouldn't have budged. Everytime she moved—even wriggled a toe—the carriage moved, frightening her. But she'd trusted Nicholas with her life once; she had no qualms about doing so again. She released the strap and eased toward him. The carriage creaked and groaned, then

Summer Storm

shifted. She touched his hand. Suddenly Nicholas's hands were on her waist, lifting her up and down to stand in front of him. His arms encircled her, pulling her as close as the spread of crinoline would allow, close enough that she rested her head against his chest. It was solid, warm, safe here. There was his strong, steady heartbeat, the scratchiness of his open brown frock coat, the smoothness of the ivory vest beneath.

"Are you all right?" he asked softly, his breath warm in her hair. "You're not hurt?"

Katherine shook her head. "I'm fine."

"You're not. You're trembling."

She couldn't fool him, though she tried to breathe evenly. "This is the second time you've rescued me, Nicholas."

"Second . . . ? Oh, you mean from the Flats?" He chuckled, a thick, rich sound that vibrated his chest and sent tremors through Katherine.

Two men came around the carriage with Mr. Jackson. "I've got her," Nicholas said. "Thank you." They nodded and walked off.

Mr. Jackson fretted over the carriage, hunching down to assess the damage, shaking his head repeatedly. "Mr. Kraus ain't gonna like this. Just spent a mighty sum getting one of those doors fixed."

"Then perhaps it's time Mr. Kraus bought a new carriage. I intend to speak with him about this," Nicholas said tightly. He looked down at Katherine. "Where is Werner today? Why would the man let you venture out in Cleveland alone? There have been a number of robberies lately. And three days ago a woman was accosted on Erie Street—not even a mile from here."

Katherine set her lips. She *had* to tell him the truth. She couldn't let him storm into Uncle Werner's house and rant about the evils of letting a woman venture out alone in the city. "He . . . Well, he didn't exactly let me."

Taking her by the shoulders, Nicholas stepped back and stared harshly at her. "What?"

"Oh, you heard me," Katherine said impatiently. "He didn't let me."

"Katherine."

She frowned. "What was I to do? Mr. Baum came this morning. By ten o'clock Uncle Werner and Mr. Baum were drunk and singing for the entire neighborhood to hear. I had shopping to do, and I would have done it without incident if this hadn't happened. Now Uncle Werner will be furious, and Peggy will be delighted. I only wanted to get a pair of stockings and a new camisole—" She paused when she saw Nicholas grinning. Exasperated, she motioned to the crippled carriage. "What in all of this do you find amusing?"

He put a finger to his chin and glanced around, appearing to ponder something. His emerald eyes sparkled. "A pair of stockings and a new camisole . . . Perhaps I could help you locate the items."

Katherine felt her neck and face heat to an explosive level. She couldn't believe she had blurted such things! She twisted away, hoping to see an omnibus that might take her home. Instead she saw only a few wagons and carriages traversing the gravel street. A woman working in a garden beyond a fence at a nearby two-story brick house paused in her gardening to stare.

"Katherine," Nicholas said softly from behind her.

As glad as Katherine was to see Nicholas, the carriage accident and his teasing left her with little enthusiasm. "Could you possibly arrange to take me home?" she requested.

"I could," he answered, "or I could take you shopping."

That deepened her embarrassment. "No. I'd prefer to go home."

"Very well," he relented. Rather easily, Katherine thought.

Nicholas led her to his carriage. It was stopped a short distance away on the side of the street. He handed Katherine up, saw her seated inside, then disappeared. Katherine heard soft voices and assumed Nicholas was speaking with his driver. Moments later, he climbed inside. The door shut, and the carriage jolted forward.

"Frightened?" Nicholas asked, his eyes going to Katherine's hand that gripped the leather strap above her.

Katherine quickly released the strap and smoothed her skirt,

Summer Storm   59

feeling foolish. "I didn't realize I was holding it."

Nicholas couldn't take his eyes from her. She was refreshing, delightfully refreshing, blushing to no end when she had realized she'd not been very delicate in mentioning the intimate items she wanted to buy. The rose and plaid of her basque and crinoline suited her. Unruly curls escaped from the confines of her bonnet to swirl gently around her ivory face. Strokes of red stained her cheeks, matching her lips. He had not forgotten his reaction to her the other evening, nor could he deny that he had thought of her most of the following morning while sitting in his study trying to sort financial figures.

"I'm not taking you home," he said.

"You're not?" she asked, so innocent, so captivating.

"No."

"Where . . . where are you taking me?"

"Shopping."

She flinched. "No. You wouldn't want to shop for what I need."

He laughed low. "I wouldn't? I've purchased women's items numerous times."

"You have?" she blurted, her eyes wide.

He nodded. "Fascinating things. Clasps and lace. Light, almost sheer cotton, sometimes silk. Delicate ribbons and bows. Hidden ties." He couldn't seem to resist teasing her, and yet he knew feminine undergarments were the last thing he should be teasing her about. The subject was definitely one that might cause any normal woman to swoon. Undergarments were, after all, so . . . intimate.

Her mouth opened slightly as if she wanted to say something, then she clamped it shut. She looked down at her hands, her thick brown lashes splaying against her skin. "I . . . I had no idea. I mean . . . you must think I know nothing about . . ."

"I'm sorry. That was mean of me. I shouldn't tease about such things. It's the way you flush, I suppose. It's charming."

She gave him another demure look. He didn't really think she meant to entice him with those looks, but they were no less irresistible. "I've instructed Harold to take us to the Exchange on Superior Avenue. He'll stay with the carriage in front of the building while I go across the street to the Weddell House, where I had planned to meet some friends anyway."

Katherine nodded. The carriage turned a corner.

"Don't go out alone again," Nicholas warned, wanting to stress the dangers of the city to her. "We have a mere handful of police officers, and they give preference to sounding the church bell when an escaped slave is spotted in the city. If you need to go somewhere and Werner can't take you, send me a missive."

"All right," she agreed reluctantly.

The Merchant Exchange was a four-story building with its name stenciled on the front door. People flowed in and out of the entrance, some carrying boxes and packages, some empty-handed.

Katherine caught Nicholas's arm as he handed her down. "This is a shop? It looks enormous!"

"Many shops. I'll be across the street," he said, motioning to an even larger building there. It totaled five stories. One corner was constructed of columns extending from the top of the second floor to the bottom of the third. Iron rails connected columns. A banner displaying the words "Weddell House" fluttered gently from a two-story dome atop the building. Horses, gigs, wagons, and people cluttered the street corner.

Nodding, Katherine turned back to the Merchant Exchange. Obviously this was the place to shop; Nicholas wouldn't have brought her here if it weren't.

He led her to the door, said good-bye, then turned and walked off, finally disappearing inside a Weddell House entrance. Harold stood leisurely near the carriage, which was parked beside the planked walkway. Katherine felt his watchful eye on her. Sensing his loyalty to Nicholas—and therefore to her— she smiled at him. He inclined his head.

Katherine ventured into the building. Brass frames, railings, and candelabra shimmered against dark, polished woodwork. The floors and staircases were marble. The place was filled with various charming stores, one advertising the finest brandies,

Summer Storm

wine, gin, and rum, and another porcelain teeth, of all things. There was a lithographer and a shop with a sign proclaiming "The finest lace mantillas and cambric may be found within." Katherine paused in a bookstore to lift the cover of a European history book, then moved on to read the title of Emerson's latest, *English Traits*, a book she knew Alexandra didn't have but would love to read. Alexandra loved anything Emerson wrote. Katherine bought the book.

Finally she found a shop containing an array of women's underclothing of silk, satin, muslin, and cotton. There were chemises, camisoles, drawers, stockings, and corsets—boned and stitched, with and without gussets. Perfumes and powders filled two small shelves. A variety of ribbons and bows, hair combs and silver-handled brushes filled a huge silver tray. Katherine was admiring a shelf of white, black, yellow, and lavender slippers when a small woman walked around a counter and offered her assistance.

Presently Katherine found herself in a small back room, where she was soon trying on items, turning this way and that way while the woman fussed with various fits.

When she left the shop, she was burdened with more than she'd intended to buy. Her boxes held silk handkerchiefs, a new reticule, two camisoles, a new pair of drawers, and three pairs of stockings. She had also purchased two bottles of perfume and of course *English Traits*, wrapped in a neat brown wrapper bound with a length of twine.

Once outside, she was embarrassed for the third time in one day when she saw Nicholas and Harold leaning casually against the side of the carriage conversing, obviously waiting for her. How long had she been in the building?

Grinning, Nicholas relieved her of the boxes. "You're going to empty Werner's accounts if you're not careful," he teased.

Katherine shot him a smart smile. "Just be glad you're not him."

"Oh, I am. I am."

"Oh, you. I didn't spend *that* much."

"No?" He placed the boxes on the carriage seat, then reached for her hand. "Good. Werner won't be angry that I took you shopping. He'll be thinking about fixing that axle. What's in the paper?"

"What?" She glanced down at her hand. "Oh. The book. It's Emerson's latest. For my friend Alexandra."

Over the many conversations, sounds of horses, and creaks of conveyances, sharp musical notes suddenly filled the air. A small crowd had gathered near the front door of the Merchant Exchange.

"What is that?" Katherine asked Nicholas.

"The organ grinder with his monkey." Nicholas took the wrapped book from her and placed it inside the carriage. Then he took her hand and gently pulled her toward the crowd.

"Organ grinder? Nicholas, what—"

Once Katherine had seen a monkey when a circus came through Sandusky, but that monkey had not been nearly as tiny as the one propped on the organ grinder's shoulder. This monkey wore a bright red satin jacket and cap. His arms were the size of twigs, and his little eyes darted here and there. Katherine stared in amazement. She smiled, then laughed. "It's so little!"

Nicholas dug into a frock-coat pocket and removed a coin. "Here," he said, placing it in Katherine's hand. "Offer it to him."

She gave him a glance of surprise and reluctance. "Is it—he—friendly?"

"Quite. Especially if you have a penny to offer. Go ahead."

"No."

Nicholas could see she needed stronger urging. He took her by the shoulders, turned her around, and guided her in direction of the organ grinder's monkey. "Hold the coin out to him."

"If he takes a finger... Nicholas..." Katherine offered the coin. The monkey took it and tipped his cap. Katherine laughed, twisting to face Nicholas.

Enchanted by her delight, Nicholas reached to brush a few stray curls from her face. They were silk threads, curling around his finger. Her face was smooth and soft. Just the feel of her hair and skin was enough to stir the same longing for her he had experienced the other evening aboard the *Morning Star*.

The distant sound of a familiar tinkling drifted to Nicholas. He was glad for the distraction. He visually searched this side of the street, didn't find what he was looking for, then looked to the other side and was satisfied. "Hungry?" he asked Katherine.

"A little. Why?"

"Come on. A moment, Harold." Nicholas pulled Katherine with him to the street. He paused until the way was clear, then crossed with her.

Katherine was baffled by his mysteriousness. "Where are we going?"

"To visit the waffleman."

Across Superior Avenue they stopped in front of a wagon drawn by one horse. The animal stood obediently still while in the back of the wagon a man opened a waffle iron. Nearby stood a small grill with smoke twisting up from it.

Nicholas held up two fingers for the man to see. The waffleman inclined his head, removed the baked waffles from the iron, and sprinkled them generously with powdered sugar. Then he handed them to Nicholas in exchange for several coins.

Katherine loved waffles. At school they were rarely served, so the powder-sprinkled waffles were a treat that made her mouth water. As soon as Nicholas handed her one, she promptly began eating it.

"A little hungry?"

Katherine glanced up to find him staring at her, amusement dancing in his eyes. "Waffles . . . delicious," she managed around a bite.

"Careful," he teased, brushing powder from her cheek. "Someone in this crowd might think you're only disguised as a lady."

She laughed. "It's been so long since I had a waffle."

Nicholas's hand drifted down. Katherine's heart paused. She enjoyed the warm strokes of his thumb as he cleaned her chin, the very fact that he was touching her. Then the strokes slowed and finally ceased.

She was disappointed. He could have stroked her chin forever, and she wouldn't have objected.

Nicholas withdrew his hand and straightened his cravat, alarmed at just how much he suddenly longed to have her in his arms. Her skin was softer than the skin of any woman he had ever touched—almost like satin. Again her eyes were clear, sparkling, lovely.

He could have stood and stared into them for hours.

6

"Harold is waiting," Nicholas said, disturbed again that she could stir him so much.

Once inside the carriage they sat opposite each other and finished their waffles. An uncomfortable silence fell between them.

"I don't want to go home yet," Katherine said. She wanted to be with him longer. Truthfully she didn't want to leave him at all. His hair was windblown, and she wanted to straighten it with a few brushes of her hand, then share conversation with him.

Surprise flickered across his face, flaring his eyes, lifting his brows; surprise and something else . . . wariness? Yes, she thought so.

"I have business at one of the piers," he said.

"Let me go with you. We had little time to talk last evening, Nicholas. Let me go. Please."

Nicholas debated her plea. He shouldn't even consider spending more time with her. He might be devoted to Sarah, but right now he wanted the woman seated across from him, and he would be a blind fool if he told himself he didn't. Still, this afternoon would be the perfect time to tell Katherine about the upcoming announcement of his engagement; by doing so, he'd put a firm end to whatever romantic notions were circling inside her lovely head.

He tapped on the carriage ceiling. "To the pier," he said, loud enough for Harold to hear.

A slow smile spread across Katherine's lips. "Thank you. I've missed you," she said.

He glanced from her to the window and back to her. "Katherine . . . I can't allow you to continue thinking . . . tonight . . ."

"Tonight should be wonderful. Since I've been back, we've hardly had time to talk. Perhaps after supper we can. I learned a little of everything at school. Composition, algebra, Latin, French, German, history . . . sketching, something I love to do."

"You draw?" Nicholas asked in surprise, distracted by her once again.

She nodded. "It's just play. I'm not an artist."

"I would like to see some of your drawings."

Her gaze faltered to her hands, placed neatly in her lap. "They're in Sandusky. I left them for Alexandra."

"Could you draw more?"

"Perhaps. And of course you know I like to read."

"Devotion to the written word," he teased.

"Yes, I'm silly that way sometimes. I'm passionate about certain things. Sketching . . . reading . . . orphans . . . particularly orphans. I look into the sad eyes of a child left alone in the world and I'm overwhelmed with wanting to help," she said, her gaze darting between him and the fingers she was now twisting nervously in her lap. "I know what having no one is like, you see. It's terrifying."

"And you said you wanted to be left alone so you could go back to the farm."

She smiled shyly. "You know I was crying for help, for someone's attention. All those things I did to Uncle Werner and Peggy I did to draw their attention. Neither had any patience for me, whether or not I acted horrid. I'd seen Uncle Werner perhaps twice in my life—the times he visited the farm. My father was too proud to accept the help Uncle Werner offered. When my father died, I needed much more than just a roof over my head. I needed someone to give me

Summer Storm 67

direction. Of course, I had no idea at the time that that was what I wanted."

"You've sorted through all that now, it seems," Nicholas said, watching the way she tossed her head this way and that way as she spoke, and finally tipped it to one side and gazed at him much the way she had around tangled curls five years ago. The difference was that she was no longer that brash girl. She was most definitely a woman, soft with curves and valleys in the right places, and an air of refinement to her. "You're amazing, do you know that?"

She stared at him.

"Five years ago you could barely read and write. You were a street urchin with knotted hair, dirty clothes, and a dirty face. Now you're anything but that. I've never met anyone who astounded me more."

"I'm glad," she finally said, and that, too, disturbed Nicholas almost as much as her occasional demure looks.

Katherine's heart sang. Every compliment he paid her, every tender look, was what she had worked to hear. She loved him beyond everything.

The carriage stopped, still bouncing slightly on its springs. Katherine heard Harold talking to the horses, heard their snorts and whickers. She didn't wait for Harold to open the door or for Nicholas to hand her down. She lifted the latch, pushed the door open, and climbed out.

The *Morning Star* was docked at a pier. Beyond the ship was Lake Erie. Sun dappled her surface, glittering on her water. Few vessels were coming in; many were going out. At the next pier cargo was being unloaded from a sailing ship—a schooner, Katherine thought. She gathered her skirts and started for the *Morning Star*.

"Katherine, wait," Nicholas called. She paused at the ramp to allow him to catch up. He took her hand and led her on board. "I have to check some repairs. Minor things," he said.

The red, white, and blue banners had been removed from the railings. The ship seemed ghostly now, empty of the crowd it had held only a few evenings ago. It stirred gently in the water, creaking slightly. Katherine walked with Nicholas along the deserted deckways, the planks solid beneath her boots. Now and then Nicholas stopped and leaned over the railing to look at something.

In the main saloon upstairs, he inspected several lamps. His effort to tell Katherine that his engagement would be announced this evening had been thwarted—unknowingly thwarted, but thwarted nonetheless. He knew he couldn't continue letting her think he had any romantic interest in her. Neither could he continue touching her now and then, wanting her.

"Katherine, this evening . . . ," he began. "I've—"

"I'm still angry that you didn't dance with me the other night," she said, pouting for his benefit, running her hand along the smooth dark wall. She was so damned lovely, wispy curls mixing with the soft lace spilling gently from the edge of her bonnet, her hand and arm graceful, smooth, elegant. Her head tilted again as she smiled. Her blue eyes were startling in the dim light shining through the windows. They were spellbinding, in fact. Her skin was unblemished except for the touches of color on her cheeks. Her strawberry lips begged to be touched. Again he couldn't take his eyes from the bewitching sight of her.

"I'll dance with you now," he said, not realizing he had spoken until her eyes widened.

"Now?"

"Now." One dance, he told himself. One chance to hold her close and stare down into those beautiful eyes. Then he would reveal a truth to her that might take some of their sparkle, something he hated the thought of doing.

Standing the length of the saloon across from him, she laughed and twisted her fingers nervously. "But there's no music, Nicholas."

"We'll pretend."

"You're crazy."

"Impulsive," he countered, watching the sparks in her eyes. He strode purposefully toward her, sketched a bow, and asked, "A waltz, dear lady?"

Catching her breath, Katherine placed her hand on his arm. This was more than she had dared to think might happen when he had offered to take her shopping. She might not have danced with him the other night. But today . . . and they were completely alone.

She felt the ship sway to one side. She swayed with it. "We're moving," she said, losing her smile.

Facing her, he placed a hand on her waist and pulled her to him. "Just some turbulence in the water. Even at the piers that's not uncommon. Ready?"

Katherine forgot the ship's movement. She lost herself in Nicholas's rich eyes and perfectly etched face. She lost herself in his deep voice, urging her to dip and sway. She lost herself in the heat of his body, in the strength of his arm that urged her closer, in his warm, manly breath fanning her cheek as his face neared hers.

There was no music. There was silence, marred only by their breathing and the clicks of their shoes on the wooden floor. Being with Nicholas like this stirred more emotion in Katherine than she'd dreamed possible. Alone with him, she forgot everything else.

"Nicholas . . . ," she whispered, staring into his eyes that were slowly deepening to evergreen. One of her hands rested on his shoulder. She lowered it, let it slide over the roughness of his frock coat, over his shoulder, and down his strong arm. Then she trailed her fingertips back up his arm. She touched his soft yet firm lips, wondering how they might taste, and she touched the slightly coarse hair at his nape, pushing her fingers into it. "I was disappointed that you didn't kiss me the other night, too. Once, I thought you would," she said.

She heard his rapid intake of breath and knew she had affected him profoundly.

"Katherine, you have no idea what you're doing," he said breathlessly.

"I know exactly what I'm doing, Nicholas Cummings."

They were barely moving now. Nicholas was unable to concentrate on the dance steps while Katherine tortured him with her touch, her eyes glazed with want.

Finally he groaned and dipped his head to brush his lips across hers.

Her reached beneath her chin, untied the ribbon there, and stripped the bonnet from her head. Her hair was pinned back, but Nicholas found the pins easily and removed them. Free now, the wild curls cascaded down her back, just touching her hips. He buried his hands in the silk, lifted a handful to his face, and inhaled its flowery scent. Lavender, he thought. "Katie," he murmured. "Oh, Katie . . ."

He nudged her hair aside, finding the tenderness of her neck, nipping the softness, tasting the sweetness. She shivered, moved her body, and pressed firm breasts against his chest. He trailed kisses along one side of her jaw, then sought her lips.

They were moist and sweet, just as he had known they would be. He slipped his tongue inside her mouth and groaned softly when it met her lips.

Her kissed her nose, her eyes, her forehead. She tipped her head back and offered the column of her neck, her eyes slitted with awakened passion. "Love me, Nicholas," she whispered, "love me."

God, but she would give herself to him here, on the saloon floor! He couldn't . . . She *didn't* know what she was doing. She didn't . . . He watched need play on her delicate features and shook his head to try to free it of her spell. He felt as Adam must have; partaking of the forbidden fruit, knowing he was doing wrong, yet unable to help himself because the temptation was just too damn great.

He squeezed his eyes shut, still fighting. "Katie, this is so wrong," he managed, his voice sounding thick and strained. "Tonight . . ." He felt the ship sway, suddenly *knew* they were moving, and grabbed her hand, pulling her toward the door leading to the deck. What the hell was happening now?

"Nicholas—what do you mean . . . wrong?"

"Come on," he snapped, angry with himself, not her.

Once they were on deck, his fear that the ship was moving out into the lake was confirmed. The *Morning Star* was approximately a half mile from shore. The water rippled and shimmered. "Captain Islington must be checking how she rides after those repairs. I didn't know anyone else was aboard. They obviously didn't know we were on board, either," Nicholas said. "I'll go tell them to turn around."

Katherine touched his arm. "Surely the captain will turn back soon, Nicholas. Until then, let's enjoy the beauty of the lake."

Nicholas watched her walk near the deck railing, her hands skimming the top rail. A second more with her in that saloon, and he might have made love to her. What the hell was wrong with him? Not only was taking a woman on a saloon floor not his usual way, he never should have allowed the passionate interlude to flare in the first place. He should be thinking of Sarah, and their engagement.

He stepped toward her. "Katherine—"

"Are you hungry?" she asked. "Where's the kitchen? I didn't see the entire ship the other night."

"Katherine—"

"We could gather some food—that is, if you have any food below right now—and bring it up here. Lake Erie is so beautiful. Alexandra and I used to sneak from the school one morning a week, usually Saturdays. We had a hidden boat we often took out on the lake. It was the only time we could be alone and talk."

Her hair curled gently around her face. Her eyes were bright. Her skin glowed. Her smile was the loveliest Nicholas had ever seen. Talking, she was captivating. Excited, she was an unbelievable vision.

"Katherine, there's something I must—"

"Alexandra might come to Cleveland to teach. Surely there are jobs for teachers. You'll like her. She's pretty. Beautiful. Fun. Smart. She has no one but me. Her father never wanted her. Oh, he pays for her schooling, but that's to keep her from his sight. It's horrible, Nicholas, the thing she told me about him." Katherine brushed the hair from her face, then gripped the railing and looked out across Lake Erie. "Alexandra was young when her mother died, but she told me she thinks her father pushed her mother down a flight of stairs. Alexandra's greatest fear is that her father may show up at the school one day and want to take her back to Chicago. She loved her mother, still does. She would kill her father if she ever saw him again."

"You care for Alexandra a lot," Nicholas said. "Kath—"

"I care about her happiness. I miss her terribly. I wrote her a letter as soon as I arrived. I'll write another tomorrow."

"How old is she?" She wanted to talk about her friend. They would. Then he would tell her about Sarah, Nicholas decided.

"Eighteen."

"What if she left the school?"

Katherine glanced at him in surprise. "You mean without her father's permission?"

He nodded.

"I don't know. Perhaps her father would be glad. He'd be free of the responsibility of her."

"Why not ask Werner if she can stay with you?"

Katherine released the rail and twisted her fingers again. "Uncle Werner? He's still getting used to having me around."

"He might say yes."

"Yes . . . he might. Alexandra could find a position at a school here." Katherine smiled at him. "Thank you. You're wonderful."

"I only suggested—"

"Mr. Cummings!" shouted a voice from the other end of the deck. "Didn't know you were on board, sir."

Damn. Another lost opportunity. Nicholas turned and caught sight of a short man with weathered skin and snow-white hair. He was walking toward them.

"It's all right, Captain. I found the repaired rail. How's the engine?"

"Good as new, sir. Better." The captain beamed. His gray eyes shifted to Katherine.

Wonderful. Nicholas knew how this might look. At least he and Katherine weren't being caught alone in the dim saloon. At least they weren't being caught making love on the saloon floor. Nicholas wondered briefly what Kevin would think of his "perfect world" now. At least part of it didn't feel so perfect anymore.

Summer Storm

He managed to collect himself and introduce Katherine and Captain Islington.

The good captain dipped his head, murmuring a quick "My pleasure, miss."

Katherine smiled. She didn't seem at all unnerved that they might have been caught in a compromising position by any member of the crew. "How is it traveling Lake Erie all the time, Captain? You must see every sunrise and every sunset."

"Make a point of doing just that. 'Cept for the winter months. Then I wouldn't brave her if Mr. Cummings here doubled my pay." He grinned, showing a few blank spaces where teeth had once been.

"You share my respect for the lake," Katherine said. "It's beautiful. So is the *Morning Star*."

Captain Islington glanced at Nicholas, then back to Katherine. "Has he shown you the ship?"

"Some of it. Is that an invitation?" she teased. "I'm hoping it is."

The man flushed.

"Come along," Nicholas said, sighing. How easily she charmed the most unsuspecting person. He held out his arm. She took it, and they followed the captain to the other end of the ship.

Near the pilothouse, Katherine saw far across the glittering lake. She admired the endless water, although she knew from studying geography that somewhere to the north Lake Erie met Canada and ceased. To the east she merged with Lake Ontario in a great waterfall. To the west she met Lake Huron. And Lakes Michigan and Superior lay beyond that, giants lying in partially unexplored, majestic beauty. Katherine caught her breath, seeing and imagining the five sisters. She wanted to travel them all one day, admire their calm and feel their fury.

At Nicholas's nod, Captain Islington invited her into the pilothouse. A muscular man stood in the center, steering the ship with a huge wheel. A nearby table contained a compass and rolled-up papers Katherine guessed were maps. The woodwork here was oiled and dark, and the windows shimmered with cleanliness.

"Where does the *Morning Star* travel, Captain?" she asked.

"Between New York and Ohio mostly. She's an excursion vessel. Carries passengers mostly, but there's space for cargo if space is needed. Finest ship in the line. Other two can't boast of fine saloons, staterooms, and passenger cabins." He opened a map on the table and soon caught Katherine's interest by pointing out the *Morning Star*'s various ports along Lake Erie's shore. "Got a ship in the line that makes runs to Canada, sometimes over to Detroit, Chicago, and other places out in that direction. Now that the canal at Sault Ste. Marie's in, the third ship's been going up Michigan and Superior way, unloading and loading cargo."

"The Sault Ste. Marie . . . I read about it in the Sandusky newspaper," Katherine said, and rattled off the exact dimensions of the canal, dimensions that were foremost in every shipbuilder's mind when he drew sketches for a vessel. She even knew the exact materials that had been hauled in to build the canal, and the number of years the construction had taken.

Captain Islington stared at her. So did Nicholas.

She looked uncomfortable suddenly, clasping her hands and averting her gaze to the pilot's wheel. "I wasn't trying to be smart. I just know, that's all."

"That's amazin'," blurted the captain.

Nicholas grinned. He couldn't help himself. "We're astonished, not insulted," he assured her. "Not many lake men know the things you do about that canal."

She smiled, but still a bit self-consciously.

"We sure needed that thing," the captain said. "We were takin' cargo up to the falls, and it'd have to be shipped the rest of the way by wagon. Same thing comin' down. We'd get it by wagon after it'd been hauled around the falls."

"Show her the old maps, the old routes," Nicholas said.

Her smile widened. "And logs. Do you have any logs? Manifests? Have you ever been through a gale?"

"Plenty." Captain Islington moved to the map and compass table. "No man who's traveled the lakes for long can say he hasn't been through a gale. Some of 'em just whip out of

Summer Storm 75

nowhere. Some we suspect are blowin' in, and we break for the nearest harbor. Sailed a schooner, *Monley,* some years ago. She broke up near Buffalo. Could see the harbor lights, but there wasn't a thing we could do. The wind picked up and tossed her like a wooden toy, drove her against the rocks."

Katherine's eyes widened. Captain Islington's had grown distant and bright. Nicholas settled himself on a chair near the pilothouse door. There was nothing a seasoned lake man liked to do more than tell his adventures. The man certainly wasn't boring Katherine. His voice was soft as he described the ship breaking up, the other ships trying to sail out and help, and it grew louder when he described the wind and the driving sleet, the ice that had formed on the outside of the ship. Katherine listened, captivated.

Nicholas sat and watched her, just as captivated.

When the *Morning Star* docked, Nicholas saw Kevin perched atop a mooring stump on the pier and shook his head in disbelief.

"Your butler told me you were coming here," Kevin explained. "Man on the next pier said the ship wouldn't be out long. I was thinking of inviting you to go to the club or to the track."

"*Was?*" Nicholas queried, knowing Kevin's invitation to him had most probably withered as soon as he spotted Katherine.

And he was right. Kevin fastened himself to her side. "Yes, was, my friend."

"Well, I was just taking Katherine home," Nicholas informed him, guiding Katherine to the waiting carriage.

"I'll ride with you. I'll send the cab on."

Without being outright rude to Kevin, Nicholas knew there was no way to get rid of him. He also knew this meant he wouldn't have an opportunity in the carriage to tell Katherine about the announcement to be made this evening. The many irritating interruptions were beginning to border on ridiculous. And the dull throb of a headache just taking hold added to his irritability.

7

KEVIN HAD BEEN all of nine years old the day his father sent him off to deliver boots to a Flats merchant. He crossed from the west to the east riverbank and was maybe a half mile from the merchant's shop when he spotted the dark-haired boy skimming stones across the river. The boy was different from him, Kevin knew. His clothes were tailored, folded, creased, and tucked in the right places. Kevin didn't think he'd ever seen such a white shirt. Saints, it was white. Like snow before it melted and mixed with dirt and turned gray. Kevin's own clothes were tattered and dirty. Of course, he'd never thought they were tattered and dirty before.

Nicholas had accompanied his father to the Flats warehouse, and while Lemuel Cummings was conducting his business, he wandered outside. He was fascinated with the way he could turn a stone just the right way and send it skipping across the water. The warehouse district was quiet today; there were not so many schooners and brigs and the appealing ships called side-wheelers. He expertly sent three more stones skipping along, then felt someone staring at him.

There were two hundred yards of grass between him and the boy with tousled and dirty reddish-blond hair. They stood assessing each other.

Both heard the sobbing from behind the old warehouse at the same time. A thick voice rose, taunting someone, then there were more sobs.

Summer Storm

Nicholas and Kevin both moved at the same time, more curious to learn what was happening behind the warehouse than they were with each other. Both were shocked when they spotted a pudgy bully twice their size hovering over a boy who couldn't have been more than six years old. The bully was demanding a coin. The boy said his mother had given it to him to buy milk for his baby sister. She needed milk, and if he gave up the coin, she wouldn't get her milk. The bully grabbed the boy by one arm, and again Nicholas and Kevin moved at the same time.

Alone they couldn't have bloodied the bully's nose or blackened one eye or made him turn around and run. Alone they might not have had the courage. But together they did the task—and doing it together bonded them together.

After the bully was gone, the boy sniffed a few times and thanked them, then wandered away wiping his eyes. Nicholas and Kevin plopped themselves in the grass by the river. Grinning, they exchanged names.

"Well, we remedied that," Nicholas said.

Kevin laughed. "Shit. He got a whoppin'. Won't be comin' round here no more."

Nicholas sobered and gave him an odd look, a disapproving look that made Kevin feel uncomfortable. Kevin scratched at the ground with a finger, not minding when dirt gathered under his already stained nail. But he did mind when he glanced over and saw that, other than the bully's dried blood, Nicholas's hands, fingers, and nails were spotless. His skin was smooth and pale, not rough and sunburned like Kevin's. Nicholas was also aware of the difference between himself and Kevin, but he didn't care. He liked Kevin.

Kevin smudged the circles he'd drawn in the dirt, then stood and grabbed the boots he'd dropped in favor of pounding that bully. "Thinkin' I'd better git. Pa be whoppin' me if I don't."

"Please stay," Nicholas said. "Where are you from?"

"Not where you're from. You're different, all clean. Manners 'n' all that."

"It doesn't matter."

"I best be deliverin' these boots. Pa complained 'bout givin' up last night with his fav'rite whore to finish 'em."

Nicholas frowned. "What's a whore?"

Kevin stared. He knew all about whores, all about women for that matter. He couldn't believe someone else who looked about his age didn't. Yes, he knew all about whores, even Irish whiskey, but somehow he had a feeling this Nicholas didn't. "Gotta git," he said again, hustling away.

"Come back tomorrow?"

"No."

But Kevin did. And there was Nicholas, sitting in the grass on the bank just where he'd left him.

Somehow in the ensuing years Nicholas and Kevin managed a friendship, despite the outward differences between them. Kevin often found Nicholas looking at him in an odd way when he spoke words Nicholas called vulgar. Once or twice they even fought over the words.

They were curious about each other's lives. But Nicholas never seemed as curious about Kevin's as Kevin did about Nicholas's. When Kevin was twelve, Nicholas secretly took him to the Cummings home. There Kevin found a different world, a world of glittering things, pretty things, nice-to-touch things. Right then he decided that someday he'd have nice-to-touch things.

He met Nicholas's mother that day. He hung his head before her stare. She asked if he knew how to cipher and read. He said no, but he knew how to make sturdy boots and some fine Irish whiskey, even Irish stew when his father could afford lamb, which wasn't but about once a year. She smiled then and said Mr. Cummings needed a boy to help the gardener and the groom sometimes and she wondered if he wanted the position. Kevin didn't really know what "position" meant, but suspected it had something to do with the gardener and the groom she'd mentioned. He said yes real quick. Hell, he just wanted to be close to this house with all its nice, glittering things. He wanted to see this woman sometimes who was different from the whores wandering the street over on his side of the river. She smelled nice. Her hair was pinned all pretty. And her dress

Summer Storm

rustled and swished when she walked.

He didn't know at first that she meant to give him money for helping and being near her and the house. But that was good, too.

Actually, as the months and years passed, he never helped the gardener and the groom much. He spent most of his days in a back room with Nicholas and a man Mrs. Cummings called Mr. Wirth, the schoolmaster. He was given the same slate and was expected to listen and learn just as Nicholas was. He soon realized that Mrs. Cummings had decided to see him educated.

The day Nicholas packed to go to college at Oberlin, Kevin also packed.

As the carriage moved away from the pier, Kevin watched Nicholas. He valued their friendship, knew he was risking it by objecting to Nicholas's engagement, but cared about Nicholas enough that he couldn't stand back and watch Nicholas commit himself to a lifetime of unhappiness.

After some thinking, Kevin had decided to try again to talk sense into him.

When he'd gone to Nicholas's home earlier today, he'd gone hoping to talk to him more about the engagement. Nicholas had avoided him these past days, possibly because he didn't want to be faced with the reality of the situation again—that his relationship with Sarah was as platonic as platonic could get, that he wanted to marry her because she'd been groomed for him, or so it had seemed. Their parents had formed an early, close friendship, and people had assumed Nicholas would marry Sarah. Nicholas, ever the socially conscientious man, apparently meant to go through with what was expected of him.

What Kevin saw developing between the lovely Katherine McDaniel and Nicholas was in stark contrast to Nicholas's relationship with Sarah.

Nicholas had told him a little of how he'd met Katherine in Werner Kraus's bank. Nicholas had taken that abandoned girl under his wing and played the role of guardian. But the heated way Kevin had seen Nicholas looking at Katherine as they'd stepped off the ship was hardly the way a guardian should be looking at his ward. The look had been a far sight different from the fond looks Nicholas often gave Sarah.

No, no. Nicholas had been longing, admiring. Kevin didn't think Nicholas had ever experienced the sort of passion that went with love, the kind that crept up and hit you right in the chest and eventually in the head so you couldn't sleep or think straight. All you could do was think of the woman you loved.

He knew.

He'd never recommend falling in love to anyone; *he* never wanted to do it again. But Kevin didn't want Nicholas marrying a woman he didn't love either, and finding out later just how unhappy that sort of situation could make a man. Nicholas at least needed to experience the sort of passion involved in a relationship that *could* develop into love; the sort that didn't exist between him and Sarah. The sort that was kindling between him and Katherine McDaniel right now.

The night of the Independence Day celebration aboard the ship, jealousy had flared in Nicholas's eyes when Kevin lifted Katherine's hand to his lips. Moments ago, when Kevin had invited himself along for the ride, there'd been jealousy in Nicholas's eyes again. Kevin wondered if adding kindling to the sparks would force Nicholas to see the difference in the way he viewed Sarah and Katherine. It might.

And I'm just the man for the job, Kevin thought. His reputation with the ladies was known throughout Cleveland, after all. Wooing yet another female wouldn't be unlike him.

"Are you attending Nicholas's supper this evening?" he asked Katherine. Nicholas sat silently beside him.

"My uncle is not feeling well today," she said, twisting a ribbon on her parasol.

Kevin leaned forward. "Could it be you don't have an escort?"

She gave him a slight smile. "You're very perceptive."

"I—and no doubt dozens of other men—would love to escort you. Of course, today I seem to be the first in line.

Summer Storm

The *only* one in line. I could arrange to pick you up, say . . . What time does the supper start, Nicholas? I forget." Kevin glanced at Nicholas, who sat with his arms crossed, looking like a storm cloud about to burst. Kevin suspected he wouldn't need to play this game long.

"Seven," came the cool response. "If you can arrange time away from the hotel. I thought you said—"

"I already made arrangements," Kevin said, grinning. "I'll pick you up at six-thirty then, Miss McDaniel."

"She hasn't agreed to go with you yet. Perhaps you should *ask* if she wants to."

"Oh, yes." Kevin chuckled. He had definitely found Nicholas's sore spot. If he'd had even a fraction of a doubt before that Nicholas wanted Katherine McDaniel, that doubt vanished now. "Terribly sorry, Miss McDaniel. Your loveliness flusters me, makes me forget my manners. Would you do me the honor of allowing me to escort you to Mr. Cummings's supper tonight?"

Katherine hesitated. How she wanted to go this evening! Nicholas had not volunteered to be her escort, for whatever reason. She wanted to be near him. Of course, she would have to take advantage of Kevin's offer—use him—and that thought caused her a twinge of guilt since she liked him. But if going with Kevin was her only chance to be near Nicholas . . .

"I'll be waiting, Mr. Riley."

Kevin reached for her hand and kissed the back of it. From the corner of his eye he saw Nicholas's glare. Most men would have taken one look at Nicholas Cummings, at his intense eyes and hard-set jaw, and not dare cross him. He was in good shape physically; he and Kevin often rode together at the track, sometimes indulging in a race here and there. But Nicholas hardly intimidated Kevin.

Kevin met his friend's gaze with an unwavering stare.

When the carriage stopped before the Kraus home—gothic-looking, constructed of dark stone, with turrets set on each side—Kevin leapt out to escort Katherine to the front entrance. There he paused to kiss her hand again. Nicholas and Harold swept past them, deposited Katherine's boxes in the foyer just inside the front entrance, then emerged, walking back to the carriage.

"Until six-thirty, Miss McDaniel," Kevin said, returning her smile, bowing away . . . backing into Nicholas.

"Let's go. Now," Nicholas said low.

Back in the carriage, Kevin sat opposite Nicholas and took the full force of his fiery glare. "My, but you're in a black mood today," Kevin taunted.

Nicholas unfastened his stock buckle and yanked the neckband off. The buckle went clattering to the floor. He made no effort to retrieve it. "I had not planned to spend my afternoon encouraging your courtship of Katherine McDaniel."

"Courtship? Now, now. It's hardly that. I don't plan to court any woman. Woo her, yes, but not court her."

"Leave her alone."

"Leave her alone? You can't be serious. Katherine McDaniel's a lovely lass. And I'm a bachelor, a free man. Unlike yourself, an engaged man who has no business being alone with any woman other than the one he means to marry."

"What I do is none of your damned business," Nicholas muttered.

Kevin leaned toward him, all humor gone from his expression and manner. "You listen to me, my friend. If you want Katherine McDaniel so bad, you'll have to be man enough to tell Sarah you don't really love her and can't marry her. Otherwise put your eyes back in your head and take your own advice—what happens between Katherine McDaniel and myself is none of *your* damned business."

With that, Kevin settled back against the seat to the sound of creaking leather. The carriage rocked slightly. There was the muffled clip-clop of horses' hooves.

Nicholas clenched his jaw and turned his head to stare out the window. "I'm not interested in Katherine in that way."

Kevin sighed, growing exasperated. "Always the gentleman, afraid to admit when a woman stirs you in the right place."

"That's enough. I never like vulgarity. You know that."

Kevin lifted a brow. "Did I say something vulgar?"

"You have a way of putting things."

"Ah! It's my honesty, my bluntness you don't care for. She doesn't stir you in the right place? Is that why you looked so startled when you came off that ship?"

"She's an acquaintance, that's all. Captain Islington and I were showing her the *Morning Star*," Nicholas said, still denying the obvious.

"An acquaintance . . . Ah. I see. And a very intimate one at that. One with whom I should like to be so intimate."

"Stay away from her," Nicholas warned again. "You'll do nothing but ruin her."

"I never knew you held such a high opinion of my private adventures."

"Damn you, Kevin! This is no game."

"Ah, but it is. I'd love to see your mask of propriety stripped away, just this once. You're marrying Sarah out of—"

"Another lecture?" Nicholas snapped. "I've had quite enough of your ill manner regarding my engagement."

"And I've had quite enough of your ill manner," Kevin said, tapping on the carriage roof. He asked Harold to stop and let him out—he would walk the rest of the way back to the hotel or find another cab. He wouldn't try to convince Nicholas again. But neither would he grasp Nicholas's hand and wish him the best in his upcoming marriage.

When he'd climbed out of the carriage and it had rattled off, he glanced up at the cloudy sky. To his surprise he felt the urge to whistle a merry tune. There was some sunshine in all of this, after all. He had just discovered he didn't need to expend much energy to make Nicholas more jealous; there might be no reason for him to say anything else at all. Nicholas was quite enamored of Katherine McDaniel. Quite.

Hours later Kevin shared easy conversation with Katherine inside a hired cab as it headed toward Nicholas's home. He told her about his hotel on Ontario Street—the Lighthouse Inn—and how he had struggled to start it, first by saving his every penny, then by rebuilding the part of it that had burned down nearly two years ago. She shared her account of how she'd first met Nicholas, and how, when she and Nicholas had reached the Flats, the "very gallant Nicholas" told her he didn't intend to let her walk back to the bank alone. He had argued with Werner when her uncle would have sent her to who knows where.

As she spoke, Kevin felt guilt creep up his spine and imbed itself in his gut. He'd thought to use her to jolt Nicholas from making a commitment to Sarah. But this woman was in love with Nicholas, as much in love as a woman could be. Considering that, he should not be encouraging anything between her and Nicholas. He was sometimes crude and brash in speech and manner, regressing back to his slum days, but he was not without conscience. He'd had no idea Katherine was in love with Nicholas, only that Nicholas desired Katherine. Did Nicholas know Katherine loved him? Surely he did. Her feelings were obvious in her pretty blue eyes. Had Nicholas told her about Sarah? Kevin didn't think so—Katherine probably wouldn't be so starry-eyed if Nicholas had. Saints. This was not supposed to happen. Love was not part of the scheme.

Kevin was so deeply involved with his thoughts he didn't realize the cab had stopped until Katherine reached across the way and tapped his knee. "We've arrived," she said.

They stepped down. Kevin wondered if he should take her aside and tell her about the engagement. Others were arriving; a carriage pulled to a stop behind the cab. Kevin was still deliberating when he realized Katherine had walked ahead and was almost to the door. He collected himself and hurried after her.

Once they were inside, Tom Jenkins pressed forward around a stylishly scrolled and curved side chair. The man was overbearing by Kevin's thinking, someone he preferred to avoid—and he avoided few people. He was courteous enough to introduce Katherine and Jenkins, but after the formality he put a hand on Katherine's elbow, urging her through the small hall and to the parlor.

An array of conversing females with crinolines and hoopskirts spread wide around them occupied green velvet wing chairs and a matching sofa with more scrollwork and curves. Men mingled behind the settee and the chairs, near tables and an ever-popular whatnot. Spread beneath the furnishings was a leaf-patterned Persian rug. Lamps cast flickering light about the room.

Katherine studied Kevin as he introduced her to several dignified-looking men. His hand remained on her elbow, almost protectively. He had become quite serious at some point during the journey here. She wanted to ask him if he was feeling all right, but more introductions were made, more smiles and polite conversation required of her. Every time Kevin told someone she was Werner Kraus's niece, eyebrows lifted and expressions became respectful. Evidently Uncle Werner was quite an important man in Cleveland.

"Where is Mr. Kraus this evening?" inquired Mrs. Laden, an elderly woman seated in a chair near the fireplace. "He always brings such life to these gatherings."

Katherine remembered her first evening home with Uncle Werner, how he had teased her, saying she would catch every male eye in Cleveland. He had taken her into his library and shown her his collection of fine books. She smiled, recalling how his and Mr. Baum's merry singing had boomed through the house this morning, and how she and Uncle Werner had poured through accounts of hot air balloon adventures the morning after Independence Day.

"Yes, I'm certain he does," she said sincerely. "Unfortunately he's not feeling well." That was a lie if ever she'd told one. She had peeked into the library when Kevin arrived at the house. Uncle Werner had been fast asleep, his head resting against one wing of the chair. Doubtless he was feeling nothing at all.

Near the door, Katherine encountered a woman with dark hair touched with gray near her face. The eyes were unmistakable—the same as Nicholas's rich emerald eyes.

"Reddish-blond hair, wide blue eyes... You must be Katherine," the woman said.

Katherine smiled. "Yes. And you're Mrs. Cummings?"

"I am. You look exactly as Nicholas described," Mrs. Cummings said, fingering the pearls at her neck. "Except he forgot to tell me you are beautiful. And there's intelligence behind those lovely eyes. Tell me, what are your plans now that you are finally home?"

Telling her she aspired to marry Nicholas would never do, Katherine thought. "Someday I hope—"

"You should join our cause."

Katherine wrinkled her brow, waiting for Mrs. Cummings to explain.

The woman took Katherine's elbow, steering her toward one corner of the parlor, away from the cluster of people. Katherine glanced over her shoulder and found Kevin aiming a grin of admiration and mischievousness at Mrs. Cummings.

"And what cause is that?" Katherine prompted, for Kevin's grin and Mrs. Cummings's words had piqued her interest.

"Voting rights for women someday," Mrs. Cummings answered in a hushed voice. "Equal status. Certain other rights that the male population of the world has denied the female sex for years. My dear, it can only serve to better your life and the lives of your female children and grandchildren. The day will soon arrive when all the women of this country will demand the same rights only a handful of us are demanding now."

Katherine had heard of the movement demanding "certain rights" for women. Several years ago, at the school, Alexandra had somehow managed to smuggle in a newspaper. They had taken it aboard their little boat the following Saturday and spent their entire excursion reading the article about "the outrageous demands some women are making around the country." While Katherine agreed that women should be allowed to vote and should be as educated as men, she was thankful the Bloomer costume—trousers beneath a skirt reaching halfway between the knees and ankles—had not become popular. The ideas Amelia Bloomer and her followers upheld were considered scandalous, but that costume was even more scandalous, from what Katherine had overheard from the other girls at the school.

"Mother, you promised . . ." Nicholas's stern voice came from behind Katherine.

"Oh, Nicholas, you are determined to hold me to that, aren't you?" Mrs. Cummings said, looking exasperated.

"Yes, I am. I understand and respect your opinions, but you said you wouldn't try to recruit forces this evening."

"And I had every intention of keeping that promise until I met this striking young woman. She has more intelligence behind those pretty eyes than most men have in a fingertip."

Kevin chuckled. "Mrs. Cummings, you have my admiration."

"You're encouraging her," Nicholas accused, his frustration obvious. "Don't do that. Not tonight. Katherine, have you met—"

"No you don't," Mrs. Cummings objected, gripping Katherine's elbow again and turning her toward the door. "Do not try and shelter her from me, Nicholas. Now that I've met her, I intend to speak more with her. Where is Sarah?"

Katherine wondered why Nicholas's brow tightened. He thrust his hands into his trouser pockets and glanced uncomfortably between her and his mother. "In the hall. She was delayed," he responded.

"Well, I suggest you busy yourself with her. Or your father. He's here, you know."

"No, I didn't know."

"You couldn't keep this from us, Nicholas. For months, we've suspected. We're delighted."

"If you don't mind, Mother, there's something I need to tell Katherine. In private. Something I couldn't seem to find the chance to tell her earlier," he said.

"No. I know what you are trying to do. Save her from me. Well *I* have more to tell her. You go see to Sarah and your many guests."

She led Katherine away from Kevin and Nicholas and out into the hall, where people were gathered around a pretty young woman with auburn hair. The woman's soft brown eyes met Katherine's briefly as Mrs. Cummings spoke highly of Amelia Bloomer and of "the God-given rights of the female sex."

"That's Sarah Preston," Mrs. Cummings interjected in her speech. "A lovely girl. There's an announcement to be made later. But I won't say more. I would ruin the surprise for the two of them."

Katherine tore her gaze from Sarah Preston. She didn't like the words that rang in her head: *Go see to Sarah,* Mrs. Cummings had told Nicholas. Then: *There's an announcement to be made later.*

Katherine didn't like what her mind pieced together. No, Nicholas would have told her. He wouldn't have kissed her the way he had. He wouldn't have allowed her to go on believing he wanted her if he wanted someone else.

Mrs. Cummings began talking about "the injustices wreaked upon females for centuries now . . . thousands of years, in fact."

Katherine stole another glance at Sarah Preston, lovely in a gown of rust-colored satin. Her heart pounded, drummed in her ears, filled her with dread.

What had Nicholas wanted to tell her?

8

LATER, IN THE dining room, Katherine watched Nicholas and Sarah together. He led Sarah to her seat on the opposite side of the long table, its edges already cluttered with people talking low, sometimes laughing. Sarah smiled at Nicholas. He raised her hand to his lips and kissed it.

Pain stung Katherine's breast. Mrs. Cummings's strong voice continued in her ears. While she didn't want to believe what she suspected, she had only to watch Nicholas with Sarah to know. She was neither blind nor stupid.

But she was a fool.

She had placed herself in a compromising position, something she had been taught never to do. She had offered her lips; Nicholas had taken them. She had offered her heart; he had taken that, too. Dear God, she had been willing to offer him everything.

She had trusted him.

From the moment of their reunion, when his eyes had raked so appreciatively over her, she had harbored the idea that he would propose someday—to her. Until now.

Apparently lust was far different from love.

Fine china and Tiffany silver gleamed and sparkled beneath the glow of a single chandelier. There were crystal goblets and pure white linen. An elegantly set table . . . beautiful enough for a celebration. And yet Katherine's disbelieving mind still wanted to thrust off the obvious truth. Her trembling hand reached for a goblet and somehow brought it to her lips without incident, but she barely tasted the sweet wine she swallowed.

A rather short, stubby man near one end of the table suddenly stood, bellowing, "Wine, Nicholas? I'll be damned! Where's the champagne? You'll not announce your engagement to my daughter over glasses of wine."

Murmurs and gasps rose around the table. "Engagement?" some exclaimed. "Oh, I knew! I just knew!" others said. Most everyone looked to Nicholas and Sarah, wanting the man's blurted words confirmed.

Katherine dropped her gaze to the burgundy-colored wine in her goblet. "I don't suppose I will, Alistair," she heard Nicholas say, and perhaps there was a touch of irritation to his voice. "You've done it for me."

Laughter filled the room. Alistair Preston chuckled. "Forgive me. I couldn't restrain myself. To the engaged couple," he boomed, proposing a toast. "For now, wine must do."

Not wanting to draw unpleasant attention, Katherine composed herself enough to lift her glass in accord with others being lifted around the table. Nicholas's gaze caught and held hers. His eyes were soft emeralds pleading forgiveness and understanding.

But she didn't understand. And how could she possibly forgive him for not telling her? For not at least letting her know the occasion for this supper so she wouldn't be fighting to piece together her dignity right now? She had assumed this dinner party was just a gathering of his friends.

Glasses lowered. People conversed. Servants moved silently in and out of the room carrying silver platters piled with roast beef, glazed carrots, and potatoes sprinkled with herbs. Wine goblets were refilled almost constantly. There were fresh rolls and little pats of butter, as well as plates of celery, radishes, and olives. At any other time the spread of food would have looked delicious. But tonight Katherine forced herself to eat.

And, for appearance sake and to pass the long moments, between tiny bites she also forced herself to talk to the men seated to her right and left. Tom Jenkins owned a thriving

Summer Storm

bookstore on Superior Avenue. Stephen Brines operated a carriage business.

By the time dessert was served, Katherine could hardly bear the thought of spending another moment amid all the gay conversations and merriment, wearing a false smile and pretending to laugh at things Tom and Stephen said. She really had no interest in the two men; she had no interest in anything but leaving this place. She wanted Alexandra's embrace, her shoulder, their little boat. She wanted to hear the gurgle of Lake Erie around her, for it offered solace. She was ashamed, outraged, wanted to bury her face in a pillow and let the tears flow that threatened to choke her every few seconds.

She didn't touch her cake topped with strawberries, and she glanced distastefully at the little bowl of cream that accompanied it. When Tom asked why she wasn't eating, she said softly, "I have a small appetite. It's probably delicious, but I'm full."

When people began rising, Katherine found Kevin behind her chair, ready to assist her. Tom had obviously expected to perform the task; he rubbed his side whiskers, giving Kevin a look of surprise. But he said nothing as Katherine took Kevin's arm and allowed him to escort her from the room.

"I'll take you home if you want," Kevin offered in a soft voice.

Katherine wasn't sure she trusted Kevin now any more than she trusted Nicholas. He was Nicholas's friend, after all. Perhaps he shared Nicholas's distasteful morals, his total lack of regard for her feelings. Perhaps he thought he could take her from here and have his way with her and she might be as willing in his arms as she'd been in Nicholas's. "I don't think so. I—"

"You really didn't know, did you?" he asked. "About the engagement, I mean."

"No," she mumbled, still in shock. "He would have seduced me, yet would marry her." She couldn't believe Nicholas capable of such an awful thing. She didn't want to believe.

"*What?*"

She turned to stare at Kevin. "Don't tell me you didn't notice that Nicholas and I were alone part of the afternoon," she finally said softly, thinking that any condemning looks he, or anyone, gave her could never possibly wound her as much as she'd already been wounded by Nicholas.

Kevin led her to the end of the hall, beyond a swirling staircase, away from the crowd. "*Did* he seduce you?"

She wouldn't lie. Inside a strange feeling of regret engulfed her. She almost wished Nicholas *had* made love to her this afternoon. Sharing only a part of physical intimacy with him had left her aching for more. She shut her eyes, overwhelmed by the memory of his passionate kisses and the various ways he had gently spoken her name.

"Did he?" Kevin demanded again, taking her by the shoulders and shaking her slightly. "If he did Katherine . . . He's my friend, but I'd be having words with him. Even I have ethics."

Katherine's eyes shot open. "I don't want him forced to marry me."

"That's not—"

"He pulled me from a carriage accident this afternoon and took me shopping. Then he offered to take me home. I didn't want to go. I wanted to be with him. I cannot lay the entire blame on Nicholas. I offered myself. I did exactly what ladies are taught not to do," she said, aware that she was sharing precious information with a man she barely knew—a man who was Nicholas's friend, at that! But she desperately needed someone to talk to, needed a shoulder . . .

"He has a bit more experience than you. He might have had the decency to restrain himself," Kevin muttered through tight lips.

Katherine stared at him in surprise. His face had reddened. He was truly angry. "A row between you and Nicholas would certainly make the evening all the more delightful, wouldn't it?" she mumbled. She placed a hand on his arm. "We shared an embrace, a few kisses. That's all. Please . . . say nothing. And please don't do this. People will notice."

Summer Storm

Backing away, Kevin straightened his shoulders. "There's a flower garden to the side of the house. Want to walk with me?"

Katherine shook her head, gazing warily at him. "I don't intend to throw myself into the arms of another man."

"Seduction is hardly what I have in mind. I know how it feels to be shot in the heart. I know better than anyone."

A haunted look passed across his face, brief and startling, but no less intense. Suddenly Katherine was confident he wasn't Nicholas's friend at the moment, but hers. She saw, too, that something or someone in Kevin Riley's past had wounded him deeply. His normally light attitude was merely a facade to disguise his pain.

"Yes, I think you do know," she murmured. "And your loss is still very great sometimes, isn't it?"

"The best thing we can do for ourselves is get the hell out of here," he said, avoiding the question.

"Then let's go."

Katherine took his arm. She didn't care what people thought about their leaving together so soon after supper. The ladies would be gathering in the parlor or drawing room, the men in the library or the study. The thought of enduring a little gossip about her and Kevin leaving early, as bad as it might become, seemed far better than enduring another hour or two of trying to make polite conversation.

Kevin pushed a nearby door open. The kitchen. Pots and dishes cluttered the room. There were stacks of dirty plates and piles of silver forks and spoons. The room was unbearably hot, stifling—probably from the heat of the formidable black stove standing on darkened bricks laid in no particular pattern. Servants scurrying around a huge oak table paused, and suddenly Katherine felt a half dozen pairs of curious eyes darting between her and Kevin. She was not unaware of the fact that servants' gossip, though it frequently began in whispers, often developed into roars.

But since the damage could not be undone—the image of her and Kevin looking frantic and angry was doubtless imprinted on the servants' minds—they might as well continue. She presumed Kevin must be thinking the same thing; he gave her a startled look, then took her arm and tugged her to a door leading outside.

When night had made them inconspicuous, Katherine realized she was breathing again.

Once they were inside the cab, Kevin blurted apologies. As often as he visited Nicholas's home, he hadn't realized that door led to the kitchen. He hadn't been thinking clearly.

Katherine settled back in a dark corner. She could only hope Uncle Werner would not be harmed by the talk about her and Kevin that would surely reach the ears of many of his friends. How many days had she been home? Not quite four.

What a mess she had made of what was supposed to have been a wonderful homecoming. Odd how she hadn't worried about her reputation this afternoon, when she'd gone aboard the ship with Nicholas. But then, the eyes of servants had not been riveted on her and Nicholas, and she'd been caught up in the thrill of just being with him.

Oh, dear. What would Uncle Werner have to say about her outrageous behavior this time?

Nicholas was surrounded by well-wishers, but over the tops of their heads he saw Katherine and Kevin dash into the kitchen. He waited for them to reappear. Minutes passed, and they didn't.

In a mad rush, they had left together.

He imagined them darting through the kitchen filled with inquisitive servants, some hired specifically for tonight. His own wouldn't talk so much, but the hired ones . . .

Good God, what had Kevin and Katherine been thinking? Yes, they had arrived together, and everyone understood that. But to leave, to *escape* like that! And through the kitchen! There would be talk, and it would not be kind.

But perhaps Katherine was angry and wanted to hurt him. She hadn't realized, in her moments of shock, that she could only hurt herself by acting so rashly.

The announcement was supposed to have come *after* supper. That would have given him one last chance to pull her aside and prepare her. Accepting the engagement still would not have been easy for her, but at least she wouldn't have been as stunned. Damn Alistair! Katherine had been unsuspecting, vulnerable, sweet, innocent.

Nicholas's mind tortured him with images of her offering the coin to the monkey, jerking her hand back, and laughing, of the sugar powdering her chin . . . of the glance she had given him from the corner of her eye while teasing him about not dancing with her the night of the Independence Day celebration.

The perfect arrangement of the engagement, even of tonight, had begun to unravel then. Why hadn't he remained in control of his response to her? With any other woman, control would have been simple; with Katherine it had been a losing battle.

She had rushed away with Kevin. She could only be more hurt. Damn, damn, damn! And if he didn't do something quick, the gossip that would follow tonight might not necessarily remain just gossip. He knew Kevin's reputation. He didn't think for a moment Kevin would force himself on any woman, but Kevin certainly wouldn't turn one away, particularly one who needed comfort.

Normally a man conscientious about adhering to social propriety, Nicholas concocted an excuse he could use to escape the house for a time. The men were shifting toward the study. A game table had been pulled to the center of the parlor for the women. His mother was busily instructing a servant to fetch chairs, and a few women were still fluttering around Sarah, congratulating her. Sarah smiled at him over the tops of their heads. Nicholas forced a smile in return. He wouldn't think of hurting her—ever.

Presently he strode toward his mother and pulled her aside. "I just received a message from Captain Gates of the *Ontario*. There's a problem with some cargo. I must leave for a while. Will you take care of things here?"

Grace Cummings wrinkled her brow. "Nicholas, can it not wait until tomorrow morning? This is your engagement celebration after all. At your home."

"It can't wait."

"Very well," she said, sighing and shaking her head in disbelief. "You'll tell Sarah?"

"I'll say good night on my way out," he assured her.

Sarah was accommodating, as always. She kissed him lightly on the cheek and wished him well. If only she knew the truth, Nicholas thought. She would be wounded.

Outside, Nicholas strode quickly to the stable and saddled a horse, not bothering to locate the groom. He swung himself up onto the animal's back, tapped his heels against its sides, and rode off.

The ride took all of fifteen minutes. He dismounted before the Kraus house and tethered the horse to the branch of a small tree. A breeze made branches scratch against a turret window.

At the front entrance, Nicholas lifted the huge brass knocker. Suddenly he paused, staring at its ornate lion's head. Should he knock? Or should he simply remount and go back home? Kevin's carriage was nowhere in sight, and that was a relief. Still, he wanted to talk to Katherine, scold her for making that dash with Kevin, then say something—he didn't know what yet—that might ease the pain he'd seen in her eyes.

He rapped. When no one responded, he rapped again.

Finally the door creaked open a mere inch. "Yes?" came a voice.

"Katherine?"

"Nicholas. What do you want?"

"We need to talk."

"There is nothing to say."

"Dammit, Katherine, there's a lot to say!"

"Be quiet!" she whispered. "Uncle Werner's sleeping. Peggy didn't feel well, so I told her to go to bed. I was going up, too."

"Let me in," he said, seeing the sparkle of one blue eye and the heavily shadowed soft curves of her face through the crack. "I'm not going away until I've talked to you and I don't intend to do that through this crack. Open the door."

"No."

"Yes," he persisted.

Summer Storm

There was a pause. Then: "Nicholas, leave me alone. Do you hear me? Just go away!"

"And have you hate me, Katie?" he queried softly, for he couldn't stand the thought, he really couldn't. He still had no idea what he wanted to say to her, but he knew he wanted to see her, see for himself that she was all right. "No. Let me in, or I'll force my way in."

"You wouldn't!"

"I would. Easily. Let me in."

At last the door swung open. She had unbound her hair, and it curled wildly around her face, spilling over her shoulders and down her back. She wore a light-blue silk robe that enhanced her eyes. She stared hard at him for a moment, then stepped aside to allow him entry.

Once he was inside, she shut the door and turned to face him. "What is there to say?" She crossed her arms and rubbed her shoulders as if cold. "You're not the man I thought you were. You should have told me about Sarah. I was a fool, a stupid, infatuated fool. But I learn from my mistakes. I'll never offer myself to another man the way I offered myself to you. That's all."

Her words cut him. She was terribly hurt. He wanted to envelope her in his arms, comfort her. He wanted to explain . . . But how stupid an explanation would sound at this point! Better to make certain Kevin hadn't worked his charm on her, then leave. "Do you really think running out with Kevin that way was a wise thing to do?" he asked. "We had barely finished supper."

Her jaw dropped open. A harsh laugh tore loose from her throat. "How very touching! Oh, how very, very touching. Concern for my reputation? When you would have made love to me knowing you were engaged to another woman?"

Nicholas felt his guilt intensify. "Did Kevin try anything?"

Another harsh laugh. "Why, if you must know the truth . . . He pretended to dance with me. Right here. He swept me around the place, lulled me with softly spoken words, kissed me. He—"

Nicholas gripped her shoulders and narrowed his eyes. She was describing what had happened between them this afternoon, substituting Kevin for him! "Don't do that. Tell me the truth. Tell me!"

She stared at him. "What right do you have to demand the truth from me?"

He went still. She was right. His arms fell to his sides.

"You ... an engaged man," she whispered. "I should not have thrown myself at you, but you—"

"You don't have to throw yourself at any man, Katie."

"Don't call me that!" she said hoarsely. She backed against the wall, turned her face from him, breathed deeply. "My parents called me that, and you called me that! I had to forget them. Now I just want to forget you. Leave me alone, Nicholas. Just please, oh, please, leave ... me ... alone."

Pain swelled in his chest—the profound pain that accompanies great loss, the same pain he had felt after being told Samuel had died. By choice, *his choice,* he didn't have a right to her. He had hurt her so much, never wanting to, never meaning to, but he had. He had caused the agony in her eyes. He had broken her heart.

He wanted so much to make things right, yet he didn't know what to do, didn't know what to say. "I never meant for ... for anything to happen this afternoon," he said, stumbling over his tongue, something he had never done. "I—Katherine, for years I've planned to marry Sarah. Things were set in motion long before you came home."

"What do you want from me? What do you want? Do you even know? You've pledged yourself to Sarah Preston, yet here you are with me. Well, I don't want you here or anywhere near me. I never thought I would say that, but I don't. Go. Go now."

"I wanted to make sure you were all right," he said, torn inside by her words. He had had everything in order, or so he had thought. Katherine would come home. He would play the role of big brother, advising her about this and that. His engagement to Sarah would be announced. Everyone would be happy. Everything would be neatly laid out and go according to plan.

She lifted her chin, and he was reminded of that willful girl of fourteen. "I will always be all right. Always," she said, and she didn't even sniffle when she said it.

Nicholas nodded, opened the door, and slipped out.

A light rain had started.

The first lifted brow came the following Sunday morning when Katherine accompanied Uncle Werner to church. While men shook his hand and talked eagerly with him, their wives avoided Katherine. At first Katherine thought she was imagining things. But as more and more women brushed by her without a word, she knew. During mass, she observed more than two female heads bent toward each other, whispers passing between them. They tossed odd looks her way.

In *church,* Katherine thought with disgust, where people were supposed to gather in love and friendship. She only hoped the gossip she had brought upon herself did no harm to Uncle Werner's standing in the community.

Days passed. Kevin visited once, apologizing again for a predicament Katherine felt he couldn't have foreseen. He wouldn't be back for a while, he said. Hopefully people would realize there was nothing more to talk about, that there never had been, and the rumors would die. Smiling, Katherine squeezed his hand.

Peggy remarked that she'd expected more callers to welcome Katherine to Cleveland. After one look into the Irishwoman's eyes Katherine knew Peggy had heard an account of the hasty kitchen exit.

Katherine raised her chin, refusing to be subjected to condemning looks from a woman who lived under the same roof. "You know the truth, Peggy. You know we were there for the supper and that two hours after it began Kevin brought me home and stayed no more than five minutes. Tell me, when did we have time to do anything illicit?"

That quieted Peggy. She gave a sniff, then stalked from the room. Presently Katherine heard her beating the upstairs carpets and suspected that was the end of Peggy listening to the cruel whispers. Peggy seemed too dignified, too proper, to involve herself in gossip. Her wish to protect Uncle Werner was probably the only reason she had given it an ear at all.

The odd looks and huddled female heads were evident during the next mass, too. Katherine wondered why Uncle Werner didn't notice and remark. Surely he'd heard the gossip by now. She was baffled.

He escorted her numerous places during the next week—to the Merchant Exchange, to the theater in Melodeon Hall, and to a supper at a prominent attorney's home. The man's wife, Isabelle Chambers, had been the first to brush by Katherine in church without even so much as a hello. Katherine soon realized what was happening.

Everywhere they went, Uncle Werner refused to let the women who had shunned her escape with a tossed head or a disapproving look. He worked in subtle ways, of course, often making them feel very small.

He accompanied her to the dressmaker's one afternoon. He and Katherine were waiting in the front room when Mrs. Lyles, the seamstress, appeared. She was a small woman with gray hair and spectacles and wore a modest black gown buttoned up to her chin. At her side was Isabelle Chambers's friend, Clara Stowes, her dark hair pinned in a chignon. Clara's steps slowed when she saw Katherine; the rustle of crinoline ceased.

But Clara was doomed—she had already stepped into the room. When she spun to go, obviously planning to leave the settling of her account for another day or time, Uncle Werner barred the doorway in the most gentlemanly fashion—with a broad smile.

"Mrs. Stowes. *Guten morgen,*" he said, greeting her in the cheerful manner Katherine had witnessed many times these past days. "Hurrying off to a meeting of the Library Association? I do know how dedicated you are to your various causes. I am dedicated to a number of them myself. But surely you would not mind taking a moment to sit and talk with myself and Katherine, my niece?"

"Mr. Kraus! Oh, yes!" The woman tittered nervously. "Good morning."

He offered a chair next to Katherine. Mrs. Stowes sat, fluttering a fan, fluttering in general. She arranged her skirt, tucking here and there, smoothing, burying her one free hand in the folds and tittering more. Somehow she found the sense to ask an intelligent question: "H-how are you, Miss McDaniel?"

"I'm well. And you?"

"Quite well, quite well. And you, Mr. Kraus? You were missed at Mr. Cummings's supper. A fine affair, it was, with the engagement being announced."

"So I have heard," Uncle Werner remarked somewhat dryly.

Mrs. Lyles drifted from the room. Clara Stowes folded her fan, produced a delicate white handkerchief, and commenced twisting it. Katherine half expected the woman to touch it to her forehead to dab at the perspiration that had gathered there. "Y-you are still planning on providing the funds to purchase those books for the association, aren't you? We've never had anyone make such a generous offer," Clara said suddenly.

"Mrs. Stowes, certainly I still plan to purchase those books," Uncle Werner admonished, drawing back in surprise. "Have you been listening to idiotic *klatsch*? Such talk often leads one to believe things that should never have been voiced at all. Do you not agree?"

She stared dumbly at him. Then she tittered yet again and finally dabbed the handkerchief to her upper lip. An instant later her head bobbed.

Katherine produced her own handkerchief to hide her grin.

Sunlight beaming through a gauzy curtained window reflected off Uncle Werner's balding head. He patted Clara Stowes's hand. "I thought you would."

Katherine wanted to hug him. He was so dear to protect her and force these women to see that she was no trollop.

That evening, when the house was very quiet, Katherine found him in his library, dozing in a chair near the empty fireplace. She eased around the chair. He started, then ran a hand over his weary eyes. "Oh, Katherine. I did not hear you come in."

"*Danke schön,*" she said softly.

He furrowed his brow. "Thank me? For what?"

She gave him a stern look. "For defending my honor, you wonderful man. I wanted to laugh aloud this morning when Mrs. Stowes looked so stunned."

"Oh. That."

"Yes, that. Tell me, did you really make her and the other members of the association believe your weren't going to purchase those books?"

The hint of a smile played on his lips.

"You did, you devil!"

"I have always intended to purchase them."

"Of course." Katherine paused. "But you can't always be my protector, you know."

"I have a suspicion you will not need a protector much in your lifetime. You learn lessons quickly," he said. Then he amended the statement: "Most of the time."

She loved him. She truly loved him. "May I bring you a glass of wine? Your pipe?"

"No, no. I plan to go up to bed in a moment."

"All right. Good night, then," she said and kissed his cheek, quickly and fondly. He blushed, not one for fussy affection.

She left him there. He was a man she had once feared because she felt he had taken every last small thing she owned in the world. He had sold the farm and brought her to Cleveland. She remembered despising him at the time as much as he'd seemed to despise her. He had never visited her at the Sacred Heart School, something that had never surprised her. He had sent her there to get her out of his sight, after all, and because Nicholas had convinced him.

Aside from the occasional dry letters she had collected over the years, she really had not known Uncle Werner well before these past weeks. She had really not even concentrated on those letters. Her thoughts had been centered on Nicholas— meeting him again, making him fall madly in love with her, and marrying him. She had not thought a great deal about

Summer Storm

Uncle Werner at all, except that he was her uncle, and that hopefully they would get along well someday living under the same roof.

As she climbed the immaculately polished staircase to her room, she paused, casting a look over her shoulder. Odd how life sometimes took many different twists and turns. Twice now, hers had. She had gone from not liking Uncle Werner and adoring Nicholas to adoring Uncle Werner and not especially liking Nicholas. Odd indeed.

9

ALEXANDRA STEPPED FROM the train and stood on the platform gazing around. There were six piers extending into Lake Erie if she had counted right. Railroad tracks branched east along the shore. To the south, east, and west stood the homes and buildings of Cleveland. A river curved and cut through the land. Several bridges connected the east to the west.

Somewhere in the midst of it all she'd find Katherine.

An elderly porter Alexandra recognized from the train approached her. "Someone comin' for you, miss?" he inquired, the gold braids on his coat shimmering in the afternoon sun.

"No. I am afraid I forgot to let my friend know I was arriving this afternoon," she responded.

"Live in Cleveland or just visiting?"

"Visiting. Do you know a Mr. Kraus?"

"Kraus? Sure do. Pretty important man, Mr. Kraus. Owns a bank near the square." The porter paused to study her. He narrowed his eyes, deepening the many lines surrounding them. "Related to Mr. Kraus?"

"No," she answered. "I went to school with his niece. I'm a friend."

"Well, let me fetch a cab. Mr. Kraus wouldn't want you standing by the depot when you could be comfortable in his parlor."

"Thank you."

The porter hurried off. A short time later, he returned, taking Alexandra's portmanteau from her hand. He led her across the

Summer Storm

train platform, through the crowded depot, and to a waiting cab. She saw a factory of some sort, a few houses, and a mill positioned on a piece of land in the middle of the river, isolated from the east and west banks.

"Whiskey Island," the porter said, apparently noticing her stare. "Got its name when a distillery was built on it years ago. Course now the big business is Cleveland Ironworks." Alexandra nodded in understanding as he handed her portmanteau to the cabdriver. The driver placed it in the trunk, then handed her up. "Off you go now, miss," the porter said. "Lots more to see in Cleveland. Have a nice visit."

Alexandra poked her head out to thank him. Moments later, as the cab moved forward, she smiled slyly. Visit? This was no visit.

She intended to stay.

Upon hearing the quarrelling voices downstairs, Katherine hurried from her room. At the top of the staircase she stopped short and stared down, unable to move, unable to believe what she saw.

Peggy stood with her back to the bottom of the stairs, hands on her hips, steadfastly barring the way of a dark-haired young woman. "No one flies in here and tells me my business, miss. I told ye to wait in the parlor, and that's where ye'd best be goin'."

"And I told you that I want to surprise Katherine," the young woman insisted.

Katherine would have known the voice anywhere. "Alexandra?"

"Katherine!" Alexandra lifted her skirts nearly to her knees, found a gap through which to shoot past Peggy, and bounded up the stairs. She virtually threw herself at Katherine.

Laughing with surprise and delight, Katherine grabbed the banister to keep her balance. Her other arm slipped around Alexandra and hugged her tight. "What are you doing here?" She was overjoyed to see Alexandra, but also curious. "I know we talked about you coming to Cleveland. But I didn't know you planned to come so soon."

Alexandra clutched Katherine to her. "I could not stand staying there without you. I do not know how I managed before you came. I ran away. I had to. My father will not care. He has never cared. They will tell him I'm gone, and he will be glad."

"She insisted on followin' me," Peggy called from below. She had turned around now to stare up at them. "Said she's a friend of yours from school. What did they teach at that school? Ye goin' out alone, comin' back with Mr. Cummin's and Mr. Riley. Now this one with no manners! Sweet Jesus!"

Katherine smoothed Alexandra's hair, choosing to ignore Peggy's remarks. "Shh. It's all right. We'll think of something. Come now." She settled an arm around Alexandra's shoulders and led her down the hall.

Upstairs Katherine took Alexandra to the huge, quilt-covered tester bed in the middle of her room and made her sit. "I'm so glad to see you," she said. "I've missed you terribly. I had two letters for you taken to the post just yesterday. Three pages each. I had a lot to tell you."

Alexandra laughed. She had run from the school, and Katherine had nearly written herself mad. "What will we ever do when we marry? We cannot seem to live apart for long."

"When we marry, we'll learn," Katherine said, laughing, too.

Alexandra glanced about the room. The wooden floor was waxed to perfection. Sheer, summery curtains billowed at the window. There was a secretary, an ivory chiffonier, a vanity, and several small, antique-looking mahogany chairs before the fireplace. Chippendale, she thought, rococo, having graceful cabriole legs, ball-and-claw feet, and deep leaf carvings. A white, tasseled spread covered the tester bed, with green bed drapes tied back at the posts. The walls were papered with a pattern of tiny swans among tall reeds.

"It's a beautiful room, Katherine," Alexandra said truthfully. "You sleep in it alone?" She really couldn't imagine such a thing.

Katherine laughed. "Of course, silly. I know—you're used to the four girls per room at the school."

"Sometimes five. This must feel wonderful. Tell me, does it?"

"Well . . . yes."

Alexandra smiled, her dark eyes shimmering. "Glorious?"

"Incomparable."

"Incredible," Alexandra said, concluding the familiar game of words.

Katherine tossed back across the bed. Alexandra joined her, and they lay side by side, staring up at the tester.

"I hope they don't come after you," Katherine said, sighing. "That would be dreadful. I can see you kicking and screaming if they do. Of the two of us, you've always been the most outrageous."

"No one will care. My father never wrote and never visited. He will be glad to be free of me."

"Perhaps he will, and perhaps they won't come after you, but I'll have to convince Uncle Werner to let you stay. *He* may send you back."

"I am never going back, Katherine. I'm finished there. I want to find a position in a nice household . . . What about here?" Alexandra asked suddenly.

"What do you mean—here?" Katherine was stunned.

"Here. As I said. This is a beautiful, big house. That formidable Irishwoman must need help. Why, just polishing that staircase must take an entire day!"

"Stop, Alexandra! I won't have you working as a servant in Uncle Werner's house. You're so smart—you could teach. Perhaps Uncle Werner will let you to tutor children in the garden or in the parlor."

Alexandra clapped her hands. "That would be wonderful."

Katherine sat up and looked around, expecting to see at least a few of Alexandra's belongings. If she remembered correctly, Alexandra had had nothing in her hands when she'd flown up the staircase. "Is your trunk downstairs?" she asked.

"Trunk? Ha! Now how is one supposed to sneak through a window and run away while pulling a trunk?" Alexandra asked, lifting her brows.

Laughing, Katherine looked back at her friend. "That would be a rather strange sight."

"Ridiculous."

"Preposterous."

"You look so pretty," Alexandra said softly, the playful moment turning serious.

Katherine smiled tenderly. "So do you."

"Ugh! I feel dusty, my clothes are rumpled, and my hair is sticking to my head," Alexandra objected. "But I am very glad to be here. I did bring a portmanteau. Not very full. It is still downstairs."

"No," Katherine assured her, moving from the bed. "By now Peggy—'that formidable Irishwoman'—has done something with it. She keeps a very clean house. Let's go see. The room next to this one is a guest room. We'll put your things in there. I'll ask Peggy to have some of the servants prepare a bath, too."

"Ah! A bath," Alexandra said with a sigh, an expression of heavenly bliss on her face.

Katherine laughed.

Peggy had indeed done something with the portmanteau. She'd placed it in a guest room at the end of the hall, the farthest room from Katherine's. "Miss Owens will be occupying the room next to mine," Katherine informed Peggy.

Peggy gave her a hard look with her sharp green eyes, then said, "Very well, miss," in her customary way. She instructed a young upstairs maid to "Take Miss Owens's bag to the guest room next to Miss McDaniel's." Then she flounced off.

Katherine watched her, thinking the woman always found little ways to irritate her. Alexandra moved up beside Katherine, mimicking Peggy's brogue: "Don't believe she likes ye, miss."

Again Katherine laughed, then hugged Alexandra tight. "I'm so glad you're here. I'm going to do everything possible to convince Uncle Werner to let you stay."

"I'm thinkin' that'd be lovely, miss."

"Oh, stop before I laugh till I'm sore! Come on."

Summer Storm 109

In the guest room, Alexandra admired shimmery blue curtains drawn back from the windows. A matching blue spread covered this tester bed, and blue-and-white-striped paper decorated the walls. In one corner sat a small secretary. A dark chiffonier occupied another, and in yet another a maid appeared from behind a beautiful oriental privacy screen, a cloth draped over one forearm. Alexandra assumed there was a tub behind the screen. It was a pleasant room, not as elegant as Katherine's, but compared to the drabness of the large room Alexandra had shared with three other girls at the school, it was quite luxurious.

Soon other maids toted buckets of hot water into the room. One of them added a sweet fragrance to the steaming water—a light lavender scent—then they left.

Alexandra bathed behind the screen, pouring the warm water over her shoulders again and again and scrubbing her body and hair.

Katherine placed Alexandra's portmanteau on the bed and unpacked it. There was a skirt, a black basque, a pair of stockings, a comb, and a thin bundle of money—a few dollars. "We need to go shopping for you," she said loudly.

"Do we?" Alexandra called.

"Yes. I hope you don't mind—I unpacked your things."

"Oh. Well, as you can see, I do not have much money left."

"I have money. Uncle Werner's very generous."

"He is also very important. I had only to mention his name to the porter, and the man scurried to get me a cab."

Katherine smiled. "I'll lend you a gown to wear during supper—we could always wear each other's clothes anyway. Things are much different here. Uncle Werner is a wonderful man. You'll like him."

"That was not what you said when I met you," Alexandra teased. "You often said that if he ever learned you were sneaking out in that boat, he would send you to some faraway school."

"What happened to the boat?" Katherine asked, warmed by memories of the times they had rowed out, spent an hour or so listening to the sounds of Lake Erie and the gulls and the breeze rustling the foliage near the shore. Sometimes they had just listened; sometimes they had talked. Always they had enjoyed themselves.

"It's probably infested with gulls by now. Or maybe it drifted out and the lake swallowed it. Pieces of it probably washed up near the pier."

"Oh, Alexandra, don't talk about our boat that way!"

"It was just a boat."

But Katherine knew Alexandra was jesting. It had been *their* boat.

"I suppose you wished I had packed it in the trunk you expected me to drag to the train station," Alexandra teased.

"Silly," Katherine said.

"You mentioned shopping. I did not see many stores during the ride here."

"The Exchange."

"Exchange?"

"Merchant Exchange. A big building filled with wonderful shops. Nicholas first took me there, then Uncle Werner," Katherine said.

"Nicholas? *The* Nicholas?"

"Yes . . ."

"How marvelous. And did you concentrate on shopping or did you stare at him all day? Perhaps the two of you found an ice-cream parlor in this Merchant Exchange and you ate ice cream together. Then he bought you a bottle of French perfume and the most beautiful gown. Perhaps . . ."

As Alexandra describe an imaginary afternoon, memories of the real one flooded Katherine with overwhelming force. Suddenly she was frozen by images of the afternoon she'd spent with Nicholas, going to the Exchange, watching the organ grinder's monkey, eating waffles together, and laughing. Then they'd gone to the dock and climbed aboard the seemingly deserted ship and found themselves a mile out in Lake Erie.

Nicholas, Nicholas . . . His emerald eyes haunted her. How she longed for his touch again. How she wanted to feel his lips on hers again!

Summer Storm

But coveting another woman's fiancé was an absolute sin.

Nicholas did not belong to her. He never would. And that was the end of it, she thought, trying to rid herself of the memories as she had so many times during these past few weeks.

But a familiar pain swelled in her chest, tormenting her eyes. She put fingers to the bridge of her nose and fought tears. The hurt was terrible, a heavy ache. How long until she could think of him without feeling this way? Months . . . years?

And then more memories . . .

After he left her in the entryway the evening of his engagement supper, she had stood and listened to the muffled clip-clops of his horse's hooves as he rode away. What would she do with her life now? she'd wondered. She had lived for Nicholas, studied for Nicholas, grown for Nicholas.

Nearly every night at the school she'd lain awake waiting for the nun's footsteps to cease in the hall and the girls in the other beds in her room to fall asleep. From beneath her pillow she would then remove the book, whichever one she had chosen for the night and hidden earlier. Beside a large, moonlit window, she would sit and study for hours, being careful not to fall asleep on the floor beneath the window.

Once she had been so absorbed in studying she hadn't heard the door open. Only when she saw the glow of light from an intruding lamp did she realize someone was looking in the room. She would be caught since she didn't have time to flee to her bed. Sister Dorothy poked her head inside and looked around while Katherine held her breath and waited. Moments later, Sister Dorothy withdrew and shut the door. Finally Katherine released her breath, then shakily climbed back into bed. But her heart continued to pound for what seemed an hour.

Nicholas, Nicholas, she had thought then, too. If she had been caught, Sister Dorothy would have written to Uncle Werner. And Katherine would have been disgraced in her uncle's eyes and, more importantly at the time, in Nicholas's eyes. She had once promised him, after all, that she would do her best. How she had wanted to please him. How she had wanted him to love her!

She still wanted him to love her. But no . . .

When Katherine was certain she'd fought off tears for what must have been the hundredth time in the space of the last few weeks, she rubbed her nose and straightened, as always. Her pride wouldn't allow her to hang her head for long. Nicholas was right about one thing. She would always have some of the willful, spirited girl of five years ago in her. During recent days she had thought a great deal about her plans for the future.

"Are you all right?" Alexandra said, stepping around the screen. She was wrapped in a large white bath blanket, her face flushed from the water's heat. Her sleek black hair hung to her waist. "I was talking to you and . . . You look pale."

"I haven't been sleeping well, that's all," Katherine said. It wasn't a lie. Since she'd learned of Nicholas's engagement, sleep had been interrupted by interludes filled with painful thoughts of him, something she had told no one.

"*Nicholas* was the first to take you to the Merchant Exchange?" Alexandra asked, having no idea that Katherine didn't want to think about the afternoon Nicholas had taken her shopping.

"Yes, I . . . I needed to do some shopping." Katherine explained about Uncle Werner's episode with Mr. Baum, trying to be fair to Alexandra. Then she told Alexandra about the carriage accident.

"He rescued you?" Alexandra asked, wide-eyed. "How very romantic! What else?"

"Then he took me to the Exchange." Katherine fastened the straps on the portmanteau and placed it on the floor beside the bed. Then she moved toward the door. "I'll go get a gown and some underthings for you." It was the perfect excuse to avoid more questions.

Alexandra grabbed her arm. "That is all? For a girl who has been in love for years, you are certainly not very excited about him rescuing you. What happened afterward? Do not leave me with that! I concocted an imaginary afternoon, but I would much rather hear about the real one."

"Don't!" Katherine snapped, jerking her arm away. Her violent reaction immediately shocked her. Alexandra flinched;

Summer Storm

she didn't understand her friend's behavior. How could she? Katherine didn't really want to tell anyone about the afternoon she had spent with Nicholas, but she reminded herself that Alexandra was no busybody who would take the story beyond these walls. They had shared many secrets.

"Something is wrong," Alexandra said slowly, eyeing her. "What is it?"

"I'm sorry." Katherine moved back to the bed and sat down, her eyes stinging with threatening tears again. "You want to know what happened. I'll tell you. Nicholas played Romeo the rest of the afternoon. That evening I learned he was engaged. That is what happened."

Alexandra was silent for a long moment. "No . . . Outrageous."

"Hurtful."

"Unforgivable," Alexandra said slowly. She put a hand on Katherine's shoulder and pulled her close. "I'm so sorry."

"It doesn't matter. I'm glad you're here." Katherine brushed escaped tears from her cheeks, refusing again, to cry. "I'm not going to mope. I'm going to get busy."

"Doing what?"

"Opening an orphanage."

"Yes! Splendid! I will help."

Katherine smiled and nodded. "I'm so glad you're here. Now," she said, sniffing and drawing a deep breath of resolve, "we'll make a list of the things you need . . ."

They spent a great deal of the afternoon doing exactly that. Later, when Katherine heard Uncle Werner's carriage pull into the drive, she began to prepare what she would say to try to convince him to allow Alexandra to stay. She practiced before Alexandra, who sometimes said, "Yes, oh, yes, that's good," and other times "No, that will never do." As close as she and Uncle Werner had become, Katherine was still nervous. He was a very honest, straightforward man. He would doubtless be shocked that Alexandra had run away from the school. And he might even insist on sending her back.

10

KATHERINE FOUND HIM in the library, seated behind his desk. A stack of leatherbound books, some cracked with age, sat to his right. An open ledger lay beneath his forearms, the pages marked with figures and script. He had been working when she'd knocked, that was clear. She hoped that disturbing him this way would not be to her, or rather Alexandra's disadvantage.

"In the letters I wrote while at the school," she began, "I mentioned a very good friend named Alexandra. I met her soon after I arrived."

He very patiently listened while she spoke. She explained Alexandra's dilemma, then waited quietly for him to respond.

He picked up a brass paperweight modeled in the form of a side-wheeler and fingered its intricate parts—the tiny masts and smokestacks, the rails. "You say she ran away from the school to come here?"

"Yes," Katherine answered, fearing his next words would be that Alexandra must go back.

"And no one knows where she is? Only us?"

"That's right. She has no one else outside the school. No one."

"No mother?" Uncle Werner asked.

"No."

"Father?"

"Well . . . yes."

Summer Storm

He lifted a brow. "I see . . . There is more to this than you have told me, Katherine. I must ask questions to get to the truth. Let me see if I understand correctly. You are requesting that I take Alexandra in and give her a home without the permission of her father?"

Katherine sighed, breathed deeply, and let her words spill. "Oh, Uncle Werner, the truth is—he doesn't care about her. He never wrote to her at the school. He only sent her there to get her out of his sight after he pushed her mother to her death and—"

"Alexandra saw this? She saw her father push her mother to her death, as you say?"

"Well . . . no . . . she didn't actually see—"

"There was a witness? *Someone* who saw?"

"No," Katherine admitted honestly.

"Then you are making serious accusations about a man you know nothing of," he said gently.

Effectively humbled, she lowered her eyes to her hands. "I know what Alexandra has told me. She heard them quarreling, then her mother's screams as she—"

"Katherine. You must not take the mere opinion of one person and form a bias against another. Think of what recently happened to you. Words, spoken the wrong way, can be harmful. Hearsay. You have no proof. Alexandra *heard*—that is what you said. Not Alexandra *saw*."

Katherine stood in silence now, not knowing what to do or say next. She believed Alexandra's story, but convincing Uncle Werner . . . well . . . she wasn't accomplishing what she'd set out to do. She supposed that if she were in Uncle Werner's position—having never met Alexandra and having this request suddenly flung at her—she would be reluctant, too. And he was right. She had no proof. What she had was more regard for him than she had ever had for anyone in her life. He was a fair man to the final word.

"I will speak with Alexandra over supper. I will ask for her father's address and write to him," Uncle Werner said.

Katherine glanced up hopefully. "You will not return her to the school?"

"For now—no. But if her father insists, you must understand. There will be no other way."

Touched by the gentleness that softened his eyes and smoothed his wide brow, she nodded. She was unable to resist the temptation to reach across the desk, over the ledger, and squeeze his hand. "Thank you, Uncle."

He flushed at the show of affection, as she knew he would, and inclined his head. Then he busily averted his gaze to the ledger. "Off with you now. I have much work. Nicholas wants these accounts by this evening."

She left him to his work and went to find Alexandra, knowing the news she had was not exactly what Alexandra would want to hear.

Upstairs, Alexandra met her at the banister, her eyes bright. "Well? What did he say? Tell. Tell!"

Katherine watched her friend as she spoke: "He wants to write to your father and ask permission."

Alexandra paled. Katherine touched her arm, soothing her, knowing how difficult this must be for Alexandra. "I'm sorry. For now you may stay with us. It'll take weeks to send a letter and get a response. We'll have fun until then. We'll go shopping. We'll make plans for the orphanage. We'll have a wonderful time, I promise. Now come. Let's see about getting you a dress to wear during supper."

Katherine led Alexandra toward her bedroom. Alexandra's gaiety was diminished, but Katherine was determined to stir it again. In the bedroom, she opened the doors of a heavy wardrobe and pulled out an array of gowns she thought would look lovely on Alexandra. There were silks, satins, chiffons, and taffetas in shades of green, blue, violet, and yellow. Alexandra picked a blue satin with a shimmery overskirt. Katherine helped her into the gown, then directed her to the vanity. Once Alexandra was seated, Katherine picked up a silver-backed brush and began stroking Alexandra's thick ebony hair.

"Your uncle will not like me," Alexandra blurted, suddenly stricken with a confidence problem. "I know he will not."

Katherine paused in mid-stroke. "Alexandra, he will. Don't think that way. Now, let's finish your hair, then I'll dress, and we'll go downstairs for supper. Uncle Werner *will* like you. Don't worry."

An hour later they descended the staircase, their pumps lightly tapping the tiled hall. They turned into the parlor, where Katherine knew Uncle Werner would be awaiting them.

He was seated in a chair near a window, a copy of *The Cleveland Plain Dealer* spread wide in front of him. He must have heard them; he lowered one corner of the paper, his soft eyes flitting between Katherine and Alexandra as they paused near a floral-patterned settee. He promptly lowered the entire newspaper, folded it, placed it on a nearby table, and rose to greet them.

Introductions were made. Alexandra's eyes kept shifting. Her face was flushed. She looked as if she wanted to flee the room and Uncle Werner.

"Miss Owens, Katherine informs me you wish to stay in Cleveland," Werner said as he guided Alexandra to a chair. She was certainly a beautiful young woman, with striking blue eyes, black hair, and soft features. She had French blood in her to be sure. He meant to acquaint himself well with her before contacting her father. He must be sure she hid nothing from him.

Alexandra felt him scrutinize her, and her heart pounded miserably with nervousness. Katherine always told her she was very bold, and yes, she appeared so on the outside much of the time, but she had her nervous moments like anyone else. She just hid them well. She knew her future depended on this evening and that she must impress Katherine's uncle somehow. She thought of something she had read in a newspaper during the train ride to Cleveland, something that had caught her eye.

"Yes," she said. "I want to stay here and teach. Teaching is something I have thought of doing for several years. I recently read that the first kindergarten in our country was just opened in Wisconsin. By a . . . a Mrs. Schurz."

When Werner Kraus lifted a brow, Alexandra knew she had his interest. "Schurz? A German?" he asked.

"Yes. In fact, the kindergarten is a German-language school."

"Indeed?"

"Yes—"

A maid appeared in the doorway to announce supper. Werner extended his arm to Alexandra. She took it, allowing him to lead her to the door. Stealing a glance over her shoulder, she found Katherine smiling as she followed.

"A German-language school...," Werner said, his interest obvious. "Tell me more. Tell me something of this Mrs. Schurz, if you would."

"Have you heard of Friedrich Froebel?"

"An educator, wasn't he? Yes, I believe I have heard something of him."

"He founded the first kindergartens in the world. His theories have had a marked effect on Mrs. Schurz. She is what some would call his follower. I am, too, I suppose."

Behind them, Katherine's smile widened more, if possible. Alexandra, with her charisma and mind, was easily winning Uncle Werner's respect and admiration. As they entered the dining room and were seated, and Uncle Werner encouraged Alexandra to tell him about Friedrich Froebel's theories, Katherine could hardly keep from laughing aloud with joy. She guessed that by the end of the evening Uncle Werner would be writing to Alexandra's father and pleading with the man to allow Alexandra to remain in Cleveland.

Through a supper of braised mutton, juicy potatoes and onions, and buttered peas, Alexandra and Uncle Werner continued speaking.

"He received little education until he was ten," she said, speaking of Friedrich Froebel. "Over the years he studied the natural sciences, then architecture at Frankfurt am Main, where he was invited to teach a model school. He even served in the Prussian army during the Napoleonic Wars."

"And how did he become so involved with children? Enough to begin kindergartens?" Uncle Werner asked.

"He conducted a boys' school at Keilhau in Germany. Later he returned to Switzerland and established schools to train women elementary school teachers. He studied, taught, observed.

Finally he concluded that children need careful training during their very young years."

Alexandra went on to tell Uncle Werner how Friedrich Froebel had founded many kindergartens. He believed that the purpose of education of the young should be the full development of their physical, mental, and spiritual natures, she said. "True development, you see, comes from within. It's not imposed from outside. It's important that children be allowed to play creatively, to observe nature, and to be within the circle of a warm family."

Uncle Werner finished his last bite of mutton, wiped his mouth with a white table napkin, and leaned contentedly back in his chair. "Fascinating. Thoroughly fascinating. You, Miss Owens, have a remarkable mind."

Katherine met Alexandra's gaze across the table. Alexandra grinned slyly as if to say: "Well, it helped that the subjects were German." Instead she said, "I've merely studied the man's life and his teachings and techniques a great deal. When I read the small article about Mrs. Schurz, I was excited."

"Quite naturally," he said, as a servant set small plates of apple pie before them. "We must take Alexandra to the Prestons' picnic in a few days and introduce her to our friends, Katherine."

Katherine's heart paused. Prestons' picnic? "Nicholas will be there?" she blurted before thinking. She hurriedly lifted her goblet to her lips and sipped wine in an effort to appear calm.

"I assume he will be. I know you have only seen him twice since you arrived home. This is a busy time for him. He is putting together plans to build a ship, his engagement was just announced, and he has various other matters he is involved in. Perhaps we will have him here one evening."

Katherine barely kept from blurting an objection. No . . . she'd seen Nicholas more than twice. She'd spent an entire afternoon with him, an afternoon she couldn't seem to forget. But Uncle Werner would never know about that afternoon. No one would, save Kevin and Alexandra. Forcing a smile, Katherine said, "Do not trouble him. I had no idea the Prestons were having a picnic, that's all."

And she wished they weren't. She didn't want to face Sarah Preston. Perhaps she was acting childish, but as much as she loved Nicholas, the pain of seeing Sarah and Nicholas together sharing gentle touches and looks would be too much to bear.

"I had set the invitation aside, as I often do with things of that nature. Peggy found it and reminded me I had an obligation since Nicholas is my business partner," Uncle Werner said.

Katherine feigned another smile, something she was certain she would become an expert at doing whenever Nicholas was mentioned in the future. She met Alexandra's imploring eyes and realized she didn't fool her friend for a second. She also knew she must prepare herself for the inevitable. Nicholas and Sarah would be husband and wife soon. Naturally they would appear together at social events, and she would invariably encounter them. She might as well square her shoulders and face them.

But the truth was she didn't want to go to that picnic. She didn't!

She must, if she wished to avoid questions.

If only she had arrived months before. If only . . .

She silently chastised herself. She could say "if only" for years, and doing so would change nothing. She had lost Nicholas. Soon he would marry another woman, and she . . . she must march forward with her courage intact. Moping, crying, and feeling forever sorry for herself wasn't like her.

Just when she began to believe she would be able to go on, something that had not occurred to her before this moment suddenly struck her as violently as a carpenter's hammer strikes a nail: Nicholas was Uncle Werner's business partner. Attending Nicholas's fiancée's picnic was the proper thing to do. Attending Nicholas's wedding would be the proper thing to do, too.

The knowledge made Katherine choke on the wine. She coughed and sputtered and covered her mouth with her napkin.

"Katherine," Uncle Werner blurted. "Katherine, are you well?"

Katherine managed to catch her breath, but her heart still pounded an unsteady rhythm. "The wine went down the wrong way."

Summer Storm

He moved to stand beside her and stare at her with concern. "You are pale. You should go rest."

"Yes, I think I will, if the two of you don't mind me deserting you," she managed, her glance darting between him and Alexandra.

"Not at all. Alexandra and I will talk more, perhaps walk in the garden. Then she will be upstairs to look in on you."

Nodding, Katherine allowed him to help her from her chair. At the doorway, she caught Alexandra's disapproving gaze.

Upstairs Katherine stood at her balcony doors, looking out at the breathtaking sunset that cast an orange-and-pink glow on the few other elegant Lake Street houses, some of stone, like Uncle Werner's, and some of wood, each having a series of bay windows and angles painted in various ways. Her bedroom and the front of the house faced north, toward Lake Erie. The water glittered under the fading sun. Ships decorated the horizon, their lanterns faint in the remaining daylight. Katherine eased out onto the balcony and pulled the pins from her hair, enjoying the soothing breeze that Lake Erie swept inland to frolic in her hair and the folds of her gown. She inhaled the fresh scent of the air, wishing more than anything for her and Alexandra's little boat right now. She'd take it out on the water and lie back. She'd watch the gulls soar—curves of white against a blue sky. She'd listen to their shrieks and to the occasional whispers of the freshwater sea, and that would be her peace. It was certainly a peace she and Alexandra had often sought when escaping the confines of the school.

Over the lake, gulls soared and dipped. To the west the harbor lighthouse, the guardian angel of the many ships that sailed in and out of Cleveland daily, stood proudly against the striking background of sunset. Katherine caught her breath, watching white-tipped waves splash huge rocks surrounding the stone foundation. So serene . . . Yet Katherine had seen Lake Erie unleash hungry fury, mostly during the month of November, when cold northern air assaulted her. Lake Erie battled back, rising, churning, roaring, often consuming ships and people who dared to brave her then.

A side-wheeler eased by the lighthouse, startling Katherine back to thoughts of Nicholas.

She couldn't attend his wedding. A picnic she would endure, but his wedding . . . No. She couldn't bear the pain of hearing him pledge himself to another woman. *She* wanted him. She wanted his love, his devotion. She wanted his children. She could only pretend for so long to herself that she didn't.

She heard horses' hooves and the grating of wheels on the street below. A carriage halted in the drive to one side of the house.

"*Nicholas,*" Katherine whispered, for she recognized the driver as Harold, the man she had met the day Nicholas had taken her shopping.

Harold pulled the door open, and Nicholas emerged from the carriage. He looked unbearably handsome in an evergreen vest and trousers of a lighter shade. His dark hair became tousled by the day's persistent breeze. A green-and-white-striped cravat was fastened around a white collar that just touched his jaw. Harold stood near the carriage door. Nicholas laughed deeply at something his driver said, then gripped a packet of papers in one hand and took a step in the direction of the stone walkway that led to the front entrance.

He paused.

Katherine realized what was happening, but before she could react, Nicholas glanced up; their eyes locked and held. Even from this distance, his were glowing emeralds. She felt their fire.

She cried out in anguish and retreated to her bedroom. How could he look at her with such open desire, knowing she wanted him yet couldn't have him?

She regressed fully to her old defiant and bitter self for a time. She grabbed a feather pillow from the bed and flung it across the room, where it knocked over a vase. The ceramic shattered on the floor. How she wished she could vent such anger on Nicholas!

An hour later, determined again to put her mind from him, she sat in the middle of her bed, clutching another pillow and going over her plans for the orphanage. Once she had a clear plan worked out in her head, she meant to approach Uncle Werner about holding a supper party or a ball to raise donations. Surely people would come—who would turn away an invitation bearing the name of Kraus? Even if the women did, the husbands wouldn't. The husbands had never treated her as the wives had.

A knock sounded on the door. Alexandra entered, pausing to stare at the pieces of shattered vase on the floor. Shaking her head in admonishment, she strode across the room to sit on the edge of the bed. "I met your Nicholas," she said softly.

Katherine squeezed the pillow. "He isn't *my* Nicholas. Don't call him that. I don't want to talk about him."

"I was not going to talk about him. I came to tell you that you are stronger than this. Pretending to choke on wine . . . throwing pillows and vases . . ."

"I didn't throw the vase. The pillow hit it. And I did choke on the wine, for your information."

"Katherine McDaniel, raise your chin and never let him know how deeply he has hurt you. You have plans, remember?"

Katherine allowed herself to pout and wallow in self-pity for another few moments. Then she smiled, squeezed back tears, and reached for Alexandra. "You're right. I'm too old to throw tantrums. I'm sorry I was short with you."

They embraced. Alexandra was the first to withdraw. As she did, Katherine saw her sly grin. "Now, what did you think of the way I charmed your uncle?" Alexandra asked.

Katherine laughed. "Amazing. Absolutely amazing."

11

THE DAY OF the picnic arrived. Guests mingled on the Prestons' back lawn, which bordered Lake Erie. The lake frolicked in the early afternoon sunshine, lapping and splashing as she warmed herself.

A train rumbled by on the Cleveland and Erie railroad, and for long moments Katherine's view of the playful lake was limited to the glimpses she caught between rail cars, but glimpse she did from beneath her wide-brimmed, flower-and-ribbon-decorated bonnet. The smell of barbecue, roasting corn, and freshly baked bread wafted to her. Behind her, people laughed and conversed. Children giggled and scampered about. Occasionally mothers scolded. A little girl with blond locks and laughing brown eyes raced around Katherine, slipped, and grabbed one of the scalloped edges of Katherine's bright yellow skirt to steady herself.

Laughing, Katherine caught the girl's arm and righted her just as a fierce-looking young man halted not a yard away. His beige trouser knees were darkened with grass and dirt stains, his chestnut hair was in no order at all, and his blue-gray eyes sparked with anger.

"What have we here?" Katherine teased the two of them—the young man on her right, the girl on her left. "A row, is it? Well, I daresay your mothers would not be nearly as amused as I, you tearing about in that lovely pink dress with all those ribbons and bows," she said to the girl, "and you—" She lifted

Summer Storm 125

a brow at the boy's dirty trouser knees and smiled. "Well, you are a boy, I suppose. And now I see that your coat sleeve is torn!"

"She ruined the picture I was drawing," he blurted, clenching fists at his sides. He itched to get his hands on the girl, Katherine thought, and with good cause if he spoke the truth.

"Oh, it was only a stupid little dirt picture," the girl snapped.

"Was not! I was drawing the cat!"

Katherine raise both brows. "Now—"

"All you draw are stupid *bad* pictures, Charles Pennington. Ugly pictures!"

"Why you . . ." Charles Pennington lunged for the girl, nearly grabbing a handful of blond ringlets before he fell face forward on the grass.

The girl giggled. "An artist. Mother says artists never amount to anything. That means you're never going to amount to anything, Charles."

Katherine hunched to the girl's level and scowled at her. "You might be pretty with all your ribbons and bows. Indeed you're very pretty until you open your mouth. I'll have you know I am something of an artist. Now you've hurt Charles's feelings. Apologize this minute, then go off and find your mother so she can teach you a few manners."

"Beth! Beth?"

Katherine glanced up to find a stout, robust-looking woman bearing down on them, her thick brows drawn together. The woman leveled a glare on Katherine. "What are you doing to my Beth? Move away from her this instant!"

The woman's manner infuriated Katherine more than the girl's had. Obviously this woman thought "her Beth" was something of an angel. And, contrary to what Katherine had told Beth to do, Beth would find no example of manners in her mother.

"I was attempting to get your daughter to apologize to Mr. Pennington here. She ruined his drawing, then said horrible things to hurt his feelings," Katherine said, straightening.

The woman's cold eyes raked over Charles, who was attempting to brush grass from his filthy trousers, then she returned her scalding gaze to Katherine. "Katherine McDaniel," she said, sniffing, "if anyone is in need of a reprimand, it is that . . . that riffraff and yourself! Now come along, Beth. Let's straighten your hair and dress. Mrs. Curtis was asking about you."

Anger prickling her skin, Katherine stood watching the woman and her daughter weave their way through the gaily dressed crowd. Once she thought she saw the girl glance over her shoulder and smile a wicked little smile. Katherine shook her head. Uncle Werner had thought *she* was bad when she'd first been dropped on him. He'd never had the misfortune of meeting that girl!

"You draw?"

At the faint sound of Charles's voice, Katherine turned her attention to him. He was seated on the ground, his knees drawn up, his arms wrapped around them. His face was smudged. "Well, I haven't in about a month, but, yes, I do. Tell me, do you have a tablet?" she inquired.

"At home," he said, avoiding her gaze.

She nodded at that. "Let's go to the house and clean you up a bit. We'll talk on the way."

He lifted himself awkwardly, a tall lad for his age. "You're about ten, I'd guess," she said as they walked across the lawn.

"Eleven."

"Sorry. I was close."

"Most people guess older. I'm big, my father says, big and strong."

"And what do you draw?"

"Animals mostly, and people. What do you draw?"

"Lake Erie. Ships. Lighthouses. I'm Katherine, by the way, and don't tell anyone, but I would have clobbered Beth, too. I wanted to clobber her *and* her mother. I've wanted to clobber many people lately. Alas, I fear I've grown into an adult and, sometimes worse, a lady," she said, a smile touching her lips.

They laughed together. "I'm Charles," he said.

"I know. I think we'll get along well, Charles. And don't mind what Beth or her mother say. Artists do amount to something. Michelangelo, for instance."

"Michelangelo . . ." He whispered the name in awe. "He was terrific."

Katherine laughed again. "Yes, that's one way of describing him."

They had just come upon one of several huge maple trees located a short distance from the Preston house when Nicholas appeared at Charles's side. He inclined his head in greeting to Katherine. She politely returned the gesture. This was the first time she had seen him since she'd stared down at him from the iron-railed balcony.

The summer lake breeze had danced in his hair; it was at least as disorderly as Charles's. Sunlight enhanced the glowing emerald of his eyes. Light shadows played on the strong lines and angles of his face as he tilted his head down to Charles. "I see you've made a friend, Mr. Pennington," he said. Then his gaze shifted to Katherine, who suddenly wondered if she could bear the remainder of the afternoon.

Today he wore a white shirt with billowing sleeves and an unadorned brown vest with matching trousers. He looked as unpretentious as a man of wealth could possibly look, and yet he was the most handsome man she had ever seen.

"You look well, Katherine," he said. "I'm glad. Rumors are dying."

She nodded, agreeing. Most of the women in the crowd today had accepted her more readily than they had as little as two weeks ago. Thanks to Uncle Werner—he had taken a steadfast stand on her behalf. Katherine caught herself searching Nicholas's eyes, something she knew she shouldn't do. What did she hope to find there? Love? She nearly laughed aloud in disgust at herself.

Flushing, she cast her lashes down, wishing he would finish the conversation, then be on his way. Shouldn't he be at Sarah's side, accepting the best wishes of their friends and acquaintances?

"She's an artist, Mr. Cummings," Charles said brightly. "Katherine's her name. She asked if I had a tablet."

"And do you?" Nicholas inquired, the richness of his voice thrilling Katherine. Did he know how he affected her? Surely he did. He possessed a certain masculine confidence, one that never failed to make her heart drum and her breath catch. She wondered if he had such an exciting effect on all women, or just her, fool for him that she was.

"At home," Charles answered.

"I thought that if he brought his tablet, I could show him a few tricks," Katherine explained.

"I'll see if the Prestons have one lying about somewhere," Nicholas said.

Katherine's gaze shot up. The last thing she wanted him to do was trouble the Prestons for something she wanted. "No—"

"That'd be great, Mr. Cummings," Charles blurted, his eyes bright with excitement. "I've never met an artist before."

Nicholas chuckled, and Charles's eagerness brought a genuine smile to Katherine's lips. "I'm not an artist, Charles, not really. I . . . well, I merely sketch. Weren't we on our way to clean you up a bit?"

He nodded, rather reluctantly she thought.

"A little soap and water is needed, eh, Charles? Been chasing the girls again, have you?" Nicholas teased. Charles scowled. Nicholas drew back in a show of surprise, forking his brows and holding up his palms to ward off the scowl.

"It was Beth. Beth Likens," Charles said in disgust.

"Ah . . ." Nicholas nodded, as if he'd had an unpleasant encounter with the child himself.

"The girl is infamous, it seems," Katherine commented.

"That she is," Nicholas agreed. He clamped his hands on Charles's shoulder. "I'll take Charles from here. We'll find soap and water and a tablet, maybe even find someone to stitch that coat sleeve."

Katherine watched them walk away together. She maneuvered her way through the crowd in search of a cool tumbler of lemonade. The plush green lawn was decorated by an array of colorful gowns. She admired blues, greens, roses, violets, and yellows in various fashions. A lady passing close to her wore an olive-green overskirt ornamented with rust-colored ruching and an underskirt of the same color. The basque was edged

Summer Storm 129

with more ruching and was simple but pretty. The sleeves were the fitted "coat sleeves" that Katherine and Alexandra had struggled to make so many times at the school, a task they'd never perfected.

Katherine looked around for Alexandra, wondering if her friend had noticed the woman's dress, too. She spotted her finally and smiled. Alexandra's mind was hardly on the latest women's fashions.

Ever the flirt, Alexandra was wooing a group of young men all sporting the latest fashion among men—heavy side whiskers. Katherine laughed when Alexandra had three glasses of lemonade pressed upon her at once by her eager band of suitors. If the example before Katherine was any indication, the bachelor population of Cleveland would be alighting on Uncle Werner's doorstep very soon.

Returning to the tree to await Charles and Nicholas, Katherine turned about and bumped into someone. Lemonade splashed from the tumbler she held. She gasped when she realized she'd just soaked the rose bodice of a very lovely gown.

"I'm terribly sor—" She found herself looking straight into Sarah Preston's very gentle brown eyes.

"Never mind. I should have announced my presence behind you," Sarah said, her voice soft. Almost like a brush of velvet, Katherine thought. "Since I'm at home, I'll simply go inside and change in a moment."

Katherine nodded. She took a few seconds to appreciate Sarah's features in a way she'd not thought of doing the night she'd learned Sarah was engaged to Nicholas. She had only wanted to flee Nicholas's house that night. Sarah's skin was pale. Long, thick, dark lashes outlined her eyes, and her lips matched her rose gown. She'd braided her auburn hair and pinned it up in a fashionable coronet around her head. She was quite slender, with long arms and fluid movements as she averted her gaze and attempted to brush droplets of lemonade from her sleeve. Feeling a twinge of jealousy, Katherine realized why Nicholas had fallen in love with Sarah Preston.

Sarah was very pretty.

Then Sarah's attention was drawn from the sleeve to her. She's assessing me, Katherine thought. The situation was almost ridiculous, she and Sarah taking turns examining each other. She wondered if Sarah knew about the time she'd spent in Nicholas's arms. Of course, if Sarah had heard the gossip about her and Kevin, how could she possibly suspect her of being with Nicholas? But perhaps Sarah thought she'd spent time in both men's arms.

"You're Katherine?" Sarah inquired.

"I'm Katherine," she responded, wanting to add, "the infamous Katherine McDaniel," but sealing her lips.

"Nicholas said I would find you waiting by this tree." Sarah said, pressing a drawing tablet and several pencils into Katherine's hand. There was no incrimination in her eyes, not one spark. She smiled, in fact. "I encountered Nicholas and little Charles in the house. Although Charles should hardly be called 'little Charles' anymore." She inclined her head to the tablet and pencils. "I took lessons for a while. Though I admit I was never any good. I made a very weak attempt at sketching. Finally Mother decided she was wasting her money. In any case, there's more where that came from if you and Charles have a busy afternoon of it. I should like to see your sketches. I'm sure they'll be lovely."

"I don't show them to many people," Katherine mumbled, wanting no more contact with Sarah than she was forced to have this day. Not that she didn't instantly like Sarah. The problem was she did.

"I would be very honored if you'd show them to me," Sarah said. "Nicholas has told me about you, Katherine. You've come so far."

Katherine wondered briefly exactly what Nicholas had said about her. Of course he would never tell Sarah about the intimate time they'd spent together, would he? He would ruin his engagement, ruin his perfect, upstanding image.

"I talked with your friend, Alexandra, earlier. She said something about you wanting to open an orphanage," Sarah continued. She clasped Katherine's hands and smiled. "If you need any help, any help at all, contact me."

Katherine nodded, not knowing what to say. She didn't *want* to like Sarah. She wanted to hate this woman who held Nicholas's heart. She sensed Sarah's sincerity and wished that Sarah Preston were some sort of monster she could learn to detest. But no . . .

She was truly relieved when she spotted Nicholas and Charles emerging from the house behind Sarah. At least she wouldn't be forced to make polite conversation with Sarah much longer.

"Nicholas," Sarah said softly, seeing them, too. She smiled at Katherine again. "We've been surrounded by so many people, we've hardly had a moment to talk."

Nicholas and Charles reached them. Charles's face was immaculate now. His clothes seemed cleaner, too; the rip on his coat sleeve had been stitched, and he'd combed his hair.

"I see you found Katherine," Nicholas said to Sarah, then looked to Katherine. "Sarah encountered Charles and me in the hall and asked what we were doing. When I told her, she insisted on fetching the tablet and pencils."

"Charles and I are most grateful," Katherine responded, noticing the affectionate way Sarah touched Nicholas's arm. A knot formed in her throat, a knot she was sure she wouldn't be able to breathe around if it swelled any more. Seeing Nicholas, meeting Sarah . . . the afternoon had already been much too eventful, and the actual picnic had not even begun. She averted her gaze to Charles. "Shall we, Mr. Pennington?"

He grinned and held forth his arm like a true gentleman.

Laughing, she placed her hand on the arm. "We're off then. There's a wrought-iron settee near the far end of the lawn, facing Lake Erie. That's where we'll go."

She held her head high as they walked off together. Neither Nicholas nor Sarah would ever know the pain she had suffered by seeing them together. But she'd done it, hadn't she? She had survived her first true test.

Unfortunately she knew there would be many, many more.

12

THROUGH THE HOLES in the pattern of white latticework partially enclosing the gazebo, Katherine observed Charles and the small crowd of children and adults—mostly men—that had surrounded him. Charles talked rapidly, and his voice carried. "She taught me how to turn the pencil sideways to make the pine boughs. Look at the horse's mane and tail. Long, quick strokes, she said. And the horse's shadow! I'll be an artist yet, thanks to Katherine. I mean, Miss McDaniel."

Katherine smiled. Charles had been quite an eager pupil. She'd spoken to his mother about having him delivered to Uncle Werner's house twice a week for lessons. His mother had hesitated, then agreed. Katherine looked forward to tutoring him.

Nicholas stepped up into the gazebo. Katherine started, not wanting to be caught alone with him. He placed a restraining hand on her forearm. Their eyes met and held.

"Don't run away, Katherine. We're in view of everyone. People would question your odd behavior. Besides, my conscience won't allow me to kiss you again. Relax. You're quite safe."

She sat. He had made his point. People would notice and question. There would be more gossip, about her and Nicholas this time.

Nicholas sat near her. He jerked his head in the direction of Charles and the boy's onlookers. "He's singing your praises."

Summer Storm

"What do you want?" she demanded.

"To talk to you."

"You might have picked a better time. Here we are, pretending again."

"When would be a better time?"

"Never. I told you to leave me alone."

"How I wish you would stop hating me, Katherine. What I did—"

"I don't hate you," she said tightly, though she was certain her face revealed no emotion. "I detest what you did to me, and to Sarah. You speak of your conscience. Well, I don't know how anyone with any sort of conscience could lead someone on the way you led me on."

"Even the most married man would have been tempted by you."

She inhaled and exhaled deeply, feeling as if she might suffocate. She didn't want to be here with him, shooting words back and forth. This was senseless. It would lead nowhere. Yet she couldn't contain the words that spilled from her mouth: "You allowed me to . . . to throw myself at you, something I acknowledge a great deal of blame for, but you . . . you said nothing about Sarah. As your friend and mine Kevin said, you might have had the decency to restrain yourself."

"Yes, Kevin does seem to have something to say about everything." There was a bitter edge to Nicholas's voice.

"He's a very good man."

"He has a reputation, you know."

"If you came here to lecture me about my relationship with Kevin, don't bother. My respect for you has taken a beating of late."

"Be careful with him. He's not a marrying man."

"What do you want?" she snapped again. "If you're hoping to continue where you left off on the ship . . ."

Nicholas sighed, heavily, wearily. "If I could withdraw my actions, I would. I do ask that you not say anything to Sarah."

Katherine snapped her head around to look at him. "My God. Why do you think, for even a second, that I would intentionally break Sarah's heart by telling her you were seconds away from making love to me? You don't know me at all, Nicholas. You think you do, but you don't." Her voice sounded shrill. She squeezed her eyes shut for an instant, fighting to regain the composure she had lost. She prayed no one had noticed her little outburst.

He started to say something. She stopped him with words. "I'm trying to maintain my sanity despite this madness. But I find your presence here, alone with me, a distraction. You've made things very clear. You want Sarah, not me. If anyone ever discovers our secret, it won't be because I breathed a word of it. Now leave me alone."

Silence fell between them. Katherine again glanced off to the crowd gathered around Charles. Nicholas didn't move.

"I only want to go on with my life," she said tiredly, sensing he didn't feel, as she did, that the conversation was ended. "A life that most obviously does not include you. Why continue this?"

Three pigeons joined them in the gazebo, waddling about, nibbling at crumbs of bread. A strong breeze shuddered the latticework. Laughter drifted from Charles's admirers. Nicholas shifted uncomfortably. "I didn't come here to ask that you safeguard our 'secret.' I blurted that. I'm sorry. Sarah says you plan to open an orphanage. You'll be needing donations. I have a draft for you," he said, holding out a note.

Chilling, Katherine stared at the paper for a moment, then flinched away from it. "Your attempt to earn my forgiveness? To ease your guilt? I'll accept donations only from people who give because they want orphaned children to have shelter and food."

She stood, ignoring his hand, a pleasant smile fixed on her face as Charles looked her way and waved. She was getting quite good at acting, she thought, so good she had no doubt she could travel to New York and earn a role on any stage there if she had a mind to. She gripped both sides of her wide skirt and descended the gazebo steps, not daring to cast a backward glance. Surprisingly she felt no threatening tears. She felt consumed by outrage . . . and perhaps something stronger. She'd

Summer Storm

faced Sarah and Nicholas together, as much pain as that had caused her, and she'd faced Nicholas alone.

The sun dipped behind a gray cloud. Katherine noticed other clouds had gathered, too, dark clouds that were coming in over Lake Erie. Summer storms on the lake could be sudden, even violent, with hail and gusting winds. She wondered if this might be one of those sudden storms and couldn't deny the thrill that rippled through her at the possibility. If so, the storm would be a subtle reminder that man would never truly subdue the magnificent Lake Erie; subtle because a summer storm could never match a bewitching November gale, the ferocious kind that always left Katherine with the thought that this awesome lake could never be tamed. Lake Erie was queen of this part of North America and would remain so, a fact the lake felt the need to rise up and prove now and then.

Katherine met Alexandra near the house. She was watching the clouds, too, with sparkling eyes. "Do you see what I see?" she asked.

"Aye, a fierce one, mate, me thinks," Katherine said, lowering her voice. "Comin' straight off the lake."

Alexandra laughed. "Incredible."

"Awesome."

"Breathtaking."

They laughed together at their excitement.

"I'm going to gather Uncle Werner, wherever he is, and convince him to take us home. We'll venture out and watch from the railroad tracks," Katherine said,

Alexandra nodded in agreement, and Katherine wandered off. The crowd had thinned somewhat; people had already left, probably wanting to be safe in their homes before the storm hit. Katherine waved to Charles as she passed him and his crowd of admirers, then she went to search for Uncle Werner in the house.

She found him in the library with a group of men smoking pipes and cheroots. The topic was the book *The Impending Crisis of the South*. Katherine tugged on Uncle Werner's sleeve, feeling a dozen disapproving pairs of eyes upon her. She thought briefly that perhaps she might be causing herself and Uncle Werner trouble again by having wandered in here among the men. She was forever ignoring convention, and realizing it too late to remedy the awkward situations she created.

"Home soon, Uncle Werner," she said softly, not wishing to stir any more interest than she already had from the group of men. "If you don't wish to leave yet, I'll have Mr. Jackson take us home, then come back for you."

"No, no. I will go," he said, not looking at all bothered that she'd sought him out here. "I have had enough of this political business. Tomorrow will be an early day."

On the way home, wind rattled the windows and swayed the carriage. The trip was a short one. As Katherine stepped from the conveyance, she felt the first raindrops. She stunned Uncle Werner by saying, "Alexandra and I are going out again."

"Where to?" he blurted. "There is a storm forming out here, in case you had not noticed, dear niece."

"I noticed. That's the very reason we're going out again. Don't worry," she said, kissing his cheek. "We're only going across the street to watch the lake."

She and Alexandra hurried into the house. They changed from their gowns into the plain gray gowns they'd worn so often at the school, all the while hearing the wind whip through trees outside.

Then they hurried downstairs and out the front door. In the fifteen minutes it had taken them to change, the sky had darkened, and a pounding rain had started. The rain and a fierce wind molded their skirts to their legs, for they wore no petticoats or hoops. Their hair quickly escaped pins, lashing their faces as they raced across Lake Street.

And there she was—Lake Erie in astonishing fury, beating at the rocks and foliage below. The temperature had dropped; the lake had risen. Katherine crossed her arms and hugged herself to ward off the chill. A surge of water struck like a lashing arm, then the cracking of a branch, or possibly a tree, split the air. An incredible gust nearly flung Katherine across the railroad tracks. Her respect for Lake Erie's elemental power great, she fought her way back to the street and yelled to Alexandra over driving rain and roaring wind.

Then the hail struck, beating, pounding, crashing, pelting. Katherine felt Alexandra's hand close over hers. Seeking the safety of the house, they fought more gusts and battering hail.

Once indoors, they laughed together, drenched as they were. *Ten minutes.* They hadn't even lasted ten minutes! Katherine thought as they dripped water on Peggy's immaculately polished tiled foyer. She'd be amazed if they had even lasted *five* minutes! She'd known Lake Erie might sweep them over the embankment and devour them. The lake spared nothing in her path during these shows of temper. Nothing and no one.

"You are mad, both of you!" Uncle Werner blasted from the doorway leading into the hall. "What possessed you to go out in that . . . that near hurricane?"

Lightning flashed throughout the house as if proving his point. Thunder rumbled. Even from inside the house, Katherine heard Lake Erie pound the shore. Uncle Werner's eyes sparked with anger, but Katherine knew he was more concerned than furious. "Notice we didn't stay out in it long, Uncle," she said.

"You should not have gone out at all!"

She strode over and kissed his cheek. "It's beautiful. Stop worrying. We're well, see?"

His eyes softened. They darted between her and Alexandra, then slowly lowered to stare disapprovingly at the floor. "You are very wet, *that* is what you are."

Katherine's gaze followed his. From the hem of her gown, water dripped onto one of his shoes, splattering softly. There was a spreading puddle of water on the floor. "Oh . . . yes," she said, glancing up, a smile playing on her lips.

Uncle Werner tilted his head back and narrowed his eyes. Smiling at his attempt to look angry, Katherine eased away from him and toward Alexandra. "Well I . . . rather, Alexandra and I . . . We'll go change now."

He nodded as if to say, "A very good idea," then Katherine took Alexandra's arm, and they crept past Uncle Werner.

From the entry doorway, Werner watched Katherine and Alexandra until they disappeared beyond the second-floor landing. He shook his head in astonishment as he walked toward the library. Then he chuckled softly. Finally, as he neared his desk, he slapped his knee and laughed from the very depth of his soul. Life had never been so entertaining before his niece and her friend had come along. Braving that storm! Not caring one moment if they were drenched to the bone and looked as if they had barely escaped drowning. They were two rather unconventional but delightful girls. They always stuck their heads together as they talked. Those two . . .

He had heard from Nicholas about the carriage accident and how Katherine had been wandering out alone. Then there had been the gossip about Katherine and Kevin. Now there was this business of Katherine and Alexandra going out in a storm most rugged lake men would avoid.

He strode back to the door and called to Peggy, knowing she would not be far away. She never was. She emerged from the dining room down the hall a ways, her dark dress and white apron painstakingly starched. "Ye called, Mr. Kraus?"

"I did, Peggy. Tomorrow we will start planning a supper party. Rather, you, my niece, and Miss Owens will plan a supper party."

She arched a fine brow. "A party, sir? I've never known ye to 'ave any sort of party. Ye go to 'em—when I remind ye it's your duty, but . . . Are ye sure, sir?"

"Now that Katherine is here, I have decided to change a few of my ways. Why should a young, lively girl be deprived because her uncle is a stuffy old man? And a German at that."

Peggy chortled. "No more days with Mr. Baum, sir?"

Werner furrowed his brows. "That is something I am not prepared to alter."

"Didn't think so, sir. The beer and the old tunes, they're almost like food, wouldn't ye say? Ye need 'em now and then."

Chuckling, Werner slipped back into the library. "Indeed I do, Peggy. Indeed I do."

Summer Storm

The next day Katherine and Alexandra ventured out to look at prospective houses for the orphanage. The first had marble floors, intricately carved fireplaces, and sparkling chandeliers. The high ceilings possessed ornamental cornices, and the walls were papered with what must be a French design—courtyard and garden scenes with young women holding decorative fans and men clustering nearby; settees and trellises and scaling vines.

Katherine tried to consider the house seriously. But it was as adult as a house could be, even if the paper were stripped away. One would hold balls and parties in the enormous rooms, not read stories and teach music and geography and other lessons children might need. Children already intimidated by the adult-dominated world would never be comfortable here.

Nevertheless, Katherine would not be rude. She met the owner's smile and humored him by taking his arm and consenting to a full tour of the house and the land surrounding it. A small pond covered an area out back. It was charming enough. She could see having picnics beneath the maples there. There was a carriage house and a large stone wall surrounding the entire residence—a stone wall the owner would include in the price of the property, considering Katherine's reason for wanting the place, he most kindly informed her, his stout chest stuffed with pride.

During the grand tour Katherine glanced at Alexandra now and then, only to find an irritating, smug smile fixed on Alexandra's face. The owner talked and talked. Katherine managed to interject the words "orphan" and "children" now and then, and once she tried to explain how she had to be practical, but the man disregarded her words with the motions of one pantomimic hand, going on forever, it seemed, about the many social events that had taken place within the grand walls of the house and on the grounds.

His brother had owned the house. How tragic Robert, his wife, and daughter's deaths had been! "The bodies were found in the pond two years ago. Murder? Suicide? Hard to say. The girl had taken up with a certain young man, and Robert was not too happy, I do know that. His wife was. She liked the young man. They quarreled about it, quite a lot. I have always wondered if they haunt this place," he said, looking up and about as if searching for the spirits of the dead. "Fascinating. No one's lived here since the deaths. I sold the furnishings. Now the house. Thought about moving in myself, but the place is too much for me."

Katherine stared at him. He meant the elegance, the hugeness of the place was too much for him, she realized. He did not mean the fact that three people—his relatives—had died horrible deaths in that pond was too much. An image flashed in her head of bodies floating facedown, hair like wet webs, skin ghostly pale. An icy chill went through her. Somewhere overhead, something slammed. A shutter? A door? It didn't matter.

"Ah . . . there. Perhaps they *are* still here," the man murmured, his eyes bright. As if she shared his macabre fascination for the house and the troubled "spirits" he obviously felt certain were occupants and made the house all the more valuable and appealing. As if the slamming door or shutter should put the final seal on her decision whether or not to buy the house.

It did.

Katherine thanked the man, lied when she told him she would consider the property, and somehow managed to ease her hand free of his—he'd been clutching it to his forearm for the better part of a half hour.

Alexandra began laughing as soon as the carriage pulled far enough away from the house that she was certain that overbearing, odd little man would not hear her.

Katherine shot her a glare. "Well, you're certainly enjoying yourself."

"You were trying to be so polite," Alexandra said between rounds of laughter.

"An inaugural ball could be held in that house!"

"*I* would have taken one look at the marble entryway and turned around."

"Well, I'm not you, am I? The man agreed to meet us there. The least we could do was be a little accommodating."

"You encouraged him."

"I was gracious," Katherine argued.

"If you have to look at ten houses before you find the right one, are you going to be as gracious to all the owners? You just spent two hours being gracious, and what do you have to show for it?"

"Images of a beautiful house."

Alexandra lifted her brows, waiting.

"All right. Images of dead people floating in a pond," Katherine conceded. "My stomach jumped to my throat when that noise came from upstairs."

"Which do you think it was—the daughter, the mother, or the father?"

"Alexandra!"

"Well, you wondered. I could hardly keep from laughing when you jumped. And you *did* jump. Shall we go see another house?" Alexandra asked sweetly.

Katherine wouldn't admit that some of the enthusiasm she'd had just a little over two hours ago had withered. "All right." She opened her mauve reticule and pulled out a slip of paper. She had skimmed the advertisements in the newspaper and managed to locate five addresses that sounded promising. "This one sounded especially interesting," she said. "Six bedrooms, a kitchen with a new stove, a parlor, and a small office at the back of the house."

Alexandra nodded her agreement. "Practical."

It was located across the river, on the corner of a not too pleasant part of what had been Ohio City before the residents of Cleveland and Ohio City had finally agreed on something—an annexation. Katherine and Alexandra exchanged doubtful looks as the carriage passed over the street, which was rutted with the tracks of other conveyances' wheels and gouged with imprints of horses' hooves—not uncommon sights on an unpaved street after an entire morning of rain.

But the houses and buildings here... For every one Katherine spotted that looked as though it might stand another fifty years, she spotted five more she felt certain would fall apart today or tomorrow; or if the residents were lucky, perhaps the day after. Vagabonds huddled in corners and on steps, looking tired and dirty. Katherine's heart went out to them. Many scrambled to their feet as the carriage passed, shouting things, begging. Katherine instinctively opened her reticule, reaching for the coins within.

Alexandra stopped her. "Are you mad? Toss those, and they will only want more. So much more, they might attack us. If you want to help them, buy food and have it delivered here."

That was a much better idea when Katherine considered it. Several men started toward the carriage, looking as though they would like to drag her and Alexandra out and—Katherine knocked on the carriage ceiling. "Mr. Jackson, hurry!"

The carriage lunged forward, leaving the men behind.

Katherine sat back against the cushioned seat, not daring to look out the window again until they reached the house.

Soon they did.

As Katherine paused in the open carriage door and stared out, her first thought was to fade back, pull the door shut, and tell Mr. Jackson to take her and Alexandra straight home. The first house had been too elegant, among other things. This one was . . . well, it seemed she was getting a lesson in contrast today.

"Dilapidated" was a kind description. The porch leaned to one side. One step of the four leading to the porch was rotted and broken, nearly gone. Katherine had no intention of buying or renting this house either.

But suddenly the owner, a ruddy man, appeared before Katherine to hand her down. He wore a dark frock coat and certainly seemed decent enough, though he introduced himself only as "Loring." He handed Alexandra down, too. Jackson had jumped down from the driver's seat. His eyes darted between Katherine, the house, and the carriage, as if he couldn't decide whether or not he felt he should go inside with her and Alexandra to protect them or stay with the carriage. Katherine gave him a reassuring smile. She meant to decline politely to go into the house, and she would not take long doing so.

Summer Storm

Perhaps the first sign that Mr. Loring was not the gentleman he had at first seemed came when he paused to pull a long cheroot from his frock-coat pocket and light it right before Katherine and Alexandra. The smoke he exhaled swirled around their heads. They both coughed at the same moment. Mr. Loring offered no apology. He made no attempt to snuff out the cheroot either.

"Do you mind?" Katherine asked, glancing at the cheroot.

He ignored her implied request. Between eyeing Katherine and her reticule, and taking more draws from the cheroot, he made his stance as a landlord very clear: for a certain sum, he would be responsible for the repair of major things, such as the roof and the stove. For a slightly lower sum, he would hold the tenant responsible for all repairs, major and minor.

The man's manner was offensive. Katherine had given no indication that she even wanted to go inside that ramshackle house! "And the step and the porch?" she inquired, dripping sweetness.

"Your responsibility if you pay the lower sum. Had to throw the last people out when they expected me to fix things."

As if asking him to fix things were an unreasonable request. "And have you fixed anything since?" She was growing more outraged every second, but was careful to not let it show, not just yet.

He narrowed one eye and studied her. "How many places have you looked at?"

"Two now."

"Look at a few more and you'll realize I'm charging a lot less than anyone."

"Yes . . . but perhaps by paying more I'll find a house that won't crumble around me."

She spun and walked away. An instant later, she heard him mumble something about her being high and mighty, and that she had the same thing under her skirts as any woman. His descriptive terms were obscene.

Alexandra gasped. In a rare moment, Mr. Jackson looked capable of murder. He glared at Mr. Loring.

"Let's go, Mr. Jackson." Katherine used the most authoritative voice she could manage. The very last thing she wanted was for Mr. Jackson to punch the man.

A moment passed, thick and frightening. Mr. Jackson finally moved to open the carriage door for her and Alexandra. "Now get on the seat and make the horses move," she told him as she settled her skirts around her.

Mr. Jackson, thank God, did just that.

Katherine sat with her back fixed firmly against the seat. She was still in shock from Mr. Loring's scurrilous comments. "That man was rude," she blurted, allowing herself to tremble a little.

"You sound indignant." As usual, Alexandra was trying to make light of a bad situation.

"Should I have been gracious again? I heard you gasp. Don't pretend you weren't shocked."

Alexandra tried to hide her broadening smile behind a fluttering fan.

"Humor is sometimes inappropriate," Katherine scolded, quoting Sister Dorothy's oft-made remark.

"Where should we go now?" Alexandra asked. "Do you have another charming address listed on that paper in your reticule?"

"I'm surprised I still have a reticule! One moment more and the man would have gobbled it."

"After he gobbled you, of course."

"Alexandra!"

Alexandra clicked her tongue. "Katherine. Well, what did you expect? That the scenery would go from deplorable to delightful in the space of a few blocks? That the manner of the people would improve? The paper, please...."

"I don't have the stomach for any more visits today. Let's go home," Katherine said, tucking her reticule away. "If you're agreeable, we'll go out again tomorrow afternoon. If *I'm* agreeable, too," she quickly amended.

She did manage to muster some enthusiasm the following afternoon, though how she didn't know. She and Alexandra looked at two more houses, neither of which equaled the

Summer Storm

elegance of the first house or the deplorable state of the second. There were no suggestions that the ghosts of the people who had once lived in the houses now haunted them. Katherine would always wonder about the noise she, Alexandra, and the owner of the first house had heard. She recalled no afternoon breeze that might have been responsible for blowing about a shutter or slamming a door.

No, there were no rude little men or suggestions of ghosts. But the rooms were either too large or too small. One of the houses was an older home that sat between business blocks on Superior Avenue near Public Square. Let the businesses have it, Katherine thought. She preferred a more residential, outlying location. The owner whispered to her the exuberant sum a certain businessman was offering for the property—for the right to tear the house down and build yet another business, of course—and Katherine promptly declined even to think about topping the sum. She wasn't quite sure how generous benefactors would be, but she didn't think they would be that generous.

A modest house on Garden Street captured her interest. It sat back from the street amid tall overhanging oaks, surrounded by a spacious green lawn. Painted pale yellow, it had two dormer windows on the third floor. There were five bedrooms—enough for now. Several other orphanages had already been established in Cleveland, so Katherine knew children wouldn't pour in as soon as she opened the place. Perhaps one or two might arrive now and then.

There was a gardener's shed and a gardener's cottage. The kitchen was adequate. So was the little office nestled between the parlor and the dining room—an odd place for an office, but Katherine was intrigued. The house needed repairs—latches here and there, a crack in a side door, a few leaks in the roof.

But this was the house. She envisioned children running through it, gathering around a table for meals, near hearths for stories, and greeting prospective parents in the parlor, where two windows fronted the house.

Yes, this was the house. Now for benefactors, people who would hopefully look beyond her muddied reputation to the fact that she wanted to stretch out her arms to parentless children.

She had time. The house, willed to the city a number of years ago, had captured the interest of no one else, it seemed.

13

DAYS AFTER THE Preston's picnic, Nicholas sat opposite Werner and Lemuel on a leather-cushioned seat inside Werner's carriage. They were going to have dinner at the Forest City House. Nicholas stared out the window as the conveyance traveled east along Center Street. There were few shops, mostly wood-frame houses. Lemuel and Werner struck up a conversation about the shipping of various freights in railcars. All in all, river shipment was cheaper, but shipping by rail to areas removed from river and lake access was certainly more expedient than shipping by wagon, Werner said. Nicholas agreed, but his mind was clouded today. Involving himself in the conversation beyond a few words took effort.

His mind wandered to places he shouldn't allow it to go. Glimpsing Katherine on the balcony that evening had been enough to set fire to his blood. She had been a vision, her hair loose, windblown curls falling wildly about her face and shoulders. She had been pale, but she still looked beautiful. Her lips had been the color of summer-ripe strawberries, and he had wanted to touch them and taste them again. He had not forgotten her flowery scent or the feel of her silken skin. He had not forgotten her heated response to him either.

These were not the thoughts that a man about to marry one woman should be having about another.

On the evening of the Independence Day celebration aboard the *Morning Star,* his illustrious friend Kevin had lectured him about passionate and platonic relationships. Kevin was right, Nicholas knew. Passionate was Katherine, skimming her fingertips up his arm and over his shoulder, burying her hands in his hair, pressing her body to his and opening her sweet mouth to him, talking about the lakes and ships and sketching, captivating him with her smile and with her excitement. Platonic was Sarah, planting a light kiss on his cheek, always speaking softly and calmly. He recognized the difference; he would have had to be blind not to see it and numb not to feel it.

He was beginning to wonder if this engagement was the best thing for him and Sarah. How could he be faithful to her when he wanted another woman? But on the heels of that thought, he considered all the people involved who would be disappointed if he ended his engagement—not only Sarah, but also their mothers, who had been lifelong friends, and Alistair, Sarah's father, whom Nicholas respected and loved a great deal.

"You have much to say today, Nicholas," Werner teased when the carriage stopped before the Forest City House. "A man deep into his thoughts, you are."

Nicholas turned his gaze from the window to Werner, managing a smile. "Yes, I suppose I am . . . deep into my thoughts," Nicholas said. "The ship occupies my mind a lot."

Werner nodded.

Nicholas had not told the whole truth. The ship *and* the tangle of deceit he had gotten himself into occupied his mind. Obviously Werner hadn't a clue that there was trouble between him and Katherine. Of course not. Most everyone's concentration had been on Kevin and Katherine. Nicholas had been angry that people had talked so viciously about her. Like Werner, he had defended her. As little as three weeks ago, he had found himself standing outside a parlor door during an evening at a friend's home. On his way to the drawing room, where the men gathered for cheroots, pipes, and brandy, he had stopped beside the doorway because he had heard Katherine's name mentioned by someone in the room. Three ladies gathered on a sofa there wondered aloud where Kevin Riley had taken Katherine the evening everyone was talking about. Kevin

Summer Storm 149

lived alone, so perhaps he had taken her to his house, one speculated. Another hinted that he certainly had enough rooms in that hotel of his to have taken her there. Nicholas had not waited for the third woman to suggest a location.

He had stepped casually into the room. Three strides had put him behind the sofa, where he kneeled and folded his arms behind the heads of two of the women, Susan Linkens and Donica Strines. The other gossiper was Rachel Stanfield. All three women gasped. His cool look wandered from one to the other as they eased forward on the sofa to escape his proximity. "Lovely . . . ," he said truthfully, "but such talk taints your beauty."

He had left them with that, and he was sure Susan and Donica had made others aware that he would not tolerate anyone talking about Katherine in such a vile manner.

The carriage stopped, and Nicholas followed Lemuel and Werner out of it. The Forest City House stood before them, an ornamental tower topping its mansard roof. Porches enclosed by rails extended above the entryways.

Inside Nicholas noted banister railings of polished mahogany. The floors were oak with blood-red carpet runners on the stairs and in the hallways. A barbershop, hat shop, clock shop, and a jeweler occupied various spaces for the convenience of hotel patrons. The dining room was huge, a place where political and civic groups gathered from time to time. The tables were covered with white linen, and silver and crystal reflected light from low-burning, glass-covered lamps in wall sconces. Nicholas knew many of the people who sat at surrounding tables. He inclined his head in greeting as he passed, following Lemuel, Werner, and the waiter, who directed them to an unoccupied table.

They ordered their food, and cups of steaming coffee were placed before them.

Werner cleared his throat. "Since my house has been blessed with the occupation of two delightful females—"

Lemuel's brows furrowed. "Two? Katherine and . . . No . . . Could it be? Have you finally done what people have whispered you should have done years ago?"

"And what is that, my friend?" Werner inquired, light dancing in his eyes.

"A woman, Werner. Marriage."

"I am quite happy—"

"Married to your bank. Much more happiness, or at least pleasure," Lemuel said in a low voice, "could be found in the arms of a loving female."

Werner blushed. Even his shiny balding head turned cherry red. "*Peinlich*. Now, Lemuel . . ."

Lemuel sat back and laughed heartily. Nicholas chuckled with him, enjoying the playful exchange. Werner sipped coffee in an effort to hide his obvious embarrassment. He chuckled, too, rather nervously.

"Now, Lemuel," Lemuel mocked in a tone much like Werner's. "My friend, I know little about your private affairs, but I cannot deny that I wonder. Do you have a woman secreted away somewhere? Not many men can do without feminine comfort now and then."

Nicholas thought he saw a grin twitch the corners of Werner's mouth. Still, the blush persisted. "So we will begin our ship. This fall the wood will be brought," Werner said.

Tossing his head back, Nicholas roared with laughter. His and Lemuel's amused gazes touched and held. "Very adept at changing the subject, isn't he?" Nicholas said. Long ago, he had accepted the distance that had grown between himself and Lemuel. There had never been a longing to have things the way they'd been before he and his father had visited that South Carolina plantation and such violent differences of opinion had erupted between them. In fact, he had done everything possible to sever his relationship with Lemuel. Still, he was enjoying these easy moments with his father, which amazed him.

"Like a sly fox, he is," Lemuel agreed. "Has a woman somewhere—I would wager my sizable accounts on it." He unfolded the newspaper he had purchased in the hotel lobby, passing over the front-page article: an account of Abraham Lincoln's latest speech. While the *Plain Dealer*'s editor did not support the Republican nominee for the U.S. Senate, Lincoln's remarks were often quoted in the paper. Perhaps the most famous—or infamous—quotes yet, made during the man's acceptance speech, were ones that rang in Nicholas's ears often: "A house divided against itself cannot stand. I believe this government cannot endure permanently half-slave and half-free."

Truth, Nicholas thought. Truth and prophecy. Civil war was in the future. He felt the sparks every time he attended a political meeting and listened to fiery remarks. Of late, there'd been a number of such meetings in various cities, their purpose to discuss peaceful settlement and even the possible separation of the North and South. None had attained positive results. The embers beneath the issues had burst into little flames all over the nation, and it was only a matter of time before the flames became a consuming blaze.

Nicholas's mind strayed back to the subject that had caused Lemuel to tease Werner about his unmarried state. "So your house has been blessed with two delightful females, Werner," he said, taking a drink of the flavorful coffee. "Katherine and Alexandra. A charming girl, Alexandra, wants to be a teacher. At the Prestons' picnic she also said something about teaching at the orphanage Katherine plans to open."

"We have a number of orphanages and schools in the city already," Lemuel commented over a corner of his paper. "Why open another? Has Katherine thought of that?"

"She is determined," Werner said. "She was a bit undecided about what she would do with herself once she came home, but her mind is settled now, it seems."

"Marry her off. She would have a houseful of children to care for without opening an orphanage."

Nicholas stiffened. *Marry her off?* How blatantly disrespectful of Katherine's desires. "You haven't listened to our women lately, Mother included. Many no longer care to be 'married off' and burdened with a 'houseful of children.' Mother, for one, frequently talks about the rights of women."

"Pah! Senseless prattle. Your mother!"

Their eyes met, Lemuel's a steely blue. Nicholas felt the familiar sparks of annoyance at his father's reluctance to listen to modern opinions or change his view on any subject. The man was dead set in his ways, the only right ways in the world, if one asked Lemuel Cummings.

"I disagree," Nicholas dared to say, as he had for years. "Mother has some very sensible things to say—particularly in defense of the rights of women."

"It is not a subject we discuss," Lemuel said tightly.

"By your wish?"

"By my wish," came the carefully controlled response. "She seems happy enough as long as she has money for this and that. I'm certainly happy enough having her at my side. She is still a beautiful woman."

"Adorning your home," Nicholas mumbled.

Lemuel's jaw jutted out. "When you stepped into that carriage, I knew something was wrong. What is it, Nicholas? What is bothering you?"

Nicholas took a drink of coffee, hoping to wash down the sharp retorts threatening to burst from his lips. "Your attitude bothers me."

Lemuel breathed deeply and studied his son. An ache rose in his breast that Nicholas despised him so. Hatred sparked in Nicholas's eyes, and revealed itself also in his crisp, cutting speech and the grip of his fingers on the handle of the china cup he held. "Perhaps a private conversation is what we need, Nicholas, away from the ears of many."

Nicholas placed the cup on the table. "How long do you honestly think you can ignore the words of your outspoken wife? She has a mind and a voice of her own, as do millions of other women. Some are talking about rights they've never dared discuss before. If they did, the conversations were held behind closed doors, away from the ears of the men."

Lemuel folded the newspaper. "You are finished?" he asked calmly.

Nicholas glanced at the paper, seeing part of the print that revealed Lincoln's latest remarks. "No . . . no, I'm not. Tell me, do you read more than the Board of Trade reports these days?"

"I hardly think what I read is your concern," Lemuel retorted.

Werner coughed. "More coffee, gentlemen?"

"Lincoln opposes slavery. Is that why you avoided the front page?" Nicholas demanded softly, ignoring Werner's question, his eyes still on Lemuel and the newspaper. The world was changing, politically and otherwise, but other than for his very modern thinking regarding the ship, Lemuel refused to change with it, refused even to give pressing issues attention. Women's rights, abolition of slavery—two issues Lemuel Cummings would never discuss and certainly did not care to read about.

Muscles twitched around Lemuel's eyes. "That is enough. You will not disgrace me by dragging our private differences before—"

"No . . . I will not disgrace you. But neither will I sit here and agree with you."

Lemuel glared. Nicholas finished his coffee in silence. The air between them was again charged with anger and bitterness.

"Always a quarrel, Nicholas. Always. Better to stay with the business of the ship we plan to build than drift off on other topics," Lemuel finally said gruffly.

Werner conveniently mentioned that he had proposed the idea of a supper party to Katherine and that she had countered with a proposal to make it a fund-raising affair for the orphanage, with a ball to be included after the supper. He asked if Nicholas would mind the affair being held aboard the *Morning Star;* after all, a lake excursion would draw more people. Nicholas, remembering Katherine's refusal of the draft he had offered, was certain she would find a way to evade the suggestion, but he sincerely told Werner he thought the idea was a good one.

Lemuel had grown quiet. Neither the heated words between father and son nor Lemuel's withdrawal from the conversation seemed to surprise Werner, and that, in turn, didn't surprise Nicholas. Werner knew about the differences that had separated Nicholas and Lemuel for years. This was not the first time Werner had been in the middle of one of their disagreements.

The arrival of plates filled with boiled codfish, peas, and carrots took the edge off the awkwardness. The conversation again turned to the ship, the proposed tonnage it would hold, and the surplus of ore in the rich land surrounding Lake Superior. Nicholas produced the plans for the after cabin. There were rooms for the engineers and the steward. There was a linen room, pantry, kitchen, the crew's mess, a dining room, closet, and washroom.

It was a safe subject where he and Lemuel were concerned, Nicholas thought, agreeing with Lemuel on at least that point. In the future he would remember that fact and try to subdue his temper.

Evening found Nicholas at the Prestons'. The back expanse of green lawn that had just days ago been filled with picnickers was now silent. The settees facing the lake were empty, as was the gazebo where Nicholas had spoken privately to Katherine. Now, as he walked with Sarah, he watched the red and gold of sunset sparkle on the water and enjoyed the cool lake breeze that ruffled his hair. Ships were plentiful on the lake this evening, some so close to shore Nicholas watched their sails billow and their side-wheels turn; some so far out they resembled mere specks on the horizon. Lake Erie seemed to merge with the sky, but Nicholas knew that was an illusion, a beautiful but deceptive illusion. Across the vast expanse of water was Canada, a land that represented freedom for many who had been held captive for years and been subjected to cruelties most people couldn't imagine. Nicholas remembered the night he had held a girl who had suffered a beating just before his contacts had kidnapped the child from Georgia. She had not survived to taste freedom; he had wept when she died in his arms.

But others . . . others did taste it. For them, the beautiful waters of Lake Erie represented the last stair step on the difficult journey to freedom. Most cried when they glimpsed the lake.

"You're very quiet this evening," Sarah said softly.

Nicholas managed a smile. "As Werner commented earlier,

I'm deep in thought today. I apologize for being a bore."

She laughed. "You're never a bore, Nicholas. Mother asked today if you had a preference as to the wedding date. I told her I would ask you."

Nicholas stiffened. The wedding date. *Finality.* "None," he answered quickly. He felt her turn to stare at him, and unease prickled the back of his neck.

"Is something wrong, Nicholas? I know you met with Werner and your father today about the ship. Did things go badly? Is it that?"

"My father was . . . how he's always been. For a time we relaxed together, but I quickly realized that was a temporary thing. Plans for the ship are going well. What about you, Sarah? I encountered a little sprite in the parlor while waiting for you to come downstairs. Your cousin?"

She laughed again, a light sound he had always enjoyed. "Andrew. Do not tell me—"

"He made a face at me, then disappeared."

She nodded. "He's good at that sort of thing, unfortunately. He doesn't like unfamiliar people. Speaking of children, I was thinking of offering my assistance in helping plan Katherine's orphanage."

Nicholas had stiffened before; he went rigid now, not wishing to subject Katherine to working side by side with Sarah. "I . . . well . . ."

"Do you think Katherine would mind? I mean, I do not know her well, but I did meet her at the picnic and would like to become better acquainted with her. She was wonderful with Charles that day and will be wonderful with other children, too, I have no doubt."

"Katherine hasn't talked to me much about the orphanage," he said truthfully, wishing the subject of Katherine hadn't arisen.

"I see," Sarah said slowly. "I saw the two of you together in the gazebo that afternoon."

Nicholas drew a swift breath and held it. Was this the moment he had been trying to prevent? Sarah had guessed that he desired Katherine, and she was hurt. He thought he had hidden his feelings for Katherine that day, but he hadn't really, had he? The first time Sarah had seen him and Katherine together, she had guessed he longed for Katherine. "Sarah, I never—"

"Nicholas, I know you have contributed to charities before. You never make a habit of telling me. I've simply discovered these things through conversations with friends over the years. I found a draft in Father's study, one you wrote to Katherine. You must have been talking with her about Charles in the gazebo and forgotten to give it to her."

"Of course," Nicholas lied, something he was not very good at doing. So this wasn't about his and Katherine's relationship after all. Guilt had nearly snared him into confessing everything—the way he had held Katherine on the deck of the *Morning Star,* the afternoon he had spent with her, the way he had kissed her and nearly made love to her. "Yes, of course," he repeated, greatly relieved. "After Katherine left the gazebo, I went inside, to the study for a drink from the sideboard there. I set the note down and forgot about it."

Sarah nodded, her smile widening. "And that's exactly where I found it, though I must admit your generosity this time astounded me."

"And the draft . . . ," he said, a new sort of dread settling over him now as he remembered Katherine's heated words about his donation. "Where is it now?"

She stood on tiptoe to give him a chaste kiss. "Never fear, Nicholas Cummings. I thought that if I'm to be your wife soon, I should start practicing. I had it delivered to Katherine this morning along with a note from me explaining how I had found the draft you had obviously forgotten to give her. At this very moment she is probably shouting your name throughout her uncle's house. The amount was enough for half a year's payment on a very nice establishment."

Nicholas flinched. If he knew Katherine—and he did—she was probably *cursing* him throughout Werner's house.

Bad enough she thought him an unfeeling seducer of innocent women, almost an adulterer. Now she would think he had used Sarah to get her to accept the donation.

Summer Storm 157

"You're not angry, are you?" Sarah asked, wearing a frown of worry.

"No, no," he said quickly.

She smiled. "We should join Father. He told me he expected a game of chess from you this evening since you beat him the last time."

Nicholas forced a smile, took her hand, and let himself be led back to the house.

14

"THE GROOM'S BOY has run off with my hat again, sir," Harold said indignantly, his noble nose outlined against a full moon in a sky filled with glittering stars.

The hour was late, at least ten o'clock. The house was quiet. The handful of servants Nicholas employed had already bedded down for the night, as was their usual custom unless he requested otherwise. There was only Harold, who had just returned Nicholas from the Prestons'. And, of course, there was David, the rowdy "groom's boy," as Harold called him with such disdain. Not that the boy himself was really all that detestable; he was just a boy with a lot of mischievousness and energy. Unfortunately his favorite pastime seemed to be snatching Harold's hat, a trick he had pulled the moment Harold stepped from the driver's seat of the carriage tonight.

Nicholas chuckled. Harold sniffed, as Nicholas knew he would. "By all means, Harold, you have my permission to retrieve your hat."

"I must object, sir. This is not the first time that . . . boy has run off with my hat. As you know."

"Nor will it be the last, I'm sure," Nicholas said, moving toward the front entrance. "By all means—"

"I know. I have your permission to retrieve my hat." Harold sighed deeply. "For your information, Mr. Cummings, the groom's boy has a collection of my hats, for I haven't caught the prankster yet to retrieve—as you put it—even one of them."

Summer Storm

"You mean to say you buy a new hat every time David snatches one?" Nicholas asked in disbelief.

"That is exactly what I mean, sir," Harold said in great frustration.

"I had no idea. I'll ask David about your hat."

"Hats, sir. Many, not one."

"Yes, of course. Hats." Nicholas fought laughter for the sake of Harold's dignity. "I'll ask David about the hats tomorrow. And how many hats do you estimate you've lost to David, Harold?"

"Ten. At least."

Nicholas chuckled, much to Harold's obvious disapproval—the man scowled admirably. "The boy does have quite a collection, doesn't he?" Nicholas teased lightly, unable to help himself. "You'll find an extra amount in your pay this next time, Harold, and, as I said, I'll ask David about the hats."

"Thank you, sir."

Nodding, Nicholas went inside the house. He shut the front door and strode to the study, where he meant to read a bit, then go upstairs to bed. He had stayed at the Prestons' longer than he had intended. He'd found himself involved in that game of chess with Alistair, Sarah's father, a longtime, worthy opponent, and the match had been lengthy.

He settled himself in a chair near a window, lit a cheroot, and opened a book.

Presently he heard horse's hooves on the brick-patterned drive just outside the window and rose, wondering who would be calling at this late hour.

At the front door he met the caller. The person wore a black cape, with a huge hood thrown over a head Nicholas couldn't even glimpse. Suddenly he realized he didn't need to see the face. He smelled her. The sweet, flowery scent was Katherine's alone.

"What the devil?" was all he had time to sputter before she stepped inside and pushed the hood from her head.

"You're always such a mannered host, Nicholas," she said, anger sparkling in her eyes. Golden curls softly framed her face. "But I fear you've taken leave of your manners this night. Why didn't you ask me in?"

"Katherine, I can't believe—"

She held up a hand, palm out, to stop him. "If you mean to admonish me as you might a child, don't bother. For years I worked to please you only to come home to . . . what I came home to. Don't trouble me with a scolding when you have many lessons to learn yourself."

Nicholas drew a deep breath, her words hitting their mark. "Very well," he said stiffly. "I gather this is about the note and the draft Sarah sent you."

"Ah, yes . . . the note and the draft. But first, your manners. Have you no wine? Not even a chair to seat a guest in?"

She was calmly furious, ridiculing him, jabbing verbally to avenge the way she'd been hurt. She also looked incredibly beautiful. Breathtaking, as she'd been on the balcony the night he looked up and saw her standing there in disheveled glory. Only now there was something even more disarming about her. Now her cheeks and lips were flushed, and her chin was tilted in defiance, as it had been when he had first met her so long ago in Werner's banking office.

One thing was certain. Just as he had refused to allow that girl of fourteen to roam the warehouse district alone that afternoon, he would not allow Katherine to return home alone on the dark streets of Cleveland tonight. One never knew who might be hiding in the shadows, waiting for a victim.

"I'll take your cape," he said, easing around behind her. He reached around to the front of her neck to unfasten the clasp there. Wispy curls teased his jaw. When he lifted the cape, her breath brushed the back of one hand like the touch of a feather, sending tiny spasms of pleasure up his arm.

Nicholas nearly leapt back to escape the sensation. He wondered if Katherine sensed his reaction. Could she hear the pounding of his heart, the way his breath had quickened?

Sarah . . . Sarah . . . , he began telling himself. When in Katherine's presence, why was his loyalty to Sarah, in heart and body, so easy to forget?

He tossed the cape over one arm, averting his eyes from Katherine's slender form clad in an unadorned, unhooped gray dress. If she had thought to be drab in the outfit, she had thought wrong. The cloth outlined the fine curves of her bosom and waist, as well as the flare of her hips. Katherine McDaniel would look enchanting in anything she wore.

She was also the last woman with whom he should be caught alone.

"Where might we go to talk?" she inquired insistently. He knew there would be no turning her away.

"I was reading in the study. The other lamps—"

"The study will do."

"This way then," he said, a hand directing the way to the hall before them.

She took the lead. Once they were in the study, he closed the door out of habit and motioned her to the chairs before the fireplace. He tossed her cape over the back of one chair, crossed the Persian carpet, and reached for a crystal goblet from the small sideboard.

"You wanted wine?" he asked, making the mistake of meeting her shimmery gaze. Desire flickered between them, small sparks, but sparks nonetheless. They both looked away at the same moment.

"I shouldn't have chided you about your manners as a host, Nicholas. I find no fault with that part of you."

Only every other part of me, is that it? he thought angrily. To think he'd had no idea her tongue could be so sharp would be a lie to himself. In some ways, Katherine had not changed at all.

He was damned sick of her laying total blame at his feet for the intimacy they had shared, making him feel as if he'd set out to be an adulterer. Hopefully she would get to her business and conclude it quickly; her sarcastic remarks whittled away at his carefully controlled temper.

He poured a goblet of rich red wine, cupped it in his hand, and carried it to her. He didn't meet her gaze this time, wouldn't let himself. He would find anger or desire in her eyes, perhaps both. The anger would only make *him* more angry.

The desire would increase his own want of her, luring him closer to a precipice that already seemed dangerously near.

But he couldn't seem to keep his eyes from the slender fingers that curved around the goblet as she took it from him. Long fingers, the nails neatly trimmed, filed, and buffed. The structure of her hand was beautiful: small knuckles, fragile-looking bones extending to her wrist. Her skin was ivory. No doubt the center of her palm contained a map of thin lines and was sensitive. His gaze followed her hand to the table where she placed the goblet. Only when she withdrew the hand and placed it in her lap with the other did he realize he had been staring at it.

He stifled a laugh of absurdity. Staring, lovestruck, at a hand! No . . . no, it wasn't the hand at all. It was the possessor of the hand. He wanted her so much that even the graceful movements of her hand had the ability to capture his total attention. An arm or a foot might have the same effect, as long as they belonged to Katherine.

"Damn," he said softly, turning away. He realized he had cursed aloud and issued a quick apology.

"Have you forgotten that my mouth was much worse when I first met you, Nicholas?" she asked. "Nothing you can say will shock me. Nobleness now—after you've plunged a knife into my heart—serves no purpose."

He turned back, narrowing his eyes. "I'm weary of your cutting remarks. Please get on with your business so you can go home and I can go back to what I was doing."

"All right," she said, undaunted.

He settled himself in a chair before the window, some distance from her, but facing her. He didn't trust himself to sit near her, not when he truly ached for her with an intensity he had never felt while merely sitting in the same room with a woman. The power of it astounded him. He longed to make love to her, and yet he also wanted to take her by the shoulders and shake her, scold her for riding through the night alone to come here. This was the second chance she had taken with her reputation and safety. Talk about the way she had escaped the supper through the kitchen with Kevin was finally dying. The hour was late and the servants were probably all asleep, but what if they weren't? What if someone had seen her arrive? That aside, *he* had told her not to go out alone again. Did the woman listen to no one? No, she didn't, or so it seemed. She decided she wanted to do something, and damn anyone who stood in her way.

"As you guessed, I came about the draft," she said.

"To return it? Give it to me then, and I'll take you home. There's no sense in drawing this—"

"Return it? Just like that? How could I possibly just return it? Sarah would be insulted, or hadn't you considered that? But I did come to *discuss* it. How clever you are. You had Sarah send me the draft after I refused it."

He shook his head. "I knew you would think that, Katherine. I knew. Sarah said she explained what happened. She assumed I had forgotten to give you the draft. I'm not usually so careless as to lay one somewhere and forget about it."

"Is *that* what happened?"

"It is."

"I don't believe you."

No one had ever called him a liar! The woman was infuriating, exasperating, sitting with her back straight, her head tilted. Indeed, there was not one sign that she was even nervous or that she doubted for a second that she might be wrong. He might desire her, something that was definitely wrong of him since he was an engaged man, but he had never lied to her. "Believe what you will then," he muttered.

"You're determined to try to ease your guilt by contributing to the orphanage," she accused.

"Damn you! That was not my purpose."

"Damn *me*?" The hint of a bitter smile pulled at the corners of her full red mouth. "Damn *you*! What was your purpose then?"

He yanked at his cravat. "Exactly what I said it was. Stop insulting me, Katherine."

"Insulting *you*? Oh, and how dare I do such a thing."

"Enough. I offered the money because I knew you would need it."

"And did you also suggest the use of your ship for a charity supper and ball because you knew I would need the money? The very ship we were on that afternoon."

He knew damn well what afternoon she was talking about. "I didn't suggest the use of the ship. Werner—"

"Of course. Uncle Werner. You didn't suggest it, he did, is that it? Is that your story, Nicholas?"

"That's exactly it!" he snapped, coming out of the chair. He paced before the window, watching tree branches shiver from the night breeze. Presently he turned on her. "What do you want? You didn't come to return the draft, so what do you want?"

She sipped wine, then returned the goblet to the table and drew a piece of paper from the sleeve of her dress. The draft.

"I want as little from you as possible, that's what I want," she answered softly. "At one time I wanted everything from you. Everything. Whether or not you had anything to do with the draft being delivered to me . . . well, the fact is, it was delivered. Not listing you as a contributor would raise questions in Sarah's mind." She paused and breathed deeply, as if gathering strength. Although Nicholas couldn't imagine her needing more strength. She seemed to possess quite enough. "I find myself in the position of *having* to accept a donation from you, a position I don't like," she continued. "Understand that I'm not trying to protect you. I'm trying to protect Sarah and myself."

He shook his head in confusion. "If you mean to accept it, why did you come here? To berate me for the many things you think I've done wrong?"

"You mentioned once that I felt indebted to you," she said, "and yes, perhaps I did. You altered my life in an extraordinary way. But after much thinking, I decided I don't want to find myself in your debt again. There's no reason the amount anyone contributes must be listed anywhere other than in financial reports. And Sarah will probably never read those."

She stood and crossed to him. Their eyes locked. Nicholas again wondered what the hell was swirling inside her lovely head. She didn't want a donation, but felt she had to accept one to avoid questions. And what was this talk of Sarah never reading financial reports? Of course Sarah would have no interest in reading financial reports! He was thoroughly confused.

She took his hand, lifted it, and placed the draft in it. "I'm returning it for one of a lesser amount, say one dollar. If, of course, you're very angry with me for making this request, you can refuse to contribute at all. In that event, I'll leave you to provide any necessary explanations to Sarah."

"One . . . ?" He inhaled a sharp breath and released it with a laugh of disbelief, of outrage. He hadn't really expected her to keep the draft, but this . . . this was insult piled upon insult! Bad enough she had refused the money in the first place, but this . . . One dollar when he was what most considered a wealthy man? When he could afford double what he'd tried to give her? "Katherine, the donation was made to ensure a healthy start for the orphanage!" he sputtered.

She stared at him, still not believing him.

He jerked a nod, not knowing what else to do. She had caught him completely unaware—exactly what she'd meant to do. "All right. As you said, you certainly thought this out well. One might think you make business transactions daily," he snapped. The remark was a stab at her confidence, but she didn't flinch. She stood unmoving before him.

He ripped the paper, vented his anger on it. Then he marched to the secretary, pulled open a drawer and removed a small pad. He reached for a pen and seconds later handed her another draft. "One dollar," he bit out, his hand trembling. "I do hope this one satisfies you."

"It does. It does indeed. Thank you," she said, taking the note and turning away. "And thank you for the wine," she added, almost as an afterthought.

"You're not riding home alone, Katherine. I told you once before, the streets of Cleveland are not suitable for a lady to wander alone."

She halted in mid-step and turned an uplifted brow on him. "I rode here alone. I'll ride back alone."

"Don't be foolish. I can't allow that," he said, gripping the edge of the secretary.

"Can't allow—?" She laughed incredulously. "And what, pray tell, do you intend to do about it? I'm hardly a child to be tossed over your shoulder anymore."

Irritated by her stubbornness, still angry over the business about the amount of the second draft and the fact that she had accused him of lying, Nicholas rounded the secretary. "I'll take you home."

"I don't think so. I'm afraid I'd feel indebted to you again," she said, spinning to reach for the shimmering brass doorknob.

He crossed the room with six easy strides, slammed an open hand on the partially open door, shutting it, and grabbed her forearm with his other hand.

"What are you doing?" she demanded.

A moment passed before he could even speak, he felt so angry and insulted. She stripped him raw, refusing even to allow him the courtesy of escorting her home. "Ordinarily I have a vast store of patience," he said through gritted teeth, "but I'm at the bottom of it."

"Let go of me, Nicholas. There's no reason—"

"I don't think so." He turned his face toward her then, leveling a heated look on her. They were so close, he felt the warmth of her breath feather his face; he noticed for the first time the tiny mole near one earlobe, the slight arch to one eyebrow. Buttons were undone at the base of her neck, and her pulse throbbed there. Her bosom curved delectably, her waist narrowed, her hips flared. No hoops. No crinoline. Just a simple matter of raising her skirts and . . . He was aroused, thoroughly aroused, and the hot sensations going through him fueled his anger, if anything. For weeks, he'd been fighting his response to her. What was it about her that weakened him so? That made him say things and do things he wouldn't normally say and do? That threatened to upset the perfect plan for his life?

"You're not stepping from this house alone," he warned.

"How dare you detain me?" she shot back.

"I will detain you for as long as I wish. With scalding remarks, you accused me of being a bad host, of lying to you, of offering a charitable donation to allay my guilt—Oh, and just days ago, you implied that I had no conscience! Obviously you think I set out to seduce you. Hardly. You tried to seduce me! Tell me, Katherine, did you ever once stop to consider, before you set your sights on me, that there might be another woman?"

She stared at him, disbelief widening her blue eyes. Finally he had pierced her armor. Finally. "Nicholas, let go."

But Nicholas was too slashed with wounds from her verbal jabs, too infuriated by his inability to remain indifferent to her. He lowered his face a breath away from hers. "You worked for five years to become a lady. Tell me, should a *lady* spend an entire afternoon alone with an unmarried man? Should a *lady* ride through a dark city to an unmarried man's home alone— ever? Things would be much better if you would act as a lady should act! And, for the love of God, stop acting so damned righteous when you were as much to blame for what nearly happened aboard that ship as I. *I* should have had the decency to restrain myself? Well, *you* should have had the decency to restrain yourself!"

"Nicholas . . . you're hurting me. Stop," she whispered, trying to wrestle free.

Nicholas released her arm and spun away, breathing deeply to try to restore his patience and calm. It had melted in a puddle around his feet, he thought, with hardly a hope of returning to its original form. "I'll take you home now," he managed.

He would. He would take her home, see her safely inside, then come back here, grab a bottle of whiskey, and drink until he passed out. He, a man who never drank whiskey. But its powerful, numbing effect would blot out thoughts of her for a while. Good God! How he wished he could blot them out forever. The woman hurled him to the brink of madness and created havoc in his life.

He turned around, ready to usher her outside, where he would saddle a horse for himself and take her home.

But the sight before him gripped and squeezed his heart, tearing at more ragged emotions inside him.

Katherine's back was planted against the door. She was bent, her face buried in her hands. She didn't make a sound, but her shoulders shook with soft sobs. Nicholas clenched a fist and put it to his mouth. He had hurt her with his little show of temper. Perhaps subconsciously he had wanted to make her feel as torn apart as he felt. Well, he'd done it, hadn't he? And he was not proud of the fact. In the space of a few seconds his anger, his total fury toward her, dissipated.

He lowered his fist and forced his hand open. He slowly walked over to her, scared to touch her for fear she would push him away. But the need to comfort her swelled within him, and he reached out anyway, taking the risk. "Katherine . . . Katie," he rasped, drawing her to him. "Dear Katie, I'm sorry. I'm sorry. I was cruel."

She pushed against him at first, palms against his chest. But they were weak pushes, and he knew she didn't really want him to release her. His hands went to her hair, buried themselves in the silk and soothed—or tried to. Her soft sobs grew louder until she cried outright, cursing him and herself. She lifted her head, her face marked with tears, her eyes red and streaked. Then she pounded his chest with clenched fists, cursing him again. In those horrible moments he hated himself for the wretched pain he had caused her.

He grabbed one fist, but she tore it away, beating at him again. He let her anger flow for a time. It poured forth in tears, in sobbed words of rage, in blows.

"Katie."

She continued.

"Katie," he said louder, knowing he didn't dare return her to Werner's house in this condition. Werner was a perceptive man; he wouldn't need to ask many questions to draw a conclusion.

Nicholas knew he must do something. She was hysterical, her sobs wracking her body. He reached down, scooped her up—and was shocked when she stopped beating and clung to his shoulders. She seemed so fragile in his arms, not at all like the clever woman of strength who had requested that he write her a draft "for a lesser amount." Good God, what had he done to her?

Summer Storm

She was light, an angel cradled against him. He loved her warmth, longed to put a smile on her face again and return the light of happiness to her eyes. Katherine... Katie... she was all that mattered at the moment. Her curling, wispy tresses swept over his arm like sensual silk. Sweet, tempting curves pressed against him. She buried her face in his neck, her hot breath shooting fire to every frayed nerve ending in his body. He wanted her, how he wanted her!

He moved across the room and sat in one of the chairs before the fireplace, still holding her close. He breathed her flowery scent, drew it into his lungs, his body. He stroked the silkiness of her hair, let it curl around his fingers, then pushed strands dampened by her tears away from her face and caressed her cheek.

"Katie... sweetness," he said hoarsely. "How I've hurt you. I never meant to... never. All I've wanted to do is love you. Oh, yes, from the second I laid eyes on you the night you returned."

Fingers touched his jaw, fingers so delicate Nicholas at first thought they were wisps of her hair tormenting him. He shut his eyes and held her. All night, if that's what it took. He would hold her all night to soothe her. In the morning... well, morning was hours away.

"Nicholas." Her voice was a whisper, a velvet caress, a plea.

He stiffened, not wanting to open his eyes... yet wanting to. Madness! Her fingers skimmed his jaw, touched his lower lip, traced the line of his nose. He couldn't open his eyes and look at her, for he knew what he would find in hers. Awakened passion. Need. Want. Reflections of emotions he knew glowed in his own eyes.

Hold her. Only hold her, he told himself.

"Nicholas, love me then," she said, her fingers slipping to the back of his neck. "Look at me."

Why in God's name was she torturing him so? "Katherine, I... we..."

He opened his eyes, a fatal mistake.

Her strawberry lips were wet and inviting, her eyes glazed with passion. A low rumble rose in his chest, a rumble of desire too strong to ignore. It consumed him in great waves. His gaze shifted to the luscious curves of her breasts, which rose and fell with her rapid breathing.

"Yes . . . yes," he rasped as he bent to touch his lips to hers. He tumbled over the precipice, taking her with him, wanting her, needing her.

They slid to the carpeted floor.

15

KATHERINE'S BODY ACHED in a way it had never ached, awakened with desires and sensations she'd never dreamed possible. She longed for Nicholas's touch, longed to mold her body to his.

Lying back, she stared up into his hazy emerald eyes, offering herself, seeing that his need for her was as great as hers for him. She wore nothing more than drawers and a camisole under her dress and she felt his hard muscles press against her. He lay beside her, his hands taunting over her breasts, teasing her waist, kneading her hips. Exquisite torture. Even all the whispering about the "act between men and women" she and Alexandra had done could not have prepared her for these suspended moments. Something incredible awaited her and Nicholas.

He kissed her, a light touch at first, then drew back to stare down at her. His lips brushed her again. Katherine opened her mouth to him. He groaned and kissed her much the way he had the afternoon they'd boarded the ship alone, only this time there was an unleashed force behind the kiss. His tongue sought hers, seared every part of her mouth, delving, exploring, searching. His hands slid beneath her, urging her closer and closer still. She felt his hard length driving against her, seeking. Her heart pounded furiously, erratically, and she drew rapid breaths, giving Nicholas most of them as she slipped her fingertips to the back of his head and sought more of his mouth. She felt that no matter how much they drank of each other, they couldn't drink enough.

His hand eased up over the mound of one breast, his fingers and a thumb teasing the peaked tip. Katherine couldn't control the cry of sweet agony that tore loose from her throat any more than mankind could control Lake Erie. She arched to Nicholas's touch, wanting more, needing more. Her body was on fire. Everywhere he touched, everywhere he kissed, he left a scorching trail. Then he retraced the path to stoke the flames again . . . and again. The feminine flesh between her legs throbbed, her heart hammered, her breath slipped in and out, in and out, catching when he gripped her hips and his mouth moved down across her stomach. She cried his name, every inch of her wanting him with a passion that threatened to erupt into a million dazzling colors. Her lips felt hot and bruised; still they throbbed for his.

Then she felt his fingers on the base of her neck, where her many bodice buttons began. Trembling, he struggled with the buttons. She brushed his hand aside and unfastened them herself, parting the material.

Drawing back, he stared down at the silk and lace of her camisole, his eyes smoldering like hot coals. He dipped his head to kiss the swells of her breasts spilling from the top of the garment. His lips seared her flesh, and Katherine gasped.

She reached for the buttons on his shirt, unfastening them swiftly, achingly, pushing the silk over his sculpted shoulders and down his muscled arms. Her fingers played in the wiry black curls on his chest, grazing his nipples. Groaning, Nicholas stiffened. She thought she'd done something wrong. Then she glanced up and saw passion surging in his eyes.

She kissed him again, brushed her lips across the coarse mass of hair. He tasted slightly salty, smelled of perspiration and cologne. His scent—there was no other like it, she knew. In awe, she ran her hands up and down his sides, tipped her head back and offered her neck. He feasted. She moaned. This was Nicholas, this was Nicholas. He was so wonderful, what she wanted, the phantom in her dreams. She planted her palms against his chest and stared into his heavy-lidded eyes.

Summer Storm

He withdrew slightly, the smoldering emeralds again admiring her with heat akin to that of glowing coals. He reached for a camisole ribbon and pulled it free. Katherine trembled. The other ribbon succumbed; strands of silk slipped through his fingers. Katherine shut her eyes, the agony of this slow torture overwhelming her. She wanted him, and she wanted him now.

Nicholas bent his head to taste the sweetness of the shoulders he'd bared and flitted his tongue up one side of her neck, tasting her rapid pulse and her soft earlobe. Her silky hair curled across his face; he inhaled its lavender freshness, became intoxicated by it. His head swirled, his body demanded. He claimed her lips again as he uncovered a breast and cupped its fullness. He drank Katie's cry of pleasure, then dipped his head to the breast. He found it swollen, firm, rose-peaked, straining for attention.

Gently at first, he kissed and suckled while Katie arched and moaned softly, her head tossed back in wild abandon. Then he lost himself in the one white mound while his hands sought the other.

She clutched his shoulders. Her fingernails raked his back. Her hips thrust up in a primal way, and she instinctively parted her thighs beneath him, seeking him. Nicholas groaned, restraining himself from spilling his seed like an inexperienced schoolboy.

He withdrew, slowly unlaced her boots, and set them aside. His heart thudded and his breath paused, while his hands reached for her skirt and drew the lengthy folds of material up. His eyes locked with hers as he reached to pull the string fastening her drawers. She breathed his name and clutched at him. He whispered her name, ran his tongue over her lower lip, then parted the undergarment. Then he withdrew to glimpse the parts of her body he had uncovered.

Soft curves. Fullness in the right places. Beautiful breasts, a tiny waist, and beckoning hips. Brownish hair swirled at the juncture of her creamy thighs. Stockings ended inches below.

"Nicholas?" she questioned. He glanced at her face and found her blue eyes imploring him.

"You're beautiful," he whispered.

She gave a cry of what seemed to be happiness, then rose up, her hands pushing him back slightly. He unbuckled his stock buckle, let it fall, slowly pulled the cravat free, then loosened his collar and tossed it aside, too. She pulled at his disheveled shirt and discarded it. Her hands touched the tops of his trousers, and her eyes sought his in question again. Nicholas reached down to unfasten and slip from the binding trousers.

Katie lay back on the carpet. In unspoken invitation, she opened before him like a summer rose. Though he suspected she was ready to receive him, Nicholas wanted to be sure. He stroked the insides of her thighs, his hands moving toward the hidden flesh that made her a woman.

She gasped when he touched her there, arched when he caressed her. She was hot and wet, wanting him. He smelled her woman's scent and groaned; his restraint was incredibly fragile.

Then he rose to hover over her, seek entrance, brush her sweet, damp flesh with his hardness. She cried out, shocked at the touch. He tentatively probed the entry, finding her barrier of innocence.

With one powerful thrust, he buried himself in her tight depths, clutching her hips to his. She went rigid, uttered a cry against his lips, then held her breath. Murmuring assurances, he kissed away her tears of pain.

"Katie . . . love . . . my sweet Katie . . ." He tasted her breasts again, sampling each, savoring the delicacies. She tossed her head back. He ran his tongue up and down the delectable white column that was her neck.

He moved with painful slowness at first. Her wet heat enveloped him, enticed him deeper. He rocked his hips, plunging in and out of her to the sound of her sweet moans as her hands grappled at his shoulders, upper arms, his back. In passion she was an unbelievable beauty, her thick-lashed eyes mere slits, her cheeks and lips flushed a fiery red against ivory skin. Her mouth parted breathlessly as uncontrollable gasps of pleasure escaped her. Instinctively she arched to meet his every stroke.

Summer Storm

The sounds and smells of their joining intoxicated him.

She trembled, and he knew she was a heartbeat away from meeting Pleasure, a force she surely couldn't imagine. He thrust deeply into her, watching her face, watching the ecstasy that tightened her features and drew the very breath from her body as she spasmed around his length and, for a few precious moments, journeyed to heaven.

The frayed line of his restraint snapped. Groaning low, his erection swelling to almost painful intensity, he gave a few more thrusts and spilled himself in her, shuddering with the force, his chest crushing her breasts, his length buried in her glory.

Their raspy breath filled the room. They lay entwined, stroking each other, neither wanting these moments to end.

But end they did.

The demons of guilt stole over them as their souls and thoughts mingled, casting a shadow on the beauty they had shared. Nicholas shifted onto his side to remove his weight from her. Her hair splayed about her head in a wild, exciting tangle of beautiful golden curls. Her eyes were on him, filled with emotion—love, tenderness, doubt, fear . . . Oh, such fear!

He brushed a few curls from her face. The demons had claimed their tongues, too, it seemed. Any words would have been awkward, stuttered. They both knew they had shared a few moments of forbidden bliss. Words would shatter the beauty.

But words came anyway, as both had feared they would.

"I do not place the blame at your feet, Nicholas, believe that," she whispered, touching his brow to wipe away droplets of perspiration. "I offered myself to you. You were right. I shouldn't have gone to the ship alone with you, and I shouldn't have come here alone, knowing how I love you and knowing how easy casting myself into your arms would be. I was going to be a tower of strength, and I was, as long as I blamed you. When you stripped away the blame and made me see my own faults, I couldn't deny the truth. I did throw myself at you. Perhaps even tonight, when I decided to come here and settle the issue of the draft, lurking in my subconscious was the thought that I needed to be with you."

His throat seemed tight, almost cutting off his breath. "I meant only to comfort you," he managed.

"I know. I know. But I'm glad I gave myself to you. Oh, yes, I'm glad."

"Ah, Katie," he whispered, caressing the smooth length of her arm. He wondered what they would do now. This complicated things—as if things had not been complicated before! He needed to think. More than anything, he now needed to think.

Silence fell between them again, the thick silence of reality. Their eyes held, searched each other's souls. "I suppose . . . ," Katherine began, and suddenly her throat felt unbelievably dry. "I suppose we should avoid being caught alone together. Neither of us had the strength to stop the other tonight."

He nodded his agreement.

They dressed each other. Nicholas's gentle touch moved Katherine to smile, rather sadly, for she felt his quickened breath brush her shoulder as he helped her, and she knew he restrained himself from possessing her again. She carefully buttoned his shirt; he smoothed the folds of her skirt. They were careful, reserved touches, for one caress between them would make them tumble to the floor again.

A name hovered between them, thoughts of a person who would suffer unbelievable pain if she ever learned of the moments of passion Nicholas and Katherine had shared. Katherine saw guilt in Nicholas's clouded emerald eyes and knew the same emotion must be revealed in hers. Their protective barriers had been stripped away; emotions were easily revealed without words.

"I'll take you home. And don't bother to object, Katherine," he said, his intimate nickname for her now tucked away somewhere. That pained Katherine somewhat, for she loved the way he called her Katie.

"Or you'll toss me over your shoulder again?" She couldn't resist.

He shot her a glare. "Indeed."

Summer Storm 177

Outside, the magic of night had settled on the city. The darkness was tempered only by the silver glow of the crescent moon. Hand in hand, Nicholas and Katherine walked across a dirt path to the small stable behind the house and saddled a horse for Nicholas. Then they retrieved Katherine's from where she had tethered it in front of the house.

Through the darkness they rode, few words springing up between them. Katherine wondered if Nicholas shared her thought of not wanting to attract attention. Of course he does, she thought, stealing a glimpse of his shadowed face, but he wouldn't voice it. She felt guilt edge into her brain, but refused to let it grow. She would keep it at bay, always cherishing the time she had spent with him. She would never allow guilt to ruin her memories.

"The draft," he said as they turned at the corner of Erie and Lake streets. "I sincerely wanted to help with the orphanage. That was my only motive. If you would allow me to write another draft for the original amount . . ."

She smiled. "Dear Nicholas. I wouldn't dream of asking you to do that."

"It would be no trouble."

"Do what you will."

"Have you looked at houses or buildings yet?"

"Yes, Alexandra and I went out several afternoons. There's a house on Garden Street. It needs some work, but Uncle Werner says he has friends who will probably do the work as a contribution. It's the old Grayson house, I'm told. Elizabeth Grayson died and left the property to the city. I'm hoping to buy it for a reasonable amount."

He nodded, then seemed to slip into his thoughts again.

Soon they reached her home. Nicholas dismounted. As she slid from her horse, she felt his arms upon her waist and turned to find mere inches separating them. His eyes searched hers. "You won't be angered by any donations I choose to make in the future?"

"No, Nicholas," she assured him.

He touched her lips, ran a thumb over the bottom one. "You mentioned feeling indebted to me. I don't want you to feel that way, Katherine. Anything I've done, I've done—"

She shook her head. "Don't. I know. I was angry when I said those things. Very angry."

They continued to stare at each other for long moments. Finally she moved away, and immediately longed for his arms again. He didn't move. "Go, Nicholas, go," she said finally. "I'm ready to accept things as they are, but that doesn't mean I'm indifferent to you. Don't look at me with such longing, or I'll toss myself at you again."

Nodding, he turned, mounted, and rode off into the night.

16

BLESSED MARY, KEVIN thought, as he guided his horse up Werner Kraus's drive. The young woman seated on a blanket with Katherine under a huge elm was a vision from heaven, to be sure. Kevin blinked in disbelief.

Her hair, as blue-black as glittering coal, was tied back with a white ribbon, the ends curling gently at a tiny waist. A white smock covered her dress of lavender-patterned gingham. All soft and feminine, the woman stirred him to his fingertips.

He dismounted and hurried over to better acquaint himself.

"Katherine!" he called in greeting, as always finding her a pleasant sight.

Looking up from some sort of book, she shrieked, bolted to her feet, and raced at him. He twirled her in his arms, then set her on her feet and drew back to look at her. "Well, you've only grown prettier while I've stayed away, I see. There's a glow about you. Someone's replaced me in your heart already?" he teased.

"Oh, Kevin! Don't feed the rumors. I've missed you." She hugged him again.

He chuckled. His gaze wandered to the beauty eyeing him from the safety of the quilt. Her eyes were like the oceans. Darker, he thought, with astounding depths. Her lips were tempting, odd-shaped roses, but roses nonetheless. Touches of color rode high on her cheeks.

"I'm at Saint Peter's gates, to be sure," he murmured, his breath lodged in his chest. "An angel awaits me, a blessed angel."

Katherine followed his stricken gaze to Alexandra, then back to him. He was positively smitten. "Allow me the pleasure of introducing you to Saint Peter's angel," she said, laughing and tugging at his arm.

Her heart fluttering, Alexandra watched the stranger approach. A breeze lifted his reddish-blond locks, and the sun glinted in his blue-green eyes. His skin was browned by the sun, from the tip of a slightly freckled nose to forearms bared by rolled-up shirtsleeves. His white shirt and brown trousers were dusty, as if he'd just come in from working on the deck of a ship or something. His look was a rakish one, one that stirred excitement in Alexandra.

"What did the lake cast upon us today, Katherine?" she inquired, seeking humor to ease the embarrassment she felt under his bold stare. Not many people succeeded in embarrassing her.

"A huge fish this time, mate," Katherine responded, laughter in her twinkling eyes. "His name is Kevin and he seems to have grown lungs, though I'm not sure they're functioning properly at the moment."

"Kevin," Alexandra repeated. She stood and offered her hand. "I'm Alexandra."

Kevin skimmed his lips over the back of her delicately structured hand, the bones so fine a man could easily crush them. A sudden longing to trace each of them with his tongue gripped him, and he struggled to free himself. An angel to be sure, or a witch stirred from the bottom of Lake Erie. He'd just met her, and already she'd cast a spell on him. He was aware that he held her hand more than the necessary amount of time to bestow a kiss of greeting on it, but he didn't seem to possess the strength to release it. She finally pulled it free.

"You were reading?" he asked, silently cursing his stumbling tongue. Could he think of nothing better to say? Of course she'd been reading!

"Yes, an old schoolbook. I'll be teaching in Cleveland soon."

"A teacher?"

She nodded. "I'm quite skilled."

Swallowing hard, Kevin felt scorching heat creep up his neck and engulf his face. She hadn't really intended a double meaning, had she? But laughter danced in her navy eyes. He sucked in a sharp breath. She had.

"Alexandra!" he heard Katherine gasp.

"Yes . . . uh . . . literature, is it?" Kevin inquired, glancing at the book that lay open on the quilt. "Thoreau. *Walden*."

Alexandra's eyes widened with interest. "You've read it?"

"I read it monthly. A lovely piece of work."

"Then you know the story behind it? That his inspiration was the way he isolated himself for two years and lived amidst the simplistic beauty of nature?"

"Aye, I know the story well, incredible as it is."

Katherine smiled at them. Their faces were lit with interest as they wandered over to the quilt, sat, and plunged into a discussion of Thoreau's life at Walden Pond. Katherine said something about going to the terrace for lemonade, but neither of them looked up. She doubted that she had even been heard. She doubted that even a ground-rumbling train chugging by on the railroad across the street would disturb them, so deep were they involved in each other and their discussion.

She slipped away, leaving them alone. But not really alone, she thought humorously. Thoreau and *Walden* were between them. Remembering the admiring looks they'd given each other, she had no doubt they would manage to get around what was between them.

Plans for the dinner and ball on the *Morning Star* commenced. Musicians were hired, a menu was planned. Katherine saw little of Nicholas except for the occasional times he came to the house to discuss business with Uncle Werner. One evening he stayed for supper. They spoke politely, but a stiff formality hovered between them. They both knew they must keep their distance. Still, sometimes when their eyes met, she saw tenderness in his, and pain always seized her heart. She loved him with every fiber of her being, and nothing would ever change that. But she was learning to live with losing him.

She felt no regret over the passion that had erupted between them, and only an occasional flicker of guilt that she'd shared moments with him she felt pretty certain he and Sarah had not yet shared. Sometimes she even viewed the unbelievable interlude as her consolation prize. She laughed in disbelief whenever the absurd notion crept into her head.

But in a way, wasn't that what it was? A consolation prize . . .

He'd been weak, as any man might have been at the moment. Sarah still held his heart, but she . . . she had shared the cup of passion with him. She suspected that though Sarah might go through the motions with him someday, as any dutiful wife might, Sarah and Nicholas would never experience the beauty of what she and Nicholas had. Never.

She consoled herself with those thoughts during days she struggled through because she was haunted by visions of Nicholas hovering over her and memories of his exquisite touch.

How differently she viewed things now compared to the way she had when she'd first returned to Cleveland a mere month ago! She felt stronger inside, as though she wouldn't crumble if—God help her—Nicholas rejected her, which he had in a sense. He still meant to marry Sarah.

Katherine would always love him, but plans for the orphanage occupied her mind so often that she didn't have much time to dwell on the thought of loving him but losing him. Charles began coming for his twice-a-week sketching lessons, and she found him immensely delightful, ever the eager pupil. He, too, helped avert her mind from Nicholas.

Alexandra began spiriting away with Kevin for occasional afternoon carriage rides to the outskirts of Cleveland. She took a bundle of books every time they went. One afternoon, when Kevin brought Alexandra home, Katherine watched from her bedroom window as they shared a kiss and a look of longing.

Her arms felt empty suddenly, and a dull ache clenched her heart, but she quickly moved from the window and went back to the small secretary in one corner of the room, where she had been addressing invitations.

Sarah called one morning—the last person in the world Katherine wanted to see, but she wouldn't let her reluctance show. Sarah spent the entire morning talking about the upcoming supper and dance. She'd been speaking with close influential friends, she said. Donations were sure to start pouring in. "Surely you've begun looking at locations?" she inquired.

"I've been looking at a house," Katherine responded.

"Oh?"

"On Garden Street. Except I've been so busy with plans for the supper and dance, I haven't had time to inquire at City Hall about the cost of the property. I wouldn't dream of asking Uncle Werner to do it. He's so busy with the bank and building that ship."

"I'm free the day after tomorrow. I'll do it then," Sarah offered.

"No . . . please, Sarah. I'll do it after the supper. There's no sense in even bothering with it until I at least have a sizable amount of money to work with."

"But you do," Sarah objected. "From Nicholas."

"Oh, yes . . . ," Katherine said, realizing her blunder. She wished she didn't have to deceive Sarah, but there was no other way, aside from blurting the truth. Nicholas had said something about writing another draft for the original amount, but that had been weeks ago, and he'd said nothing more on the subject since.

Sarah smiled. "I'll check on the cost of the house then. You finish planning the supper, and if you need any help with the plans, *any at all,* please tell me."

Katherine was glad when Sarah rose to leave. In the entryway Sarah suddenly turned and embraced Katherine. "We'll make wonderful friends, I just know," she whispered fiercely. "I've liked you from the moment I first laid eyes on you."

Katherine had tried to avoid feelings of guilt. Now they settled on her with a vengeance. Seeing Sarah, watching her talk and laugh openly, feeling her embrace, seemed to rip into Katherine's guilty conscience. The way Sarah strove to help made the wounds fester. And the card Katherine received the following day on which Sarah further remarked how grateful she was to have met such a caring, honest person as Katherine made Katherine nauseated when she thought of how she was deceiving Sarah.

Guilt plagued her even more whenever she thought of how precious her time spent in Nicholas's arms had been. She couldn't deny that she longed for those arms again . . . the arms of the man Sarah was going to marry.

"He's Sarah's, damn you! Sarah's!" Katherine actually cursed aloud at herself once. She knew Sarah might be dealt a mortal blow if she ever learned of the time she and Nicholas had spent in each other's arms.

That was a thought that chilled Katherine like a gusting winter wind.

Days later, as the summer heat gave way to fall coolness, Sarah returned, looking baffled.

"I've just been to City Hall," she said, as Katherine ushered her into the parlor. "It's the oddest thing, Katherine. That house has sat for years. Why, the woman who owned it died at least five years ago. Now that you've expressed an interest in it, someone else has bought it."

"What?" Katherine sank into a side chair. She did not want to start searching for a house all over again, meeting ridiculous people, wondering if ceilings or porches would fall on her and Alexandra. "You're right, that house *has* sat for years," she mumbled.

"At one time there was talk of just tearing it down. But no one bothered and . . . well, I cannot imagine who would have bought it out from under you."

"Perhaps this is fate telling us something. Perhaps it wasn't meant to be," Katherine said, sighing heavily. "Well, I'll think about looking for another house after the supper and ball."

"I'll help," Sarah volunteered.

Katherine wanted to scream at her, rail at her with cruel words like "I wish you wouldn't be so helpful! Don't volunteer to do me any favors, because I certainly haven't done you any. Don't send me cards declaring our friendship. Don't!"

But she didn't. She couldn't. Again, Sarah was the real victim in this horrible web, and she didn't want to hurt her.

17

LAKE ERIE GENTLY rocked the *Morning Star*. Obviously in a good mood this evening, the lake stirred with occasional white-capped waves. She lapped at the edges of the triple-decked ship that glided along her surface, propelled by huge wheels on either side. Katherine mingled in the crowd of people, her guests. Only one invitation had been declined, and that was because the family had long ago planned to be away tonight. Enclosed in the note expressing their regrets had been a generous check to be used for the orphanage. So tonight's gathering was a huge success.

Women wore a variety of colorful gowns—reds, blues, pinks, yellows, lavenders, and maroons. Elegantly dressed as well, men mingled among the ladies. Katherine made sure everyone had a glass of punch or wine. She had the help of Alexandra, Nicholas, and Sarah as well.

Sarah was an expert hostess. No doubt she would serve Nicholas well once they were married, Katherine thought.

The dining saloon brimmed with people during supper. Plates of braised lamb, herbed rice, and buttered corn were served. Uncle Werner stood at his place beside Katherine and drummed a spoon against the rim of a crystal glass to draw attention to himself. The crowd quieted. Uncle Werner held up his wineglass.

"A toast," he boomed, "to the incredible woman who pu

this together. My niece—Katherine McDaniel."

Katherine flushed cherry red, she was certain. She'd had no idea he'd planned to do that. A cheer of agreement went up from the crowd. A hundred crystal goblets clinked, and people drank in her honor.

"Thank you very much for that. Now sit down, would you?" she gently scolded him. He tossed his head back and laughed heartily. She wanted to hug him, his heart was so huge.

"Sit down, she says," he said to further embarrass her. "The business of the moment is not concluded just yet, dear Katherine."

She clicked her tongue impatiently. She was forced to endure more praise.

"Nicholas? Where are you, Nicholas?" Uncle Werner boomed across the spacious saloon.

Katherine searched the saloon also, wondering what in heaven's name Uncle Werner and Nicholas were up to.

Nicholas emerged from the shadows of one far corner, his hair combed neatly, his black evening coat, vest, and stock in striking contrast to his snow-white shirt and high collar.

Uncle Werner chuckled. "There you are, hiding yourself away to force me to take sole credit. Come here."

Grinning, Nicholas strode across the saloon. Katherine watched him, feeling her heart increase its rhythm, a reaction that no longer amazed or shocked her. Years from now, she was certain, her response to him would be the same.

As he approached the table, she saw that his jaw was clenched although he wore a half grin. Muscles twitched in his cheek as he regarded Uncle Werner.

"Werner, you devil," he swore softly under his breath. "You had to make this a big affair."

"Hah! He calls me a devil!" Uncle Werner announced.

Nicholas shook his head. He was in the same uncomfortable position she had been in moments ago, Katherine observed with some amusement. She caught his warm emerald gaze, a gaze that never failed to pierce her soul and make her long for his strong arms once again. Recalling his expression of supreme pleasure and his groans of release during their lovemaking, she looked down at her plate so he wouldn't know what she was thinking. Surely everyone could see her wanton feelings in her eyes.

"Most everyone here knows Nicholas Cummings," Uncle Werner said. "Over the years, Nicholas and I have made a number of business ventures together. Considering that, it was quite natural that we would make a combined effort to purchase the property my niece has been looking at to house the orphanage."

Katherine gasped. They'd bought the house! Uncle Werner and Nicholas! She sat in stunned silence, tears filling her eyes when she thought of their generosity. One minute she wanted to jump up and hug them both. Then next she wanted to berate them verbally for the worry they'd caused her. She'd lain awake several nights wondering where to look next for a suitable house. She'd dreaded resuming the search. Now here stood Uncle Werner and Nicholas, handing her the papers to the Garden Street property!

She didn't know what to say, and even if she could think of something, she wasn't sure she could speak. She covered her lips with her fingers, gazing in disbelief at the two men she loved beyond words, beyond everything, and whispered, "God!" It was all she was capable of getting beyond her lips.

Murmurs rose from the tables surrounding theirs. Whispers spread, laughter rose, then excited words spread throughout the saloon like spilled wine on a linen tablecloth: "They bought the house! Look, she's crying! Isn't it wonderful?"

Nicholas placed a burnished folder before her and said softly, "A copy of the deed. Just so you have it. We'll talk more later, about future taxes and repairs."

She nodded. By the time she gathered enough sense to thank him, he was halfway across the dining saloon, amid the cheering and clapping of the many guests.

Smiling, Sarah placed Nicholas's hand on Katherine's. "I told him I couldn't believe he hadn't danced with you yet this evening."

The luring notes of a waltz filled the room, lit by low-burning oil lamps. Katherine's unsure gaze flickered from Sarah to Nicholas, who stared at her, masking well any emotions roiling inside him. And Katherine knew there must be many. She felt them. She was fairly certain he did, too.

"Go. Dance, you two," Sarah urged.

A second later, Katherine was in Nicholas's arms, relishing his closeness but silently cursing herself for that, too. Surely there must have been some way of declining the dance. What excuse might she have used? Sore feet? Yes, she most certainly could have used that one since she'd danced for hours already.

"Stop that. You couldn't have refused the dance without creating suspicion and you know it," Nicholas scolded gently, reading her thoughts.

She managed a smile for outward appearances. "Sore feet, you know."

"Don't do this to yourself, Katherine. You had no more control over dancing with me than either of us had the night we . . ." Nicholas's eyes flared in shock at his lack of restraint.

Katherine stiffened. "The night we what? Plunged a dagger into Sarah's heart without her even knowing? For God's sake, she thinks I'm her friend," she whispered, Sarah's sincere desire to befriend her and to help with the orphanage having whittled at her conscience. "Under normal circumstances, I would be. As things are, I only pretend to be. She visits me nearly every other day now. She talks about you, about plans for your marriage, and I'm forced to sit and listen and nod politely. Oh, Nicholas! At first I regarded the time we spent together as my blessed gift since I couldn't have you in marriage. Now I regard it as treachery. How could we have done it? How could we have hurt her so?"

"Look at her," Nicholas said as they twirled, unnoticed among the others. "Does she look like she's hurting?"

Katherine stole a glance at Sarah, who stood near a wall and sipped wine. Sarah smiled. Katherine returned it. "No, but—"

"No buts. No regrets. Stop it, Katherine. I've done much thinking these past weeks. Every time I look at you, I ache to touch you. Even now I want to draw you close."

She gasped. "Nicholas, don't! I thought we agreed—"

"To hell with agreements. I've something to say to you and I want you to listen," he said huskily.

She stared at him, waiting, hoping others didn't notice the look she gave him, for she feared her heart was in her eyes. His certainly was.

He bent over her, his hand resting lightly on her waist, and whispered a vow: "I'm going to marry you, Katie. I'm going to marry you."

She tore free of his arms, pain searing her chest and stomach. She fled the saloon, fought her way through the throngs of people, raced down a flight of stairs, and sought the middle deck. There she gulped lake air and clung to the rail.

Marry her?

Damn him to hell!

Didn't he realize she desired nothing more in the world than to be his wife, than to share a lifetime of bliss with him? But his engagement to Sarah was already announced, plans for *their* marriage were already being made. And she had accepted that, *damn him!*

She pressed clenched fists to her chest to try to still the pain there. A cry of sheer agony tore from her lips. She was thankful the upper deck was free of people and that most of the crowd remained gathered in the main saloon; she was certain the cry had carried far.

She heard footsteps behind her and smelled the spiciness of cologne.

She spun around. "Get away from me."

"I told Sarah you became ill," Nicholas said, his eyes like twin emeralds glistening in the moonlight. "She wanted to check on you. I insisted on doing it myself."

Katherine clenched the rail, her weak legs alone unable to support her. "How very convenient for you."

"Katie, listen to—"

"No, Nicholas."

"I won't marry Sarah after the time I spent with you."

"Dear God! I thought we'd settled our futures. I'll have the orphanage. You and Sarah will have each other."

"No. I'll tell Sarah somehow."

"You will not!" she blurted. "I can't believe you think it's a simple matter of telling Sarah what happened between us. When I first came home, that might have worked. But not now, not when Sarah and I have become friends. You'll break her heart."

He grabbed her shoulders and tried to pull her to him. She struggled and turned her face away. "Don't," she said, gasping. "Oh, don't! Don't . . . touch . . . me."

"You don't mean that, Katherine."

"I do. I will not hurt Sarah any more than I already have. And neither will you. Now leave me alone."

His held his face an inch away from hers. His hands gripped her upper arms. She felt the warmth of his breath, the heat of his body. Weakness rushed through her. Only Nicholas had the power to make her feel this way. Only Nicholas.

"What about me, Katherine?" he whispered fiercely. "For once, what about me? You've been hurt, Sarah *would* be hurt. Do you think *I* don't hurt? Do you? And wouldn't telling Sarah be fairer to her than marrying her and wishing every day for the rest of my life that I had married you?"

He grabbed her chin, forced her to turn her face and look at him. He kissed her, anger and passion driving him. If he persisted, Katherine knew she would not be able to resist him.

"I love you, damn you!" he murmured, kissing her again. "Do you hear me? I love you! I would risk everything for you."

His lips . . . so firm, so moist, so promising. His words lured her down a path that could only bring more heartache to everyone involved—to Sarah, to her, to *him*. Oh, yes, he didn't realize the pain breaking Sarah's heart would bring him; he was so caught in passion he wasn't thinking clearly. And he was trying to snare her in his ardor, too. He would succeed if he kissed her much more.

"Seduce me into saying yes then, Nicholas," she said breathlessly, melding against him. "Yes, seduce me into it. Do you think I won't have regrets later?"

He stiffened and caught his breath. His lips went still against hers. His hands slid down her arms, caressed her hands briefly, then fell to his sides as he stepped back. "Do you think I have ever been one to give up on anything in my life?" he demanded. "You won't agree now, but one day you will, Katie. One day you will say you'll marry me."

Which meant he still intended to break his engagement. "No, Nicholas. Even if you break the engagement, I won't marry you."

He turned and walked away, his footsteps sharp and quick on the deck. He jerked open the door leading to the saloon. It snapped shut behind him. Katherine gripped the railing again and sobbed softly.

Poor little crying fool, she told herself. She had his heart, didn't she? Something she had always wanted. He had said the words she had always wanted to hear him say—*I love you*. He had said he wanted to marry her, something else she'd always wanted to hear.

She should be happy. Life should be wonderful.

Tucked in the shadows, Kevin and Alexandra gripped hands, hearing most of Katherine and Nicholas's conversation.

Alexandra squeezed her eyes shut. She loved Katherine so . . . She felt a mere twinge of the pain Katherine must be feeling. Nicholas Cummings was a beast of a man! Weeks ago, when Katherine had ridden to his home and not returned until much later, Alexandra had guessed what had happened between them. She felt Katherine had made a horrible mistake, succumbing to Nicholas Cummings's charm, but she had said nothing. Nor would she say anything now or in the future. It was Katherine's business, and only Katherine could summon the strength to resist the man.

Alexandra heard the swift breath Kevin inhaled through thin lips. "I'm going to her. She needs someone."

He started from the shadows.

Alexandra placed a restraining hand on his arm. "No. It would embarrass Katherine terribly. I know her well. Leave her alone. She knows she can always talk to either one of us. Let it be her decision."

Summer Storm

Kevin swore softly, then settled. "I never knew she would be so miserable or I wouldn't have...," he whispered, the heaviness of regret edging his voice.

"You wouldn't have what?" Alexandra asked, tracing his jaw with a fingertip to try to soothe him. So fine a jaw, so strong and proud. He possessed an inner, simple beauty. She was beginning to think that perhaps she loved him, this man who had snared her interest with his talk of Walden and Thoreau. Only yesterday they had lain together on a quilt beside a stream and read Emerson's *Hamatreya* and the poetry of Longfellow. Of late, she had turned away a number of other suitors to spend more time with Kevin. Peggy sometimes made snide remarks about how often she went out with Kevin, that he was the last person with whom Alexandra should be seen, particularly since all the rumors had been about *him* and Katherine. Alexandra always ignored Peggy's remarks, and Peggy always flew off in a huff.

"I wouldn't have encouraged it," he finished.

Alexandra withdrew her hand. "You... you *encouraged* it?"

He nodded. "When Katherine first came home, I thought I could make Nicholas see that he didn't love Sarah by proving to him how much he wanted Katherine. So I set out to make him jealous."

"How?"

"I snatched Katherine from his side a few times, and he was jealous. Anger burned in his eyes. But I'm thinking he wasn't jealous enough then."

"Apparently not," Alexandra said. "He's just now decided he wants to marry her."

Kevin raised her hand to his lips. Alexandra felt a thrill ripple through her as he kissed it. Their eyes met and held.

"You're more beautiful than the night," he whispered as stars blinked and twinkled above.

She smiled. "And you are a poet, Kevin Riley, always enthralling me with words."

Kevin drew her from the shadows to the opposite side of the ship. The September air chilled her; feeling her shiver, he closed his arms about her. The lake lapped at the side-wheeler, playing in the moonlight, causing the air to turn cool as it swept over the water. Lake Erie was speckled with silver, a breathtaking beauty. Almost as breathtaking as the woman in his arms.

His lips whispered over Alexandra's, and soon desire burned in his veins. Until now, he'd not been what he considered ardent with her, in fact he'd barely kissed her, and never deeply. Saints, he'd never even explored her mouth with his tongue. They'd spent so much time reading to each other, enjoying the beauty of nature these past weeks ...

But tonight ... Ah, tonight there was something extraordinarily different about her, something almost magical. She was swathed in baby-blue silk, bursts of flowers at her shoulders and at the valley between her creamy breasts. Her blue-black hair was braided and pinned in a coronet; its sleekness had caught his eye the moment he walked into the dining saloon earlier. For hours he'd longed to touch her. They'd danced, then come on deck. He'd just pulled her into the shadows, drawn her to him, when they'd heard Katherine's cry of agony.

His tongue parted her lips, sampled the sweet juices of her mouth. She moaned softly, melding against him. His hands cradled her face, swept up and down her satin arms, touched her silken hair, and settled on her shoulders. "Angel," he whispered against her mouth, kissing her again. Then he lifted his head and stared down at her, wanting to measure her reaction once passion settled a bit. He'd kissed more than a few women in his lifetime, and a number of times he'd been bitten by a sharp tongue afterward.

Alexandra could scarcely catch her breath. Her heart drummed, her skin tingled, her feet felt as if ... well, as if they were suspended inches above the deck. An incredible sensation, one she had never imagined in all her dreams and had never even come close to imagining during all the secret conversations she and Katherine had shared about what love must feel like. She stared up at Kevin, wondering why he had stopped kissing her.

Summer Storm

"Angel?" He murmured the fond name he called her occasionally, his voice like a gentle night breeze blowing across the lake.

"I have never been kissed like that," she said.

"Never?"

"Never."

"It can be done again. Easily," he said, and there was a touch of humor to his tone.

Smiling, she tilted her head. "You are a rogue, Kevin Riley. A devilish rogue. Still . . . *would* you do it again?"

"My pleasure, miss. My pleasure," he said, chuckling deeply. He dipped his head and stole her breath again. But Alexandra did not mind. No, not at all.

Part Two

He has lost credit ... from accidental circumstances. It does not appear that his position was ill chosen.

He looked as if he could sit there a great while patiently, and live on his own mind biding his time; she, as if she could bear anything ... but would feel the weight of each moment as it passed.

—*Summer on the Lakes, in 1843*
MARGARET FULLER

18

DAYS LATER, WEARING only her shift, Katherine was seated at her vanity one morning, absently stroking her hair with a brush. She reached back to pull a section of hair over her shoulder and gave a muffled cry at the sharp pain that radiated in her breasts. Yesterday she'd noticed they were tender, felt heavier, and that the bodice of her dress fit differently, as during her menses, as Sister Dorothy had always referred to the monthly time.

Her menses.

She couldn't remember the last time she'd had one. She stared wide-eyed at herself in the mirror, and she touched a breast, wincing when another sliver of pain took her breath. A tremble of dread went through her.

Her notebook. She jerked herself from shock, dropped the brush, and yanked open one of the three vanity drawers to her left. She rummaged through her personal things: a journal she had kept during her last year at school, the pink and blue braided hair ribbons she and Alexandra had worked together the first time they'd gone out in their boat, some tiny shells she had collected the one time Sister Dorothy had taken some of the girls to Kelley's, one of the Lake Erie islands. Finally she found the little leatherbound notebook pushed to the back of the drawer.

She clutched it and pulled it out, fluttering her way through pages. Sister Dorothy had always encouraged the girls to keep the dates of their menses, and Katherine had dutifully complied. Now, as she paused at the page on which she had last written, she froze and wished she hadn't been quite so dutiful. She didn't want to know, not really, but knew she must.

2 Aug.

God.

She remembered writing the date, tossing the book back into the drawer, putting a hand to her aching stomach, then easing her way to the bed. That seemed such a long time ago, which it was.

This was almost the end of September.

When had she been with Nicholas? The middle of August? The third week? She poured through thoughts in her head, trying to remember the date of the Prestons' picnic. She'd gone to Nicholas's home, where they'd made love, within days of that event.

No.

She thrust the notebook back into its remote little corner and slammed the drawer, telling herself that her breasts were sometimes very tender just before her time, that she'd been late before . . .

But never more than five days. She'd never been over three weeks late. Never.

Trembling again, she moved to the window and stared across the street at the lake as it stirred slightly. She pressed a hand to the side of one breast, then let the hand slip to her belly. She really had no idea if a woman's breasts became tender during pregnancy. She knew nothing about pregnancy at all—the nuns had not taught anyone about that. It was something, she supposed, that women learned from mothers and older sisters, neither of which she had, of course.

Oh, God, what was she to do? Who could she confide in? Who would know? Who? Peggy?

Dear. She could *not* consult Peggy. The woman didn't like her. Peggy might take great joy in clicking her tongue and shaking her head, as if to say, "I knew you would come to no good."

Who then?

Summer Storm

A knock sounded on the door. "Are you awake yet?" Alexandra asked brightly.

Alexandra?

No, not yet. Not until she was certain. Alexandra knew as much about pregnancy as she—which was absolutely nothing except that after nine months a baby emerged. Besides, what if she bled tomorrow? What if she worried Alexandra needlessly? She wouldn't.

"I'm awake," she said, turning from the window. "Come in."

The door opened, and Alexandra bounded in, her eyes still glassy from sleep, her hair pulled back and bound with a white ribbon. Her red dress was free of wrinkles, but not for long, Katherine thought as Alexandra plopped onto the bed, settling herself in the middle of it. "Kevin and I found this charming stream yesterday . . ."

Katherine wandered over and settled near her, listening for a time. But her mind never completely stayed with Alexandra and the charming stream. Every time she moved, her breasts gave tender objections, and her head was filled with the image of the date she'd scrawled in that notebook.

What was she going to do?

September had passed with the swiftness of a thunderstorm, Nicholas thought one morning as he opened his front door to admit Lemuel. Moments later he was wishing he hadn't opened the door, hadn't even placed his hand upon the knob. Not that not admitting his father would have altered things. At the most, doing so would only have delayed the horrible news that left Nicholas standing in shock.

Alistair Preston was dead.

It wasn't possible. Nicholas had played chess with Sarah's father just last night. Alistair had put him in checkmate so fast, he had sat staring at the game table in much the same way he stood in his entryway staring at Lemuel right now.

"No, I . . . I was with him last night," Nicholas stammered. "He was . . . he was laughing, toasting himself that he'd cornered me so fast. No . . ."

"He is dead, Nicholas. Less than two hours ago, Myra tried to wake him."

"Good God." Nicholas turned away, tightening the sash on his dressing robe. He had been sitting in the dining room, enjoying breakfast. He had looked out the window and seen his father riding up the drive.

"Grace is with Myra," Lemuel said. "Sarah has been asking for you."

"Yes, of course," Nicholas said around the huge knot that had formed in his throat. Alistair . . . dead. "There's coffee and biscuits in the dining room. I'll go dress."

Upstairs, he dressed, barely managing to fasten a cravat around his collar. It was all wrong, but his appearance at a time like this hardly mattered. He slid his stockinged feet into a pair of boots, combed his hair, then joined Lemuel downstairs. Lemuel had instructed someone to bring a horse for Nicholas.

They rode to the Prestons' home.

There were several carriages in the drive. Nicholas slid from his horse and handed the reins to a waiting boy. He started to hurry toward the house, knowing Myra—Alistair's wife—and Sarah must be in agony. He felt a hand on his arm and turned to find Lemuel shaking his head. "Slow, Nicholas. Be calm. You will not help the women by rushing in alarmed."

Nicholas nodded, knowing Lemuel was right. He concentrated on gathering his composure, a difficult thing since he was in shock. He wanted to rush inside, greet Alistair in the library, settle across the table from the man for their occasional, sometimes irritating game of chess. Alistair Preston had been a lifelong friend, often reminding Nicholas, when Nicholas sometimes got the better of him during those games, that he had witnessed Nicholas's first steps. "So don't be thinking you're wiser than I am," Alistair had often said.

Werner and Katherine were seated in the parlor. Both stood when they saw Nicholas. Katherine had been crying; her eyes were swollen and red. Werner jerked his head toward a window. Sarah stood there, her back to them, gazing out. As Werner and Katherine moved toward the door, Nicholas went to Sarah.

Summer Storm

He placed a hand on her shoulder. She turned, crying silently. He wrapped his arms around her, comforting her. She clung to him.

He had planned to come here tonight to talk first to Sarah about breaking the engagement, then Alistair, explaining only that after much thinking he had decided he couldn't marry a woman he regarded only as a close friend. But now, with Alistair dead, he knew he would have to wait some time before telling Sarah he couldn't marry her. One terrible blow at a time was all she could bear, and this one might prove too much.

He cradled her head against his chest and rocked her, wondering how she would possibly go on without the father she had adored so very much.

Alistair was laid to rest the way he would have wanted to be laid to rest, with a huge showing at his funeral and at the wake. Alistair had always enjoyed a party; Nicholas envisioned the man smiling in approval, his head resting comfortably on that silk pillow inside the casket.

Instead of crumbling the way Nicholas thought she would after her father's death, Sarah was a pillar for Myra, who began spending most of her waking hours locked away in what had been her and her husband's bedroom. She would let only Sarah in, and Sarah spent hours trying to talk Myra out of the room, eventually convincing her to take morning walks on the back lawn that faced Lake Erie. Nicholas walked with them sometimes, through colorful falls leaves that curled, crackled, and crumbled as the days hurried into October.

For the last year, Sarah had volunteered one day a week at the Sisters of Charity Hospital; now she volunteered two days a week. She also took over running the household her mother had always run. The woman Nicholas had thought was so fragile, the one he had thought might crumble like the crisp fall leaves if dealt any hardship, astounded him.

Nicholas began spending a great deal of time at the Erie Line shipyard. The keel block and keel plank were in place. Ribs and frames were being assembled. Soon they would be bolted together in a U shape. Nicholas watched a number of planks, keel, and bilge cut from a flitch—a long strip of timber. He spoke with carpenters, engineers, and shipwrights regarding the various aspects of construction. Werner came one afternoon and told him he should go home, that he looked as weary as a man could possibly look.

Still Nicholas worked, taking time to go to affairs such as a gathering to mull over the recent Lincoln-Douglass debate. He had thought about not going, but he had received an invitation scrawled and signed by the governor himself, Salmon Chase, who was familiar with Nicholas's involvement with the Underground Railroad. Governor Chase had expressed his eagerness to meet him, and Nicholas could hardly have bowed out.

The affair was held in the grand dining room at the Weddell House. There he and hundreds of others listened to the orations of Governor Chase and Professor Henry Peck of Oberlin College, a man Nicholas had conspired with many times to help fugitive slaves. There was a reception afterward, complete with raw oysters and other delicacies, and the finest wine. Nicholas talked intimately with the governor, who, in hushed tones, congratulated him on his work with the Underground. The affair ended with one last speech by another Oberlin professor, then Nicholas went home to strip away his coat, vest, cravat, and collar, and settle himself with a glass of port in the study.

The following evening at the Kraus house, Werner went off in a friend's carriage to a German Society meeting. Alexandra wandered off to her bedroom to read the Emerson book Katherine had bought her this past summer at the Merchant Exchange shop.

Moments later, in the privacy of her own bedroom, Katherine undid the clasps on her corset, thinking that doing so might help ease the cramps that assaulted her stomach now and then. The sensations were mild, but enough to be annoying. She hadn't felt well all day actually. She'd been dizzy at times and nauseated, but the twinges in her stomach hadn't started until right after she'd eaten that bowl of chicken soup less than an hour ago. Something in the soup then? She wished she hadn't eaten it.

Summer Storm

She tossed the corset over the back of the vanity chair, not caring to put it neatly away as she usually did. She'd already removed her boots and stockings; they lay strewn on the floor near the vanity. She gave them a sour look—Peggy would have something to say about her sloppiness, but the boots and stockings could stay right there until later. Her stomach was beginning to knot, and her back ached. She eased herself toward the bed, wanting to sleep, wanting the irritating cramps to leave her alone.

Instead they worsened.

She turned on her side and pulled her knees up, hoping that would help. Hot pain tore at her insides, seared, settled below her stomach. She moaned, unable to help herself. This was too much . . . something was wrong . . . terribly, terribly wrong. More than a simple stomach illness. Waves of nausea wracked her. She clamped a hand over her mouth and fought her way from the tangle of sheets and the quilt to the edge of the bed.

She couldn't straighten. She couldn't. She rolled onto the floor with a loud thump and gave a shrill cry as pain jolted her again. Wetness gathered between her thighs, and suddenly she knew what was happening.

The child. Oh God, the baby. She had decided just yesterday that she would tell Uncle Werner soon. It had been nearly three weeks since she'd realized she was pregnant. Together she and Uncle Werner could decide what to do, where she could go to stay, give birth, then raise the child. She had to go somewhere. She couldn't stay here. She had begun to make plans, to accept the pregnancy.

No, oh, no . . . She clutched her shift to her groin, clenched her thighs. She wouldn't let this happen. She wouldn't!

An insistent knock sounded on the door, then Peggy asked if she was all right. Katherine sobbed. No, she wasn't all right. She hurt everywhere. Wasn't it enough that she couldn't have Nicholas? Must their child be taken from her, too?

The door opened. Katherine blinked. There was the flicker of a lamplight, a shadowed figure drawing near. A softly spoken "Sweet Jesus" then a cool hand on her face. The hem of her shift was bunched at her knees. The lower half of the garment was wet and sticky in places and smelled of sickly sweet blood. Katherine didn't want to look down, wouldn't. She stared at the vanity instead, frozen with pain and horror, clutching her stomach.

"What is it, Katherine?" Peggy asked, bending near her.

Katherine moaned. Peggy. Peggy didn't like her. She couldn't tell Peggy. Peggy would turn the pregnancy into something vile and dirty. No . . .

"Don't be stubborn. I'll help, miss. Believe me," the Irishwoman whispered. "There's blood. What's happened?"

Katherine had no choice, it seemed, but to reveal what was wrong. If she didn't tell someone, if *someone* didn't help her, she might lie here and bleed to death. There was Alexandra down the hall, but Peggy, older and wiser, would know more of what to do. "I'm . . . I'm with child," Katherine mumbled.

"Oh, lass," Peggy said. She glanced down at the stained shift, crossed herself, then moved away. Katherine heard the patter of feet, a scramble of activity out in the hall and on the stairs, then Peggy's distant shouts: "Jackson? Mr. Jackson? Fetch a doctor. It's Miss Katherine. She's sick. Her stomach."

There was Alexandra's voice, then Mr. Jackson's, then Peggy's and Alexandra's, clamoring. Then Mr. Jackson's again. There was more horrible pain, then spots. Then darkness.

Oh, blessed darkness.

When Katherine surfaced from the darkness, Peggy and Alexandra were lifting her to the bed. Her thighs were sticky with what she knew was blood. Her abdomen was one great knot of hot agony. She groaned, sinking down onto the bed, wishing this were over. If it had to happen, why couldn't it just be over? How long did a miscarriage take? She sobbed more and swiped at tears, ashamed that she was crying. She was always brave and strong, courageous. She shouldn't cry. Peggy leaned over to touch a cool cloth to her face, and Katherine thought she saw tears swell in Peggy's eyes, too. But no, why would Peggy cry for her, for her lost child?

Summer Storm

Peggy had resented her from the day she had come home from school. To be so gentle and caring wasn't like Peggy. The woman's manner with her had always been gruff.

Peggy thanked Alexandra for her help, as if expecting Alexandra to leave now. When Alexandra withdrew from the bed a bit and cast a look at the door, hesitating, Peggy said, "Go. You don't need to be seein' this. Send one of the maids."

"What *is* going on here? Why all the blood? Did she cut herself?" Alexandra demanded. When Peggy didn't answer, Alexandra glanced at Katherine. *"What's wrong?"*

"Baby," was all Katherine could say around the pain that seized her.

Alexandra stared for an instant, then paled as her eyes widened. "Oh, Katherine!"

"If you're goin' to swoon, do it somewhere else," Peggy snapped. "If you're not and ye mean to stay, help me wash her and change her gown."

"No," Katherine whispered. She didn't want to be moved again. Moving hurt. Breathing hurt. Thinking hurt. She wanted to be unconscious again.

"Yes," Peggy said, and Katherine couldn't find the strength to argue more.

Holding her breath, she somehow raised her bottom while Peggy pushed her shift up over her hips, clear to her breasts. Alexandra helped raise her shoulders, and Peggy stripped the garment away, but not before Katherine caught a whiff of the sickening odor of blood again. "Oh, God," she gasped. "I'm going to be—"

Peggy produced a basin, and Katherine managed to rise on one elbow and lean over it. She was going to die. She just knew it. She was going to die.

When she finally settled back on the pillows, Peggy was everywhere suddenly, washing her thighs, between them, washing the floor where she had fallen earlier, pulling away stained sheets and the quilt and producing new ones, stroking her face with a clean damp cloth, whispering things that sounded, oddly enough, like understanding. Like compassion. "I know it hurts.

I know. It'll be over soon. Oh, lass, I do know."

Peggy was comfort.

Nicholas had eaten a late supper with Sarah, Myra, and Sarah's uncle, who had been in Cleveland since shortly after Alistair's death. The four of them were now gathered in the parlor for conversation. A short bundle of a man, Lawrence Preston was a doctor in Erie, Pennsylvania, where he had practiced medicine for the last ten years. He was full of accounts about the many patients he had seen with this ailment and that ailment. Myra picked up an embroidery hoop and began stitching while Sarah listened to Lawrence with sharp interest.

Nicholas watched Sarah and listened to her. Judging from the many questions she asked Lawrence about cures and treatments, her interest in medicine was greater than Nicholas had known. Lawrence noticed, too, apparently, for he asked if she ever thought about attending medical college.

She flushed, glancing first at Nicholas, then down at her hands. "I hardly think there will be time once I'm married. A woman cannot expect her husband to run the household while she is attending medical college."

Lawrence gave Nicholas an imploring look, perhaps expecting Nicholas to say he either did or didn't agree with what Sarah had said. Since Nicholas planned to end the engagement one day soon, he didn't feel he had the right to give an opinion either way. Certainly if he still planned to marry Sarah, he wouldn't object, but he knew another man might. Disillusioning Sarah about that fact wouldn't be right. Oberlin College might have opened its doors to women students, but the Western Reserve College had not, and it followed the standard of many colleges. Besides, women doctors were not widely accepted by the population.

Lawrence had just begun another account when an insistent, continuous pounding on the front entrance, just outside the parlor, drew Sarah from her seat.

Myra stood. "No, I'll see who's calling. You rest for once," she said. Sarah smiled in pleasant surprise, then settled back in her chair and turned her smile on Nicholas. He was just as surprised. Myra issued an apology, wondering aloud what had happened to the butler, then she swept from the room.

Nicholas heard her hushed voice outside the parlor door. He also heard the unusually high-pitched voice of a Negro. Jackson? Werner's driver? What the devil was the man doing here? And why did he sound so frantic?

Nicholas started from his chair. He hadn't lifted himself three inches when Jackson burst into the room, followed by a wide-eyed Myra.

"It's Miss McDaniel. Terrible sickness," Jackson sputtered. "Mr. Kraus went to some German Society meetin'. Can't 'member where he told me now. Told Peggy I'd get somebody. Miss Preston, you'll come, won't you?"

"Katherine's ill?" Sarah said sharply.

Jackson nodded. "In a bad way. Real bad."

Nicholas froze for an instant, then bolted toward the door. "Couldn't you or Peggy get your senses together enough to fetch a doctor, Jackson? Is this the best you could do?" he snapped, meaning no insult to Sarah. He was just so irritated and alarmed. He spun about. "Lawrence?"

But Lawrence and Sarah were already out of their seats, too. "I'll get my bag," Lawrence said. He and Sarah shot past Nicholas into the hall. Lawrence went one way; Sarah went another.

"I'll come, too," Myra said.

"No," Nicholas responded, instinctively wanting to protect her. Jackson might be the panicky sort, but if Katherine was indeed deathly ill, Myra, just recovering from the shock of her husband's sudden death, didn't need to see her. "You should stay here."

She cast a weak look of reluctance his way, then sank into a side chair, a delicate black handkerchief lifted to her mouth. "Heavens. You're right. I'm a bit weak already just thinking of someone else being ill. How Sarah works at that hospital, I don't know."

Moments later, Sarah and Lawrence reappeared, she with a dark shawl tossed around her shoulders, he clutching a black bag in his right hand. Jackson led the way to the carriage waiting in the drive. Everyone scrambled in. Soon Jackson had the conveyance moving along Lake Street.

The trip took only moments. When the carriage stopped, Nicholas pushed the door open, climbed out, then helped Sarah down. Lawrence followed. Jackson took the rear as the party filed into the entryway, where Alexandra awaited, her face etched with worry. Peggy was just coming downstairs.

"Terrible stomach pains, but she'll be jus' fine. She will," Jackson mumbled, shaking his head and trying to convince himself. "Jus' fine. Sorry to be draggin' you here, Miss Preston. Didn't know who else to get."

"It's all right, Mr. Jackson," Sarah said.

"Wait in the library," Alexandra told Nicholas. There was an odd look leaping in her dark blue eyes, one of hostility, he thought.

He nodded. The hall was furnished with several long tables. A floral-patterned carpet runner extended halfway down the passage, to the mahogany staircase, which was always polished to perfection. A shrill cry of pain seemed to hurl down the stairs and pierce Nicholas. "Katherine," he whispered, starting for the staircase. What in God's name was wrong with her?

"No!" Alexandra cried, seizing his arm. "To the library."

"Take us to her," Lawrence told Peggy. An instant later, he, Peggy, and Sarah brushed by Nicholas.

"The library," Alexandra ordered again, once they had disappeared upstairs.

This time Nicholas followed her.

The library was lit by a number of lamplights. At any other time Nicholas would have paused to admire Werner's collection of books filling shelves that spanned two walls. Not this night. He paced for what seemed an hour while Alexandra sat in a chair. Jackson had gone back out to look for Werner, but so far he hadn't returned, either alone or with Werner. What if something was so terribly wrong that Katherine died? A gut-wrenching thought. But what if? Werner would never forgive himself for not being here.

Pacing more, Nicholas realized his forehead was beaded with perspiration. He jerked at his neckband.

"Where the hell is Werner?" he blurted suddenly, clenching a fist. His nerves felt twisted and mangled.

Alexandra appeared at his side, pressing a snifter of brandy into his hand. "Calm yourself," she said. "Do you really think you are doing Katherine any good pacing and ranting this way? If anything, you will only make the situation worse for Mr. Kraus when he comes. For once think of others, not yourself. Sit down!"

Nicholas lifted a brow, taking the snifter. He had sensed her dislike the first evening he met her. She was skilled with sharp looks and edged words; he saw a different Alexandra from the friendly, gentle friend Katherine had described to him a number of times. "You're a split second away from giving me a lashing, I believe," he said softly, watching her.

"And one you truly deserve," she shot back. "Then I've a mind to give Mr. Jackson one for bringing you here." She moved to stand behind a brown settee near the room's one window.

"What was he to do?" Nicholas demanded.

"Bring a doctor."

"He brought Lawrence Preston, even if Lawrence's appearance here came about in an odd way. The man *is* a doctor."

"He brought Sarah. And you. You're Katherine's worst enemy. You don't belong here."

Nicholas's fingers tightened on the snifter. He drained it, needing it filled a dozen times more. "Indeed? Her worst enemy? Loving her the way I do?"

"Indeed. She would never be so ill if it weren't for you!" Alexandra's eyes widened immediately, as if she'd meant to bite back the words and failed.

Nicholas caught his breath and narrowed his eyes. "What are you saying? What exactly is wrong with her? You seem to know a great deal more than any of the rest of us."

Alexandra stared at him, silently refusing to say more. Sarah appeared in the doorway, looking pale.

"What is it? Will she be all right? What's the matter with her?" Nicholas shot the questions in rapid succession, needing immediate answers.

Sarah sank into a chair near the small fireplace, over which hung a modest painting of Werner. "I . . . I don't know. She's in such pain, yet she refused to allow Uncle Lawrence to look at her unless I left the room. I waited in the hall for a time, hoping she would change her mind. Finally Peggy asked me to come down here. I'm Katherine's friend and yet . . . Why would she want me to leave?"

Nicholas stood in stunned silence. Thoughts skittered through his mind, thrust hints at him, dangled a conclusion he didn't want to believe. He dared another look at Alexandra, at the hostility in her eyes. "Stomach pains," Jackson had mumbled. Alexandra's voice echoed in Nicholas's head, too: "She would never be so ill if it weren't for you!" Why would Katherine refuse to allow Sarah in the room? Unless she didn't want Sarah to see and hear certain things?

Was Katherine pregnant? Losing the child?

"Good God, what have I done to her?" Nicholas whispered, forgetting Sarah and Alexandra's presence for a stricken instant. He ran a hand over his rough jaw, over his mouth.

Sarah was still so stunned that Katherine had not allowed her into the bedroom that she seemed to have missed his exclamation entirely. But Alexandra, on the heels of a sob, fled the library.

Nicholas knew he had guessed right.

Hours and many snifters of brandy later, he stood at the library window watching the sun descend over Lake Erie. Katherine loved the water so. She was lying somewhere above his head. He had no idea whether or not she teetered on death. He had not seen Lawrence since the man had taken the stairs two at a time behind Peggy upon hearing Katherine's cry of pain.

Sarah asked something so softly Nicholas couldn't define her words. He turned a questioning gaze on her. Her eyes rested gently on him from where she still sat in the chair.

Summer Storm

She twisted a handkerchief in her lap. "I said, you're in love with her, aren't you?"

He leaned against the window frame, hands in his trouser pockets, and listened to an autumn breeze rustle the crisp leaves on the ground just outside the window. He had never expected to have to tell her the truth during such dark circumstances, but the time had come, it seemed. "I am," he said.

She smiled sadly. "I've known, you know."

He inhaled deeply. "Have you?"

"Oh, yes. You spoke of her so fondly before she came home. Yet after she returned, you suddenly stopped mentioning her to me. I saw you in the gazebo looking at her the afternoon of the picnic. I even told you I saw you with her, then I waited. But you said nothing about it. And while you were dancing with her the night of the charity ball, the look on your face said she was the woman for you." She twisted the handkerchief more, pausing to brush a tear from her cheek. "Dear Nicholas, why didn't you just tell me? I'm not as fragile as you think. We've spent our lives together until now because our families have been close, but that does not mean we must marry. I realize you're a man devoted to your work and causes, but I don't want you to feel duty-bound to me."

Nicholas straightened, stunned by her revelation. All the time he and Katherine had been struggling to keep their feelings for each other from her, Sarah had known? "The day you told me you had seen me with Katherine in the gazebo, you knew?" he asked incredulously.

She nodded. "I knew."

"What a fool I've been," he said, shaking his head. "I was so scared that you knew. You paused as if—"

"As if giving you a chance to tell me?"

"Yes. But . . . I didn't know. Then you talked about the draft, how you had sent it to Katherine."

"Does she know you love her?" Sarah asked.

"Yes. She knows. I had planned to tell you soon that I couldn't go on with the engagement. I was waiting for some of the pain from your father's death to ease. Our marriage would have been a lie, for myself and you."

"And does Katherine love you?"

"I—"

Lawrence coughed as he entered, as if knowing they were discussing a private matter. Wondering how much the man had overheard, Nicholas opened his mouth to ask how Katherine was. Lawrence stopped him with an upheld hand as he settled in a chair near Sarah.

"Influenza. A terrible case. But she'll live," he said, and Nicholas knew by the way the man avoided his gaze that he had spoken a lie for Sarah's sake. But then, there was no reason Sarah should ever be told. If she knew he had made love to Katherine during his engagement to *her*—Nicholas looked away, disgusted with himself. More deceit. It was like a spool of thread. When the unraveling began, it seemed infinite.

"I'll stay, if the two of you don't mind," Lawrence said. "I want to look in on her now and then until morning."

Sarah nodded. "I'll go see if there's anything I can do to help Peggy and Alexandra." She quietly left the library.

Nicholas strode to Werner's desk and found paper and an ink blotter. Then he searched for a pen, finally finding one in a side drawer. "I'll write a note to Werner explaining. You will, of course, notify me if Katherine's condition changes?" Nicholas said, writing the explanation.

"I'll notify Sarah."

Glancing up, Nicholas found the man's cool gaze fastened on him.

"She cries your name in her sleep, are you aware of that?" Lawrence asked. There was a hard edge to his voice.

Nicholas stared at him an instant more, then turned his attention back to writing the note, not caring to discuss his and Katherine's relationship with Lawrence.

"You're the father, aren't you?"

Nicholas inhaled and exhaled deeply, glancing up again. He was grateful that the man had protected Katherine by claiming she was suffering from influenza, but he didn't think Lawrence would be receptive to his words of gratitude at the moment. "To answer your next question before you ask it—yes, I do plan to marry her."

Summer Storm

"Even now that she's lost the child?"

"I would marry her if there hadn't been a child."

Lawrence seemed to consider that. "She . . . uh . . . the pregnancy that is, was not far along. Perhaps not even three months."

Nicholas nodded, not knowing what to say. He wished to hold Katherine, to somehow soothe her and make everything all right again.

"Take Sarah home, then go home and rest yourself. I'll notify you," Lawrence said.

Nicholas finished the note, signed his name to it, and left the paper lying on Werner's desk. He met Sarah near the staircase, and they walked the half mile to her home since Jackson was still gone with the carriage.

"Will you be seeing her?" Sarah asked softly.

"I think I'll wait for some indication that she wants to see me," Nicholas answered. Katherine had been hurt in ways he couldn't possibly reveal to Sarah, first by his rejection of her, and now by the fact that months ago he hadn't been able to control his lust for her.

Sarah placed a hand on his arm. "You love her so. I wish you much happiness, Nicholas, you know that. I would be lying if I said I'm not disappointed, perhaps hurt, too. But I do wish you much happiness. Katherine is a wonderful person."

Nicholas nodded. They parted at the front entrance, Sarah looking after him, Nicholas going for the horse he had ridden here hours ago because he had given Harold a much deserved night off.

So it was done.

Sarah knew. And she wasn't crumbling as Nicholas had thought she might. As he swung himself up onto the horse, she waved good-bye.

Nicholas returned the gesture, then rode away.

19

ALEXANDRA BEGAN TUTORING three children almost every morning in a little back room Werner had once thought to use as an office. The children—two young boys and a girl of ten—were delighted with her. They learned rapidly, and that in turn delighted their parents.

The orphanage opened. The Garden Street Orphanage, Katherine called it. She spent much time there, despite Peggy's objection that only weeks had passed since the miscarriage. She cared for the five-year-old twin girls who had been delivered to her by Father Garrity from the Sisters of Charity Hospital where Sarah volunteered sometimes. The girls' parents had died during the long voyage from Ireland. Alexandra found time not only to continue her tutoring in the Kraus house, but also to take turns with Katherine teaching the Irish girls. Several nuns also volunteered to devote a great many of their days and nights to the orphanage.

Thanksgiving came and went, celebrated with a bounty of food spread across the dining room in the Kraus house. One evening Katherine sat in the parlor, staring at a glowing fire in the fireplace, her mind wandering to what Sarah had told her this afternoon: Sarah and Nicholas's engagement had been dissolved. The news had been kept quiet; people probably thought that since Alistair Preston had died, plans for the wedding quite naturally would be put off for some time. Sarah planned to start telling people the truth, however, knowing there would be some lifted brows and some skeptical looks, which would then cease with time. Sarah had enrolled in Oberlin; Nicholas was busy building his ship and never called. Sarah called less often of late, but when she did, she was always the same—talkative and filled with future plans to become a doctor, not at all the attitude Katherine expected of a woman whose world had recently been turned upside down.

"*You* broke the engagement?" Katherine asked hesitantly.

"Nicholas and I agreed that getting married would not be the best thing for us to do," Sarah said.

After that, nothing more was said on the subject. Sarah spoke of her nervousness about starting classes at the college. She was proud of the fact that she knew she would have had her father's support. "Most men expect women to do no more than stay home and do trivial things. Father was never like that."

Katherine was happy for Sarah, she really was. Sarah missed her father, probably always would, but at least she had found something to fill the void his death had left in her life.

Winter made its presence known.

Ice decorated the iron balcony railing outside Katherine's bedroom. The lawn, once so green and lush, barely peeked through the snow now. Trees were dark sentinels with powdered branches. The houses on Lake Street looked beautiful, their roofs and awnings sprinkled with white; snow clung to fences and piled on steps, covered walkways, and gathered in small drifts beside the houses. Horses and people inhaled frigid air and exhaled white smoke.

Lake Erie rose in fury at the assault. Northern wind roared across her, and she lashed at it, throwing herself at rocks, lurching at the embankment on the other side of the railroad opposite the Kraus house. Several times Katherine and Alexandra dared to cross the railroad and watch the lake. The great lady stretched, spotted them, and drove a blast of water at the bluff. As high up as Katherine and Alexandra were, the icy spray still reached them.

Katherine often wondered about Nicholas—what he was doing, if he was courting anyone now that he and Sarah had severed their relationship. She missed seeing him, she truly did, but as long as Sarah didn't seem to know that she and Nicholas had feelings for each other, she didn't want to see him any more than as friends for a time. Simply friends—if and when he ever called. If she and Nicholas suddenly took up with each other within months of his breakup with Sarah, wouldn't Sarah wonder if the two people she held in such high regard had deceived her while she and Nicholas were still engaged?

He came to the house for supper one evening. Finally. She hadn't known he was coming. She neared the bottom of the staircase, heard his laughter coming from the parlor, and paused. Suddenly the evening she had looked forward to spending with Alexandra and Uncle Werner was disturbed by the sudden pounding of her heart. She hadn't seen Nicholas since before the miscarriage. She wondered why he hadn't called; always before, he and Uncle Werner had gathered in the library here occasionally for business discussions. She wondered, too, if he knew about the pregnancy and the miscarriage from Kevin, who always called—Alexandra had confided in Kevin. But no, Kevin wouldn't have said anything to Nicholas. He knew how she felt about not wanting Nicholas forced to marry her.

She finally found the sense to set her feet in motion.

"Katherine," Nicholas said, as she quietly entered the parlor, almost as if saying it, seeing her, brought him a rush of relief. He seemed to feast on the sight of her.

Katherine gave him a weak smile, refusing to hold his warm gaze or encourage him. She really did not wish to take up with him again just yet.

Uncle Werner and Alexandra didn't seem to hear his odd, almost intimate tone, or else didn't perceive it as being so; Alexandra gave a sweet smile and moved to make room for her on the red-velvet settee. Uncle Werner greeted her with a nod and his usual comment about how lovely she looked. Nicholas's eyes were now fastened on the brandy swirling in the glass he held.

Soon they all moved to the dining room.

"How are you?" Nicholas asked Katherine over supper.

"Fine," she responded. "Recovered from that bout with influenza." She lifted a wineglass to her lips and watched him over the rim, needing to know if he knew she had not suffered from influenza at all but something very different.

He nodded, then forked another piece of glazed pheasant and casually lifted it to his mouth. Uncle Werner said something about having some remodeling done at the bank. Nicholas agreed that it would be a good idea.

Katherine sipped her wine. So he didn't know about the pregnancy or miscarriage. She felt strangely disappointed. She would have been embarrassed for Nicholas to know that she hadn't been able, for whatever reason, to carry their child—though Lawrence had assured her there was no reason she could not have other children—and yet she longed to find comfort in his embrace. The child *had* been theirs after all.

She and Alexandra exchanged glances. Alexandra didn't like Nicholas, had made no secret of her feelings after the miscarriage. Her gaze darted between Katherine and Nicholas. She looked as if she wanted to leap up and pull Katherine from the room, to safety from the man Katherine loved. How absurd. Katherine hoped Alexandra would stay quiet. And in her chair.

"Seeing you, and Alexandra and Werner, at the New Year's gala at the Forest City House would be nice," Nicholas said, speaking to Katherine again.

It was just a suggestion. Though a rather strong one, Katherine thought. He wanted to be with her socially. He wanted to escort her places. How she would love to go with him. But it was too soon after his engagement—she wanted no scandalous talk—so she declined, dropping her gaze to her plate. "I'll be spending New Year's Eve and Day at the orphanage," she said.

Nodding slowly, Nicholas abandoned the subject and turned his attention back to Uncle Werner.

He came twice more for supper during the next few weeks. Always he asked how she felt. Always she answered with short responses, tiring of his queries about her health and not wanting to encourage his attempts to become intimate with her. The atmosphere between them was awkward to begin with; it grew more so. Dear Uncle Werner cast odd looks her way now and then, as if realizing that something had happened between her and Nicholas. But he was tactful enough not to ask questions, and respectful enough of her obvious discomfort not to leave her alone with Nicholas.

Nicholas came for more suppers, and more, obviously not content to have him and Katherine appear just friends for now. He wanted to hurry into much more. For the first time since coming home, she wanted to abide by the unspoken constraints of society.

So she began to avoid him, conveniently being absent from the house at the supper hour. She spent evenings instead of days at the Garden Street Orphanage with Colleen and Margaret, the Irish girls. Other than that, she didn't go out to do much more than shop sometimes with Alexandra or Peggy. Weeks passed during which she didn't see Nicholas at all. At the theater she most certainly might have or at Chapin Hall, where popular concerts were held on occasion; but the whole appeal to Katherine, months ago, of Cleveland's social side had been in the thought that she would go to every theater production, every ball, every picnic, every supper or party, on Nicholas's arm. But since that simply wouldn't be the right thing to do yet, she didn't attend the affairs. She ignored invitations and often declined to accompany Uncle Werner and Alexandra to events. They simply smiled and went about their business. No one asked questions, no one demanded anything.

Except Nicholas.

Uncle Werner convinced Katherine to go to dinner with him one day. She was to meet him at Kraus Saving and Trust, and from there they would go to a quiet place. But when she arrived, there was Nicholas, leaning casually against a window frame. He had folded his arms across his chest and had removed his coat, revealing a green brocade vest. Uncle Werner leaned back leisurely in the chair behind his desk, his hands clasped behind his head. The two men had obviously been sharing an informal but nonetheless entertaining conversation.

Summer Storm

"Oh, I'm sorry," Katherine said, starting to back out. "We'll make it another day, Uncle Werner. You look busy."

Nicholas straightened. His eyes shone, as if he might be somewhat angry or at least irritated. "Don't let me run you off. I was just leaving."

Katherine paused.

He snatched his coat from the back of a chair before the desk, and his top hat from the chair seat, placing the hat on his head at a slant. This was the only time she had ever seen him wear a hat; she'd only seen him carrying one. But now he seemed to need to make a big show of preparing to leave, arranging not only the hat on his head, but his coat about his shoulders as well, smoothing the sleeves, yanking at the ends. "Have a good afternoon, Werner. Katherine." He moved across the room toward her and the door and paused at her side. "We *will* talk soon," he told her in a low voice. "With or without others about."

He sounded determined, which only made her more reluctant to see or talk to him. She didn't want an angry confrontation, with him demanding to see her on a social basis, her not wishing to see him just yet. Surely, at some point of frustration, he would simply give up. But the words he'd spoken the night of the charity supper and ball flashed through her mind: "I've never given up on anything in my life." She wished he would, just this once.

Uncle Werner never asked what Nicholas had said as he passed her, or why Nicholas had left in such a hurry, or even why *she'd* been eager to leave when she'd first walked in. Again, Uncle Werner was a dear.

One evening as she sat in the parlor at home, she stared into the orange and gold flames in the fireplace. Uncle Werner had gone out. Alexandra had gone up to bed, complaining of a cold.

The fire popped. Peggy's voice came from somewhere behind Katherine. "Married or not, ye wanted the babe?" The gentle tone of Peggy's voice revealed that the question was not one of condemnation, but rather one of concern.

Katherine and Peggy's relationship had taken a turn the night of the miscarriage. Peggy was patient, even pleasant, much of the time. Katherine was relieved but still uncertain why the change had taken place. She didn't think a little compassion could alter such a stubborn Irishwoman's thinking. But compassion was the only reason to which she could attribute the delightful change. She had moments when she marveled over the fact that Peggy knew her deepest secret, and could have ruined her with a few words in a way even Uncle Werner could not have remedied, but had told no one anything.

Katherine fought tears. Married or not, had she wanted the babe? Oh, yes . . . Oh, yes. The pregnancy had been nearly three months along, Dr. Preston had told her. She had never even felt the child move, had known nothing more than the fact that it had been growing inside her womb. And yet . . . a great sadness sometimes gripped her when she least expected it. Perhaps when she was reading a book, or writing a letter, never when she gazed at a small child or a bundle she knew was an infant.

"I did want it. Very much," Katherine finally answered truthfully. "Even if I had to go away to avoid talk that might have hurt Uncle Werner."

"I lost a babe once."

Katherine turned to look at Peggy, who was standing just inside the door. Shadows fell across her, but Katherine saw a flicker of emotion in her eyes. Their gazes locked. The moment was one of deep understanding. Peggy had lost a babe? Peggy, who as far as Katherine knew had never been married? That explained the change in the housekeeper of late. That explained her compassion, the tears Katherine had seen in Peggy's eyes that terrible night.

"Ye must love Mr. Cummin's a great deal, to risk the disgrace," Peggy said. "Ye were lucky that evil-mouthed Dr. Birk didn't come along. Had ye uncle been here, miss, that's how it would 'ave gone. Mr. Kraus can't see the viper's tongue. But I can. I can."

Katherine was shocked that Peggy knew who the father was. Love must have shown on her face countless times; that, and perhaps she had babbled in feverish sleep those nights after the miscarriage when Peggy alone had cared for her. Many times she had awakened to Peggy's gentle hand, touching her brow, bathing her with cool water, changing soiled sheets.

"Thank you for not saying a word of anything you saw that night. Thank you for helping Dr. Preston. Thank you for not condemning me."

"How could I condemn ye? Ye're a good strong Irishwoman, Katherine McDaniel. No matter that only half Irish flows in your veins. Ye're Irish to be sure and you'll find a way through this. The Irish 'ave been through worse," Peggy said, then slipped from the room to the sound of a winter wind rattling the windowpanes.

20

NICHOLAS FLUNG AN unfinished cheroot at a spittoon in a corner of his study and spun around in disbelief. "Are you sure, Harold?"

Harold stood stiffly near the closed door, gripping his hat before him with both hands. "Quite sure, sir. Disturbing news, I know—"

"Thirty-seven men," Nicholas muttered. "Thirty-seven!"

"Including Professors Fitch and Peck, and most of the others who conspired to kidnap the fugitive from the slave catcher in Columbus and ship him on the Underground," Harold said.

Nicholas crossed to the sideboard and poured a goblet of port. He lifted the glass to his lips with trembling hands, then anger got the better of him. He hurled the glass at the fireplace. It crashed on the stones and shattered to the hearth in a million pieces. "*Most,*" he bit out. "*That* is the word here. Tell me why I was not arrested, Harold. Tell me, would you?"

"Only a few know that you are a conductor, Mr. Cummings. And you will serve the fugitives better if you leave it so."

Rounding the sideboard, Nicholas narrowed his eyes. "While thirty-seven of my colleagues are awaiting arraignment, I should keep my mouth shut? Is that what you're advising me to do?"

Harold fidgeted with the hat, looking decidedly uncomfortable. "Yes. I have been told to advise you to do exactly that, sir, if you wish to continue to be of assistance to the fugitives.

One word that you were involved—"

"Advised? By whom?"

"By someone who has been working with the Underground for more than a decade. Like yourself, sir, he's quite an influential man in the community. He risks a great deal to provide havens for the fugitives."

Nicholas often had no idea where the fugitives had been before Harold brought them to him for transport to Canada. Definitely some came from Oberlin, but what about others? He had never wondered before—his aim had always been getting the fugitives to safety—but Harold's mysteriousness made him curious now. "Who is the man?"

"Sir, I . . . I would rather not say, sir," Harold said, faltering in speech for the first time in the three years he had been with Nicholas.

"Can I not be trusted?" Nicholas demanded, rather offended.

"It is not—"

"You've no idea what I'm feeling right now. No idea! Thirty-seven people are sitting in the city jail at this moment, and this man, this . . . *advisor,* wants me to stay quiet. Thirty-seven lives I care about. My first thought was to go yank them out, put them back where they belong. They're good men who tried to help other men. By doing so, they may have put nooses around their own necks. I at least want to see them."

"That would not be a wise thing to do."

"As you have been *advised* to advise me." Nicholas's voice dripped sarcasm.

Harold again fumbled with his hat, rolled the narrow rim, pushed the top in a bit. Nicholas scowled at it. Harold hid the irritating, distracting object behind his back and cleared his throat. "You should not accept any more fugitives until next fall either. By then the trials will have been held, excitement will have died some."

Nicholas's jaw dropped open. *"Next fall?"*

"Yes, sir."

"More advice?"

Harold stared straight ahead.

Nicholas strode back to the sideboard. This time he drank the glass of port he poured, glancing intermittently from the painting of Public Square hanging above the fireplace to Harold.

"May I go now, sir?" The question reached Nicholas just as his eyes returned to the painting.

"Go then," he said, his mind set. He had always disliked anyone telling him what to do. His next words came more out of defiance than anything: "Go and tell your contact I plan to ship every fugitive who comes my way during the next year. I plan to enlist counsel for my friends, too."

Harold inhaled swiftly. "Mr. Cummings, you risk—"

"I damn well know the risk. Go. Now."

Harold nodded, then turned and exited the study.

Nicholas moved to the window, sinking into an upholstered chair there. Thirty-seven men... arrested for breaking the Fugitive Slave Law, arrested for helping a man to freedom. The law had been passed by a hypocritical government, a government that had been so since its beginning. Not one hundred years before, a roomful of men had signed their names to these words: "We hold these truths to be self-evident, that all men are created equal, that they are endowed by their Creator with certain unalienable rights, that among these are Life, Liberty, and the pursuit of Happiness." Some of the men who had signed had been slave owners. Why then had the sentence not been written "... that all *white* men are created equal..."? Why?

Nicholas was still sitting near the window, debating the question, when he heard the clip-clop of a horse's hooves and turned in time to watch Harold ride away on horseback.

The next evening, Harold came to the study again. "He wants to see you, sir."

Nicholas looked up from a ledger, brows arched "My advisor?"

"Yes, sir."

Nicholas closed the book. "Then let's not keep the man waiting."

Out in the hall he tossed a woolen greatcoat over his shoulders while Harold waited patiently by the front entrance.

Summer Storm

Nicholas soon found himself standing before his parents' home, staring at the classical structure he visited rarely. "Harold, I'm in no mood for jokes," he said. "Either take me to meet the man or take me home."

"You will be meeting him right here, sir. You see," Harold said, stepping up beside him, " 'the man' is Lemuel Cummings."

Moments of thick silence passed. Nicholas stared at Harold. "My father?" he finally managed to say. "A man who has upheld slavery all these years? The very man who lashed me with angry words because I embarrassed him after his friend ordered the death of a Negro man? No, Harold, you're mistaken."

"No mistake, Mr. Cummings. He is waiting for you, sir, in the library. I am certain he will explain everything, how he came to be doing this, why he kept it from you . . ."

Nicholas started for the front steps. The library of his parents' home was the last place he wanted to be. But he also wanted to get to the bottom of this. He breathed deeply. "This should be interesting," he mumbled, still not believing his eyes or his ears. "Quite interesting."

He found Lemuel seated behind a huge desk. Sharp memories came back to Nicholas. He was a boy of fifteen. He had been summoned by the all-powerful man who was his father, and he was coming before this desk for yet another tongue lashing, this time for missing supper last evening. By preferring to be off at a shipyard with his friends, he had also missed the guests. And he had embarrassed Lemuel Cummings. Embarrassment always enraged the man. Always.

But this room was different from the one Nicholas remembered well. This one had two windows, not three. Thick curtains, not wisps of material billowed from a morning breeze. A scant supply of shelves, not walls of shelves, were filled with books. Nicholas's shoes clicked across the bare floor. The room he remembered had been carpeted. Only the desk was the same here. Oh, yes . . . the desk. It was the one Lemuel Cummings had lurked behind for years.

Nicholas blinked. This was the house on Euclid; the earlier one, the one containing the library with three windows and the walls of shelves and the carpeted floor, had been on Superior Avenue, back when it had been Superior Street. And some years ago Lemuel had donated much of his collection of books to the Library Association.

Still, Nicholas *had* been summoned by the man, and the figure behind the desk *was* as dark as ever; dark and hazed by swirling smoke. Nicholas fought a shiver of apprehension as the deeply shadowed figure of Lemuel Cummings rose, rounded the desk, and held forth a hand.

The gesture spoke of Lemuel's respect. The way he had come around to this side of the desk did, too. His eyes were not lit with a father's fury. No . . . this time they were lit with admiration.

"I am honored that you have come. You are highly respected by those involved with the Underground," he said.

Nicholas stared for another instant, then took Lemuel's hand.

"Come. We will sit together. I have wine, brandy, whiskey, whatever you prefer," Lemuel said, as they parted hands. He moved to a small table cluttered with decanters.

Nicholas took a chair opposite another near a shelf. "Port, if you have it."

Moments later, Lemuel joined him, holding forth a goblet of wine. Nicholas waited for his father to settle himself in his chair, a million questions threatening to spill from his lips.

"I offered my assistance to the Underground the year you went off to Oberlin," Lemuel said, his raspy voice filling the dim room. "For years I had listened to you talk about the bondage of Negroes. I was as horrified as you were when Justin Shannon ordered that slave whipped in South Carolina."

"Samuel," Nicholas whispered.

"Samuel . . . I had forgotten his name. But like you I never forgot his screams. I had never seen a human . . . tortured like that. I was horrified."

"But you watched."

Lemuel jerked a nod. "I watched. By Justin's side, I watched. I asked him to end it, to give the word and end it. He refused. His property, he said. If he did not show the other slaves what would happen if they ran, they would run."

Nicholas's hand nearly crushed the goblet. "You asked him to stop?"

"I did."

"Then why were you so enraged when I called him a murderer that evening? Why did you drag me from the room? And what of the many arguments that followed?"

"I was trying to convince myself that Justin was right. He had been a friend for so long. I did not want to believe him capable of such a thing, of murder. You were right. And because you were right, I unleashed my anger on you, not on Justin. For four years I lived with the guilt of that man's death. Still, I tried to convince myself that Justin had had every right to do what he had done. I never succeeded."

"So you joined the Underground," Nicholas said, piecing facts together. "Why didn't you tell me?"

"I met Harold. You met him years later, of course, and hired him. Why did I not tell you? When you came home from Oberlin, you were filled with more stubbornness than ever. You told me you wanted nothing more to do with me or Cummings' Ironworks. Then you proceeded to *prove* that you wanted nothing to do with either. You would hardly talk to me, much less listen to anything I had to say."

"Why now? Why?" Nicholas had to ask.

"Because the years have tempered you some . . . You are still determined, but not as stubborn. And because you asked to see me," Lemuel said.

Nicholas sipped wine, watching the lamplights flicker on his father's deeply lined face. The man was old, old and weary. As he reached for his pipe and tobacco box from a nearby table, he moved more slowly than Nicholas remembered. Or perhaps he moved that way for years, Nicholas thought. He's been old for some time, and I'm just now noticing. The years had rolled by, leaving a skeleton of the strong, vibrant man Lemuel Cummings had once been.

Nicholas recalled his sharp words to Lemuel in the Forest City House some months ago, when they had been dining with Werner, and guilt singed him. He had jumped to conclusions, assuming the only part of the newspaper Lemuel ever read was the Board of Trade reports. Perhaps the man read the front page during quiet moments.

"The years have hardly 'tempered' me," Nicholas mumbled, feeling a stab of what could only be called shame.

"Oh, they have tempered you. You do not jump as quickly as you used to," Lemuel said, as if reading his thoughts.

"What's being done for the men who've been arrested?" Nicholas asked.

"Volunteers are coming forward to defend them. Keep quiet about this, Nicholas. Observe. Do not ship fugitives for a time, at least until eyes are taken off the Underground. We all knew the risk when we got involved. I know that does not make this any easier, but what good will you do the Underground if you are sitting in jail with those men?"

"I gave that man passage."

"And you will be available for others if you keep quiet."

Lemuel went on to speak about the success of the Underground in Cleveland. As soon as the many sets of condemning eyes were taken off this part of the country, movements would begin again. Lemuel named at least ten friends who had, at one time or another, hidden fugitives in the basement of their homes, entrusting them to Harold, who then took them to Nicholas. Putting the Negroes in the *Ontario*'s hold had worked well, Nicholas said. Lemuel agreed.

They were co-conspirators, Nicholas thought, finally facing each other respectfully, agreeing on the one issue that had seared them both to the soul so many years ago.

Night deepened, but Nicholas was in no hurry to leave. He drank more port and smiled at Lemuel's story of how he had met Werner some forty years ago. Lemuel had lifted Werner from the mud out near where the track was now, after Werner had gotten himself into a scrape. "Over a woman!" Lemuel said, chuckling. "I would never believe it if I were just meeting Werner today."

"That is hard to believe," Nicholas agreed.

Lemuel sobered, studying him. "You have done well for yourself," he said. "I have never told you that, but you have done well."

The words touched Nicholas more than he had thought words from his father ever could. "Thank you," he said through his constricted throat. "Thank you."

21

ON CHRISTMAS EVE morning, Katherine awoke to Uncle Werner and Mr. Baum's robust singing. The men had secluded themselves in the library and were having a jolly time if the sound of their festive German songs was any indication.

Over breakfast, with the voices booming through the house, Alexandra gave Katherine a look of amused confusion. Katherine laughed and said, "Mr. Baum. He comes to share beer and the old songs with Uncle Werner. That's all I know. I've never met the man. I've no idea what he even looks like."

"It is a wonder they do not go hoarse," Alexandra said, smiling.

Katherine gave Alexandra a box of pearl-studded combs she and Peggy had selected. Alexandra gasped with delight, embraced Katherine, then pressed a gift into her hand. Katherine untied the green ribbon around the small white box, opened it, and stared at the brass model of a simple boat without masts or rigging.

"Very much like the one we used to spend Saturday mornings in, don't you think?" Alexandra asked, her devilish blue eyes sparkling.

"Oh, yes, very much," Katherine murmured, emotion catching in her voice. The expensive combs seemed like nothing compared to the inexpensive paperweight.

Kevin called that afternoon and convinced Katherine to go skating with them. She had a marvelous time, whizzing across the ice in the most unladylike manner, with first Kevin, then Alexandra. Kevin amused them by skating backward, then on one skate, then by making circles on the ice. He and Alexandra were Katherine's best friends. They had lifted her spirits many times during the weeks after she'd lost the baby, making her smile when she didn't especially want to smile.

Kevin placed a hand lightly on Alexandra's waist, and the two skated off together. Katherine smiled, watching them. They were so happy, obviously so much in love. Remembering the rumors she'd heard about Kevin and her own first encounter with him aboard the *Morning Star,* she knew what a womanizer he could be. Alexandra had heard stories, too, but often laughed about them and said, "Kevin seems so devoted, I can hardly believe the things some of the women whisper about him. He excites them, I know that. I've seen the looks in their eyes when he bends over their hands."

"Are you jealous when he does?" Katherine asked on one occasion, feeling certain Kevin's womanizing days had ended as soon as he'd laid eyes on Alexandra.

"Jealousy is most unbecoming, Miss McDaniel," Alexandra said, repeating the favorite saying of one of the nuns at the school.

"Oh, most, Miss Owens. Most." But the flicker in Alexandra's pretty eyes was revealing: She most certainly was jealous, despite the teachings of Sister Dorothy.

When Katherine and Alexandra tired of skating, Kevin took them to the ice-cream parlor on the street level of a three-story brownstone building known as The Chapin Block. The ice cream was delicious, but more chilling than the frigid wind outside.

"What a mad thing to do!" Alexandra said, laughing. "Ice cream in the middle of winter!"

Katherine and Kevin laughed with her as the three of them started out the door of the building, to join the crowd of people traipsing through the snow-covered walkways and streets.

"Ooh, that dress!" Alexandra's eyes fastened on a shop across the street.

Kevin grabbed her hand and pulled her along. "Let's go see. Katherine, come on!"

"Oh, no," Katherine said. "I'm going to the carriage to escape the wind."

Kevin and Alexandra raced off. Katherine smiled at their eagerness, then turned to walk toward the carriage.

Suddenly her smile withered and died. Nicholas and an older man walked straight toward her, or rather walked toward the front entrance of The Chapin Block, the shoulders and sleeves of their greatcoats powdered with snow. Was the man Nicholas's father? Yes. Katherine remembered the face from the night she'd learned of Nicholas and Sarah's engagement, though how she managed to remember a face from that terrible night, she didn't know. Both men's strides were long and quick. In a moment, Nicholas and his father would reach her.

Nicholas's eyes found hers. His steps ceased, while the steps of the elder Mr. Cummings continued, then slowed as he looked back in question at Nicholas. Finally he followed the path of Nicholas's eyes and gave Katherine a studied look.

Then Nicholas moved again, coming toward her. He paused to say something to his father. The man strode toward her, gave a nod of acknowledgement, then swept past into the building.

Nicholas approached. "Hello, Katherine," he said, halting before her. "You look well."

She lowered her eyes to her gray muff and sighed. Conversation about her health again. "I am."

A moment passed.

Strong fingers lifted her chin. She tried to move it up and away, but his hold was tenacious. "Look at me," he said softly, firmly.

"Do you mind? We're in the middle of a busy walkway. Must we—"

"We must. There seems to be no other way with you."

"Oh, Nicholas."

"I said look at me."

She did. And she found herself staring into his most beautiful emerald eyes fringed with dark lashes. "What do you want?" she asked, annoyed by the excitement that shot through her jaw and down her neck to slither along her spine. What a stupid thing to ask. She knew what he wanted. He wanted to see her more. Now. Take her places. Act as if nothing had happened, as if Sarah's feelings didn't matter, as if people wouldn't gossip. How easily he drifted from one woman to another, unconcerned about decency. He might at least wait until spring or even summer.

"Are you? Well, that is." His breath, soft puffs of white, swirled not four inches from her face.

"We've had this same conversation numerous times. Do I look ill?" she demanded, exasperated.

"You look pale. Let me take you to the New Year's gala."

"The implication being that allowing you to do so will bring a flush of happiness to my face?"

"You're being stubborn."

"You're being persistent. I already declined."

"You could change your mind."

"Could, but won't." She finally wrestled her chin free. "I plan to have an open house for the orphanage benefactors soon," she said. "You'll be invited to that, of course."

He nodded. Another moment of silence ensued. The usual noise of mingling people, hawkers, horses, and opening and closing doors swirled around them.

"I have a meeting inside . . . ," he said, leaving the information hanging as if waiting for her to change her mind about the New Year's festivity.

But she wouldn't. She was determined to be everything she was expected to be as the niece of an important Cleveland citizen. "Then go. I won't keep you."

"No, I don't imagine you will. Are you really so cold inside, Katherine? Have you really become so . . . indifferent to me?"

"I'm not cold at all," she murmured, hurt by his remark. "I'm simply putting my life together the best way I know how. Please permit me to do that."

"Please permit me to be part of your life. No one could have predicted what happened. No one is to blame."

Her gaze snapped to his, so deep, so soft, gentle, loving, and she saw that he knew . . . He knew about the pregnancy and the miscarriage. Her heart quickened. "This isn't the place. I don't want to talk—"

"Of course not. You would rather run."

"I'm not running," she objected. "I'm merely trying, for once, to abide by what people expect of me. You're making things difficult."

He gave a laugh that sounded strangely like a snort of bitterness. "I'm making things difficult for *you*? You've no idea the hell you're putting me through," he whispered fiercely. "My God. I want to see you. Hold you."

Katherine flushed, despite the frigid temperature. People were beginning to stare. She was doing her best to avoid gossip; standing here quarreling with Nicholas would cause it.

She turned away, started off. The cab, where was the cab? Others were lined up before the building. She stood on tiptoe to try to see over the tops of them. She couldn't.

Nicholas grabbed hold of her elbow. "I am sick to death of you avoiding me."

"Then stop trying to see me. And let go before I call to an officer." She felt as if she were unraveling inside. Her stomach had tightened, and she could hardly catch her breath. She was too vulnerable to his touch, his mere gaze. *Where is the cab?*

"You would do that?" he asked, obviously a bit flustered himself now.

"I would."

"What will it take to make you want to see me again, Katherine? Me making a total fool of myself? I'll do that if—"

"Wait, Nicholas! Can't you wait?" she snapped, jerking her elbow from his grasp. She spotted the cab finally and hurried toward it, hoping she didn't slip on a patch of ice or tumble forward into the snow. She held her breath, half-expecting Nicholas to pursue her. He didn't.

Once inside the cab with the door shut, she tried to slow her breathing, tried to compose herself. She was trembling. The

Summer Storm

heavy, dank smell of leather, silk, and velvet was a welcome one, a haven. God. Why did he persist?

Presently Kevin and Alexandra joined her. "What's the matter?" Alexandra asked almost immediately.

Katherine forced a smile. "I'm too easy to read, I think."

"You're pale," Kevin said.

Katherine rolled her eyes. "I saw . . . an acquaintance. He said the same thing. I do wish everyone would stop worrying about my health!"

Alexandra's eyes widened. "Nicholas."

Katherine glanced out the cab window, at the people flowing in and out of The Chapin Block. Greatcoats were powdered with snow. Folds of pelisses and wraps were gathered close to ensure warmth. Cashmere shawls were wrapped two and three times around necks. Heads were lowered to ward off the wind.

"The devil! I would shoot him myself, if I did not think you should be the one to do it," Alexandra hissed.

"Oh, stop," Katherine scolded.

Kevin gave Alexandra a sharp look. She settled back on the seat. "What did he say? Anything?" he asked Katherine.

"Hello. You look well. I have a meeting inside. Trivial, inconsequential things," Katherine lied, removing her hands from her muff. She didn't care to go through the scene again. She rubbed her cheeks for warmth. "Let's go. I want to go home."

Kevin tapped on the ceiling. An instant later, the cab jolted forward. "I'm thinking you sound like a child," he said, watching her. " 'I want to go home.' Home . . . to hide yourself away forever, girl? How long do you think you can hide behind walls and doors?"

"Kevin!" Alexandra objected.

Katherine glared at him, unable to believe he was speaking so sharply to her. He had never done such a thing. "As long as I want! What would you have me do? I am trying—"

"You could run back to Sandusky and live among the nuns," he said softly, evenly, without so much as a blink.

The words hung in the silence that followed.

"How dare you!" Katherine finally found the sense to gasp. His words rudely reminded her of Nicholas's.

He tossed his head about, then finally brought his heated gaze back to hers. "Oh, poor Katherine. The pretense that you're always working at the orphanage or that you're still recovering from influenza will only be believed so long. It's been two months since your 'illness.' People want to see Werner Kraus's niece. Stop ignoring invitations. Stop feeling sorry for yourself. Live again, as an 'acquaintance' once said to me," he said fiercely.

Katherine couldn't hold his gaze any longer. Not when she knew he was right. Until recently, she'd never hidden herself away—and that was exactly what she had been doing. Kevin was risking their friendship to jolt her back to reality. He was making her see that by trying to avoid gossip, she was going to cause it.

Alexandra stirred on the seat beside her. Katherine glanced over, knowing Alexandra well enough to realize what the flush to her fair complexion meant. Alexandra opened her mouth to scald Kevin with words. Katherine stopped her with a sharp "No," then turned her gaze to Kevin again. "Thank you," she said sincerely.

He jerked a nod.

The remainder of the ride to the Kraus home was spent in silence.

In January, Lake Erie slept. Ice flows wandered dangerously in her water, and ships could not sail or steam without the very real threat of succumbing to her frigid depths. They huddled together in the ice-coated Cuyahoga River, sometimes shivering when the wind whistled over the lake and whipped down the channel. Katherine and Alexandra often braved winter to cross Lake Street, gaze at Lake Erie, and listen to tree branches scratch together overhead. Their boots left prints in the snow; their white breath wandered away on the soft whispers of swirling winds.

Kevin and Alexandra saw Emerson at Melodeon Hall. They bubbled about the event for days, in between poring over

Summer Storm 239

editions of *Harpers,* the popular magazine. Katherine would be seated in Uncle Werner's library reading and suddenly hear their laughter and merry conversation coming from the parlor just down the hall.

February brought an invitation to the annual mayor's ball to be held in late April. Katherine remembered Nicholas's and Kevin's words and without consulting Uncle Werner or Alexandra, she answered the invitation before she had a chance to shrink back into her protective shell.

She forced herself to drop a note into Mr. Jackson's outstretched hand, thank him quickly, then turn away. Moments later she drew aside a brocade parlor curtain and watched him ride off on horseback, her acceptance tucked in his pocket.

Days later, Katherine stepped from the parlor at the precise moment Peggy was closing the front door. Peggy glanced down at the envelope she held. The color drained from her face.

"What is it?" Katherine asked, feeling the first cold trickle of alarm along her spine.

"It's . . ." Peggy paused as if digesting the enormous meaning of what she held. "Well, it's from a James Owens. Alexandra's father, I'm thinkin'."

Katherine inhaled deeply. Whatever was inside that envelope could decide Alexandra's future. "Is it?"

Peggy nodded. "It's addressed to Mr. Kraus."

"We'll leave it on his desk then," Katherine said, having too much respect for Uncle Werner to pry into something addressed specifically to him. But the thought did cross her mind.

It crossed Peggy's too, apparently. Her eyes skittered about too much, from the letter to the tiled floor to Katherine and back to the letter. "Yes, that's what we'll do then," Peggy finally said softly. "I want to know, but I don't, ye know?"

Katherine nodded. Then Peggy left to place the letter in its rightful place.

Early that evening Uncle Werner summoned Katherine and Alexandra to the library. Katherine knew, by his solemn expression, that the news was not good. Still, her jaw dropped open when Uncle Werner, shifting in his chair, stated James Owens's demand.

Alexandra said nothing at first. Katherine drew a cashmere shawl more securely about her shoulders, folded her arms, and paced before the fireplace. The man was cold and unfeeling . . . cruel, just as Alexandra had always said! He couldn't be serious. He couldn't be!

Alexandra eventually sank into a chair before Uncle Werner's desk. Her face was colorless, her hands tangled in her lap. "I will not . . . no . . . never! He is mad!" she said, finally finding her voice.

The man *is* mad, Katherine thought. "Marriage to a man she's never laid eyes on!" she blurted, not aiming the outburst at anyone in particular. "How can he demand such a thing? For his own gain, no doubt. There must be money involved, perhaps a favor or two. Perhaps many. I don't imagine he even thought to ask if she's met anyone during the time she's been here?"

Werner Kraus tapped a forefinger on the unfolded letter lying on his desk, wondering what he could do. Judging from Owens's harsh tone, the man had no use for his daughter. But Werner would not tell Alexandra or Katherine that. He could not imagine why any parent would speak so hatefully about his own child. The two-page letter described what a disobedient girl Alexandra had been and would always be. "Marriage will help," Owens wrote, "and one to a man named Simon Hastings has been arranged for her here. Pack her things and send her this way."

Werner agreed with Katherine's assumption: James Owens was eager to make this match, which meant something beyond the ordinary marriage arrangement must be involved. A *schema*.

"I will not go," Alexandra said again, shaking her head slowly as if stunned.

Of course the girl was stunned, Werner thought. He more than suspected that she was in love with Kevin Riley. He knew. He had seen them gaze at each other enough times. She and Katherine had a theater engagement planned with

Mr. Riley this evening. Knowing Alexandra was promised to another man, Werner knew the right thing to do would be to tell Alexandra she could no longer see Mr. Riley. But Werner did not have the heart to do that.

"I will write back and ask him to change his mind. I will do what I can, Alexandra," he promised. Then he asked boldly, "Has Mr. Riley proposed?"

"No," she said, glancing up. "But he will. I know he will."

Werner coughed, not liking what needed to be said next, but he wanted her to be prepared, in the event Kevin Riley was not leaning toward marriage. "Mr. Riley has been known as something of a charmer of women. I would not want you to—"

"That stopped when he met me. He loves me, I know it." Her eyes flashed. "Perhaps I should look for a room at a nice boardinghouse, Mr. Kraus. I know I have put you in an awkward position. I could take a teaching position somewhere and stay with the family of one of the children. That is done often."

He shook his head. "No, no. Stay here, Alexandra. You have never been a burden. I will do what I can," he promised again.

But he was not sure how much influence he could wield over a man he didn't even know.

22

ALEXANDRA LEFT MR. KRAUS and Katherine in the library. Never! She would not go to Chicago and marry that man! She did not know how she would go about marrying Kevin without her father's permission, but she would find a way.

She thought of telling Kevin about her father's demand. What would he say? Would he propose?

She did not know, she just did not know.

Other than an occasional passionate kiss, he never made any overtures. But he cared, she knew he cared! She had seen love in his eyes during the many times she had caught him staring at her. But she had seen something else now and then, too.

Fear.

Yes, no matter his light attitude much of the time, Kevin Riley was deeply frightened of something.

What was it that flickered in his eyes and made him grow quiet whenever she whispered that she loved him? She wished she knew. He was always a gentlemen, taking her here, taking her there, reading to her and listening to her read. But there was always that fear when she encouraged Kevin to share things about himself.

She wanted to break through whatever kept all of him from her. She wanted to penetrate what sealed his lips at times when she was certain a proposal was about to burst from him. She wanted to convince him that he could confide in her about whatever frightened him so.

Summer Storm 243

Dear Kevin, she thought desperately as she dressed for the theater, you can trust me!

All through the first, second, and third acts of *The School for Scandal* she watched him from the corner of her eye. He sat to her left, Katherine to her right. Not one of them laughed at the comical scenes.

Alexandra tried to concentrate on the movements and voices of the actors and actresses. Soft gaslights flickered about the theater. Plush red curtains had been drawn to either side of the stage, which sloped toward the orchestra pit. There, a shadowed conductor presided. So many things with which to distract herself, and yet she never really succeeded. Numerous times throughout the evening her eyes drifted back to Kevin. His slightly crooked nose, his full lips, the freckles splashed here and there, the hair curling at his nape . . . He was wonderfully handsome in a distinct way, having the rather harsh Irish features, but a certain gentleness lurked beneath the harshness. A part of her would die if she lost him. She loved him desperately, more than anything.

She was glad when the play ended. All she wanted to do was go home and spend some private moments with Kevin before he left her for the night. She met Katherine's gaze as they filed out of the theater. Katherine smiled gently, sympathetically, as if knowing her thoughts and fears.

Once they reached the Kraus house, Katherine bid a hasty good night and disappeared upstairs, leaving Alexandra alone with Kevin in the parlor.

Alexandra took his hand, stroked the masculine fingers, then kissed his palm. Kevin drew a swift breath. He cupped her chin, drawing her gaze to his. He stared, searching . . . For what? she wondered. Surely her love of him showed on her face and in her eyes. If he couldn't see it, he was blind. She felt excitement for him in the rapid beat of her heart, in the way her blood warmed in her veins as his hand caressed her jaw, then slipped to her neck to touch the pounding pulse there.

His eyes slitted, became glazed. They shifted to the swell of her breasts above the decolletage of her dark blue gown. The brazen look stole Alexandra's breath.

"I'm thinking you're filled with fire tonight, girl," he said, his gaze drifting back to her face.

"Yes . . . oh, yes," she whispered. "For months you have had only to touch me, Kevin Riley, and—"

Alexandra lost her remaining words in a swirling storm. His hand was moving with torturous slowness down, over her collarbone and lower still. Her breasts swelled, strained, ached for his touch. His fingertips lightly skimmed the flesh above the material, then slid to the valley between her breasts. Finally they found a hardened tip and teased. A soft moan escaped Alexandra. Her knees weakened. Kevin's hand on her back steadied her.

"Do you know what you do to me when you look at me like you've been looking at me all evening, Angel?" he asked, burying his face in her neck.

She laughed, a throaty sound. "I love you, Kevin. I love you."

A second later, she wished she could withdraw the words. She felt him stiffen, felt his hand fall away from her breast. He lifted his head from her neck, then stepped back.

She stared at him, frustrated, feeling as though he had suddenly built solid walls around himself. "Dear God, Kevin, what is it that keeps you from me?" she cried.

"Love's never a lasting thing, girl," he said, shaking his head. He mumbled something about having an early day tomorrow at the hotel. Then he was gone.

Alexandra listened to the click of his shoes in the hallway outside the parlor, then to the brush of the front door opening and closing. She was always a breath away from having all of him, yet a breath away from losing him, too.

She sank into a nearby chair.

Love's never a lasting thing, girl, he had said. Well, at least she had gotten that much from him. It was a place to start. Why did he think love never lasted? Why did it frighten him so much? Had he been wounded so deeply once that loving her scared him so terribly?

Whatever was wrong, she meant to reach inside him and cradle it gently, nurse it back to health, then replace it, healed.

Summer Storm   245

She loved Kevin Riley and would not let him continue to run from her and his profound fear of love.

Kevin glanced impatiently around the modest banquet room that was being prepared for a wedding reception tomorrow. Finally he tapped a shoe on the carpet and looked fully on the little man to his right. "For one hundred, Mr. Lowry. The reception is for one hundred, not fifty, one of the largest receptions the Lighthouse Inn has ever had. The party will need both rooms. More tables, more silver, more linen. I told you that a week ago and I've reminded you twice since. Yet it's still wrong."

Lowry issued a string of apologies, then backed into one of the tables. He spun around in time to save several teetering crystal goblets from certain death. Kevin sighed through thin lips, unable to remember what had convinced him to hire Lowry. The man was incompetent, and Kevin certainly had no tolerance for him today.

In fact, he had no tolerance for anyone or anything. He'd growled at one of the maids because she'd left a pile of linen on the floor outside one of the rooms on the second floor. He'd growled at a cook for scorching a batch of eggs. And he'd growled at the door frame after he turned around and walked into it. No patience for anything. Saints.

Kevin Riley. Always a jest tumbling from his lips. Always a laugh. Always a word of patience, even on days when nothing seemed to be done right. But today he hadn't even smiled, much less shared a laugh with anyone. And to make things doubly worse, as the hours came and went, employees began tiptoeing around him, averting their gazes if he happened to look their way, dropping their voices to whispers whenever he walked around a corner, busying themselves or making excuses and hurrying off whenever they spotted him. The word that Kevin Riley was in a rare foul mood today had apparently spread like fire throughout all three stories of the hotel.

He was falling in love with Alexandra. He purposely hadn't been to see her in three days. He ached for her—for just her smile if nothing else. And there was plenty else.

He'd vowed several years ago not to fall in love again. Why subject himself to more heartache? He much preferred to play the charmer, safeguarding his heart behind a merry facade.

But Alexandra had charm of her own. Dark, dancing eyes. Hair of pure black silk. Skin of satin. A velvety voice he could hear even now. She read to him as often as he read to her, and he'd caught himself watching her too many times, watching her dusky lips, wanting to touch them . . . kiss them. What had shocked him of late was the suspicion that he wouldn't be content having her in his arms for just one night. He'd begun thinking about having her there forever.

A hell of a frightening thought.

She could betray him, too. Then he'd be damned again, wouldn't he? Damned to months, maybe years, of missing her. As before . . .

How the hell had this happened? He'd vowed never to fall in love again. When he loved, he poured too much of himself into the emotion. Every ounce of himself. He created his own hell, which was exactly what this was, because he wouldn't see Alexandra again now that he knew he was falling in love with her. Why not forget her now, while he still could? Why not close and stitch the cut she'd made to try to crawl into his heart?

The problem was he suspected that forgetting her wouldn't be easy. Alexandra was like a spark singeing him now and then. And sparks often led to fire, didn't they?

23

NICHOLAS STOOD JUST inside a partially open side door leading to the Forest City House, waiting for Harold to bring the carriage and take him home. His gaze fell on a small figure huddled in a corner near the door, the tatters of what had once been a warm coat fluttering around the boy. The awning gave scarce protection from blowing snow and occasional gusting wind.

A clerk swept by Nicholas, clicking his tongue and shaking his head. "Sorry about this, Mr. Cummings. We've run him off more than once this week. I'll get rid of him." The clerk reached for the door.

Nicholas grabbed his arm. The man paused, forking his brows. "You've run him off? To where?" Nicholas demanded.

"Well, I don't know, sir," the man replied quickly. "I've been told to get rid of them if—"

"In this weather the poor cannot even seek shelter beneath an inadequate awning?" Nicholas asked angrily.

The clerk looked meek. "I've been told—"

"Do you think I give a damn what you've been told?"

Nicholas received a stare, one he met evenly. An instant later the clerk sputtered, "I'll bring him in, Mr. Cummings. This moment."

Nicholas swept his greatcoat from his shoulders. "Don't bother. I'll take care of him myself." On the heels of the biting words, he shoved the door wide open, fighting a sudden, powerful gust of wind to hunch beside the boy and drape the coat around his small frame. Wide, hollow brown eyes lifted to him. The boy's breath was ragged and wet, and his sunken cheeks looked ghostly pale.

"Good God," Nicholas swore softly. The boy would be lucky if he lived past nightfall. The carriage pulled up and stopped not four feet away. Nicholas scooped the boy up and shouted for Harold to get the carriage door open.

Nicholas placed his precious bundle on a seat, tucked the greatcoat securely around the boy's bony shoulders, then sat on the edge of the opposite seat. The boy was half-frozen already. His lips were blue; so were the shadows beneath his eyes. Nicholas leaned over and rubbed a frail hand to warm it. "Stay alive, boy. Stay alive to taste the warm broth waiting for you, one of life's pleasures you probably haven't experienced in some time, if ever."

A sigh escaped the discolored lips. The weary eyes closed, and for a heart-stopping instant, Nicholas thought the boy had slipped away. But no . . . He whispered a thank you, snuggled deeper within the greatcoat, and sighed again with relief.

Releasing his own breath, Nicholas settled back on the seat. Thank God. *Thank God.*

At his home, the housekeeper turned down a bed for the boy, and Nicholas lowered him onto it. She then hustled away to tell the cook to prepare a bowl of hot soup. Nicholas began the task of removing the tatters of cloth from the boy's frail body.

"Where do you live?" he asked. "Who shall I tell you've been brought here?"

"Fire," the boy managed to rasp through the sickness that had attacked his lungs. "Dead . . . brother, mother . . . father."

Nicholas stared. The boy couldn't be more than nine. Already he knew more about tragedy and grief than most adults. "You're all right now," Nicholas assured him. "There's no more fire, no more cold. You'll find warmth and comfort here."

Clothes were borrowed from David, Harold's "groom's boy." The soup arrived. Harold had gone back out for a doctor. He finally returned, accompanied by a stout man wearing a tall, rumpled hat and heavy side whiskers. When the doctor examined the boy, then withdrew shaking his head, Nicholas knew the news was anything but good. He followed the man out into the hall.

"By an act of God, he'll live. It's pneumonia. In the boy's weakened condition . . . well, I don't know what more to say, Nicholas. Keep him warm, fed, comfortable. You've at least given him hope, and that's more than most have at this time of year."

Nicholas nodded. He offered a mug of steaming coffee in the dining room downstairs. Nicholas drained a mug himself, then saw the doctor to the front door.

Some time later, he stood at a window, staring beyond the frosted glass at an ever-increasing snowdrift near the carriage house. He didn't like the thought of having to leave the boy during the day tomorrow, but that was exactly what he would need to do. He had several meetings to attend, one with a shipwright, another with the investors of the Cleveland Iron Mining Company. The cook and the housekeeper would be here, but both were stern women whose company a boy would hardly enjoy. Nicholas had no choice, it seemed. He would just have to get through the meetings as quickly as possible.

He withdrew from the window and went to look in on the boy one last time before retiring for the night.

"His name is Lewis," Sarah told Katherine as they sat together in the parlor. "It has only been four days since Nicholas found him, but he gets stronger every day. Nicholas says he knew Lewis would live when the boy began getting bored. He climbed out of bed only yesterday and took the newspaper Nicholas had left on a table in the room. When Nicholas joined Lewis for supper, the boy showed him the mats he had made by folding and weaving the newspaper. He said he used to collect old newspapers with his mother. They would make mats to place on the earth floor during winter. A tragic story. Despite very little education, he amazed Nicholas only this morning by finding the sum of a lengthy list of figures printed in the Board of Trade reports."

"He sounds like a bright boy," Katherine remarked.

"You should go meet him. Nicholas mentioned he was thinking of turning Lewis over to you when the boy is completely well."

"Perhaps I'll meet him when Nicholas brings him to the orphanage," Katherine said, not wishing to sound too eager about going to Nicholas's home.

Sarah sipped her tea, studying Katherine over the cup. "If you wish to avoid Nicholas, go during the day, when he's frequently out on business. If you wish to avoid hurting me, make Nicholas a happy man," she said softly.

Katherine's eyes widened. Sarah had read her mind! She quickly dropped her gaze to her lap, where she folded her hands. "Make Nicholas a happy man? Going to see Lewis will do that?"

"In a way, yes. You'll see Nicholas, too, I'm certain. He's the finest man I know, Katherine. He loves you, and you love him. It's quite obvious."

Katherine stared at her. Sarah knew. Sarah *knew*, and she wasn't upset as Katherine had thought she might be. "You're very . . . calm about this," Katherine mumbled.

"I was hurt, but not anymore."

"How long . . . how long have you known?"

"Months."

Months? Katherine could hardly breathe. She'd wanted to avoid this day forever. She'd never wanted Sarah to know. "Why . . . why have you still been coming here, being nice to me, being a friend?"

"Love is not always something that can be controlled, Katherine. Mother was supposed to marry someone else. Then she met my father. Unexpectedly. Suddenly. But it happened. I've never thought you and Nicholas ever set out to hurt me. In any event, please do not let your apprehension of Nicholas keep you from Lewis."

So Katherine, feeling greatly relieved, decided to go see the boy. And Nicholas, too, of course, though very discreetly, for she still did not wish to see him a great deal publicly until at least spring. Half of her reluctance, after all, had stemmed

Summer Storm

from her desire to avoid hurting Sarah, and Sarah had put her mind to rest about that.

She took a basket of books to read to Lewis and a slate on which he could write or cipher if he wanted to, even a few pieces of hard candy. Nicholas wasn't there when she arrived, but the servants knew her and took her directly upstairs.

She told Lewis that she was Nicholas's friend and that she'd brought some things for him. He was trusting, wide-eyed, possessing all the eagerness of a child, laughing at silly things she said. She breathed a sigh of relief that the disastrous events in his life so far had not taken the laughter from him. As a girl with difficulties of her own, she had been so very different when Nicholas had found her. She had felt slighted. Things and people had been snatched from her, and she had wanted to be left alone so she could muddle through what remained of her life. Lewis had fared better; still, his life had just been wonderfully altered by the very man who had altered hers.

Katherine and Lewis smiled together as she read from James Fenimore Cooper's *Leatherstocking Tales*. Later she told him about how she had lost her father, and how she had thought the world was ending, that she'd felt cold inside and so alone, filled with stubbornness, but so very, very alone. Then, of course, Nicholas had given her hope.

Nicholas had dinner at the Weddell House with a merchant interested in shipping on canal boats this summer. The man was quick with his business, and Nicholas was silently thankful, wanting to return to Lewis.

Outside the Weddell House, the merchant had just said good-bye and walked away when Nicholas spotted Kevin approaching. Kevin didn't seem to see him, that was clear. There was no recognition in his blue-green eyes, no expression of either anger or annoyance, which was all Nicholas had gotten from Kevin since the night his engagement to Sarah had been announced. Nicholas was weary of allowing sharp words and misunderstandings to hang between him and the only man he had ever considered a true friend.

He stepped directly into Kevin's path and waited.

Kevin bumped into him, a man totally unaware of his surroundings. He glanced up, looking startled. "Nicholas."

"For a man walking on a busy street, you're not very observant. It's not like you to daydream," Nicholas said.

Kevin straightened his coat. "Well, I'm fine now. Don't trouble yourself." His stare was definitely a cool one.

Nicholas sighed. "Isn't it time we stopped this foolishness? Being furious with each other? I realize what you were trying to force me to see when you opposed my engagement to Sarah. I'm grateful. At the time I couldn't—"

"You have a few more lessons to learn, my friend. Such as when to keep your trousers buttoned," Kevin said angrily.

Nicholas was speechless for a moment. Finally a harsh laugh tore loose. "Good God, you're crass. Of all people to be telling me—"

"I don't fuck innocents. Over the years I've bedded a few widows, lonely women, a maid now and then, even a few whores from time to time, but never innocents. Never. I—"

"That's enough," Nicholas said, chilling with outrage. "It was nothing like—"

"I'm thinking it isn't enough. You wanted this confrontation. You have it."

"I don't care for your gutter language. This wasn't a good idea after all," Nicholas said, turning away.

Kevin grabbed his arm. "My beginnings, you know. They've never completely left me, despite your mother's refinement and the theological approach of Oberlin. I won't apologize. If you were so determined to bed Katherine, you might have considered a precaution. Withdrawal perhaps. There's something called a condom, a sheath if you're wanting me to talk delicately. A rather handy object."

Nicholas wrenched his arm free. "Get the hell away from me." He started off, using quick, long strides to put needed and desired distance between them. Kevin's words would have offended him in private; spoken on the corner of a busy street, before a respectable establishment like the Weddell House, they seemed worse. He didn't intend to stop walking until he reached the hostelry a block away where he had left his horse. He had given Harold the afternoon off.

"That's the difference between us, you know," Kevin called, yanking Nicholas from the haven of distraction. "I'm uncouth, and you're polished. It will always be that way."

Setting his jaw, Nicholas paused, turned back, and approached Kevin. He noticed things he had not noticed moments ago: Kevin's crumpled neck-cloth, the smudges on his coat, the hollows beneath his eyes. Kevin looked positively disheveled, not a good thing for the owner of a reputable establishment, someone who would undoubtedly be recognized. "The difference only shows when you want it to," Nicholas said, "when you want to offend me, drive me away. I'm very sorry I stepped in your path."

He left Kevin standing at the corner. Nicholas tried to restore some of his dignity by fumbling with his neckband and straightening his greatcoat, but he failed. The shocking exchange had left him with a churning stomach, and no amount of fumbling with his clothes would remedy that. Good God, what was wrong with Kevin?

Nicholas rode promptly home. There he dismounted and handed the horse's reins to the groom. Once inside the house, he tossed back several snifters of brandy in the study and breathed deeply to try to calm himself. Nearly a half hour passed before he felt composed enough to go upstairs and visit Lewis for a time.

He heard her voice the instant he reached the second floor. Light. Smooth. Gay. His heart quickened. Lewis said something. She laughed. Nicholas's breath caught. Such a wonderful sound, her laughter, like a favorite melody he had not heard for a long time. He could stand here and listen forever. But he wanted to see her, too. God, how he wanted to see her.

He moved down the hall, paused near the open door, and listened to her finish telling Lewis how he had taken her back to the bank and talked Werner into sending her to the Sandusky school. That event seemed so far in the past, so much had happened since, and yet he envisioned it as clearly as if it were happening again right before his eyes. She had been such a ragged, defeated little thing when she had peered at him around her tangled curls and asked if he expected her to walk back alone. He still found it hard to believe that the woman talking had once been the urchin he had wanted to dunk in the Cuyahoga River.

Smiling, he stepped into the room.

"Nicholas!" Lewis's brown eyes shimmered.

"Well, you don't appear too bored, Mr. Harting. And to think I was worried," Nicholas teased.

Katherine sat in a chair beside the tall tester bed. She stood, turned, and locked gazes with him. Her eyes were as bright as Lewis's. She was dressed in a blue habit; obviously she had ridden here, either alone or with someone. "Hello," she said, quite amiably.

"Hello."

"Sarah told me about Lewis. I decided to come and meet him for myself."

"I see you brought your basket of charm along." Nicholas shifted his gaze to the basket resting near one leg of the chair. She certainly didn't need a basket of charm; listening to her talk was enough to charm most anyone. He had thought her gay attitude might change when he stepped into the room. Not so. He didn't know what had happened, if anything at all had happened between the day he had met her outside the Chapin Block and now, and he wouldn't risk ruining the moment by asking questions. He walked over to have a look in the basket.

"Just books, some pencils, and a few games," she said.

"A miniature backgammon set. I haven't played backgammon in quite some time. Do you know how to play, Lewis?"

"No, sir."

"Then we'll teach you. Katherine and I will play, then you and Katherine, then you and I. You'll know the game well by the time we're done," Nicholas said, hoping he wasn't pressing Katherine too much. Would she run again . . . or stay?

Katherine had been about to leave, having spent a good two hours with Lewis already. He appeared delighted by Nicholas's suggestion. Nicholas looked rather delighted himself. Katherine couldn't help the smile that touched her own lips. This wasn't at all the uneasy encounter with Nicholas she had thought it would be.

"I'll have the cook bring up soup and bread for supper," Nicholas suggested further, pulling a small table from the fireplace to the bed. "We'll make an evening of it."

"I'll need to send a message to Uncle Werner, explaining where I am, and one to Mr. Jackson. He expected me to send for him when I was ready to leave," Katherine said.

"Going out alone again?"

She gave him a sheepish look, not caring to respond.

He shook his head. "I'll take care of it. You put the game on the table."

He was gone before Katherine could respond. She looked at Lewis, thinking he must be tired. "If you need to rest . . ."

"I'm all right. Really," he said.

She shook her head, then took the wooden box from her basket and placed it on the table.

Moments later Nicholas returned. He won the first game. She narrowed her eyes as he took his last playing piece from the board. "I thought you said you hadn't played in a long time."

He held up a hand, palm out, as if to ward off her suspicion. "I haven't."

"Such an innocent man you are, Mr. Cummings," she teased.

He swept a dash of black hair from his brow, giving her a grin that took her breath. Then he fiddled with his neck-cloth. She watched his fingers work, flushing and glancing away when the sight jarred free the memory of him undressing the night he had made love to her in the study downstairs. She shouldn't be having these thoughts. She should leave. She forced herself to stay; she wouldn't run from him again. No matter the reason.

"You play her now, Lewis. I'll go see how the cook is progressing with the soup," he said.

"Yes, sir."

With Lewis's help, Katherine replaced the pieces on the board. She took a few moments to show him various moves he could make using the combination of numbers on the die, then she arranged the pieces again.

Nicholas returned with a tray in his hands. He insisted they take a few moments to eat the soup while it was hot. Katherine carefully moved the game board to the floor. Nicholas placed the tray on the table, then settled in the chair across from her.

The soup was flavorful, chunks of carrots, onions, beans, and potatoes boiled with pieces of beef. The bread tasted fresh and delicious. Katherine ate two pieces rather quickly. She caught Nicholas grinning at her as she eyed the last piece on the plate he'd placed in the middle of the table.

"Take it," he said. "Lewis is done, and I'm full. Besides, no one here will give you a disapproving look."

"But one that will make me uncomfortable nonetheless," she retorted.

He chuckled. "Then I won't look."

He made a show of standing, turning his chair around, and sitting again, his back to her. Lewis laughed. "Turn back around here, Nicholas Cummings!" she objected, blushing.

"Eat the bread. Go ahead."

Laughing, too, she took the bread.

"Is she eating it, Lewis?" Nicholas asked after a moment.

"She sure is. In big bites," Lewis said, joining in to tease her.

"I knew it! I knew she wouldn't disappoint me."

Katherine nearly choked. "Stop. You two . . ."

Nicholas turned the chair back around, devilishness twinkling in his eyes. "You missed a crumb. Oh, no, two."

She threw her napkin at him. It caught him in the chest. He chuckled more, then sobered. "You've no idea how glad I am to see you smiling and laughing," he said.

She dipped her head slightly, glancing at him from beneath her lashes. Then she smiled again.

Soon they placed the empty bowls and the plate on the tray, put the tray on the floor and the game board back on the table. Lewis was very good for a beginner, but Katherine won. Still, Lewis was eager to play again. Katherine pushed the board toward Nicholas, and soon Nicholas and Lewis were embroiled in the game.

Summer Storm 257

Katherine stood to walk around a bit. She'd been sitting for hours and felt stiff. She admired brass bookends shaped in the form of wing chairs. They held a collection of books on the top of a chiffonier. She wandered to the fireplace and warmed her cool hands near the fire Nicholas had fed after returning with the tray earlier. Then she walked back to the table to help Lewis along a bit. She felt Nicholas's eyes on her from time to time, warming her much more than the fire, rekindling the flames that had sparked between them months ago.

And how easily they rekindled! She wanted to be with him, in his arms, as much this night as she had the night she had come here to request that he write her another draft. But she would think things out clearly, not rush into his arms. Certainly she would never be as bold with him as she had been right after she had returned to Cleveland. She would never again invite him to kiss her, never again invite him to make love to her. She had learned a few lessons, the most important being that a woman should never throw herself at a man.

Still, she felt his gaze...

The game ended. Nicholas won, but only by a few pieces. Katherine insisted that Lewis rest now. He'd had hours of excitement. He objected, as any boy his age would, then settled under the coverlet. Katherine tossed the pelisse she'd shed hours ago across a forearm, took her basket of charm, as Nicholas had called it, and waited near the door as he extinguished the lamps.

"Lewis is delightful," she said, walking toward the staircase with Nicholas. "From what Sarah told me, he seems to be recovering well, too."

"Very well," Nicholas agreed. "He would be running around this house right now if he thought I would stand for it."

He took a moment to fetch his greatcoat from the study, then they moved to the entryway. There he took her pelisse and settled it on her shoulders, reaching around to fasten the clasps. He smelled faintly of spicy cologne. Katherine stared down at his hands as he worked, the nails well manicured, the fingers moving deftly as they completed their task.

His hands grasped her shoulders and turned her to face him. He lowered his head as if to kiss her.

Gasping, Katherine turned her head. She felt his warm breath on her cheek. "Please . . . I . . . I came to see Lewis."

A moment passed.

"Only Lewis?" Nicholas asked softly.

She didn't move.

"You're trembling. Good God, I'm not going to swallow you up."

She wriggled her shoulders free and stepped back. "Won't you? It's easy for you, isn't it? One kiss and we're right back where we were, or so you think. The study is, after all, right down the hall. I remember. That is where we made love before. Things must be different now, Nicholas."

He stared at her. "I only wanted to kiss you."

"And a kiss leads to touches, touches lead to caresses. We know what happens after that."

"I'm very sorry," he said, his voice dripping sarcasm. "I should have asked your permission."

"Yes, you should have," she shot back.

"I wasn't thinking—"

"I was. I've thought a lot of late. I am no longer an idealist."

He drew his brows together and narrowed his eyes. "I wasn't aware that you ever were."

"Weren't you?" She laughed somewhat nervously. "No matter. I plan to be very practical in the future where we're concerned."

"I only wanted to kiss you, Katherine," he repeated in disbelief.

Katherine nodded, but said nothing, allowing him to keep trying to convince himself. Nicholas propped himself up with an open hand on the wall and drew his other hand across his mouth. The planes and angles of his face alternately caught shadow and light.

Katherine dropped her gaze to the basket she held, ran a thumb over the smooth weave, and stared at the backgammon box, studying a dark line that ran through the oak. "We can't just begin again, Nicholas. Not like—"

"Why not . . . begin again?" he asked immediately.

An awkward silence fell between them. She felt that more explanation might exasperate them more. She felt strongly that she shouldn't be in his arms just yet; he saw no reason why she shouldn't be there. "I . . . I want to see Lewis more," she said finally, looking up at him.

He lifted a brow. "And you're wondering if I intend to keep my hands, and my lips, to myself?"

Silence was her answer again.

"I will. You have my word," he said angrily, moving to the front door. He jerked it open. "Stay here. I'll fetch horses and take you home."

When he returned, they rode to the Kraus house in heavy silence.

Sometime during the middle of the night, Nicholas awoke to the patter of rain on the roof and on the brick drive. Something else, too . . . the sound of voices quarreling?

He rose, tossed on a dressing robe, and deserted his room for the hall, then the head of the staircase and the balustrade. The voices came from below, sometimes murmurs, sometimes shouts. Nicholas thought of Lewis, sleeping in a bed just down the hall. Who the devil was arguing in the middle of the night? Servants who wanted to look for other employment?

Nicholas bounded down the stairs. He reached the entryway just as Kevin stuck a pointed finger in the face of the disheveled butler. Alfred Howe had been with Nicholas little more than a year, but already the Englishman was fiercely protective. And dignified most of the time. He had obviously had his hands in his hair. Patches of it stood straight up. His nightgown was crumpled. One trembling hand held a low-burning lamp. He spotted Nicholas, and his eyes flared.

"Oh, now you've gone and done it," he muttered, presumably directing his scathing remark to Kevin, though his eyes remained on Nicholas. "You woke him. Hope you're happy."

"It's all right, Alfred. Go back to bed," Nicholas said, trying to soothe the man.

Alfred scowled, then started off, muttering as he went. His words—something about the indecency of American brutes, *Irish*-American brutes at that—faded.

"You've had a wonderful effect on people today," Nicholas told Kevin, staring coolly.

Kevin winced. "He's English."

"You're rude."

"I'm in love, that's what I am," Kevin said raggedly, falling back to put his weight against a wall. Again his clothes were crumpled. He wore no coat or waistcoat or vest. Only one side of his white shirt was tucked into his trousers.

"In love? Passionate or platonic?" Nicholas asked. He jerked at the ties on his dressing robe. The very last person he wished to see was Kevin. And in the middle of the night, looking so wretched. Kevin might at least have had the decency to don clean clothes, an appropriate set of clothes, if he had to call on anyone at this horrid hour.

"I deserve that. I owe you an—"

"You deserve much worse. If you hadn't roused me from a sound sleep, I might give serious thought to shoving you right through that door," Nicholas said, indicating the front door. "But since my brain is still a bit foggy, I have an excuse for offering you the comfort of my study. Provided, of course, you keep vulgar remarks to yourself."

Kevin nodded. Nicholas waved the way to the study and followed Kevin into the room.

"It's Alexandra," Kevin said, sinking into a chair. "I'm thinking I don't know what to do. After Alicia's betrayal, I vowed I'd never fall in love again."

"What? Where is Kevin the philosopher?" Nicholas pulled a cheroot from a box on the table between the hearth chairs.

"Nicholas, don't."

"After what happened this afternoon, I can hardly resist."

"I'm scared," Kevin said. He ran a hand through his already tousled hair, leaned over, and buried his face in his hands.

Nicholas looked away. He was still angry with Kevin, but a man's dignity was a fragile thing, after all. Besides, his anger had begun to dissipate. The sight of Kevin this afternoon,

Summer Storm

looking slovenly, and right now looking even more so, his emotions in tatters, affected Nicholas. He tossed the cheroot back in the box and strode to the sideboard. There he poured a glass of whiskey, then carried it to Kevin. "Take this," he said softly. "But understand I am not advocating you try to kill yourself with drink again."

Kevin straightened and took the glass. Nicholas clamped a hand on his shoulder. "I'm here if you want to talk."

Kevin talked.

24

TWICE A WEEK for the next two weeks, Katherine visited Lewis at Nicholas's home. Each time the three of them made an evening of it, playing games, supping together, laughing and talking. Nicholas behaved, as he'd promised her he would. Soon they moved Lewis to the Garden Street Orphanage, assuring him that although a delightful couple might come along someday wanting to adopt him, they would never loose touch with him.

Katherine spent lengthy afternoons and days at the orphanage. She introduced Charles and Lewis, hoping the boys would get along well. They did. Charles began taking his sketching lessons there rather than at Uncle Werner's home on Lake Street, with the twins and Lewis observing. Nicholas visited often.

One day Katherine was playing a tune on the pianoforte and singing along with the children gathered around, and when the tune ended, there was clapping from behind them. Katherine turned. Nicholas stood in the doorway, smiling.

"A fine song if I ever heard one," he said, stepping near.

Katherine blushed. "How long have you been standing there?"

"Almost the entire time."

She rose and excused herself to get refreshment from the kitchen. When she returned, Nicholas, of all people, was rollicking with Charles and Lewis on the floor. The girls were giggling.

Summer Storm 263

Nicholas had shed his coat. His trousers were rumpled. So was his hair. Katherine smiled at his unusually unkempt appearance, then fixed her face in a stern expression.

Nicholas saw her and went still. "We've been discovered," he whispered to the boys with a wild look, as if he, Charles, and Lewis were co-conspirators in crime.

Charles and Lewis tried to look serious, but the looks soon gave way to giggles. When they spotted the little cakes on the tray Katherine held, they jumped up and settled themselves on the sofa. Nicholas made an effort to smooth the wrinkles from his clothes.

"It's futile," Katherine said, laughing. He scowled playfully, then joined the children on the sofa.

Much later, after Charles's mother had come for him and after Lewis and the girls were settled for the night, Sister Mary came for her usual nightly stay. Nicholas had begun taking Katherine home the evenings he visited. Tonight was no different. He helped her with her pelisse, and once they were outside, handed her up to the carriage.

When their hands touched, she felt the same thrill she always felt when she and Nicholas had any sort of physical contact, however brief. He had not tried to kiss her again since the day she'd met Lewis. She told herself she was content with his companionship. She preferred that things stay, for a time, exactly as they were.

And so things did. She caught him looking at her from time to time with longing in his eyes, yet he never made an effort to draw her close when they found themselves perfectly alone, such as during the carriage rides home. He was always a gentleman, keeping an appropriate distance, letting his hands fall away after the fitting amount of time spent setting her wrap on her shoulders.

But one evening his hands remained.

Katherine made no effort to move away; she didn't want to. No. She found she wanted him to tug her back against him. She felt his breath in her hair and closed her eyes, giving in to the warmth racing through her.

"Good God, I love you," he said.

Her breath lodged in her throat. She stood perfectly still, discomposed, wondering what he would do next.

He moved away.

She was dizzy, breathless, stunned. Why had he withdrawn? Why had he not kissed her? Enclosed her in his arms? Because you chastised him, you fool, she thought, turned him into a man filled with the utmost respect for maxims. She, of course, had had no intention of being so bold as to turn in his arms, touch him, or do or utter anything to encourage him. She had vowed to herself that she would never again be so bold with him. And so she was left with frustration, determined to abide by the rules of propriety for once herself, yet wanting Nicholas to kiss and touch her.

That evening, the carriage ride home seemed to last an hour. A blessed hour. Nicholas withdrew to a dark corner. Katherine sat in silence, gathering the folds of her wrap about her.

One evening Nicholas found himself in the uncomfortable position of staring across the orphanage's dining room table at Alexandra. She was looking more and more pale of late; pale and thin, with dark hollows beneath red-streaked eyes. Despite their proximity, she gave him only dismissive glances that irritated him more as the minutes ticked by on a mantel clock, the same annoying little glances she had been giving him for weeks now. Lambasting him would be far better, Nicholas thought, shifting in his chair.

A simple dislike of him would have been tolerable; others had disliked him. It was her disapproval of him where Katherine was concerned that was *in*tolerable. The situation was difficult and awkward. After all, she was Katherine's closest friend. He didn't want Katherine feeling torn between him and Alexandra, which she undoubtedly did; Alexandra must have said something to Katherine by now, advised her in some fashion. The night Katherine lost the baby, he had learned that Alexandra usually said exactly what was on her mind. But perhaps she hadn't said anything to Katherine about him. Perhaps she preferred to keep quiet, giving him these infuriating looks in hopes that he might just go away. *Zip!*

Summer Storm

Exasperating.

Later, while Katherine was upstairs settling Colleen, Margaret, and Lewis for the night, Nicholas found himself alone with Alexandra again, this time in the parlor.

He sat in a chair near a window, the curtain drawn back with a hand so he could watch the stars and the moon against the deepening, rich blue-black of night. Now and then he stole glances at Alexandra from the corner of his eye. She had settled before an ivory-colored table in a matching chair with maroon velvet upholstery. She was four feet away perhaps, against a wall. Nicholas's view of her and the table revealed that she had produced a deck of cards and was playing solitaire.

But all wrong. Terribly wrong. A black queen on a black king when the order should have been black, red, black, red, down the scale of face and number cards. Shadows created by dancing lamplight frolicked about the room, making Nicholas wonder if he was seeing the cards right. He let the thick, smooth curtain slip through his fingers and centered his concentration on the spread of Alexandra's game.

No, he saw right. Black on black. Well, she'd made a mistake, that was all. Easily remedied once I point it out to her, he thought. Teaching her to play solitaire the right way might put them on speaking terms at least. She placed a red seven atop a red seven, turned up a black six and placed it on a red ten.

Nicholas grimaced. "An avid player of solitaire, I see."

A card slipped from her hand, as if he had startled her, roused her from some deep thought. "What?"

"Are you an avid player of solitaire?" He expected a negative response, of course.

She glanced his way briefly, then went back to her cards, reaching to put the red jack that had escaped her hand atop the black queen. Finally she had put a card in the right place. Objects in the wrong places always troubled Nicholas. "Yes, I am," she answered. "I learned when I was a little girl. I used to play for hours."

"Did you?" he couldn't help but ask. Incredible.

She flipped another card and placed it on the jack. A black two. He saw the pips as clear as if he held the card himself! Either she was entirely serious and purposely cheating or entirely serious and very distracted. He wasn't sure which. And of course there was always the possibility that she was trying to trick him, drive him a little mad.

"You're doing it all wrong, you know," he said.

Her head jerked. She paused to study the rows of cards she had laid on the table, a portion of the deck still in her hands. Moments passed. Then she laughed at herself. "What polished Chicago gentleman would want me? A woman who cannot even play solitaire?"

Nicholas blinked. What was she talking about? Chicago? Polished gentleman? Bad enough she claimed to be adept at solitaire, now she confused him with her ramblings. He sat staring at her.

"Of course, the man *couldn't* marry me if I married another man. The man wouldn't want to marry me if I chopped off my hair, perhaps dirtied my face, ripped my clothes," she said, her head wobbling with the words. "No, that would never do."

She seemed to be talking to the cards, and Nicholas found that not only baffling, but unsettling. He had half a mind to go back to watching the moon and the stars.

"Of course, I'm not going to Chicago anyway, so why worry?" she continued. "I plan to stay here. Right here. Perhaps play solitaire for the rest of my life. Perhaps that is what Kevin expects me to do. He walks across a lawn into my life and leaves me playing solitaire. All wrong, of course. All wrong. I would marry him in a second if he asked."

So that was it. Kevin. Nicholas didn't understand the part about the lawn, but he did understand that a polished gentleman in Chicago wanted to marry her, and that she wanted no part of it—she preferred marriage to Kevin. He understood, too, the significance behind the game. Solitaire represented the way she felt—alone. Obviously Kevin had not taken his advice and asked Alexandra to marry him. Kevin was still too busy being afraid. Alexandra and Kevin were driving each other insane.

Summer Storm

"How is Kevin?" Nicholas asked, wondering if she had even seen him during the past few weeks.

"I have no idea. You've probably seen him more times than I of late."

"I saw him at the club yesterday."

"That's more than I have seen him. He didn't mention me?"

"No," Nicholas answered truthfully. Kevin hadn't. They had played a few rounds of billiards, then they'd gone separate ways.

"Weeks ago, we were seeing each other regularly," Alexandra mumbled, flicking her hand. "No more, it seems. If I said anything about love, he fled. Only this time he's decided to stay away."

Her honesty with him, when she so obviously disliked him, surprised Nicholas. She seemed to need someone to talk to, and he was the only one available at the moment.

He rose, poured a glass of water from a pottery pitcher on a table near his chair, and carried the glass to her. She stared at it for an instant, then took it.

"You should cry. It might help," he said as she drank. He instantly regretted the words, realizing that he was expecting her to act as most any woman might—burst into a river of tears that only a gentleman's handkerchief, touched to the nose and eyes in just the right way, could dam.

"Cry?" she said, her eyes widening. "I have only cried twice in my life that I can remember. When Katherine left the school in Sandusky, and when she mis—caught influenza."

Nicholas looked away briefly. She knew he knew about the loss of his and Katherine's child, but she had the good taste not to talk about it. Sister Mary was expected at any moment. For all they knew she had already entered and was putting away her wrap. One never knew when unsuspecting ears might overhear things.

"And crying helped neither time," he said, assuming that it hadn't.

"Oh, but it did. Some. I usually have terrible headaches when I am upset. Those are the only two times I can remember not having the headaches."

Nicholas nodded, glad he could be of some help at least when he felt so helpless. "He was married once, you know."

She wrinkled her brow. "Who?"

"Kevin."

"No, I didn't know," she blurted, spilling the cards. At least twenty fluttered to the floor. Neither she nor Nicholas made a move to pick them up. Her eyes lifted to rest on him. "What happened? Do you know? Did she die? Is he a widower?"

"No, nothing like that. That would have been easy compared to the hell she put him through. Her name was Alicia. She took up with a man she'd met in Pittsburgh. Kevin divorced her. I don't know any more details."

Alexandra stared at him.

"Kevin was emotionally devastated. He began drinking whiskey heavily, neglecting his hotel and other private affairs." Nicholas paused here to study Alexandra. He was at a disadvantage, knowing many personal things that had happened between her and Kevin that she surely didn't know he knew, and knowing things about Kevin that Kevin might not want revealed to Alexandra. Or if they were to be revealed, Kevin should be the one revealing them. And yet Kevin seemed to have made his choice; because of his fear of marital involvement, he preferred roaming from woman to woman to marrying Alexandra, the woman he loved. That was no decent life, to Nicholas's way of thinking. He didn't take long deciding to tell Alexandra more of what had happened two summers ago.

"I kidnapped Kevin, locked myself in a bedroom with him, allowed only food and water and coffee inside, occasionally a book. I wanted his head and veins clear. We resorted to fistfights a few times," Nicholas said, rubbing his jaw. "Did we! I thought he would kill me for not allowing him to wallow in self-pity, for not letting him ruin his life. I kept telling him to live again, to go on. He had a hotel to run, he had friends. He survived, though I'm surprised I did."

"But he wasn't the same," Alexandra whispered.

Nicholas gathered the cards on the table and began trying to make some order of them, as much order as he could make with half the deck scattered around the legs of the table and chair. "He wasn't. He no longer wanted to kill his pain with whiskey, but he was different nonetheless. Kevin has always had a weakness for beautiful women. But he would never make the mistake of falling in love again, he said. He felt much safer bedding women but not allowing them close emotionally."

Alexandra flushed. Nicholas felt heat creep into his own face. "I'm sorry. I should have worded that differently, more delicately."

"No. No, it's all right." She traced the gilded trim on the edge of the table. "You are being honest with me. That is what I want—need—right now. I need to understand."

Nicholas flipped a card, frowned at it, then gathered the remaining cards on the table into a neat stack. He stepped back and shoved his hands into his trouser pockets. "Of course, there is always the possibility that Kevin might be brought to his senses. Only the situation—Kevin running scared from you—is a bit more delicate than a man not wanting to live after a wife's betrayal. I cannot very well lock him away in a room again and bully him to his senses. He's not inebriated, not with drink anyway. I spoke with him. I didn't get anywhere obviously. Perhaps you should try."

Alexandra glanced at the cards scattered about the floor, some faceup, others facedown. Nicholas didn't think she was really seeing them. No, she seemed to be piecing something together in her mind. Presently she slid from the chair to the floor and began gathering the cards. "That explains it."

"What?" he asked, kneeling down to help.

" 'Love's never a lasting thing.' "

He was baffled again. But her eyes were shimmering, and that delighted him. "Well, you've obviously found a major piece of the puzzle."

She smiled. She actually smiled at him. "Yes. Thank you."

He dipped his head. "You're welcome."

They finished gathering the cards. Nicholas returned to his chair just as she said something about going to see if Katherine needed help.

"I'll make her very happy, Alexandra, I want you to know that," Nicholas said, still bothered by the fact that she didn't approve of him.

She paused at the door.

"I love her. Her beauty, her compassion, her grace, her charm. The sound of her laughter. I want always to hear it, evoke it. Can you understand?" he asked.

She didn't move for several long moments. Then she turned slowly and nodded. "That's beautiful."

Exhaling heavily, Nicholas settled back in the chair and rubbed his rough jaw. "You don't know how relieved I am. She talked about you a lot before you came to Cleveland. She talks about you a lot now."

Alexandra smiled again. "She has *always* talked about you."

Nicholas lifted a brow. "Indeed?"

"Indeed." Her hands disappeared in the folds of her skirt, lifting the material. An instant later, she was gone from the doorway.

The trial of the men accused of the Oberlin-Wellington slave rescue began. Nicholas read the accounts in the newspaper, staying clear of the Federal Building. Even if he had had a notion to attend the trial, he would have had to fight his way through tremendous crowds, according to the paper. One man had come all the way from New York, another hailed from St. Louis, and yet another had come from New Orleans by way of the Mississippi and Ohio rivers and the canal. Business in the city had almost ceased. The eyes and ears of the country were riveted on Cleveland.

The accused were found guilty. The major offenders were sentenced to sixty-day jail terms and fined six hundred dollars each. Nicholas was relieved. Sixty days was a consequential space of time in the lives of good men, and six hundred dollars was not a sum to simply wave off, but the sentence, in his mind, might have been harsher.

He thought it was over—the waiting, the breath-holding, the masses of people. The terms would be served. Life would go on.

Summer Storm

Not so.

Protest meetings began. Trains and wagons brought more people, those not willing to allow life to simply go on. They insisted on gathering before the jail, making martyrs of the prisoners within. There were marches in Public Square, clashes between abolitionists and pro-slavery advocates. Nicholas did his best to carry on as usual, not an easy task in a city suddenly thrown into upheaval.

The evening of the mayor's ball arrived. When Uncle Werner handed Alexandra, then Katherine, down from the carriage in front of the Weddell House, a dozen other carriages lined either side of the street. Flakes of snow, the last shreds of winter, glittered in the lamplight. There were quick greetings as friends and acquaintances spotted one another, clustered for conversation, and eventually drifted to the hotel entrance. A hawker peddled a supply of wares across the street, before the Merchant Exchange, from which people were coming and going. The organ grinder was there.

Katherine paused to watch the tiny monkey. He was clad in a full red woolen suit this time. A child, perhaps all of five years, was urged by his mother to hand the monkey a coin. The creature took the offering and tipped its hat. The boy, squealing with delight, jerked back. Katherine smiled, recalling the warm July afternoon she had encountered the monkey and delighted in him, too.

She turned to take Uncle Werner's arm, expecting that Alexandra had already taken the other. She placed her gloved hand on *an* arm, but it hardly felt like Uncle Werner's. His was short and rather thick; this arm was lean and muscular, even through the thickness of a woolen greatcoat sprinkled with snow.

She looked up into emerald eyes.

"Shall we?" Nicholas asked.

Katherine smiled in surprise. Snow fluttered, landing softly on his dark, wavy hair. She suppressed the urge to reach up and brush it away. "Where did you come from?"

"I've been waiting for you," he said, urging her toward the hotel entrance.

Uncle Werner and Alexandra waited just inside the door. Servants collected their greatcoats and fur-lined pelisses, then Uncle Werner and Alexandra went on to the ballroom, leaving Katherine with Nicholas. The people she loved had conspired against her, Katherine thought, another smile tugging at her lips. Uncle Werner had long ago guessed that there was something between her and Nicholas. Alexandra, of course, had always known, and since Alexandra's attitude toward Nicholas had changed, Katherine wondered if the entire plot had been Alexandra's idea.

As always, Nicholas looked striking in black evening dress, a few golden chains dangling from a white satin waistcoat, a white collar grazing his smooth jaw. He yanked at the ends of his coat sleeves to straighten them, then offered Katherine his arm again.

This time she couldn't resist reaching up and brushing a few still unmelted snowflakes from his hair. He looked startled, one of the few times she had seen Nicholas so. He caught her hand, held it for a moment, then properly placed it on his arm, a move she found irritating.

After all, sometimes there were right moments for a tender touch.

He led her across the rich red carpet toward the ballroom. The mayor and his wife stood just inside the door, receiving their guests. Eyes shimmering, the mayor kissed Katherine's hand and murmured, "Charming."

Chandeliers glittered. People mingled. Conversation wafted. Musicians had gathered in one corner, behind barriers of long red braids, their tassels dangling from waist-high golden stands. Waiters in the pure-white Weddell House dress wove in and out of the crowd, offering trays of scalloped oysters and tiny crackers, caviar and champagne. There was laughter and the twinkling of jewels, the swish of satin and the magic of a waltz.

Grace Cummings smiled and waved, elegant in a gown of rust satin, her hair swept up and caught back with diamond-studded combs. She said a quick word to the woman at her side, then hurried over. Nicholas was just handing Katherine a crystal goblet filled with bubbly champagne when Grace reached them.

Katherine had not seen Nicholas's mother since the night of the charity ball last September. Grace took a few moments to scold a sheepish-looking Nicholas for not visiting her in weeks, then asked Katherine if she would like to attend a little event at the home of one of her friends. Katherine didn't need to ask what the event was all about; since Grace was asking, she assumed it had something to do with the rights of women Grace had spoken about the night of the supper at Nicholas's home. And indeed Katherine was interested. She might not care for Amelia Bloomer's attack on feminine dress, but she wholeheartedly agreed with the cause behind the attack.

"A little affair, nothing more," Grace said. "Day after tomorrow."

Katherine agreed. Grace drifted off. Sipping champagne, Katherine spotted Kevin coming toward them, weaving his way through the crowd. She knew he'd not been to the house in weeks to see Alexandra. Alexandra had confided that she thought Kevin was scared to fall in love. He got so close, just close enough to reach out and feel the flames, then he withdrew. Katherine wondered if Alexandra had told him about her father ordering her to marry the man in Chicago.

After greeting Nicholas, Kevin claimed the first dance with Katherine. She had thought Nicholas might ask her, and she was irritated again.

"It's good to see you out," Kevin remarked as they began to dance.

"I have you to thank for jolting me from self-pity."

"Did you arrive with Nicholas?"

She studied him. He looked peeved; his jaw was set, and there was a truculent look in his eyes. "So soon after he and Sarah decided not to marry, you mean?" she asked, taken aback by his sour disposition.

"Katherine . . ."

"No, Kevin, I didn't."

"People will talk if you start seeing him right now."

She stared at him, not caring to tell him that Nicholas was a frequent visitor to the orphanage, that in fact she and Nicholas often traveled together in a dark carriage. If he was so set against her seeing Nicholas, revealing how much time she spent with Nicholas would certainly spark his embers, wouldn't it?

She didn't need to say anything. Kevin shook his head and sighed heavily as they twirled, his hand resting lightly on her waist.

"He hasn't asked to see me on a regular or irregular social basis," she said. "Stop worrying."

That did nothing to soothe him. "I'm thinking the two of you should stay away from each other for a time," he said gruffly.

"Really? I won't ask your reasoning behind that. Not long ago you implied that I should stop hiding myself away. I've done—"

"I didn't say you should start seeing Nicholas."

"I don't remember asking your permission. Besides, I told you—I'm not 'seeing' him," she said, feeling her own surge of anger. "Don't try to ruin what happiness may or may not be waiting for me. Worry about your own life for once, Kevin. Worry that you may lose Alexandra because you're acting so odd."

Indeed there was no sign of the normally humorous, lighthearted Kevin Riley tonight; that man had been replaced by one who was obviously troubled, one who snapped at her and gave her penetrating looks.

"I made a sensible choice," he bit out. "Alexandra will be fine. She's a smart lass, a—"

"Fine?" Katherine blurted. For appearance sake, she hid her anger behind a tight smile. "Alexandra will be fine? Oh, you! You were once so condemning of Nicholas. You still are. You're a hypocrite, preaching to others what you don't practice yourself. Did you ever have an honorable intention toward Alexandra? Did you? Or did you just think to steal her heart, then break it?"

He fell silent. "I never knew her heart would become

involved. Or mine," he finally said softly as the dance ended. Couples parted, turned toward the musicians, and applauded. Katherine and Kevin applauded, too.

"You're a frightened man, Kevin. But I think you'll agree, after some consideration, that whatever you're frightened of may very well be less frightening than losing Alexandra."

Kevin didn't respond. He returned her to Nicholas, bowed away, then faded into the crowd.

Nicholas pressed another goblet of champagne into Katherine's hand. She glanced, unsure, at the glass. "I'm not accustomed to drinking much champagne."

"You'll dance away the effect," He said. "Are you aware of the numbers of men staring at you?"

Sipping champagne, she glanced around and found that he was right. Pairs of eager eyes here and there . . .

Had the date been last July when she had first returned to Cleveland, naive, wanting to throw herself at Nicholas and not thinking of the consequences, she would have teased him about dancing with her and not letting the pack of wolves come any closer. But she wasn't the same Katherine she had been then.

The wolves grew bold and drew near. Katherine finished the champagne and accepted the first dance of what she suspected would be many she didn't particularly want to accept, but would. She might not have minded accepting them if she hadn't thought, when she'd turned from watching the organ grinder and his monkey outside, that Nicholas wanted to spend the evening dancing with her. She didn't know what to make of what she perceived as his reluctance to do that now.

She was thankful for the two quick goblets of champagne; they numbed her enough that time seemed to pass faster than it might have otherwise. Still, the effect didn't last. Minutes persisted, swelling into hours. Quadrilles, waltzes . . . One man after another cut in, each trying to entertain her in his own way with tales of things he'd done and places he'd traveled. She caught glimpses of Nicholas, sometimes in conversation with various people, sometimes lounging against a wall, watching her and leisurely sipping champagne. She gave him a tight smile every time she caught his gaze, wanting to ask—sarcastically, of course—if he was enjoying himself.

She certainly was not. His nonchalant manner infuriated her.

Nicholas watched her. She looked elegant, gliding effortlessly through waltz steps, the gold threads in her otherwise beige gown catching the glitter from the crystal chandeliers. She was a beauty, her skin glowing a soft peach, curls wisping around her face as she talked and smiled, bewitching every man with whom she danced, including the mayor himself. There were scores of other women present, but she might as well have been the only woman in the room as far as Nicholas was concerned.

He wondered how long he could resist doing more than touching her occasionally to hand her up or down from a carriage or to position her pelisse on her shoulders those nights he took her home from the orphanage.

But he had made his decision. He would make no advances. He would not "seduce" her into marrying him. That remark of hers had cut into him. She'd made it the night of the charity supper and ball aboard the *Morning Star*, when he had told her he intended to marry her, not Sarah. She had insulted him, too, by denying him a kiss in the entryway the evening she met Lewis. He wanted her to fall in love with him so completely, so irrevocably, she wouldn't give a thought to saying no when he again asked her to marry him. She would never again think of denying him a kiss. She might even become bold enough to kiss him. She was reserved, and he didn't like the change in her. He meant to draw out the real Katherine.

They never spoke of her miscarriage, but he felt a sense of loss when he thought of the tiny life that had been growing within her. His loss could not cut as deeply as hers for how well he knew that Katherine loved children. Still, he felt an ache that crept up on him at the most peculiar times, when he inspected the partially built ship, when he stood before a mirror fastening his stock, and as recently as this morning,

Summer Storm   277

when he had been looking at figures summing up the tonnage of ore shipped from the Marquette mine last year. What would the child have looked like? Would it have possessed her golden hair, her blue eyes? He didn't know, but he sometimes wondered.

If he had just wanted a child, he could have married most any woman and had one. But that wasn't the problem. The child had been his and Katherine's, a result of their loving, of the most exquisite hours of his life. That was why he felt the loss.

He claimed the last dance of the evening with her, cutting in on a rather indignant-looking man. Luckily the man gave him no more than a sour look, then faded into the crowd.

Nicholas held Katherine at a distance, a bit more than propriety required. She gave him a severe look, sighed with resignation, then settled into the dance. One hand rested lightly on his shoulder, the other fit perfectly in his hand.

"I didn't know you knew how to dance," she said, not a hint of amusement in her expression. If he hadn't known her, if he had been meeting her for the first time, he might not have realized she was being sarcastic. But he knew Katherine.

He grinned. "You've been wanting me to dance with you all evening, you say?"

"I suppose you're going to make some excuse about how you couldn't have gotten a foot in front of all the men lined up to—"

"And if I do, you'll tell me I should have cut in hours ago the way I just did?"

She smiled finally, and he knew she was no longer angry. At least not very angry. "We're tossing questions back and forth, getting nowhere."

"We have gotten somewhere. We've drawn a conclusion. You're angry because you wanted me to dance with you hours ago, only I didn't think there was a way to get a foot between you and your line of admirers."

"There's more. Go back a bit," she said, looking annoyed again. "There would never have been a line if you hadn't allowed one to form. After hours of being handed from man to man, I now know the intricacies of chipping blocks of ice from the river, fitting a pegbox, and fas—"

"A what? Fitting a what?" he asked, thoroughly confused and intrigued.

"A pegbox. The place where the pegs fit on a violin." She looked more than annoyed now; she looked exasperated that he hadn't known what a pegbox was. "I danced with Mr. Cartina, the instrument maker."

"He explained that to you?"

She nodded.

"How did Mr. Cartina get on that topic? Did he think an explanation of fitting pegboxes would thrill you?"

"It is his vocation," she said dryly. "And at least he had a topic."

"We have a topic." Nicholas wrinkled his brow, trying to look wounded.

She sighed. "Oh, please, never audition for the theater."

"What else did you learn?" he asked, straightening his face, though he found her growing impatience amusing, even encouraging.

"To fasten a stock."

"What?" Now this was even more appealing than the pegbox, not that Nicholas didn't know what a stock was—he wore them all the time. He wanted to know *how* someone had taught her to fasten a stock. "Did the man realize he had forgotten to wear one? I suppose he pulled one from a pocket somewhere and demonstrated?"

"Hardly." Her eyes fastened on *his* stock. She looked reluctant to discuss the subject suddenly.

"Well? How did he teach you to fasten a stock?"

"I . . . I noticed Mr. Schnabel kept tilting his head to one side, then the other. I asked what was wrong. He apologized and said his neck was uncomfortable because he had fixed his neckcloth all wrong. Then he went on to explain how to do one the right way."

"So now, based on an explanation, you know how to fasten one," Nicholas said, chuckling with disbelief that any man would bore a woman with such an explanation.

"Do you think I couldn't do it?" Katherine asked, looking put out once again. "I could do yours."

His? No, no, he would only want her to *un*do his. He envisioned her performing the task, her slender fingers slipping to the back of his neck, grasping the buckle, detaching it, slowly removing the cloth. And as her hands worked, as her fingers fumbled around his highly sensitive neck, he would watch her lovely face, which became solemn when she concentrated on a task. Her eyebrows would be slightly drawn together. Her strawberry lips, so often parted, would be pursed.

"Mine?" he asked somewhat huskily, knowing he should never have allowed his mind to go off in that direction.

"Yes, that is what I said."

"I do my best to avoid challenges of that nature."

"It would be a challenge for me, not you. I've never fastened a stock," she said, looking thoroughly baffled.

"Oh, I disagree. It would definitely be a challenge for me, too."

Then he saw that she realized what he was trying to say. Her eyes flared, then settled; her breath caught, then expelled. "Nicholas, I didn't mean to—"

"I know." He smiled. For all the changes Katherine had undergone since coming home, one thing remained—her innocence. Almost instinctively, he drew her closer and said low, "While I may seem dispassionate sometimes, I am anything but dispassionate where you're concerned. Through no fault of yours. You just seem to be a weakness of mine."

She blushed, averted her gaze, missed a step.

The music ended. Nicholas withdrew and offered his arm, watching her. The month was April. Perhaps by the end of summer he could propose to her without creating a stir over the fact that his engagement to Sarah was barely in the past. Perhaps by then Katherine would be more than ready to accept.

25

KEVIN HAD LEFT early. Alexandra had watched him weave his way through the crowd, then disappear, not to return to the ball again. He had made no attempt even to say hello to her. The one time their eyes had met across the width of the ballroom, he had given a slight nod, then turned away.

She must do something. She didn't believe he was content "going from woman to woman," if indeed that was what he was doing. She believed he loved her; she had seen the emotion in his eyes too many times not to believe. She rode home with Katherine and Werner Kraus and lay awake most of the night thinking about Kevin and ways she could help him get through his fear of loving.

The next day she taught her pupils at the house and at the orphanage, and spent quiet moments deliberating about Kevin more. By the following morning she had reached a decision.

She swept down the hall to knock on Katherine's bedroom door. She waited for an answer, then entered.

Clad only in a corset, camisole, and drawers, Katherine sat at her vanity, brushing and pinning her hair. The middle of the vanity was lifted, displaying an upright mirror and below that a compartment that contained brushes, hairpins, and several pearl necklaces. A dress of gray barege had been removed from the wardrobe and tossed across the white-tasseled coverlet on the huge tester bed. Green bed drapes were secured to the posts.

Summer Storm 281

"Going out?" Alexandra asked, fingering the woolen barege.

"Yes. Mrs. Cummings invited me to go along to a friend's. Don't you remember? I told you yesterday afternoon. I asked if you wanted to go, too. You declined."

"Oh, yes," Alexandra said, though she didn't remember. Her mind had been so occupied with solving the dilemma of what was troubling Kevin and how she could help him that she had scarcely thought about anything else of late. "Well, I would like to go with you, but not exactly *with* you."

"What are you talking about?"

"I have the address of Kevin's establishment. The Lighthouse Inn I believe it's called."

"Oh, Alexandra." Katherine stopped brushing and turned on the chair. "You can't be thinking—"

"You and Mr. Jackson may leave me at the hotel," Alexandra said, determined. "I will find a cab to bring me home later."

There was a moment of silence.

"Are you sure you want to go see him?" Katherine asked.

"I'm sure."

Katherine turned back and finished her hair. Alexandra moved from the bed to admire a shelf of bric-a-brac, particularly the ceramic girl in pink taffeta who held an open book. She then drifted to the beautiful antique Chippendale side chairs with their graceful curves, padded seats, and leaf engravings on the upper part of the front legs. These chairs always distracted her whenever she entered Katherine's room.

When Katherine rose to finish dressing, Alexandra reached for the steel collapsible hoops waiting near the bed and opened them. They were held together by broad lengthwise strips of tape and were a much more lightweight way of forming a hoopskirt than running reeds into the casings of a cotton petticoat. Alexandra helped Katherine arrange the hoops around her, then together they began smoothing the skirt of the dress over the hoops.

"As long as you're sure . . . ," Katherine said, obviously still doubting.

Alexandra moved around to smooth the back of the skirt. "I've thought this out very well. I'm going to talk to him."

"If you're sure."

"I'm sure. I've realized he certainly does not mean to call on me. Which means I must call on him."

"I just want things to go well for you."

"Well, there is no predicting how it will go."

"What if he won't talk to you?"

"Stop," Alexandra admonished, giving one last tug at the back hem of the skirt, then straightening. "If I give up on Kevin, I might as well get on a train bound for Chicago tomorrow and marry that man. Hastings . . . whatever his name is." She scowled. "The thought of letting any man but Kevin touch me makes me ill."

Katherine embraced her. Alexandra gave her a quick hug, then withdrew. "We just spent all that time arranging your skirt, and you are going to ruin it being silly," she said.

"Loving."

"Fretful."

Katherine shook her head.

They gathered their pelisses and went downstairs, where Mr. Jackson waited beside the carriage in the drive. He had been whittling at a piece of wood. When he saw them, he tucked the knife and wood away.

Some time later, Alexandra stepped down before The Lighthouse Inn. Katherine, still worrying, leaned out of the carriage to squeeze Alexandra's hand and give her a long look.

Alexandra sighed in exasperation. "If you are waiting for me to change my mind, you will be waiting a long time."

Katherine withdrew. "I'll see you at home later then."

Soon the carriage pulled away to the rattle of springs and the muffled clip-clop of horses' hooves on the muddy street.

Alexandra faced the hotel. Three stories, a brown front, dark blue awnings over entryways, rows of windows, some with curtains neatly tied back. It was not so formidable, a modest hotel compared to the Weddell and Forest City Houses. Another carriage approached, and people wandered in and out of a two-story sandstone building across the street, but other than that, there was not a lot of activity around The Lighthouse Inn, thank goodness; perhaps she and Kevin might easily find a quiet place to talk.

Alexandra stepped onto the wooden-planked walkway to avoid mud tossed by the horses' hooves. One of the hotel's double doors opened as she reached for the knob.

The doorman was dressed in dark blue. In fact, that seemed to be the dress of all the male employees. Several worked with papers behind the lobby's long oak desk. Another swept around a cluster of leather chairs. A woman dressed in the same shade of blue was descending a wooden staircase. She carried a tray cluttered with pottery pitchers and an assortment of glasses and mugs.

Alexandra stopped at the desk and asked where she might find Mr. Riley. He was busy with a matter on the above floor, she was told. She informed the clerk that she would wait in one of the leather chairs.

Two men with copies of *The Cleveland Plain Dealer* spread before them sat opposite her. She watched as three trunks were carried in from outside. No, four trunks, a hatbox, *and* a carpetbag, carried by two employees who were followed by a woman and a man. The man fussed at the woman for having packed so much.

A patron had approached the desk and started to quarrel about his bill. "There were only four baths," he said, "and my son and I were at a friend's home dining the afternoon of the date listed here."

Alexandra didn't want to stare at the man, so she busied herself arranging her crinoline skirt around her, smoothing wrinkles and adjusting folds.

"Mr. O'Malley, if there's been a mistake—"

"A mistake if I've ever seen one!"

"If you would wait a few moments, sir. I cannot make this much of a change without approval."

"Callin' me a liar, are you?" Mr. O'Malley demanded.

"No, sir, I am not." Oh, dear. The clerk was indignant now.

Only so much arranging of the skirt could be done before Alexandra would become almost as conspicuous as the man at the desk. She shifted her attention to her reticule, fingering it, keeping her gaze on it while Mr. O'Malley barreled scathing remarks at the clerk for calling him a liar.

Ridiculous man, Alexandra thought. There were discreet ways to negotiate a bill, even she knew that. His embarrassing fuss had drawn the attention of other people besides herself. One of the men holding a newspaper lowered a corner and stared. The doorman stared, too, and a maid who had appeared in the lobby paused near the staircase to observe the commotion being played out at the desk, then hurried off.

Moments later, Kevin appeared, trying to calm Mr. O'Malley. It was finally agreed that the man and his son had not eaten dinner in the hotel's dining room the day in question, and that perhaps there were only four baths, not five. Then there was another, minor question having to do with laundry. Kevin settled the three issues within ten minutes, scratching through this and that on the bill. Mr. O'Malley looked satisfied—finally. He surveyed the revised bill one more time, produced a purse, and paid the correct amount. Moments later, he wandered away, to the obvious relief of everyone in the lobby.

Alexandra started to rise, but Kevin was still concentrating on the bill, making more marks with his pen. Just when she thought he had finished—he pushed the bill toward one of the clerks—another paper was put before him. Then there were questions about ordering this and ordering that. Sighing, Alexandra settled back in the chair.

This was certainly not the quiet place she had assumed it was when she had stepped out of the carriage.

Finally the clerk she had spoken with what seemed an hour ago glanced her way and said something to Kevin in a low voice. When Kevin's eyes found her, she managed a nervous smile.

Eventually he settled all pertinent issues and questions. But no, there was one more . . . There is me, Alexandra thought, wondering what sort of a mood he was in after negotiating with Mr. O'Malley.

He approached, wearing an unreadable expression that did little for her confidence. She had hoped to see a smile or

Summer Storm

an expression of pleasant surprise. They had never had an argument, after all. He had just stopped calling on her. But disappointment was all her hopes seemed to have accomplished.

Nevertheless she clung to other threads, hoping to say something that would bring him to his senses. She accepted his offered arm, certain he would take her to an office or other private room where they might talk. When she realized he was leading her in the direction of the hotel's front doors, she blurted, "Where are we going?"

"Walking."

Yesterday a rainstorm had saturated Cleveland. Everything that could be muddy was. Today was hardly the day for a walk. But Kevin seemed determined, urging Alexandra outside first with the light touch of a hand on the back of her waist. She lifted her skirt slightly in an effort to keep the hem clean.

They walked, strolling at first. Once they were nearly a block from the hotel, Kevin's steps slowly increased and soon became long strides. Alexandra struggled to keep her skirt from the mud while clinging to his arm. She grew more irritated every second.

He's doing this purposely, she thought, glancing at him. His jaw was set, his face red. He was obviously angry that she had come to see him. Looking at him instead of ahead, she tripped off the edge of a walkway.

"Are you all right?" he asked, pausing to right her with a hand on her elbow. For an instant, genuine concern flashed in his eyes.

She inspected her hem. Splashed with mud, just as she had feared. She glared at him. "Could you please slow your steps?"

"What are you doing here?" he shot back.

"I came to talk to you. Could we go back?"

"I'm thinking we'll talk while we walk," he said, and resumed walking briskly.

She caught up, not an easy task with the skirt encumbering her. "I'm hardly walking! Besides, look at the mud out here—or are you blind?"

"You could always go back."

"Without you, you mean."

No response.

"Surely you have an office in the hotel? We could talk there."

"You already lifted the brows of the desk clerks just by coming here. What would the employees whisper if I took you into my office and closed the door? I have a reputation, yes, but I'd rather not soil it much more."

"Leave the door open," she suggested.

"No."

"Is there a restaurant nearby? *Someplace* quiet and suitable?"

"No."

"What about your home?"

His steps slowed. He glanced over his shoulder. The fear she had seen numerous times was there again, darkening his blue-green eyes. "No. That's not a good idea," he said, and turned his attention back to the walkway ahead.

"It is. You know it is."

"I'd rather go for a ride and talk in the cab."

He was being accommodating all of a sudden, which made Alexandra suspicious. The idea of her being in his home made him nervous, obviously. The intimate Kevin was there, after all. His personal belongings and tastes filled the place. But as much as he didn't want her there, she wanted to be there.

"Take me there, Kevin. To your home," she pressed. "You never have. I want to see it."

"No."

"Yes."

"Damn you, Alexandra!" he said through gritted teeth. "Isn't it enough that I've ignored you? Why don't you go away?"

"Because I love you." She waited for him to digest that, if he could.

He kept walking, so fast, in fact, she fell behind again.

She searched for something else to say, anything that might bring him to an abrupt halt. "And . . . and because I know about Alicia!" she called.

That did it. He stopped mid-step and rocked back onto his heels. She almost collided with his back. A second later, once the shock wore off, he started moving again.

She caught him and grabbed his arm, not caring if he dragged her through the mud. "No. No, please, Kevin. No more running. I cannot believe you are the man who lectured Katherine about not hiding herself away. You have been hiding yourself from me for months. Is this fair? To me or yourself? Yes, Alicia sought the arms of another man, but I am not Alicia. You cannot continue to be so frightened of loving someone just because she treated you so cruelly. I love you, and I am not Alicia," she repeated.

Long moments passed. Kevin touched a hand to his forehead to wipe at beads of perspiration. He *was* nervous; he must be to perspire so. The day was cool, and he had not even paused long enough in the hotel lobby to fetch a coat.

"I'm . . . I'm sorry," he said.

For a stricken moment Alexandra thought he was apologizing because he could not accept what she had said. Then he glanced at her, fear in his eyes still, but now there was gentleness and love, too. She realized he was apologizing for the way he had been treating her, and she gave a little cry of happiness. "It's all right. Yes, it's all right. Please, let's talk more," she managed.

"At my home?" He looked doubtful, and very, very afraid.

"I would like that. I'm different, Kevin. I would never do what she did."

"There's . . . there's no one there today. I have a housekeeper who comes three days a week. Today isn't one of those days. There's only the groom, and he keeps irregular hours."

"Which means we would be alone," she said, liking the idea more each second.

"Yes . . ."

"Well, I cannot think of another man with whom I would rather be alone."

Kevin spotted a cab across the street and hailed the driver. Moments later Alexandra settled on the seat beside Kevin, her heart beating fast. Very fast.

* * *

The house sat at the curve of a long U-shaped drive. Small and unpretentious, it was attractive somehow. Vines scaled the dark bricks, and two huge fireplaces rose at either end. Charming dormers, possessing little roofs of their own, interrupted the steep slope of the roof. Four windows fronted the bottom story, and large bushes huddled on either side of the front door.

When Alexandra entered with Kevin, she noted the parlor to the left. It was sparsely furnished, having all of two chairs—a side chair and a wing chair. There were two tea tables, one in the middle of the room near the wing chair and the other set against the wall near a corner fireplace. The open curtains on the one window, to the other side of the fireplace, revealed sparkling mullioned glass.

The dining room might have seemed plain compared to the grand one at the Kraus house. There was an oak table instead of a glistening mahogany table, and small pictures of the lakeshore in wooden frames instead of huge gilded portraits. The floor was uncarpeted and unpolished, the window unadorned, and there were no lamps, only candles set in a small brass chandelier. It was truly as unremarkable as a room could possibly be, and yet Alexandra found it attractive.

The kitchen was much the same, plain and unremarkable. Kettles and skillets cluttered the bricks around a huge black stove. Utensils dangled from hooks extending from the stones of the fireplace. There were cabinets and a chopping table, stacks of pottery plates, and a basket filled with potatoes.

"And upstairs?" Alexandra asked Kevin, eyeing the staircase with its carved banister and handrail. It seemed out of place in the house somehow, almost as if whoever had built the place had had to settle for it, having nothing of a plainer design.

"Bedrooms," Kevin answered softly.

She turned her gaze on him. "Yours?"

He nodded. His breath had quickened; his chest rose and fell rapidly. And his eyes were glazed.

Alexandra couldn't deny her own thrill at the wickedness of just being here alone with him. Her heart seemed to have leapt to her throat suddenly—she felt it drum there. And she was light-headed. She backed against the curved end of the handrail and gripped it to keep her balance.

Kevin followed her. His hands found the clasp of her pelisse, soon parted the dark, fur-lined wool, and let it slip from her shoulders and fall back across the handrail. An arm encircled her waist, pulling her body to his. Alexandra gasped.

"I've been a fool, a damn fool," he said huskily. "Katherine was right." He dipped his head and touched his lips to hers.

"Wait," she said, having no idea what he was talking about when he mentioned Katherine. But that was not what made her hesitate. No, there was something else. Oh, God, how to tell him? But she must be honest with him. She could not allow him to believe they could now live happily ever after. Not when her father might crash down on them any day.

Kevin cocked his head and stared at her.

"Remember I once told you about my father in Chicago?"

"I remember, but—"

"He sent Mr. Kraus a letter some time ago. He's arranged a marriage for me in Chicago." She closed her eyes, waiting. Would Kevin still want her? Would he want to face her father? Or would he want to avoid trouble? She thought she knew him well, but there was still that trickle of doubt. There were still those inner parts of him she didn't know at all. He had never revealed anything about his childhood or his family—if he even had a family. She had been so caught up in the whirlwind of romance, she had simply never pressed him. She had wondered at times, but never enough to ask.

"No. Never," she heard him whisper fiercely. Then his voice grew louder: "We'll go away together, Angel. I'll sell the inn, everything here, and we'll go away together. I'm thinking I'm the only man who'll be marrying you. Unless you want something different."

She caught her breath, laughed, opened her eyes, and flung her arms around his neck. "Why would you even wonder? I want only you. Only you."

He lifted her, sweeping her into his arms as easily as if she were a doll, and carried her upstairs. There he placed her on her feet in an open doorway.

A bedroom. His bedroom. A spread patterned in blocks of brown and green covered the bed. A sliver of sunlight stole through heavy green draperies, shooting a beam across the uncarpeted floor. There were chairs, several trunks, a chiffonier, and a table, none of which held her attention more than a second. Alexandra turned her gaze back to Kevin.

"You can change your mind, Angel. I won't be faulting you for it," he said, his voice thick. "I'll wait until the wedding night."

She smiled—a facade for the nervousness that churned in her stomach suddenly. "But I thought you were such a rogue . . ."

He traced her jaw with a slightly rough finger, sending shivers of anticipation through her. "I'm wanting to make sure you're sure."

She entered the room and heard the door shut behind her. The sound made her catch her breath for an instant. She remembered hearing whispers about the pain involved, the sheer animalistic nature of the act. And yet the night they had returned from Melodeon Hall, when Kevin had touched the tops of her breasts above her decolletage, she certainly had not felt revulsion. This ache she felt, this profound want that made her heart beat so fast and her breath catch, could not possibly lead to anything horrible.

Still, there was a certain apprehension that made her tremble.

She whirled, suddenly not so confident, feeling much like a bride must feel on her wedding night, wanting to be with her husband in the most intimate way, but . . . She rubbed her damp palms against the panels of her quilted skirt. "I might seem sure of myself, indeed very sure at times. I know I've touched you . . . kissed you a lot, much more than a proper lady probably would, and I've enjoyed your touches, but . . . well . . . I suppose you could have tried anything, at anytime, all those afternoons we wandered out alone, you know—to complete things." She paused to wet her lips. "I'm not sure what I'm asking of you. I know I am asking something. I've certainly no mind to run from this room. I love you. I want to be with you, but—"

"You're frightened, Alexandra?" he queried softly. He stood beside the door, his back to the wall.

"Yes, yes, I suppose I am. I'm just not very good at admitting it."

"We'll get through this together, Angel—my fear of loving and your fear of the unknown." He approached, extending his hand to her.

She took it.

He drew her close and kissed her, lightly at first, deepening the kiss when she sighed and moved against him. She felt his strong fingers push into her hair, find the pins, and pull them loose. She felt the loose braid that had been coiled and pinned hours earlier slither down her back.

"That's it, love. Slowly. Give in to the feelings rushing through you," he murmured, dispelling her every hesitation. "It'll be uncomfortable at first, but then . . . ah, then I think you'll like it."

His lips seduced her. They were hot, oh so pleasantly hot, on her lips, her chin, her neck. There was no "giving in" to the feelings. They claimed her. Desire flared, fiery, scalding, building in intensity. And he was right. She did like it.

He unbuttoned the row of buttons on her bodice, then pushed the dress and chemise off her shoulders. He caressed a breast, taunting the tip, kneading the flesh. She moaned, feeling her breast swell and fill his hand. Then he dipped his head and took the peak in his mouth. Alexandra tossed her head back, gasping for air. Oh, God, she was being devoured. But she did not mind. No, not at all.

The intensity was unbearable—only because she wanted more, more kissing, more suckling, more caressing. She whispered his name; he drew her dress over her head. She lifted her arms, helping him toss the material aside; his masterful fingers removed drawers, then stockings and boots, leaving her chemise, but lingering on the curves of her calves and the insteps of her feet, teasing. Exquisite torture! She reached for his shoulders, breathing more rapidly than she had ever thought possible, afraid she would swoon, something she had never done.

He straightened. "Sshh. Slow, love. Slow. Remember that."

He kissed her again, his hands on her face now, and her breathing calmed some. Then he withdrew and stepped away. He slipped off his vest. She stood staring, watching the flexing of his shoulder muscles beneath the white shirt and the deftness of his fingers as they struggled with his neckcloth.

"Help me," he whispered.

But he had it undone before she took the first step toward him. She pulled the slithering cloth free, then reached for the buttons on his shirt. Her hands trembled. She couldn't do the task fast enough. But finally the shirt opened.

She touched his chest, splayed her hands across the coarse hair and the muscles beneath. He touched his lips to hers again. Then suddenly she was in his arms, being carried across the room, being placed on the bed.

A hand, strong and masculine, slid beneath her chemise and crawled its way up her thigh, stealing her breath as it pushed the cotton material along. She felt a slight urge to scoot away, to avoid the most intimate, shocking touch. Kevin must have felt her tense. He whispered more words: "Relax. Let me touch you. I love you, Alexandra. God help me, I love you."

She smiled and settled back on a feather pillow ... and surrendered.

His lips fluttered over her. They were everywhere suddenly. On her forehead, her eyes, her jaw, her neck, nudging her chemise down one shoulder, closing over a breast and forcing a cry of unbearable delight from her. He had pushed the chemise hem to her waist. He kneaded a hip, her bottom, then played in the curls covering her most private feminine place. She gasped, parted her thighs, wanting more, so much more, wanting something to fill the ache that throbbed deep in her womanly flesh.

He touched her there. Fingers slipped over her again and again, setting a rhythm. Alexandra arched, strained, cried his

Summer Storm

name as something pleasurable yet painful in intensity flooded her and left her panting.

He moved beside her, freeing himself of his trousers, working at something else for a time, she didn't know what. She had a million questions, but none she wanted to ask at the moment. There was more to this, she sensed. She knew.

He slipped between her still parted thighs and covered her. There was pain, stinging and burning but brief. He began moving, thrusting in and out, filling her so she thought she would burst. His hands slid beneath her bottom to cup, caress, knead. Then Ecstasy, mystical and beautiful, began swirling around her, evading, teasing. She wanted it, needed it. She arched a final time, reaching . . .

And finally . . . the explosion, deep and wonderful. *It* was the perfect peak she had sought so aggressively. Kevin had reached it, too, apparently. His groans mingled with her cries to create a lovely, primitive duet.

Moments later, they shifted to their sides, staring at each other, their bodies still joined.

"It wasn't anything like I thought. What was that?" Alexandra asked, unsure if she should be asking such a thing at all. Why question the pleasure they had so obviously given each other? A flush began at the base of her neck and engulfed her face. She covered her head with a pillow. "I shouldn't ask. I'm sorry."

Kevin chuckled and fought for the pillow. "Come out from under there."

"No."

"Alexandra. Come here. I'll attempt to explain. It's not wrong to want to understand."

Curiosity finally lured her out.

He slipped from her and turned on his back. He removed something from himself, from the part of him that had entered her, she thought. She was too shy still to dare a look. Shy Alexandra—who would have imagined? She laughed at herself, instinctively resting her head on his shoulder. He began talking, explaining things that embarrassed her slightly, but things she wanted to know. In all their girlish whispering back at the school, she and Katherine had been wrong about some things, about the pain mostly. It really had not been so bad, and it had been brief. Neither of them had had a clue that so much pleasure was involved, nor that there were so many different ways a man and a woman could be together, nor that there were ways—not accepted by genteel men and women—that pregnancy could be prevented. Kevin didn't explain the different ways to make love. He said he would much rather show her. She saw the devilish glint in his eyes and laughed.

"Are you thinking I won't try?" he asked, a brow lifted.

"Oh, sir, no, no! I'm hoping you do," she whispered dramatically, kissing him.

Growling, he pushed her back against the pillow. Soon his hands skimmed her body again, in a thousand different places, and in a thousand different ways.

26

SUNSET HAD BEGUN to display its wondrous colors when Nicholas stepped from the house. Harold stood beside the carriage in the drive. He looked different this evening, as dignified as ever, but different somehow. His hands were clasped behind his back. His dress was impeccable. (How Harold always managed to keep his clothing so clean while driving through Cleveland's frequently muddied streets, Nicholas could never guess.) Still, *something* was different. Harold's mouth was turned down, but it wasn't quite a frown. No, it was rather like an upside-down smile.

That was the difference then. Harold's demeanor was different.

"Good evening, sir," Harold said. He was obviously in a more pleasant mood than Nicholas had seen him in for a long while. There were no scowls, no sharp words about David, who had snatched a frightening number of Harold's hats of late. Nicholas wondered if something had happened between David and Harold then, if Harold had perhaps set David straight in some tactful fashion, for Nicholas couldn't imagine Harold lacking tact. Harold was simply not the type of man to take a child by the scruff and shake him.

"Your sister is in Cleveland, isn't she?" Nicholas inquired.

"She is. For the next two days, sir."

"I had planned to give you the evening off. Business occupied me earlier, and I forgot to tell you. Would you like the evening off, Harold?"

"But you look ready for an evening yourself, Mr. Cummings."

Nicholas shrugged. "Supper with Katherine and Werner."

"Permit me to at least take you there, sir. I'll tether a horse to the carriage and leave it at the residence for you."

"That would be fine," Nicholas responded. He smoothed his coat and smiled. Being with Harold sometimes brought forth his own store of dignity. For a time. Burying his hand in a trouser pocket, he studied Harold again, for now he thought the differences might not just be his demeanor. There was something more. Not in his posture, not in his clothing . . . What was it then?

Harold pulled a hand from behind his back and touched his jaw. "A little . . . addition to the hat," he said.

And then Nicholas saw it. A chin strap fastened to the top hat. He stared for a moment, then chuckled.

"Buttons, you see, on either side," Harold said, fumbling with one side of the strap and pulling it down to reveal a buttonhole in the pliable leather. "My sister thought of it. Ingenious, I think. The groom's boy will not take another of my hats."

"No, I don't suppose he will. Unless he takes your head along with it."

Harold refastened the leather and swung open the carriage door. "Now, sir, for your evening."

Grinning, Nicholas approached the carriage door, pausing with a hand on it to assess the chin strap again. It certainly held the hat firmly in place. "Quite . . . ingenious," Nicholas said. Then, giving a hearty laugh, he ducked his head and stepped up into the carriage.

"My, aren't you a sight," Alexandra said, sauntering into Katherine's room.

"Help me, please," Katherine said, exasperated. She was seated before her vanity, trying to twist and pin difficult curls into place.

Summer Storm

Alexandra completed the task within minutes. Then she watched Katherine fuss with hoops, step into a blue-green gown, and nervously fumble with buttons.

"I would offer to help with that, too. But I'm not sure I could do it as quickly as you seem to want it done," Alexandra said, slightly annoyed. "And now you've done one all wrong. Oh, here, let me try." She stepped forward to help.

"Nicholas was due here ten minutes ago," Katherine mumbled. "My hair is so difficult to handle when it's humid."

"Nicholas is already here. He has been here for fifteen minutes. You may as well calm yourself."

"Fifteen—?" Katherine jerked. A button went flying.

Alexandra frowned. "Now look what you've done. I should not have told you. I'll get a needle and thread."

"No. I'll wear another gown," Katherine said, twisting.

"How do you expect to be pleasant company, fussing around like this? I haven't seen you this nervous in a long time. Not since the day you left the school." Alexandra found Katherine's back again, and unfastened the two buttons she had managed to slip through buttonholes before Katherine jerked.

Katherine sighed. "Hurry, please. I'm not usually late!"

A yellow gown of shimmering silk replaced the blue-green one. Alexandra watched Katherine dig around in the wardrobe for slippers and finally emerge with a black pair with tiny black velvet bows.

"I'm going to Melodeon Hall with Kevin," Alexandra announced.

Katherine paused. "Things must have gone well the other day."

"They did. Now, smooth your skirt and calm yourself. Nicholas looks very, very handsome tonight," Alexandra teased softly over Katherine's shoulder.

"Ooh! One second you tell me to calm myself. The next you say something to make me more nervous," Katherine scolded. "I'm rattled enough, don't you think?"

Alexandra laughed mischievously, then slipped away.

After one last glance in the vanity mirror, Katherine started for the staircase leading downstairs. Then she caught sight of

Nicholas from the corner of her eye and she paused.

He was just emerging from the upstairs parlor at the end of the wainscoted hall. He stopped in the doorway, seeing her.

She approached him. Distant sounds drifted from downstairs—Peggy singing, the clinking of crystal, presumably from the dining room. Katherine halted, leaving perhaps a foot of distance between herself and Nicholas. "Hello," she said.

His emerald eyes skimmed her. His look was a lazy one; lazy and dark. "You look ravishing," he said finally, just when she was about to ask if he meant to speak at all.

She laughed nervously. "Well, that's quite a greeting. Ravishing . . . what a word."

"It suits you."

"You look quite . . . ravishing yourself." He did. He wore black broadcloth. The buttons on his waistcoat were oblong and mosaic, and the tails of his coat hung nearly to the back of his knees. He looked more striking tonight than he had at the mayor's ball.

He chuckled. An instant later he raised a hand and adjusted his stock. "Thank you. But . . . I had a bit of trouble with this. It's still not too comfortable. Perhaps you could help."

Katherine's heart quickened. She hid a smile of delicious shock behind her hand. "And what, pray tell, would Uncle Werner say if he came upstairs and saw me helping you dress? Or Peggy, for that matter?"

Nicholas seemed to consider that, twisting his lips this way and that way. Finally he jerked a nod. "You may have a point there. Later then."

She didn't respond to his suggestion one way or another. The issue of whether or not she could fasten a stock properly seemed to have become a challenge between them. And yet she knew that if the time ever arrived to face the challenge, her own nervously fumbling fingers might defeat her. "What are you doing up here anyway?" she asked, digressing.

"Werner sent me up to look at the new portrait in the parlor, the one of the horse."

"And what do you think?"

"My honest opinion?"

She nodded.

"I think he wanted to see if I would encounter you. The portrait is almost exactly like the one hanging in the bank lobby. Werner knows I've seen it before."

Katherine laughed. "That was exactly my thought. So what was his real motivation?" She shook her head. "Does one ever know what Uncle Werner is thinking until he has progressed somewhat with his projects?" she asked, thinking of the way her uncle had set the gossipers of Cleveland straight when they would have ostracized her.

"Perhaps he was growing impatient," Nicholas suggested.

"Impatient . . . yes . . . I am rather tardy. My hair was difficult."

He made a show of assessing her hair. He walked around her, inspecting it from the sides, then from the back. Then he leaned slightly over her shoulder, which was bared by sleeves clinging to her upper arms. "You should have left it down. It's thick and silky, unruly, left down, but perhaps that's why I find it so beautiful that way. The unruliness suits you—or did. Ten months ago you wouldn't have cared if someone had caught you helping me dress."

His breath was warm on her skin, warm and thrilling. Pleasurable chills shot through Katherine, up her neck, down her arms, settling in her chest and below her stomach. She thought of the evening of the mayor's ball, when Nicholas had caught her hand as she'd tried to brush snowflakes from his hair. He didn't want her to touch him . . . and yet he was speaking to her in the thick, low tone that never failed to unnerve her, that never failed to make her *want* to turn and place herself in his arms. "I don't know what to make of you sometimes," she said.

"No?"

"No."

His hands found her shoulders, and his thumbs made swirling motions near her shoulder blades. She could stand here like this for only so long before her knees would weaken. Already she felt breathless. She closed her eyes, certain he was about to kiss her.

"Do you know what I want?" he asked softly.

She could only imagine. "W-what?"

"I want the old Katherine," he murmured. "The unruly woman not afraid to ask me to kiss her. The woman not afraid to say certain things or do things most people would consider outrageous, scandalous if you will, like wanting to make love on a saloon floor. Good God, you did shock me with that. But you excited me, too. And the night you suddenly appeared on my doorstep, sweeping that hood from your head . . . I didn't know whether to admire you or throttle you for riding through the streets alone. I wanted to do both actually. Until the night of the mayor's ball, I didn't realize what was bothering me exactly, why I've felt the need myself to keep some physical distance between us. It wasn't just your request that when you came to see Lewis I not touch you or try to kiss you. I kept remembering your words 'Seduce me into it. Do you think I won't have regrets?' Remember? You said that the night of the charity ball when I tried to convince you to marry me."

She nodded. "I remember." Her hands buried themselves in her skirt. What was his purpose for saying all this? He had certainly frozen her in place. Surely he meant to make a point. What that point was, she had no idea.

"Even before the mayor's ball I realized that not touching you or kissing you or taking you in my arms—not seducing you into a decision—is only part of what's troubling me, troubling *us*. What troubles me more is the armor you've built around yourself, the reserve. I want it stripped away— it's not you. I want your total trust again, perhaps more than the physical act of making love. That may take time—how much, I don't know, but I'll wait. I saw some of the old you the night of the mayor's ball, and remembered how much I love it. It's a matter of honesty, you see. The true you. The true me. Our true feelings. Before we give in to the passion." He released her shoulders and stepped back, taking the heat of his body with him.

Katherine stood in profound silence, breathing deeply to ward off light-headedness. She had wanted to know his point. He had certainly revealed it. "Well, that was quite an outpour-

Summer Storm

ing," she finally found the sense to remark.

"Don't take my words lightly, Katherine."

She *had* placed armor about herself. Kevin, with his sharp statements, had helped her fight her way through most of its thickness. But the remaining plates . . . to destroy them would leave her vulnerable, open to possible hurt again. She was the only woman Nicholas was seeing, she felt certain, but to strip away her reserve . . . She didn't know if she had the courage to bare herself. He had, after all, been angry that she had tried to seduce him last summer aboard the *Morning Star*.

Nicholas moved up beside her. He braced an open hand against the wall to her right. He drew the other hand across his mouth, then pushed his coattail back and buried the hand in a trouser pocket. "I've done a lot of thinking."

"Obviously," she remarked. "Well, I haven't given any thought to stripping away my reserve—as you call it. At one time, the trust you speak of was so completely destroyed. I didn't want to see or talk to you. You were the one person in the world I trusted, and that trust was—"

"You had placed me on an elaborate pedestal fit only for a god," he said tightly. "I was the image of perfection in your mind. There was no one else who could equal me. Well, I am no god, as you now know. And I am not Perfection. I am merely a man, as faulty as any man. As vulnerable as any man."

"You certainly came here with a purpose tonight." She was so filled with emotion she thought she would burst—anger and unease that he would expect her to simply shed her reserve when it had led to her total humiliation once; love for him greater than any she had ever known; frustration that he wanted more from her than she thought she could give.

"I did," he responded.

Moments of near silence passed. There was, of course, Peggy's singing. And the echoes in Katherine's head of Nicholas's poignant words.

"You want me," he murmured.

A whoosh of breath expelled from her lungs along with a short laugh of disbelief. "That's arrogant."

"It's the truth."

"I think this conversation has gone far enough. I was looking forward to spending a delightful evening with you and Uncle Werner. Now you—"

Nicholas shifted and took a step that placed him right in front of her. He caught her chin in his palm, lifted it, and kissed her. "Is that what you've wanted? What you've wanted for days and weeks now?"

She stared into his eyes. They were so intense, filled with yearning . . . She averted her gaze. She couldn't deny that she wanted him to kiss her, to do much more than kiss her, but she couldn't voice her want. She was too afraid.

"You see?" He stepped back. "The old Katherine would not have looked away. You were trusting, bold—"

"And that boldness caused me all sorts of trouble!"

"I loved that boldness."

"Is it fair to expect me to be as I was? Things . . . events change people," she said.

"And people sometimes recover from illness. But not if they have no desire to."

"I am not ill. This is not—"

"In a sense, you are."

"Oh, please, let's not argue."

"Would you like me to kiss you again?" he asked. "Would you?"

Katherine's heart pounded. Warmth circulated in her veins, poured into muscles, vital organs, toes, and fingertips. "Nicholas, please . . ."

"Would you? Answer me."

"I . . . We really should go downstairs. Peggy . . . Uncle Werner."

"Katherine." His hand caught her chin again.

"All right. Yes. Yes, damn you! Kiss me. Please," she whispered.

He did.

The kiss was moist, brief. His tongue ran lightly along her lower lip, eliciting a gasp from her, then delved into her mouth to lightly frolic with her tongue. A moment later he lifted his head and gazed at her. "Well, that's a beginning," he said breathlessly. "Now we'll go downstairs."

Another laugh of disbelief tore lose from her throat. She was trembling, could barely stand her legs were so weak! "You unravel me emotionally, then think to take me right downstairs?"

He grinned with all the confidence of a cavalier. "I'll go then. You come when you're ready."

Katherine nodded. An instant later he was gone.

She sought the quiet of her bedroom for a time. She sat at the vanity, staring at herself in the mirror, thinking that his words and actions near the parlor door had been some sort of ultimatum. Just as she had demanded that he make no advance when she visited Lewis, he, too, was making a demand. He knew that she loved him, that he was the only man she wanted, just as he knew her other option—not trying to regain her old confidence and boldness—was really not an option. It would mean losing him.

And that was a thought she truly could not stand.

"Ah, there you are, Katherine," Uncle Werner said, replacing a half-filled decanter of brandy on the sideboard in the library. "I was beginning to think something had happened to you."

Nicholas sat in a wing chair to her left. She gave him a tight smile. He inclined his head.

Uncle Werner swirled the brandy in the snifter he held, looking thoughtfully into the glass for a moment. Then he lifted his head. "I have been thinking of going to the islands, Nicholas, to see about that property we bought there. You should think of going, too."

"Kelley's Island, you mean?" Nicholas asked.

"Not far from Sandusky?" Katherine couldn't help interjecting. She couldn't help the thrill of excitement that surged within her either.

Uncle Werner nodded.

"It's beautiful out that way. Trees and beautifully etched land rising out of the lake. It's incredible," she said, taking a chair opposite Nicholas. "The one time Sisters Dorothy and Ruth took me, Alexandra, and four other girls, I fell in love with the islands. We went to three actually."

"Then you should go again. With us," Nicholas said.

Katherine grew thoughtful. And solemn. "I couldn't. The orphanage."

"Talk to Sisters Mary and Elizabeth. They'll volunteer extra time. Surely Alexandra will, too."

"No, I couldn't ask them. Sister Mary stays every night already, and Sister Elizabeth comes three days a week."

"Perhaps they know of others who will volunteer."

Now that was a thought.

"You want to go," Nicholas said. "I can see it in your expression."

"Of course I want to go. But I must settle things at the orphanage first."

Peggy appeared at the door to inform them that supper was ready.

Throughout the meal of baked herring with a lemon glaze, tender, buttered potatoes, and squash, Katherine spoke more about the islands. She told Nicholas and Uncle Werner how she had eaten nearly a bucketful of grapes while visiting Kelley's. Sisters Dorothy and Ruth had taken the girls during the grape harvest. "Sister Dorothy, who was always stern-faced, smiled at our excitement over the grapes. She didn't smile when we ripped our dresses climbing on the rocks, however. She was always one for ladylike behavior. If there was a rock in the way, a lady lifted her skirt and went around it, not ever over it. I'll never forget the night Alexandra slipped into Sister Dorothy's room and dropped handfuls of—" Katherine put a hand to her mouth and laughed. "Perhaps I shouldn't tell this," she said, unsure if Uncle Werner would find it humorous.

He leaned forward and squinted one eye. "Do tell. *Alles.*"

Katherine caught sight of the smile twitching one corner of his mouth. She laughed, remembering Alexandra's many antics, then wrinkled her nose. "Worms. She put worms and mud in Sister Dorothy's boots. Poor Sister Dorothy. I felt half-sorry for her when she came screeching down the hall the next morning."

"What happened to Alexandra?" Nicholas asked, unable to take his eyes from Katherine. Her cheeks were stained with the pink glow of excitement and happiness, and her eyes were glowing pools of blue. The gold strands in her hair shimmered in the lamplight. He wanted her to keep talking and laughing forever, though he knew the hours were passing. He wanted to stop them, stop time, if such a thing were possible. He could sit right here for the rest of his life and watch her. Just watch her. And wait, very, very patiently.

"What happened to Alexandra?" she repeated. "Nothing. No one but me knew she did it. And I was not going to tell. Shocking, I know, but I was not about to tattle on my best friend. She would have been granted no privileges for months."

They finished supper. Nicholas suggested an evening walk. Werner graciously declined, as Nicholas had known he would, saying something about a book calling to him from the library.

Outside, the sun was dying, spilling breathtaking shades of orange and red. Lake Erie glistened. She was calm tonight, languidly stretching her great waters. Rain had turned the grass a lush green once again and brought a variety of colorful flowers out from winter havens. The trees were fully dressed in greenery.

Nicholas took Katherine's hand and led her to a settee on the front lawn. There they sat, watching the great lake in reverence.

"I've spent my life on the shores of Lake Erie," Nicholas said after a time, "and yet I've never been to Canada."

"Never?" Katherine asked in awe. "A man of your means?"

He chuckled. "Yes, ironic, isn't it? I've spent years building a business never stopping long enough to enjoy the scenery. Building those side-wheelers and establishing my independence became an obsession—my struggle to rid myself of my father. For years I detested him."

He felt her studying his profile. "I never knew," she said. "Werner did."

"He never said anything."

"He wouldn't."

"No, I suppose you're right. What happened between you and your father? That is, if you don't mind my asking."

He turned to gaze at her. "I would share my deepest thoughts with you. Everything."

Katherine was touched. As she sat gazing back at him, his words seemed to bond them together in a most profound way.

He talked about his father, told her the heart-wrenching account of what had happened on the South Carolina plantation the summer he'd turned fifteen. His father's every action, every word, had made him believe Lemuel Cummings upheld slavery. Nicholas had been a young man struggling to see what could possibly be right in something he found totally unacceptable. As he talked, Katherine saw his devotion, his passion, his pain.

The sun spread myriad colors over the water. They pooled, ran together, then parted in long, thin lines, melting and finally fading. The moon claimed the sky. Night deepened. Light glowed in the windows of the house to their right. Still Katherine sat watching Nicholas, her eyes widening when he spoke of his involvement with the Underground Railroad. "I've seen atrocities you cannot imagine, things that only make me more determined to end slavery."

He told her about the Oberlin men being arrested and brought to trial, how he had been told to stay quiet and not give fugitives passage to Canada for a time. And he told her of the night Lemuel Cummings had revealed his involvement with the Underground.

Katherine drew a swift breath of surprise, for he'd not even hinted at Lemuel being involved before. "That's incredible," she whispered.

Nicholas shook his head. "No one was more surprised than I. I might have wondered if he was trying to trap me into admitting my 'illegal activities,' as Harold so fondly calls them, if he hadn't already pointed out that if he had wanted to ruin me, he could have years ago, when I was really just

Summer Storm

beginning to build my own life. Last summer I found myself in the awkward position of having to go into a shipbuilding venture with him, an idea I didn't relish." He explained that there had been no other investors besides Werner, Lemuel, and himself to be found in Cleveland. "He made me aware that he had watched my business progress over the years, and that he had watched proudly. I was not, and still am not, proud of my attitude toward *him* these past years. I now feel very small indeed."

"You had no way of knowing that he was troubled, too, that he was attempting to understand his friend's cruelty," Katherine said.

"We've been seeing each other often. We had dinner with Werner at the Forest City House yesterday. It went much better than our last dinner together. The ship will be launched later this summer. Having my father beside me when it slides into the Cuyahoga will be a pleasure. We even went to the track today. Werner was there. He won a large purse."

"Did he?"

Nicholas nodded. "He didn't tell you?"

"No. How did you do?" she asked.

He grinned sheepishly. "One out of ten. I could have done worse—none out of ten."

They grew silent. Katherine wanted him to touch her, anywhere, everywhere. A breeze whispered through the branches overhead and swept through the grass. June evenings could be quite cool in Ohio. There had been a rare frost and unusually low temperatures just last week. This night was rapidly growing chilly.

"I should take you back inside. You're shivering," Nicholas said.

"Yes. Peggy's rather protective at times. She might be watching from a window," Katherine said, studying the shadowed lines of his face. "Put your arm around me," she requested softly.

"Do you think Werner will ever consider marrying her?" Nicholas asked, easing his arm around her. If her request surprised him, the emotion didn't show.

Katherine smiled. "I've wondered the same thing myself at times. He seems quite fond of her."

They drifted back to the house together. Peggy had gone to bed. So had Uncle Werner, Katherine discovered when she peeked in the library and found it empty. Alexandra was not home yet, but Katherine felt certain she would be soon.

She suggested they take a bottle of wine and go into the parlor. Nicholas said he had to leave soon, but a glass of wine sounded inviting. He followed her into the dining room, where she took a bottle from the huge sideboard there. She found goblets in a corner cabinet and handed them to Nicholas.

In the parlor lamps still burned. Shadows danced and writhed. Katherine stood near the fireplace and opened the wine. She poured the dark liquid into the glasses Nicholas held, then placed the bottle on the mantel.

The wine was sweet, rich, like the grapes she had eaten in the Kelley's Island vineyard. She wanted more. She poured herself another gobletful and drank again.

"Slow down, love," Nicholas said, watching her.

"I know, I know, wine should be sipped," she teased.

He grinned, lazily, seductively, watching her, watching her lips.

"You shared so much of yourself with me tonight," she said, "I thought I should share at least one of my little secrets. I love to guzzle wine."

"Guzzle . . . ," he said, as if considering the word. He chuckled.

"From my childhood, I suppose. My father was as Irish as Irish could be. He liked draining a bottle."

She reached for the bottle again. Nicholas placed his hand over hers to stop her. Katherine froze. It was the first real touch in hours, one she had longed for, one she wasn't about to disturb.

Nicholas knew the feelings rippling through him. How well he knew them. He had been living with them for months now, struggling to act like a perfect gentleman and touch her as little as possible. But now . . . the atmosphere—the low dancing light, the wine, the woman he wanted—threatened to

Summer Storm

be his undoing. He remembered telling her he wanted honesty between them—the true her, the true him—before allowing passion to flare. Well, it was flaring now, and he seemed to be rapidly losing his ability to hold it off. He should turn and leave while he still could.

But no . . . She turned those enchanting blue eyes on him, and his control shattered.

He skimmed his fingertips down her satiny arm, teasing the inside of her delicate elbow. He met her sleeve and touched the cool silk, touched her soft shoulder. He caressed the smooth white column of her neck, too, and traced her jaw as her head fell back and a rush of breath escaped her. Then he tugged her to him and feasted on her lips, her neck, burning a trail down to her breasts. He had been too long without. He was famished for her.

"Not here, Nicholas. Oh, God, not here," she whispered, her hands in his hair now.

That jerked him from his daze, from the powerful desire that had claimed him. "I must go," he rasped, knowing that if he didn't, they would be tumbling to the floor.

He withdrew from her, from the room.

She followed, catching up with him in the entryway. "Nicholas, stay longer, please."

He turned a lifted brow on her. "And take you right here on the tiles rather than in the parlor?"

She gasped, but he thought the gasp was more from excitement induced by the thought, perhaps the image, of turned-up petticoats, discarded drawers and trousers, and flesh meeting flesh, than shock for propriety's sake.

He faced her. "Is that it then? Are you thinking of the cool tiles? The feel of my hands caressing your body?" Good God. *He* wanted to gasp now. He was shocking himself. He couldn't believe he, Nicholas Cummings, was speaking this way. But then, he was learning that passion sometimes caused the most delicious scandalous behavior.

Her eyes were as wide as they could possibly get. "Go, oh go," she whispered, clenching her hands and backing to the wall. "I can't stand this."

Outside he was thankful for the cool night air. It chilled his skin, but hardly touched him inside, hardly thawed the heat in his groin. He managed to swing up onto his horse without damaging himself.

Just as he straightened, grasping the reins, there was an explosion from the direction of the lake. Nicholas felt the force of it vibrate through his body. The horse whinnied and skittered about. Nicholas bent to stroke its neck, trying to soothe it. An eerie orange light flashed somewhere out in the darkness of the water.

He studied it. His first thought was that the light was merely the glow of a lamp. But how foolish that thought was. No lamp glowed like that. Besides, he had spent his life learning about ships, how to make them seaworthy and safe. When he was a boy, he'd watched one burn near the harbor entrance after a similar explosion. A chill went up his spine. Alarm pumped through his veins. There were shouts from somewhere down the street; others had heard the explosion, too.

"What was that?" Katherine asked from the front entrance.

"A boiler," Nicholas responded with certainty. "There's a ship on fire out there."

"Oh, God. Are you sure?"

He nodded, shedding his coat. "Come here." As she raced toward him, he quickly unbuttoned his waistcoat. He handed her the garments and asked her to keep them for him, then he reined his horse in the direction of the Flats and kicked his heels against the animal's sides.

All three side-wheelers comprising the *Erie Line* were away in other ports. When Nicholas reached the Flats, men were scrambling toward ships and working busily on decks. The sails of the schooner *Oak Leaf* were rapidly unfurled, and the vessel soon moved through the channel amid shouts and a clamor of activity. Nicholas joined the crew of the side-wheeler *Arrow*. Cool night air whipped beneath his collar as the ship steamed out into Lake Erie. He smelled burning wood now, heard shouts and screams and prayed the sounds were only figments of his imagination.

Summer Storm 311

More ships followed the *Arrow*. The *Dean Richmond*, the *Amaranth*, the *St. Albans* . . . Oil lanterns dangled from hooks. Frowns marred faces; eyes stared intently at the vast water. These were lake men, and there was a certain pride in being classified as such, a certain dedication to one another and the cargos they shipped and passengers they transported.

The blazing ship was more than a mile out from Cleveland. Nicholas swore under his breath as the *Arrow* neared it.

Objects bobbed in the water—chunks and pieces of burnt wood, bodies, chairs, trunks. An unopened wine bottle drifted by. There was a plate, a shimmering piece of what had been a brass oil lamp. Nicholas pulled his gaze away from it and joined the lake men in tossing things that would float to people still alive and struggling in the water. Some of the *Arrow*'s crew had lowered small boats. To the objection of the captain, Nicholas climbed in one and helped row out to pluck survivors from the water.

How horrible that people had died. And the ship . . . Good God, the ship. Nicholas had seen the one burn. He had seen others blown onto shoals during lake gales, their hulls splintered, but he had never seen one *consumed*. The destruction was total, or would be in less than ten minutes, Nicholas guessed. Blackened beams, masts, and spars crashed, splintering and spraying water. Only the paddle house of the side-wheeler tipping precariously in the water was still intact. But flames, encouraged by the wind that whipped, dove, and swirled, were rapidly licking and lapping their way toward the word *Illinois*.

Nicholas knew the ship. It was an excursion vessel that traveled ports between Chicago and Buffalo.

More wood cracked. Fire popped. The ship shifted, heaved, struggled for one last breath. It rolled and groaned. Then Lake Erie swallowed it, paddle house and all.

Voices fell silent. Men stared. Small fires still burned here and there, eating various things in the water, pieces of furniture and wood that had once formed planks and beams and other parts of the ship. Nicholas sat in stunned silence.

"Jesus. Sweet Mary, mother of God," whispered a lake man seated to his left.

A woman Nicholas had pulled from the water buried her face in her hands and began sobbing softly. Nicholas managed to swallow the knot in his throat.

Then he and another man began rowing the boat back toward the *Arrow*.

Survivors were lodged in riverside inns and taverns, even in a few homes. The following afternoon a list was made naming those presumed dead, names survivors remembered. Reports of the disaster would eventually appear in newspapers in major lake cities. And, of course, the owners of the *Illinois* would be notified.

Werner was with Nicholas at the shipyard when Nicholas reviewed the list printed in the *Cleveland Plain Dealer*. It numbered one hundred so far, and names were still being added since bodies were still being plucked from the lake and washing up on the miles of shore.

Though he was skimming the names, Nicholas knew the moment Werner recognized one. Werner went completely still, not even a breath rose in his chest or slipped from between his lips for a stricken moment.

"Who is it?" Nicholas asked.

"Owens. *Gott*. James Owens. Alexandra's father."

27

"ARE YOU SURE?" Nicholas asked, gripping the paper and peering closer. Indeed he saw the name himself, scrawled beneath William Webster, the names being in no particular order.

Werner's gaze remained transfixed by the paper. "The ship came from Chicago?"

"Yes."

"I must talk to some of the survivors, see if they knew him. If not, we must wait for a copy of the passenger list for some sort of confirmation." Here he hesitated, as if deliberating on what he should do. He seemed to need to know for certain if the James Owens listed was indeed Alexandra's father.

"Write to his address in Chicago," Nicholas suggested. "There is nothing more you can do. Surely someone there will be taking care of his personal affairs. A friend, an attorney."

"Yes, one would think so."

"Of course."

"There's no need to breathe a word of this to Alexandra until then," Nicholas advised gently.

"No, I . . . I suppose not. Not that she will be terribly disturbed by the news," Werner said, pushing the list away at last and glancing off. "She despises the man."

"I know. Katherine told me." Nicholas folded the paper. Then he and Werner turned away from the shipyard and walked toward Werner's carriage, waiting a short distance ahead. Jackson stood leaning against a door, his arms folded and his eyes closed. "Are you interested in dinner at the Forest City House, Werner?" Nicholas asked, wanting to take Werner's mind from the name on the list.

"Ah, yes!" came an immediate response. Werner narrowed his eyes and cast a sour look at the gray, threatening sky. "Always the food is fine. And there must be some sunshine in a cloudy day, *ja*?"

Nicholas chuckled. "Yes, indeed. Yes, indeed."

Only some sort of deathly illness would have kept Uncle Werner and Mr. Baum from the *Saengerfest* that was held in Cleveland a few weeks after the ship exploded in the lake. Uncle Werner began talking excitedly about the song festival a week before a host of Germans started to descend on the city. The Cleveland *Gesangverein*, the choral society of which he and Mr. Baum were members, would be represented by over four hundred voices, he and Mr. Baum among them, of course. When Uncle Werner spoke of the large band, The North American *Saengerbund*, that would be joining them, he often became so excited he could not even sit still in a chair for long. Katherine smiled and laughed at him.

The day before the festival was scheduled to begin, she met Mr. Baum. The meeting was certainly the highlight of her week, perhaps even her year so far.

Mr. Baum was a tower of a man, standing at least six feet and three inches. Katherine estimated him to be approximately ten years older than Uncle Werner, which would have placed him near sixty. His white hair was thin on top, and his eyebrows and whiskers were bushy, giving him a menacing look at times. But when he conversed and smiled, he was not so formidable at all. His gray eyes sparkled and somehow curved, smiling along with his lips. If he had ever wanted to hide his merriment, he would have needed to cover his entire face, for one had only to see his eyes to know he was smiling.

He was as German as any German could be—proud, dignified, noble. He possessed a powerful baritone voice, a barrel of a laugh, and a love of beer. He had emigrated with his family to the United States during the revolution of 1848, when he, along with other revolutionaries, had faced imprisonment. His love of the old country and the men who had made it great was profound. With Katherine, Nicholas, Alexandra, and Uncle Werner gathered around him in the parlor, he spoke of the great German dramatists Friedrich von Schiller and Gotthold Ephraim Lessing, and of the philosopher Johann Gottlieb Fichte. And music . . . ah, yes, music! There were, of course, the masters like Beethoven, Johann Sebastian Bach, and others, less known but talented nonetheless. The architecture of the old country was unchallenged, too, according to Mr. Baum, and the land was rich in history and charm.

So was Mr. Baum.

Nicholas escorted Katherine to the festival one evening, along with Kevin and Alexandra. The perfectly blended voices truly amazed the audience. There were impressive fugues and chorale melodies. And the *Saengerbund* was astounding. The old baroques were beautiful, and the suites and sonatas of Bach were captivatingly done; swelling concertos were powerful and enthralling.

For days afterward Uncle Werner, Mr. Baum, and a gathering of their German friends frequently assembled in the library of the Kraus home, toasting and barreling more tunes, those more festive than baroques and concertos. Doubtless the lyrics had been learned in less refined settings than concert halls or palatial German residences. The men had a merry time, and Katherine often found herself pausing on the way up or down the staircase to listen and lift a brow in surprise now and then when words shocked her. Sometimes she smiled or laughed.

Peggy was always about, bustling here, bustling there. Once when Katherine passed the library on her way upstairs, the door stood open and Uncle Werner and Peggy were alone within. Not meaning to spy, Katherine glimpsed Uncle Werner pat Peggy's hand in a most affectionate way, and she wrinkled her brow in surprise. Uncle Werner had never been fond of fussy affection. Katherine was fairly certain he would marry Peggy someday. But for now the two of them seemed content. Uncle Werner loved having Peggy about; Peggy loved just being about.

There was one last evening of *Saengerfest*, then the German celebration was over. Mr. Baum boarded a train for Toledo. The house, indeed the city, suddenly seemed very quiet. Very quiet indeed.

July arrived with unusually mild days. A now annual Independence Day celebration was held aboard the *Morning Star*. The side-wheeler was crowded with gaily dressed people laughing and conversing. Shortly after the festivities began, Katherine was speaking with Grace Cummings when Nicholas approached.

"I won't disappoint you this year," he murmured huskily, his breath hot on Katherine's bared shoulder. "Let's waltz. I'll even take you out on deck later and kiss you thoroughly."

Katherine gasped. His mother was standing right there, watching! What was he thinking, if he was even thinking at all?

Grace smiled broadly, mischievously, as if she knew exactly what he'd said. She certainly knew his intent. "I shall leave you to my amorous son," she whispered, then drifted away.

Flushing, Katherine turned and found herself in Nicholas's arms, her open hands splayed on his deliciously solid chest.

"You look bewitching," he said hungrily as his heavy-lidded gaze raked over her.

God, what he might do if they were alone right now! Katherine was enthralled by the suggestiveness in his voice, lured by the scent of him—spiciness and the masculine smell beneath that. She'd become thoroughly spellbound by the love glowing in his beautiful eyes.

They spent the evening precisely as he'd said they would, first waltzing, then out on the middle deck. There he kissed her until she wondered if she would ever catch her breath again. They stood at the rail together, watching the moon rise higher and higher in the sky, watching it dapple the lake with silvery late-evening magic. Nicholas's arms encircled her and drew her back against him. Katherine shut her eyes and squeezed back tears. Never in her life had she been more content.

She slept better that night than she had since her arrival in Cleveland. The following morning she awoke to a squeal outside her bedroom door. She rubbed her eyes and prepared to toss back the light coverlet. Then the door flew open.

Alexandra flew across the room, stumbling slightly over evergreen crinoline. She waved a newspaper and blinked rapidly, firing words: "Owens. James Owens, Chicago attorney. Survived by a daughter, Alexandra. Look! Oh, look!" She plopped on the bed and unfolded the paper. She was so frantic, so eager, she tore an edge, but managed to smooth it. "Here!" She was breathless now.

Katherine had managed to sit up. "What are you talking about?"

Alexandra tapped the paper. "Look! Your uncle just showed me. A list of people who died in that explosion. Then another list of *upstanding* people who died. Oh, they wasted space. They did. On him. Upstanding? No, *horrid. Inconsequential!*"

Katherine stared at her. Her head was foggy with sleep still. "Your father?" she finally asked, realization dawning.

Alexandra gave a quick grin. "Papa." Then she was off the bed, flying toward the door.

"Where are you going?"

"To see Kevin. Read!"

The door slammed shut. Katherine stared at it for a moment, then turned her attention to the newspaper. The information was there, just as Alexandra had said. James Owens had died with that ship. Katherine rubbed her eyes again, wanting to be certain she was fully awake. This changed everything for Alexandra. She could stop worrying—everyone could stop worrying for her. How tragic that so many people had died in that explosion, but Alexandra was now free to marry Kevin.

Some afternoons later Katherine and Charles had been settled on the lawn beneath a huge oak no more than an hour when his mother arrived.

"She's early," Charles grumbled, scowling at his sketching tablet. "The lesson's suppose to last two hours."

"Perhaps something happened," Katherine suggested. Shading her eyes with a hand, she watched Mrs. Pennington, protected from bright rays beneath a lavishly ribbon-decorated parasol, amble her way across the modest expanse of green lawn.

"Hello, Charles dear, Katherine."

"You're early," Charles said.

"Charles," Katherine admonished, tossing a severe look his way.

Mrs. Pennington fiddled nervously with her parasol handle. "I'm sorry, Charles dear, but I need to speak with Katherine, if she could spare a moment from the lesson."

"Certainly," Katherine said, not giving Charles a chance to respond. She knew how he valued his lesson time, and she knew how his mother's doting often peeved him. His brow was drawn tight; he was most definitely irritated. "Remember, Charles, soft strokes to create the grass. Swirls will give the effect of the wind blowing through the tree branches."

She and Mrs. Pennington found a quiet place on a settee close to the house. The shutters had been replaced. The new ones were snow white, easily opened and closed, unlike the old. The wood had been so swollen and rotted, Katherine had feared that forcing the shutters either way would leave them crumbling in her hands. In the distance, beyond a line of trees, Colleen and Margaret, along with Sister Mary in her flowing black habit, were feeding pieces of bread to the ducks who often gathered along the wooden fence separating the Garden Street property from the property behind it. Flaming red braids hung down the twins' backs. They were lovely girls. Doubtless someone would come along and adopt them

Summer Storm 319

someday. Although Katherine had recently turned away one couple wanting only Margaret. She did not want the girls separated. They had lost their parents; she did not want them to lose each other. For now, they were perfectly happy here at the orphanage.

"Charles and Lewis seem to enjoy each other's company a great deal," Mrs. Pennington began, folding her parasol.

"Yes, they do," Katherine agreed. The boys often ran about the lawn together and took turns riding the pony Nicholas had had delivered to the orphanage. They even read to each other at times. Cooper's *Leatherstocking Tales* had become Lewis's favorite. He frequently shared Natty Bumppo's adventures with Charles. Over the course of the four tales, Natty became a frontiersman. Lewis would undoubtedly go west one day and find his own exploits, Katherine thought.

"Where is Lewis today, anyway?" Mrs. Pennington asked. She tucked the parasol beside her on the settee.

"Inside with Alexandra. Ciphering, I believe."

"Lloyd and I have been talking about Lewis. Lloyd is my husband, you know."

Katherine finally put distractions aside and gave the woman her complete attention, sensing the direction the conversation might take. She hoped it would take that direction. Lewis and Charles were best friends. "Yes, I met Mr. Pennington one afternoon when he came for the boys."

Mrs. Pennington nodded. "I had such a time giving birth to Charles. Obviously I've not had any more children since. Not that I don't want them, they just haven't come along."

Katherine waited.

"We have been thinking of adopting Lewis, and wondered . . . Well, we wondered what you might think," Mrs. Pennington said, almost cautiously.

Katherine didn't hesitate. "I think that would be wonderful."

Mrs. Pennington clapped her hands together and laughed with delight. "Marvelous. Oh, that's marvelous! I do not know what is involved in the legal process, but Lloyd knows, I'm sure. He's an attorney. But first we should speak with Lewis and see how he feels. Charles, too, I suppose. Oh, this is truly marvelous."

With the flutter of many more words of delight, with interjections of "thank you," and "you're truly a wonderful woman," and even a covert "I never believed those horrid rumors about your character," Mrs. Pennington wandered back to her awaiting carriage. She would return for Charles in another hour or so, after she and the maid did the marketing, she said, waving at Charles. He blushed and waved back, though not with the enthusiasm his mother displayed. He was a boy teetering on uncomfortable adolescence. In truth, he adored his mother. He talked about her frequently. She had won some quilting contest only last month, and that had made him proud. She played a fine tune on the pianoforte, he had bragged on occasion, and she made the best applesauce, adding just the right amount of cinnamon to spice it. Katherine had no doubt that Mrs. Pennington would learn to temper her doting. Already she had gone from patting Charles's cheek two months ago to patting his hand instead. And she really didn't call him "Charles dear" so much anymore.

She returned a little later, as promised, thanking Katherine again. She would speak with Charles and Lloyd this evening, she said, and have more to tell Katherine in a few days.

Katherine put her mind to the afternoon and evening project she had planned. The painters Uncle Werner had hired to paint one of the orphanage's back rooms were supposed to have come three days ago. Uncle Werner had worked late at the bank the past two evenings, so Katherine had not had a chance to mention to him that the painters had not come. She had requested that Mr. Jackson meet her and Alexandra at the orphanage at three o'clock to take them shopping for paint. He was prompt, as always. He took them to a company on Superior. There a man most graciously mixed paint and provided brushes.

"You are not thinking of painting that room yourself?" Alexandra asked, giving Katherine a disapproving look from the corner of her eye.

Summer Storm

Katherine smiled.

Alexandra sighed. "Oh, I can see you now, hoops, petticoats, and all, climbing a ladder, splattering paint all over that pretty poplin dress."

"Hoops and petticoats can be removed," Katherine said, "even the dress if no one is about and the children are asleep."

"You're impossible. Just like the days we went to look at houses for the orphanage. I should know better than to try to stop you from doing anything."

"Yes, you should."

Alexandra scowled and sank into a corner of the carriage as it moved along, rocking gently.

"I'd ask you to help, but I know you're seeing Kevin this evening. More wedding plans?" Katherine asked, smiling. She knew they had both been bubbling with plans since learning Alexandra's father was no longer a threat.

The change of subject brought Alexandra from her corner. "At his hotel next spring. And we will honeymoon in New York and see all the sights there. Isn't that grand?" Her eyes sparkled, flitting here and there. She put a hand to her mouth to keep from giggling with delight.

"But six months from now . . . that seems so long."

"Oh, don't say it in such a sour tone. I'll hardly be mourning. Kevin and I are waiting six months because society demands it. One can hardly be married within a few months of one's father's death, after all."

"It's almost like Fate intervened, isn't it? I still can't believe it . . ."

"What, that he's dead? Just like that?"

Katherine nodded.

"Well, believe. There was his name. It *was* Fate. Kevin and I were meant to be together. Papa must have been coming to shackle me and take me back to Chicago. Your uncle's letter must have infuriated him. Well, no matter. Finally, Mama's murder is avenged."

"Alexandra," Katherine admonished softly, a bit shocked that Alexandra thought of the violent demise of her father as retribution for her mother's horrible death.

"I will not pretend. I listened to the sounds that night, remember? Their shouts, her pleas. I will never forget the sound of her tumbling down those stairs. Never. I am delighted, and I will not pretend. Not with you."

Katherine didn't blame her. How bitter Alexandra must have felt after her mother's death. How desolate and filled with fury! Then to be shipped off to some school where she knew no one . . . Katherine reached across the carriage and squeezed Alexandra's hand. "I know. It's over now. I'm glad for you. Truly. Marry Kevin and be happy. Always be happy."

Alexandra smiled, then frowned playfully. "I will be . . . unless you fall off a ladder."

Katherine rolled her eyes. "We're back to the ladder. Stop. I won't fall."

"What about you and Nicholas?"

Katherine settled back on the seat. "Things are progressing. I think. I love him. He loves me. I know that. We were both hurt in little ways by everything that happened right after I returned to Cleveland. The events created a lot of mistrust. He says I'm reserved, and he wants the old Katherine back. But, oh, Alexandra, I'm different now. I'm not carefree and daring anymore."

"Yes, you are. Buying the paint and painting the room yourself, for instance. Not too many ladies would do a thing like that."

Katherine laughed. "You're right."

"I am. You are stifled, that's all. Perhaps you should practice doing outrageous things. In private, of course."

"And have you scold me?"

"I will not say a word, if you do not place yourself in too much danger. But I do have reservations about that ladder."

"I'm going to paint the room."

Alexandra sighed. "I know," she said as the carriage slowed before the Garden Street Orphanage. "Be careful."

Katherine smiled as Mr. Jackson handed her down, then carried the paint into the house for her. She was still smiling when the conveyance pulled away. Alexandra stuck her pretty face out the window and called, "Do not forget the hoops and

Summer Storm

petticoats. Remove them before you climb! And do not ruin the dress. Remove it, too. Wear your camisole and drawers!"

Behind Katherine, Sister Elizabeth gasped. Katherine hid her smile behind a lifted handkerchief. Oh, God. Alexandra had her own outrageous ways.

"What the devil are you doing?"

Nicholas's demand, just the sound of a voice in the house that had been quiet for an hour and should have been quiet for at least another, made Katherine jerk. She splattered blue paint on her white camisole. The ladder creaked.

She stared at the camisole. Ruined. She had tossed petticoats, hoops, and dress in a pile in one corner. And here she stood perched atop the ladder in only her underclothes.

"Oh—!" Holding the paintbrush in one hand, she used the other hand to pull at the tops of the camisole and the corset beneath—she might not be able to reach the dress, but at least she could try to cover herself a little better. And as she tried, she also somehow managed to balance herself on the ladder step.

"Would you—Katherine! Would you hold on?" Nicholas sputtered, nearing the bottom of the ladder. "I have seen you in less."

He'd seen . . . her eyes widened. "Most men would have the decency not to mention that fact!"

"Now is not the time to play the embarrassed maiden."

"Would you mind?" She wobbled and grabbed the edge of the ladder to keep from falling. She uttered an involuntary cry of fright.

Nicholas steadied the ladder. "Come down from there. This instant. Werner told me he would send painters over. Why didn't you wait for them? Where did you *get* this rickety contraption? Where did you get the paint?"

"Stop firing questions at me," she snapped, placing the brush beside the can of paint on a piece of dark cloth lying on the top step. "The painters never came, the ladder is from the gardener's cottage, and Alexandra and I went for the paint this afternoon."

"What is the date?" he demanded, confusing her.

"The tenth of July. What does it matter?"

"It matters because Werner told me they would arrive on the fifteenth."

"No," she argued. "The tenth."

"The fifteenth."

That date hung in the air.

Katherine frowned. She hadn't really been paying attention when Uncle Werner told her the date. She'd been sitting on a settee on the front lawn, sketching the bluff. He had casually mentioned the date, then strolled away. "Are you sure?" she finally asked Nicholas, feeling a little foolish.

"I'm afraid so."

She sighed and reached for the brush again. The damage was already done; he'd already caught her in her underclothes, and as he'd pointed out, he had seen her in less, as embarrassing as that thought was. Of course, at the time it had not been embarrassing at all . . . "I was anxious to have the painting done, I guess," she said quickly. "And since I've nothing better to do with my time, I'll continue. Sister Mary will be late. She sent a missive. And I forgot to bring the book I've been reading in the evenings."

"I'm here," Nicholas objected, sounding wounded.

She shot him a knowing glance. "Meaning you could provide me entertainment?"

He grinned. A lock of dark hair hooded one eye.

If she descended, she knew what might happen. Right here, in this back room of the orphanage, with children asleep upstairs. Her heart pounded mercilessly.

"I saw Jackson when I delivered a packet to Werner," Nicholas said. "I told him I would bring you home."

"How accommodating of you."

"Oh, don't sound so annoyed, Katherine. I usually come for you."

"You don't usually walk in while I'm undressed."

"I wish I did." His voice had thickened. "All those ribbons and ties and delicate lace . . . Not to mention the woman wearing them."

"Nicholas." The man! His mention of ribbons and ties brought images of him tugging them loose, pushing them aside. The blue strokes she made on the wall did not follow the pattern of the neat, even strokes she'd made earlier. She struggled to concentrate on the brush, struggled to steady her hand.

The ladder trembled the tiniest bit. Katherine gasped, glancing down. Nicholas was still gripping the ladder, looking up at her. "Katherine. Come down."

"Trying to rattle me down?"

"If need be. This thing is not safe. Come down before I come up and get you."

"In a moment."

He took the first step. Then another. And another. The ladder groaned.

Katherine winced. It *was* a bit old and worn. She'd been excited about the thought of painting the room herself and hadn't noticed the ladder's decrepit condition earlier. "Nicholas, get down. It certainly won't hold both of us!"

"With you in my arms."

"Stubborn man," she mumbled, replacing the brush on the cloth. She started down the ladder. As humiliating as facing him in her underclothes would be, she would rather do that than land in a pile of splintered wood and paint.

"Stubborn . . . precisely what I was thinking about you." His voice was husky; playful yet serious.

Nicholas watched her, studied her, relished her. He had a wonderful view of her bottom, free of hoops, crinoline, and even the petticoats and dark-red-and-blue poplin draped over the back of a chair in a corner to his left. Quite an extraordinary view, when he considered it. And he did consider it, tilting his head first to the left for that luscious angle, then to the right for another. If she thought he would remove himself from the ladder just because she was coming down, she was very mistaken.

She didn't even look back. She took step after rickety step. He shifted his gaze to the one right in front of his face, knowing . . . First a black-booted foot appeared, then another, then came stockinged ankles. The lace edging the hem of her drawers brushed his nose. He grinned lazily. Embroidered linen covered calves and thighs, clung to the delectable roundness of her bottom, narrowed with her waist, and followed the flare of her upper back. Nicholas caught his breath, released it, then inhaled deeply. He hoped he inhaled a bit of restraint along with air. He could easily give a yank on the ties holding together the two overlapping pieces of her drawers and . . . Her bottom touched his groin and wriggled slightly against him.

She went still. "Nicholas!"

"You should be thankful it's only me," he murmured near her ear. "Are you aware that all three doors were unbolted? Anyone might have entered. Any man might be standing here on this ladder right now, watching you, thinking the same thoughts I'm thinking."

Her bosom rose and fell rapidly. "Sometimes . . . sometimes I think you're the most dangerous man I know."

"Indeed?"

"Indeed. You make me feel . . . odd."

"Pleasantly odd, I hope. Tell me, are these the . . . garments you bought the day I took you shopping at the Exchange?" he asked, admiring them and the luscious swell of her breasts above the camisole and corset.

"Get down, please."

He took one hand from the ladder and fingered the camisole's undersleeve. "Delicate. Slightly scratchy but soft at the same time. And such tiny flowers," he said, easing his hand beneath her arm, to the curve of one breast and the embroidery there. "Fine. I can feel the bones in the corset, the fullness of you beneath that. You smell like lavender. I've an urge to kiss you."

Her head fell back against his shoulder. She was suddenly breathing quite rapidly. "Oh, my God, Nicholas, get down."

He encircled her waist with an arm and stepped back, taking her with him off the ladder. She spun, twisted free, and glared at him. "That was mean."

"Ooh, I believe she's angry," he teased. "And what a sight she is, standing before him in her fine camisole and drawers, red-faced, looking indignant."

Summer Storm

Her scowl deepened. "You're delighted with yourself, aren't you?"

"Hardly. I'm miserable. Very miserable. Restraining myself was difficult enough when we had a chaste relationship, sharing conversation but scarcely a touch."

"It was never chaste."

He stared at her, at the darkness of rose nipples showing through the delicate material. He felt the tightness of his trousers, the pain of his erection. Since spotting her standing alone near the *Morning Star*'s rail in July of last year, he had desired her. And how many times during the months he'd played gentleman had he wanted to touch her, drag her into his arms, and ravish her? Many, too many to count. "You're right, love. It was never chaste. You should marry me, you know, so I might at least get you to a bed and make love to you the proper way. I keep wanting to make love to you on floors."

Her eyes widened. She folded her arms across her bosom. Her hands clutched the tips of her shoulders. "But I thought . . . trust before giving into the passion . . . the real me, the real you."

"Do you trust me?"

"With my life," she said without hesitation. "I always have really. I was just so frightened. I had a fairy-tale life planned for myself, but when I came home, nothing was as I'd planned. Nothing. I lost a lot of hope for a time. But once again you've restored it."

"Yes . . . things do not always happen as planned. You'll marry me, then?"

"When? Tonight?" she blurted.

They both laughed at the same moment. "That would never do," he said, stuffing his hands in his pockets. "But within say . . . a few months? September? That's still a short amount of time, but I don't care. We will announce the engagement immediately if that's all right."

She nodded, then sank back against the wall, staring at him for a time. "Tell me I'm not dreaming. Oh, tell me," she whispered, shutting her eyes and tipping her head to one side.

Nicholas neared her. The lamplights cast a glow about her. Shadows flitted about the room and on one side of her neck and face. Loose golden curls touched one shoulder. He caught one of the wisps between the first two fingers of a hand, loving the silkiness of it. A tear spilled from her eye onto her cheek and began to roll. He caught it, too, on the tip of a finger, and stared at the droplet. For him, a tear of happiness. "No dream, love. This is no dream," he assured her.

He trailed a finger along her delicate jaw and kissed another tear away, tasting, loving its saltiness. She turned her face to him, tipped her head back, offering her neck. But no, he wanted the jaw. Of course, the jaw led to her small but proud chin, the chin to her lips—rather, that was the path he took. The lips were there, parted and waiting for him. He nipped at the bottom one, licked the top one, then claimed both. Their tongues met, writhing together as he knew their bodies would again soon, joining, dancing, mating.

She moaned. He felt her reach between them and fumbled with the ties on her drawers. The drawers didn't need to be untied and removed really; he had only to part them, part her thighs, and lift her up to him, steady her against the wall . . .

"No," he gasped, catching her hand. "No, Katie. We'll wait. Somehow we'll wait." He lifted his head and stared down at her; she stared back in glazed confusion. He attempted to explain: "I will not compromise you again. There might be another child, born months before people think it should be born. I will not do that to you, to us, to our child."

The confusion cleared. She smiled. "Oh, noble Nicholas. I do love you."

He smiled, too, and stepped back. "Look at you. Paint splattered on that pretty white linen. But I don't suppose you look as bad as you did the first day I encountered you in Werner's office."

She lifted her chin. Small, well rounded, it represented everything she was—proud, determined, rebellious, zestful . . . "I don't look bad at all," she said, giving him an enchanting smile.

Good God, he loved her. He loved her nature, her spirit, her lavender scent, which right now, mixed with the scent of her womanhood, seemed about to drive him mad. He crossed the room, snatched her dress from the back of the chair, and tossed it at her. "You're right and you damn well know it. Now, get dressed before I start acting less noble."

To the sound of her laughter, he hurried from the room.

Epilogue

LAKE ERIE FROLICKED beneath a bright September sun, splashing at the *Morning Star*. The first hints of sunset revealed themselves in tiny orange flecks on the water. Katherine stood at the railing. Nicholas stood behind her, his hands gripping the railing to her right and left. They admired the beautiful Great Lake together, commenting on its vastness, its depths, its serenity. The Ohio shore was but a shadow in a clear day now. There was the churning of the engine, the cries and flutters of a flock of gulls suddenly casting shadows on the ship. The air was cool, as September lake air always was.

Nicholas dipped his head, nudged a few blond wisps from Katherine's neck, and skimmed his lips along the column, working his way up to her jaw. He nipped at her earlobe. She tossed her head to one side and back against his shoulder. He trailed kisses down her neck to its base, unfastened the clasp of the wrap she'd tossed around herself, pushed the material aside, and found the tender, creamy flesh of a shoulder. She had removed her hoops and petticoats—so she could feel the wind whip her skirt against her legs, she had said. Well, the absence of the articles gave him an advantage: He pressed his groin against her lower back, dipped and pressed himself against her buttocks.

"Nicholas, the crew!" Katherine gasped.

Summer Storm

"I told them to be as inconspicuous as possible, that I didn't want to see them at all, nor have them see us," he growled near her ear.

"Surely they hold you in high regard," she said sarcastically.

He chuckled. "They are men. They understand." He nibbled more, pushing the sleek sleeve off the edge of her shoulder, nipping the delectable curve. The cloak slipped away completely, falling silently into a pile at their feet, revealing the white satin skirt of her wedding gown and her lace-covered bodice. The gown rustled with her every movement, toying with his senses. How easily the satin would slide along her skin, up over her thighs and buttocks, her waist and breasts. It would slip right off her arms, leaving her in only her undergarments. Those could be discarded as easily as the dress.

"Good God, how hungry I am for you," Nicholas murmured. "I seem to have very little control over—"

Somehow she escaped the trap he had made of his arms and body. She ran a hand over the rail, backing away, tilting her head and smiling in her demure way while gazing at him out of the corner of her eye. The evening sun enhanced the gold in her hair. Her gown glinted orange as she moved.

Nicholas groaned in frustration. He found that look of hers charming yet highly seductive; he always had. He eased toward her. She backed away more. "Now, love . . . don't tease me. I've been miserable enough these past months."

Her smile widened. It was no *natural* demure look then, not this time! She knew exactly what she was doing.

"Come here," he said.

"Oh, and be ravished right here on the deck? In daylight?" Her eyes sparkled.

"Can you deny that you want to be?"

"Nicholas!"

"Katherine. A man can only endure so much. If not here, then make your way to the stateroom."

"But we . . . we promised to have supper with Captain Islington in a while," she objected.

Nicholas frowned. "Yes, we did, didn't we?" He groaned again. "How long have we been married?"

"Hours."

"And we couldn't have spent some time in the stateroom by now?"

"Well . . . there was dinner in the dining saloon earlier, and I wanted to visit the pilothouse again. And then we came here to admire the lake."

He shook his head. "We are the only passengers aboard this ship. I purposely saw to that, and yet there are still distractions!"

"Oh, Nicholas, don't be grumpy." Katherine lifted her skirt, turned, and raced along the deck near the rail, glancing over her shoulder and smiling as if daring him to catch her.

He caught up easily enough. His hand lashed out and grabbed her arm. He spun her about, drove her up against the railing, cupped her buttocks, and pressed himself against her front this time. There was no escape. "You tease me, then run and tell me not to grumble. I've a mind to simply lift your skirt and take you right here, right now," he said breathlessly. He tossed his head back, inhaled the sweet air, and felt her warm body and the cove between her thighs that harbored secrets meant only for him.

Katherine planted her palms flat on his chest. Hours ago, he had removed his coat and waistcoat. He wore black trousers and a white silk shirt with billowing sleeves. She slowly made circles with her palms, loving the firm feel of his chest. She ran her hands up over his shoulders, slipped them to the back of his neck . . . and easily clicked open his stock buckle. It fell neatly into one hand. With the other hand, she pulled the cravat from around his neck and dangled it in front of his face, smiling mischievously.

He grinned. "What are you doing?"

"I've done it."

"Are you going to undress me completely? Right here on deck? You were so concerned about—"

"Later, if we both last that long."

"There will be no later. We're going to the stateroom now."

Summer Storm 333

She laughed, but breathlessly Nicholas thought. "Are we?" she teased further.

"We are. There's the island. Take one quick look, love, for you won't see it again until tomorrow. Supper with Captain Islington will wait until tomorrow, too."

He took her by the shoulders, stepping back just enough so that he could turn her around. She could barely see the outline of the island, but enough that she recalled its jagged rows of trees, the many wild turkeys and quail she'd spotted in the forest the day the sisters had accompanied her and Alexandra and the others to Kelley's. She remembered specifically a pond they had stopped near, and its swampy edges with patches of tall grass rising here and there. She remembered the rocks, the quarry they had visited, the dark red brick building ruling over the limestone loading dock, the lush churchyard where they had picnicked and rested during the afternoon.

"We'll be staying in a small cottage on the land Werner and I bought together," Nicholas said softly. "It's near the shore, so you can glimpse the lake as much as you want, make as many sketches as you want. You can wander the shore. You may even climb on the rocks and tear your dress."

Katherine laughed again. "Sister Dorothy won't be hiding in the shadows spying on me?"

"Only I will be spying on you."

He took her hand and tugged her away from the railing. He led the way to a door that led to stairs, a hall, and staterooms. The woodwork was dark, the wall sconces brass and immaculately polished. The eerie glow of the oil lamps was bewitching, hypnotizing almost. Of course the eagerness of the man clutching her hand had something to do with the spell rapidly stealing over Katherine. She had teased him, had put him off, not because she had wanted to, but because she had been embarrassed that the crew might know what they were doing if they rushed to the stateroom as soon as they boarded the *Morning Star*. But that was a silly thought; they were newly married, ecstatically, happily married, and whether they were in the stateroom morning, afternoon, evening, or night, everyone would know what they were doing anyway. Katherine giggled at that thought and at the way Nicholas rushed along the hall, pulling her with him.

"You're possessed," she said, halfheartedly objecting.

"Obsessed is a better description," he shot back. "I should be given a medal for restraint after all these months. I've never worked so hard at anything in my life."

They reached the stateroom.

Nicholas turned the brass handle and shouldered the door open. Then he stood aside and made a wide, sweeping motion with his arm, indicating that she should enter first. Her eyelids felt heavy, not with sleep, with something much more powerful. But her every sense was keen and alert. She smelled his spicy cologne, something Nicholas used sparsely. There was a tiny twitch in his left cheek, a spark to his emerald eyes, beautiful eyes that never failed to snare her gaze with their intensity. There was a shadow to his jaw that had not been present that morning at the small but elegant wedding held in the Kraus house. Black hair waved gently over his collar. She remembered the slightly coarse feel of it when she had removed his stock, and her fingertips tingled. She held the stiff object in her hand now, along with the cool buckle. She let both slip away. She heard the buckle clatter on the floor, heard the light brush of the stock. Surely sometime during her life with Nicholas she would find time to *fasten* his neckcloth, to show him she could do it properly. That is, if they weren't kept too occupied with other things.

She moved languidly, turning her back to him.

"What are you doing now?" he asked roughly.

"The placket. Unfasten it," she murmured.

Not a half second passed before his hands worked at her back, loosening the gown. His tongue found a shoulder blade, traced it, then blazed a trail along the upper portion of her spine and finally her neck.

She stepped away, moved inside the room, and found herself near a small secretary. It was uncluttered, but several pens had been tossed carelessly to one side. As she drew the voluminous folds of her skirt up, she heard the door shut. Moments later, while she was still struggling with the material, trying to

Summer Storm

draw it from her arms and over her head, she felt Nicholas's hands on her waist. They traveled up, skimmed the mounds of her breasts, the sensitive undersides of her arms, and finally pulled the gown free and tossed it aside. She had removed her petticoats earlier; now she slipped from her chemise and camisole. Nicholas turned her about and reached for the front clasps securing her corset.

He unbound her breasts as skillfully as he had slipped the gown from her body. There was no working at it. The clasps seemed to dissolve with his touch. The boned corset joined the heap of white satin on the stateroom floor, and she stood before him, naked from the waist up. Their gazes caught and held.

Katherine could hardly breathe, her mouth and throat having gone completely dry. Instinctively she put her hands to her breasts to cover them.

He reached for her hands. "No, Katie. Let me see you. Every inch of you," he whispered. "There is no one else. Only us."

Her hands slid away with his. His gaze dropped to her breasts and lingered there, kindling a heat between her thighs that made her gasp and want to squirm. She wanted him, wanted the fullness she remembered well, wanted to watch pleasure flicker across his masculine features and haze his eyes. She wanted to hear the wet sound of him slipping in and out of her, wanted to hear his groans of release. And she knew no shame for having the thoughts, the wanton desires.

"Nicholas . . . ," she whispered desperately.

He lifted a hand to cup a swollen breast. He caressed the outer curve of it; his fingers swirled their way to its tip, where a thumb and forefinger taunted the peak. Katherine breathed deeply as sensations of pleasure yet throbbing desire flamed through her. She realized his other hand was working at trouser buttons. "Yes . . . Oh, yes," she whispered hoarsely. Oh, God, in a moment he would free himself and . . .

He covered her mouth with his and lifted her. She wrapped her arms around his neck, parted her lips, and welcomed his ravishment. Hands on the backs of her thighs separated them, pulling apart the pieces of her drawers at the same time. Her buttocks touched the edge of the secretary.

She felt his hardness brush her, probe her the slightest bit. "What are you doing? What?" she demanded. Why didn't he just give one thrust and fill her? How she wanted him!

And then he *was* in her, quickly, taking her breath. She moaned, let her head fall back, and wrapped her legs around him. He lifted her and carried her to the edge of the bed.

He filled her again and again, rocking over her, whispering her name. He plunged, dove, undulated, bracing himself with his hands propped on either side of her. His mouth sought her breasts; she arched. Pleasure rippled through her, stopping her heart, stopping time. She heard her cries, but they seemed distant. She felt him stiffen, groan, and pump into her.

She enjoyed the feel of his weight on her. How many nights had she lain awake, thinking of making love with him again? She had thought of feeling the solidity of him, of hearing his heavy breathing in the lazy aftermath of their loving, of watching his eyes slowly flutter open and settle on her.

"We've been through a storm, I think," he said softly.

She cradled his head against her shoulder, smoothed his hair, felt his heart pound. She thought of the past fourteen months. So much had happened. There had been so much pain, so much heartache, so many looks of longing, so much healing.

"Haven't we?" she murmured. "But we're through it. Oh, yes, we're through it."

Author's Note

WITH RESPECT FOR the history of Clevelanders, the people of lakeshore Ohio, and the "iron" and "lake" men of the region, notes must be made regarding certain fictional liberties I took while writing this book.

The Weddell and Forest City Houses were popular, elegant hotels of the day in Cleveland. Since other buildings and establishments have now taken their places, I had only sketches and photos of their exteriors to aid me. I reviewed the material, ever mindful of historical accuracy. I relied on my imagination a great deal, however, while describing interiors and even minor things like the dress of hotel staff.

I reviewed 1858–1859 issues of *The Cleveland Plain Dealer* and found no account of Abraham Lincoln's acceptance speech. But since the major conflict between Nicholas and Lemuel was their opposing views of slavery, since Nicholas felt certain the nation teetered on civil war, and since Lincoln was rapidly becoming a model for abolitionists, Lemuel skipping an account of Lincoln's remarks seemed the perfect thing to use to anger Nicholas.

I spent hours studying the old ways of wooden shipbuilding. My most reliable source was Captain H. C. Inches's book mentioned in the Acknowledgments. If I have erred in any way, I apologize.

Finally, while the Erie Line and its vessels are products of my imagination, the ships that responded to the burning

Illinois are not. (There was a real steamer *Illinois*, but the one mentioned in this work is fictitious.) I toyed with dates, however, because these ships captured my interest. With the utmost respect for the vessels of the past and their crews, I list them and their actual launch dates.

Amaranth, 1864
Oak Leaf, 1866
Dean Richmond, 1864
Arrow, 1848
St. Albans, date unknown.

Teresa Warfield
Cleveland, Ohio
January, 1993

New York Times Bestselling Author

Nora Roberts
HONEST ILLUSIONS

From carnival tents to the world's greatest stages, Nora Roberts sweeps through the decades to create a shimmering novel of glamorous mystery and intrigue.

"Her stories have fueled the dreams of twenty-five million readers." —Entertainment Weekly

"Move over, Sidney Sheldon: the world has a new master of romantic suspense..." —Rex Reed

"Roberts combines...sizzling sex, a cunning villain, a captivating story, some tugs at the heartstrings—and then adds a twist...and the result is spellbinding."
—Publishers Weekly

__0-515-11097-3/$5.99

For Visa, MasterCard and American Express ($15 minimum) orders call: 1-800-631-8571

FOR MAIL ORDERS: CHECK BOOK(S). FILL OUT COUPON. SEND TO:

BERKLEY PUBLISHING GROUP
390 Murray Hill Pkwy., Dept. B
East Rutherford, NJ 07073

NAME_____
ADDRESS_____
CITY_____
STATE_____ ZIP_____

PLEASE ALLOW 6 WEEKS FOR DELIVERY.
PRICES ARE SUBJECT TO CHANGE WITHOUT NOTICE.

POSTAGE AND HANDLING:
$1.75 for one book, 75¢ for each additional. Do not exceed $5.50.

BOOK TOTAL $ _____
POSTAGE & HANDLING $ _____
APPLICABLE SALES TAX $ _____
(CA, NJ, NY, PA)
TOTAL AMOUNT DUE $ _____

PAYABLE IN US FUNDS.
(No cash orders accepted.)

Nationally bestselling author
JILL MARIE LANDIS

___COME SPRING 0-515-10861-8/$4.99
"This is a world-class novel... it's fabulous!"
    —**Bestselling author Linda Lael Miller**
She canceled her wedding, longing to explore the wide open West. But nothing could prepare her Bostonian gentility for an adventure that thrust her into the arms of a wild mountain man....

___JADE 0-515-10591-0/$4.95
A determined young woman of exotic beauty returned to San Francisco to unveil the secrets behind her father's death. But her bold venture would lead her to recover a family fortune—and discover a perilous love.

___ROSE 0-515-10346-2/$4.50
"A gentle romance that will warm your soul."—**Heartland Critiques**
When Rosa set out from Italy to join her husband in Wyoming, little did she know that fate held heartbreak ahead. Suddenly a woman alone, the challenge seemed as vast as the prairies.

___SUNFLOWER 0-515-10659-3/$4.99
"A winning novel!"—**Publishers Weekly**
Analisa was strong and independent. Caleb had a brutal heritage that challenged every feeling in her heart. Yet their love was as inevitable as the sunrise....

___WILDFLOWER 0-515-10102-8/$5.50
"A delight from start to finish!"—**Rendezvous**
From the great peaks of the West to the lush seclusion of a Caribbean jungle, Dani and Troy discovered the deepest treasures of the heart.

For Visa, MasterCard and American Express orders ($15 minimum) call: 1-800-631-8571

FOR MAIL ORDERS: CHECK BOOK(S).
FILL OUT COUPON. SEND TO:

BERKLEY PUBLISHING GROUP
390 Murray Hill Pkwy., Dept. B
East Rutherford, NJ 07073

NAME_____
ADDRESS_____
CITY_____
STATE_____ZIP_____

PLEASE ALLOW 6 WEEKS FOR DELIVERY.
PRICES ARE SUBJECT TO CHANGE WITHOUT NOTICE.

POSTAGE AND HANDLING:
$1.75 for one book, 75¢ for each additional. Do not exceed $5.50.

BOOK TOTAL	$ ____
POSTAGE & HANDLING	$ ____
APPLICABLE SALES TAX (CA, NJ, NY, PA)	$ ____
TOTAL AMOUNT DUE	$ ____

PAYABLE IN US FUNDS.
(No cash orders accepted.)

National Bestselling Author
PAMELA MORSI

"I've read all her books and loved every word."
–*Jude Deveraux*

WILD OATS

The last person Cora Briggs expects to see at her door is a fine gentleman like Jedwin Sparrow. After all, her more "respectable" neighbors in Dead Dog, Oklahoma, won't have much to do with a divorcee. She's even more surprised when Jed tells her he's just looking to sow a few wild oats! But instead of getting angry, Cora decides to get even, and makes Jed a little proposition of her own...one that's sure to cause a stir in town–and starts an unexpected commotion in her heart as well.

_0-515-11185-6/$4.99 (On sale September 1993)

GARTERS

Miss Esme Crabb knows sweet talk won't put food on the table–so she's bent on finding a sensible man to marry. Cleavis Rhy seems like a smart choice...so amidst the cracker barrels and jam jars in his general store, Esme makes her move. She doesn't realize that daring to set her sights on someone like Cleavis Rhy will turn the town–and her heart–upside down.

_0-515-10895-2/$4.99

For Visa, MasterCard and American Express ($15 minimum) orders call: 1-800-631-8571

FOR MAIL ORDERS: CHECK BOOK(S). FILL OUT COUPON. SEND TO: **BERKLEY PUBLISHING GROUP** 390 Murray Hill Pkwy., Dept. B East Rutherford, NJ 07073 NAME ADDRESS CITY STATE ZIP PLEASE ALLOW 6 WEEKS FOR DELIVERY. PRICES ARE SUBJECT TO CHANGE WITHOUT NOTICE.	POSTAGE AND HANDLING: $1.75 for one book, 75¢ for each additional. Do not exceed $5.50. BOOK TOTAL $ ____ POSTAGE & HANDLING $ ____ APPLICABLE SALES TAX $ ____ (CA, NJ, NY, PA) TOTAL AMOUNT DUE $ ____ PAYABLE IN US FUNDS. (No cash orders accepted.)

Winner of the Golden Heart Award

ANITA GORDON

__THE VALIANT HEART 0-515-10642-9/$4.95

By birthright, Brienne was Baronne de Valseme—but the black-haired maiden was robbed of her legacy by plundering Norsemen. Offered against her will as a bride to Rurik, the enemy, their people are joined in a delicate and uneasy peace—but destiny decreed that Brienne and Rurik would join an everlasting, enthralling life...

> "Anita Gordon gives the ring of authenticity to her first Medieval Romance."—LaVyrle Spencer, *New York Times* bestselling author of *Bitter Sweet*

> "An exciting confection; I read it with avid enjoyment!"—Roberta Gellis, bestselling author of *Fires of Winter*

__THE DEFIANT HEART 0-425-13825-9/$4.99

A fiercely handsome Norman lord stole the ravishing Irish beauty from a life of slavery, angered to see the lovely maiden treated as a possession. But soon there stirred within him a powerful desire to possess her himself—as only a lover could...

For Visa, MasterCard and American Express ($15 minimum) orders call: 1-800-631-8571

FOR MAIL ORDERS: CHECK BOOK(S). FILL OUT COUPON. SEND TO:	POSTAGE AND HANDLING: $1.75 for one book, 75¢ for each additional. Do not exceed $5.50.
BERKLEY PUBLISHING GROUP 390 Murray Hill Pkwy., Dept. B East Rutherford, NJ 07073	BOOK TOTAL $ ____
NAME_____	POSTAGE & HANDLING $ ____
ADDRESS_____	APPLICABLE SALES TAX $ ____ (CA, NJ, NY, PA)
CITY_____	TOTAL AMOUNT DUE $ ____
STATE_____ ZIP_____	PAYABLE IN US FUNDS. (No cash orders accepted.)

PLEASE ALLOW 6 WEEKS FOR DELIVERY.
PRICES ARE SUBJECT TO CHANGE WITHOUT NOTICE.